The Age of Gifts

TALES FROM ELORA

By Kaitlyn Shell

To Todd and Stephanie,

who always push me to do hard things.

THE CONTINENT

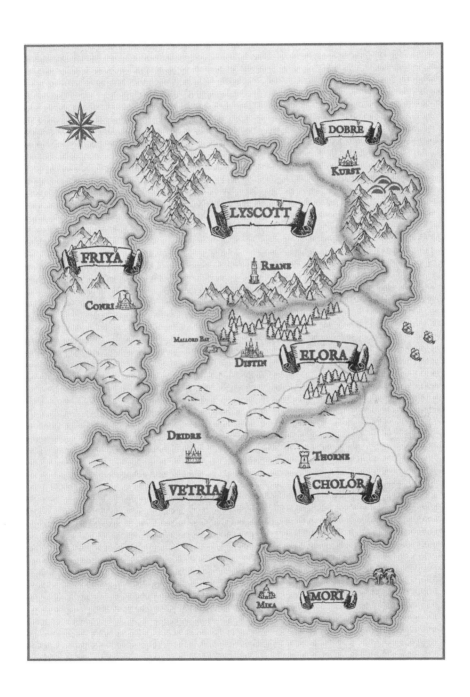

Prologue

Four hundred years ago.

A bolt of white, hot energy shot across the open field.

Drawing his hand back, Lukoh gasped for air. Golden light shone over both entities, reflecting off Lukoh and searing Akar's skin. Akar hissed, slithering away from where the blast had only just struck and reading his own, icy blow.

The battle had been ongoing for nearly two weeks; a brutal, relentless exchange of power. Once blanketed by a layer of lush, green grass, the expanse of land was now covered in frost and ash. A mile to the east, the city of Distin was under siege. War cries rang through the late afternoon air, yet the Lukoh could not let Akar go free.

Oh, how Lukoh wished for his home. There, he would not be so drained. There, he could use his power at will, with no fear of depletion. He could only do so much for his people in his physical form. Akar, too, was limited. Even as the sun began to set, Akar's ice melted faster and faster with every exertion.

Lukoh hardly had to move to avoid the stream of frost that shot out from Akar's fingertips. He paused, struck by grief and anger in equal measure. He could hear his people raging against each other. He could smell the sharp tang of metal and salt. He could see, in his mind's eye, what

Akar had once been. An ally. Not quite a friend, but perhaps the closest thing a god could have to one. Lukoh also remembered when, at the dawn of humanity, Akar began to shift. Lukoh remembered watching as Akar was consumed with wrath against the people that Lukoh had created. Thousands of years had been spent pursuing such a foolish vendetta, and it all led to that very battlefield.

"You have to stop this," Lukoh said, gathering his strength. There was only one place that would keep Akar bound, and it was going to take a considerable amount of power to send him there.

Akar scoffed, the sound deep and guttural. His skin, so pale it was almost gray, was speckled with burn marks. He lobbied another shot of ice, heaving, "Stop me *yourself.*"

Covering his mouth with his hand, Akar whispered in a foreign tongue. He blew out a heavy breath, and tendrils of darkness stretched from his palm into the neighboring town. There, the cries grew louder.

Agony gripped Lukoh. He would help his people, but they would have to hold on for a little longer.

Lukoh cupped his hands together, forming a ball of pure, white light. It hummed beneath his tanned fingers as he willed direction into the glowing orb. *The Caves of Dobre.* The ball burned brighter, as though it too was ready to see justice served.

At that, Akar's empty eyes widened. He laughed, but Lukoh could hear the mock confidence in his tone. "You know that place won't hold me."

No, it wouldn't. Not forever. But long enough for Lukoh to regain his strength, to recover his people, and to prepare them for what was coming.

"Akar Hanofel," Lukoh released the orb, striking his enemy in the chest, "you are banished to the Caves of Dobre from now until the lock is broken. You will neither harm nor influence any soul that does not seek you out. The only power you may have is that which is asked of you." Akar was encased in bright, liquid energy. "Now *leave.*"

The wicked being was given no time to argue as he vanished in a blur of light.

Lukoh fell to one knee, sighing. The sounds of war subsided, albeit slowly. He would heal their wounds in time. Distin would recover. One day, they would have to be ready to fight again, but generations would pass before that day arrived. And, fortunately, the god had a plan.

When his people finally quieted, Lukoh returned home.

Chapter One: Selah

It had been years since I'd entered a Lukonian cathedral.

The ceiling stood impossibly tall. Vast, reaching arches connected each side of the chapel to the next. Panes upon panes of stained glass had been masterfully worked into every flat surface. Rows of dark, vacant wooden pews almost seemed to glow in the fading evening light. It was a beautiful, empty place, dedicated to a god who had long since passed.

What a strange place to meet.

I'd accepted Sylvia Callahan's odd request for two reasons. First, curiosity had gotten the best of me. In my half-decade of experience, no one had ever asked to confront their spouse in a cathedral. Taverns were the standard. Public parks, near groups of soldiers, or privately in their homes were the most common orders. On my personal favorite occasions, we'd meet at a location that a mistress would happen to stumble upon. Objects were thrown every time mistresses made an appearance. In the time since the woman's inquiry, I'd been plagued with wonder.

Second, and more importantly, Sylvia Callahan paid exceptionally well.

I leaned against the pew closest to the door. While it had been quite the challenge to find an outfit that was both appropriate for a cathedral and that would conceal the four small daggers I carried, it had been more than worth it. The steel practically hummed against the bits of skin it touched. The nearness of the blades, though I hardly ever used them, soothed the subtle nerves I always felt before such meetings.

The clicking of heels against marble flooring announced the woman's arrival.

She was adorned by a long, silk, navy gown. Her braided brown hair fell in waves past her shoulders. Her expression was set, firm and unyielding, as she clutched a weighty satchel underneath one arm. Gentle creases were beginning to form around her eyes, but her dark skin remained flawless. By all standards, Miss Callahan was stunning. Especially in the city, beauty was often wasted on careless men.

She greeted me with a stern nod. We had only written, but she'd known who to expect.

"Are you ready?" I asked.

Her ebony eyes narrowed, "I am ready to live in peace." With a quiet huff, she handed me the satchel. I felt a strange mixture of pity and gratitude as I slung it over my shoulder. It would be a hard day for Miss Callahan but the satchel was noticeably heavier than I'd anticipated. She'd manage, I figured, and I'd have plenty of time to count the coins later. "Stay only as long as your gift is necessary. Let Lukoh be the sole witness to the bitter things I've waited to say to this man."

I merely nodded my acknowledgement. The god was archaic and notoriously distant, but her statement was striking.

Fortunately, we didn't wait long before her husband arrived. The rotund form of a man stumbled into the chapel, windblown and hurried. His ill-fitting green and gold uniform was one of a palace guard, though he was clearly not a very important one. The sleeves were far too long and the buttons were struggling to hold him together. Perhaps he'd been something close to handsome once. Not nearly good-looking enough to tempt someone into being with a married man, but moderate. How fortunate. He was both a liar *and* one of the king's soldiers.

Recognition lit in his eyes as soon as he entered the cathedral.

Hmmm. Very few people knew of my gift. Even fewer people knew my description. If he knew who I was, when I had never met him, then someone warned him about me. If knowing my gift worried him, it was a bad sign.

His expression turned pleading as he looked to his wife. "Sylvia. Don't do this."

That doesn't bode well for him, either.

To her credit, she remained steady. Eyeing her husband, she held out a small, golden chain.

"Who does this belong to?"

The man blanched at her question, glancing between us. His hand twitched at his side, inches away from his kingdom-issued weapon. Heavens above, I couldn't stand the Eloran king's men. They somehow managed to be over-eager and completely spineless all in the same breath.

"I don't know."

Lie, my gift whispered.

Over decades, heated debate raged concerning how gifts were allotted and where they came from. Religious theories were the most popular. Others believed that they were simply a mark of adaptation. However, it was widely agreed upon that genetics were the most important aspect of whether or not someone would be granted an ability. Those lineages usually led to people with gifts being put in positions of power or later being commandeered by the king.

I far preferred remaining rich and unbothered, so I kept my distance.

I shook my head at Miss Callahan.

The pursing of her lips was the only sign of her disapproval. "That'll be all, then, Miss Aster. Enjoy my husband's wealth."

The man began sputtering a stream of curses as I left but made no effort to stop me.

Distin was especially cold for May. The cool evening breeze did nothing to warm me, and the gown I'd worn to meet in the cathedral didn't help either. The path home was a short walk, crossing over a river that gave you a clear view of the Eloran palace. After passing over the bridge, it was only a few more minutes stroll down the pavement to reach my apartment.

I'd lived in the capital city longer than I'd ever stayed anywhere. Even though it was dreadfully close to royalty, there was enough life in one corner of the city to keep me occupied for weeks. More than that, where there were people, there was work. Everyone wanted to know who was deceiving them. Some were willing to pay quite a price, well enough to keep me comfortable.

Eventually, my etched wooden door greeted me. It wasn't lavish in a way that would draw too much unwanted attention, but the carvings made the apartment feel more like home. The lock clicked open quietly. Slowly, I breathed in the scent of my rug, my office, my bed, *my home*. Every bit of it had been paid for by my gift. Shelves of books I'd never read and weapons I didn't entirely know how to use decorated the entryway walls.

There was no one there when I arrived. There usually wasn't. I'd never been one to keep friends, and most of the visitors I did receive were bitterly angry for one reason or another. I understood being angry. Despite that, I was always relieved to find an empty home.

8

I plopped onto my bed with a sigh. My chest ached with a feeling I didn't entirely know how to name. Years of effort to get myself in a home that was warm and safe, yet still all I felt was hollow.

So, in lieu of sitting with my vacancy, I counted the coins.

****

The next morning, the market region was bustling. Distin was known as the city of commerce for good reason. The Torrid Market was always stuffed to the brim with vendors, each selling livestock, salves, produce, or anything in between. An overwhelming number of stands stood between me and my destination. Because, more importantly, it was where you could find some of the best strawberries in the entire nation of Elora, even on the market's busiest day of the week.

I barely dodged a boy running past. He was younger than I was, and he was certainly not paying the same amount of attention. Mariah and Eli Aster's shop was on the far side of the market, so I had little choice but to risk a tumble for the fruit that awaited me.

"Over here, over here! Cloaks for sale!" *True.* I silently wished my gift knew that there was no need to state the obvious.

Shifting around another hazard, Mariah's face came into view. Her apron was tied neatly around her waist and her salt and pepper curls were tucked carefully out of her face. She was short and heavy set and full of life. Mariah grinned wryly at me upon my approach. Even though she was the closest thing to family I'd ever had, she was still going to make me pay full price for the berries.

"Awfully late start, ey?" she taunted, meticulously arranging her fruit.

"I am a creature of the night," I sighed, stealing a blueberry as she tried to bat away my hand.

"You are a creature of *immense* drama, and I will be adding that to your tab," Mariah bristled, teasing.

She and Eli were the first to find my shaking form upon my arrival to Distin. I was young, far too young, and I had no one there willing to take me in. I had no memory of my parents, just of being handed off between those who felt pity. Occasionally, I ran when those who had originally been kind began to show their true colors. Other times, since I was not old enough to be sold to the king for use of my gift, I was tossed back onto the street waiting for another bleeding heart. It was a cycle I'd long since grown out of.

Mariah and Eli never took me in, which was likely for the best. I'd made my home in a corner of a less than wealthy side of town and slept there until I discovered ways to use my gift. However, they were quick to notice that every time I passed by their tent, a handful of fruit would go with me. I was no subtle thief. Mariah caught me the third time. With no money to repay them, and Eli's disdain for the local guards, they made me scrub every surface of her booth until it was spotless. It took two weeks to clean everything to their liking, and my fingers had torn with the effort.

In the end, she allowed me to work with them for a period. Eventually, my gift developed and I was ready to go on my own. We were not close, and they knew little about my story. But they were kind, and Eli had never laid a finger on me.

I had not forgotten their mercy, and I visited whenever I needed some extra sweetness in my day.

"That'll bring you out to 12 silvers, Selah. And I should've charged you more for the inconvenience, but you've caught me on a good day," she pulled the strawberries from a hidden shelf. "I don't save this kind of product for just anyone, you know."

Lie. I rolled my eyes. I had hoped it was true, if only for the fact that it meant she cared. But lovely Mariah was known for holding onto items for her regulars, and I happened to be one of them. "With that cost, I'd hope you'd expend some effort. You are bleeding me dry," I remarked. I passed her some of the payment I'd received the night prior, and she was content to number the coins in front of her.

"Bleeding *you* dry? That's half of our harvest for the season," Eli snickered. *Lie.* He passed me from behind, carrying his own load of produce in his sun-kissed hands. He was typically coated in a layer of dirt and grime, and always smelled faintly of grass and sweat. He never complained, though. They were well off because of his work.

"Fine, then. I won't take any more of your time. It's always a pleasure, Mariah, and thank you for the sample," I nodded towards the blueberries, and she glared at me in response.

"Pleasure's mine, young lady. And get your hair out of your face! No wonder no gentleman has swept you up. You can't be even bothered to look presentable at this hour," Mariah griped, and Eli gave her a pointed glance. She was a fussy one, especially when it came to the matter of my lack of suitors. I suspected she merely wanted the extra business.

I tucked a lock of ebony curls out of my face. She was right, it was a mess, but she was wrong in her assumption that it was the reason I wouldn't have a successful relationship. It is not enjoyable for a man to always be called out on his lies, and there were very few I even deemed to be worth the trouble. The men that I had been with either wanted more than I was willing to give or weren't patient or honest enough to last.

While I could not track my lineage, my parents had to have been from one of the ten gifted families that resided in Elora. That, or maybe one from a neighboring nation. Gifts did not merely *appear*. Well, not usually.

But what difference would knowing the origin of my ability even make? Investigating my parentage could only lead to undesirable outcomes, and I'd done well enough on my own.

I walked back through the market towards my home, letting my gift stretch itself out at will.

"I promise I'll give it right back!" A child's voice promised. *Lie.* I smirked slightly, knowing.

"You look beautiful, my love. Positively stunning," a man promised to his wife. *True.* I ached a bit. Not that I wished for it myself, but it was painfully sweet to hear someone's kind thoughts.

"It's the best deal you'll get on this side of Distin," a vendor swore. *Absolute lie.* He wasn't even subtle about it. The least he could do was convince himself.

"If you don't move along at this very *instant*, I'll be speaking with your father," a mother hissed, sounding rightfully exhausted. *True.* It wasn't even midday, and the poor woman had three children tugging her each and every way. Apparently, a report to their father was a good enough threat, and they trudged along.

"Come on, sweetheart. You'll be fine." *Lie.*

I cocked my head, searching for the bitterly rough voice who had said such a thing. I'd been spoken to like that before.

What?

"C'mon, now. I won't hurt you," the same voice promised in a strange accent. *Lie, lie, lie.*

I whirled once more, finding him looming in an alley I'd somehow missed before. He was a burly, beast of a man, covered in hair and arrogance. The man had on some sort of uniform, a navy and silver version of what an Eloran soldier would wear. A sword swung idly at his side. He

12

had his hands on the waist of an obviously frightened young girl. Her eyes widened beneath her blonde hair that she was using as a shield. She was young, just too young to defend herself. The man wasn't much taller than me, and I had faced worse.

There was no second thought, no amount of consideration that was going to make me leave her. I had *been* her. I set the strawberries down and palmed a dagger in my hand.

The man was too busy ogling the girl to notice that I was behind him. He was especially caught off guard, much to my delight, when I held my knife at his ribs, "Leave her be."

His breath caught. I watched his hands twitch towards the sword at his side. It was only appropriate that I relieve him of that as well, and I tossed it far out of his reach. The young girl adjusted her big, glossy eyes to meet mine, and I nodded my head for her to move, "Take the sword to one of the guards. We surely won't be bothering you anymore, will we?" I pressed my knife ever so gently further in for emphasis.

With that, she ran. I was left to deal with the man myself.

"Who do you think *you are*?" He snarled, still unwilling to move.

"I think," lowering my voice to a whisper crooning my threat into his ear, "that my graciousness is the only thing standing between you and an untimely death. And you are making it awfully tempting for my knife to dig *just* a little deeper." I pushed the blade ever so slightly further into his skin. I had never ended a man's life. I wasn't overly eager to start, either. "Is that what you want?"

"I am going to kill you," he threatened. *True.* Ah, look at that. First honest thing he had said.

I spun him around, aiming to get the knife at his throat but not moving fast enough. He shoved me out of reach. I slammed against the opposite wall. My head hit with a *thunk*, but I was still armed and it wasn't the first street fight I'd ever been in. Not that I tried to make a habit of it.

Like the brute I was expecting, he pulled back for a punch. His size made him incredibly slow. I ducked before his fist hit, and he met the wall instead. All it took was a quick slice across the back of his leg, and he was down for a moment.

He whirled, anger shining in his eyes as he took in his wounds. I could've run. Perhaps I should've, actually. But the sharp pulse of adrenaline in my veins demanded just a little more. I palmed my dagger again, waiting for him to earn another injury.

He moved to grab me, even slower than the time before thanks to the tear in his leg. Poor man practically fell into my knee, and it slammed into his stomach. I was not even particularly good at hand-to-hand combat, but he was clumsy and hurt.

My lack of talent showed, and he grabbed my leg before I could pull it all the way back. He pulled it straight up, leaving me without balance. I landed with a thud. For a moment, I couldn't breathe. He took the opportunity while I was still gasping to climb on top of me. It was my fault for choosing to continue the fight, I supposed. Although, if there was any position that I had learned to defend myself from, it was on the ground.

He landed one hit, and my head jerked with the force. I laughed. I couldn't help it. For whatever type of soldier he was, he hit like a child. And, you don't have to be good at fighting to enjoy it every now and again. Especially when it involves fighting arrogant imbeciles who absolutely deserve a healthy amount of pain.

His hands were on the ground at either side of my head, and I took the opportunity he granted. I snatched his wrist, wrapping my arm around his elbow and twisted his hand behind his shoulder. It was a deceptively

14

simple move, but one that not many were familiar with. It was also an effective way to pop the joint out of its socket.

He roared, and I tightened my grip even more. I began to hear voices moving toward us, but I couldn't be bothered to let go and see who was coming. He squirmed and tried to escape my grip, but it was of little use.

Strong hands yanked me away from him, and a pair of arms lifted me up from the dirt. The king's guards had arrived and grabbed the man up as well. He was limping, and his shoulder was bent at the wrong angle, but he would live. It was better than I had left others.

"That is quite enough," a woman pushed past the rest of the guards. She stood straighter than the lesser soldiers, with more badges on her outer coat than the rest of them combined. I recognized her, with her dark skin and watching gaze. Her reputation as one of the key overseers of Distin preceded her. I had never met General Pearce myself, mostly just measlier guards every now and again. They were fun, but so encompassed by duty that they never stuck around.

She took a moment to assess the situation. I had dropped my weapon when they grabbed me, but they had to know that it was mine. The man was clearly more hurt than I was, but I was smaller and usually appeared to be less of a threat. The man I had beaten glowered at me as we awaited the general's judgment.

"Take them both to the Vaults. We'll let the king decide what to do with them. Lucas, send for a medic to meet you there." With no other order needed, we were dragged away.

It was my first visit to a prison, but it certainly wouldn't be the last.

Chapter Two: Haven

I, too, had been shocked to discover that, despite the many skills I'd be trained to develop as a second-born prince, event coordinating would be one of the most utilized.

"Your Highness, the chairs. The vendor only delivered 1300. We *needed* 1400. Do you mind writing to him –"

"Prince Haven! I really am not sure that we have enough hors d'oeuvres. Shall we ask again about –"

"The king is asking for you, Your Highness."

"Prince Haven, the cook has fallen ill. I understand Princess Faye's gifting ceremony is over a month away, but perhaps we should plan –"

Elliott stifled a groan beside me as I hurried to write down their requests. Heavens above, the frenzy was giving me a headache. The event was indeed still weeks out, and already there was chaos. My dearest friend and lieutenant colonel had arrived to review security placement. Really, though, I think Elliott was finding an excuse for me to get away.

I rubbed my temple, "I'll reach out to the vendor. Miss, review the list again and I'll revisit that later. And the cook has weeks to rest, I'm sure we'll figure something out by then. Send him to Genevieve if needed. If you'll excuse me."

Elliott and I ducked out of the room without any further chatter. I sighed heavily. It was much easier to breathe when I was not so busy suppressing all the temperaments of however many people had been assigned to plan Faye's ceremony. I could sense Elliott's irritation, but years of tolerating his emotions had made them seem entirely manageable.

We didn't dare linger on the way back to my bedroom. It was, perhaps, the only area where I'd be free of requests until her ceremony was over. I loved my sister. I really did. She deserved a fun and memorable gifting ceremony. I just wished my parents had found someone else to oversee it.

The map of the castle was sprawled across most of my desk. In the small area it did not cover, Elliott sat. His brown eyes were largely hidden by dreads of hair so dark they were nearly black. They all fell carefully around his head as he processed the information with that supernatural speed of his. It was quite a gift. His poor parents, though, had spent far too much of their time when he was young trying to track him down. Somehow, he had always been found with me.

He pursed his lips, snatching a quill, "Don't put those two together. They're decent soldiers on their own, but they talk too much. Assign him to the front gate, I'll send someone else inside."

I waved a hand, "Arrange it however you please. It's your mother who will be bothered if something's amiss."

General Pearce was a force of a woman. I still got shivers down my spine when I recalled the winters I'd be sent to her to train. I'd nearly lost half my toes from frostbite when she left Elliott and me to survive in the wilderness alone for a week.

The lieutenant colonel smirked. "I think you're just scared of her."

I rolled my eyes. "A different prince would have you demoted for implying such a thing," I answered, looking over the roster again.

"A different prince wouldn't miss me as much. Who would save you from all the servants' nagging if I weren't here?" Evidently, Elliott had stopped by the kitchen on his way up to visit me, as he bit a large chunk out of a loaf of bread that had appeared in his hand. His gift left him always hungry, and left his parents with a massive food payment each month.

I reached for a piece of his bread, but he tucked it away with a disapproving look. "No, they're just doing their jobs. It's no fault of theirs. Event planning is simply not where my skills lie."

He snorted, "If you can't plan parties, and your combat abilities are lacking, what are you possibly good for?"

He was baiting me. I was at least as good a fighter as he was – if not far better – especially considering he had the advantage of speed. Officially, he was my tutor. Unofficially, it had been years since he could take me down without use of his gift or a great amount of effort. Due to the nature of our assigned tasks, his being with his parents, knowledge of our own defense and the defense of the kingdom wasn't optional. It was also the most enjoyable part of my work. There was a kind of release in fighting a friend. It was even better when you won.

"I must've had a dreadful tutor, then."

A persistent knock at the door cut off the snarky reply Elliott was preparing.

"Your Highness," Lars poked his head around the door wearing a grim expression. Of all the servants, he was one we'd known the longest. He was remarkably thin for having a castle-funded salary, with spindly limbs and gaunt features. His worry filled the room like a scent, "The king is asking for you. It's urgent."

Elliott and I exchanged a glance before rising to follow him. I sensed Elliott's apprehension and struggled to untangle it from my own.

Lars' pace was faster than his typical saunter. It only took a few moments for me to understand that we were heading to the meeting room. Was there something planned that I'd forgotten? That wouldn't have garnered such a response from Lars. We rapidly passed the meticulously decorated palace halls. Portraits of my father's predecessors lined the walls. I always got the impression that they knew more than I did.

Lars slid the large cedar panel aside, his slim figure blending into the background. There was a wave of emotion in the room that almost knocked me back from its sheer volume. There was anger. Plenty of it. It was a familiar burning in my chest, like a fire had settled beneath my ribcage. There was worry, a nagging, aching wound that had not quite healed. There was also a layer of embarrassment, the kind of shame that came from having everyone's attention for an unfortunate reason.

My father and mother sat together at the head of the table. The king's face was coolly calm, but I could tell even without prying that my father was troubled. The queen's brows knitted themselves together, somewhere between anger and fear, and she tried very little to hide her concern. I pulled my gift back on itself so I wouldn't be overwhelmed with their feelings, and my emotions were my own again.

"Haven, Elliott," my father acknowledged us both. Exhaustion lined his eyes like it always did. Perhaps the reason why the king and I got along was because he couldn't hide much of how he felt from me. Even when I didn't try, he had always been easy to read. "Sit."

We joined them at the vast oak table that awaited us. It had been designed for such a thing, court meetings that the throne room was too grand for. My family happened to be the only ones who arrived, save for a few others who would just be listening in. Elliott had been considered part of our family unit since before either of us had come into our abilities.

Alaric sat next to my parents, sword resting across his lap. He fiddled with it in one hand and rested his chin on the table with the other. He was completely stoic. The only thing that gave away his concern was the ease that his weapon was drawn to his fingertips. The move was surprisingly natural for someone who hadn't been trained to fight like Elliott and I had. His amber eyes matched my own, but his paler skin and darker hair lended to him looking more like our father.

My brother was not much older than I was, but his age revealed itself in the heaviness with which he sat. Alaric was always burdened by something. It exuded from him. Perhaps the weight of being next in line for the throne made his shoulders sag. I was in line after him, but my rule wasn't inevitable. Maybe it was simply the blood that still stained his sword if you looked at it closely. For someone who maintained the regal air of royalty, he held none of the joy that came with protecting his people. He was a seer, but he rarely shared with anyone but the king.

Adjacent to him seethed Genevieve, her wrath apparent. Her usually sweet features were contorted with anger, and the back of her maroon gown never deigned to touch the back of her seat. Fortunately, her gift was not fire, although there was a hint of something burning in the blue eyes she'd inherited from our father. Gen was a healer, an ability that was universally adored. Her brown hair was the same shade as Alaric's but she had all the passion he lacked.

Last, on the other side of Elliott's chair, Faye shrunk in her seat. That's where the embarrassment had originated from, I concluded. She had inherited our mother's blonde hair, just like I did. She was young, painfully so for having so many eyes on her. Not weak, just a bit naive. We had yet to discover if she had a particular talent. The rest of ours appeared shortly after we turned thirteen, and if Faye had one, it hadn't surfaced.

"Faye," my mother's voice was soft, but something bitter resided in her tone. "Please explain to them why we're here."

My youngest sister turned a stark shade of red, burying her face in the table, "Lukoh, spare me."

Alaric waved a hand, "A Lyscottian soldier – one of King Castillo's men – tried to kidnap Faye."

"What?"

"It wasn't like that, I was *fine* –"

"After," the queen hissed, "she evaded her guards!"

"I was *fine*," Faye piped. "I was about to leave, but then a girl came and said she would handle it. It was nothing." Her emotions betrayed her. I was getting the impression that it was anything but nothing.

My mother pinned down the princess with a sharp glare. Oh, how I remembered being on the receiving side of that look as a child. It was the sort of gaze the queen reserved solely for her misbehaving children. "You are dismissed, darling. We will discuss the importance of *staying with your guards* later."

My youngest sister left the room with a huff, her distaste evident.

Lyscott. Elora hadn't interacted with Lyscott in ages. I had only visited once, and that was as a small child. Faye hadn't even been born yet the last time I could recall any international correspondence.

"I'm sorry, but I don't understand. Why is King Castillo's soldier still breathing? He tried to abduct a princess. He has more than earned his death," Alaric spat. My father cocked his head, assessing Alaric's attitude. He was prone to occasional outbursts, but usually not ones asking for someone's head on a stake.

I didn't entirely disagree with him.

"Do we know what exactly happened?" I asked.

The king finally spoke. "We have the girl Faye referenced in the Vaults. I want you to ask her yourself." He glanced far away, and I sensed that there was something he wasn't saying.

"Why are we holding her if she saved Faye's life? Isn't that worth some sort of reward?" I countered.

I often took for granted how free we were to challenge our parents' judgment in the Eloran palace. I wasn't sure what it was truly like in other countries, but my father had implied on multiple occasions that different nations were more severe. In fact, I felt more fear arguing with Elliott's mother than I ever had my own. Though, in fairness, Elliott's mother could inflict far more physical damage than mine was capable of. Our father's lenience was something I hoped that Alaric would remember when he had children of his own.

"I've heard certain rumors," the king replied, "concerning a young lady with the supernatural ability of detection. There are whispers of how generously she has been compensated for her gift, reports of a woman who has ruined lives with her accuracy. She has not offered up her services to the castle yet, so all we had were stories. One of my men was able to identify her. Truthfully, if this were anyone but my own blood, I wouldn't care much aside from the political ramifications. But with this, tell me that you can see how she would be a valuable asset."

I searched Elliott for his opinion, for a read on what he was feeling. While I didn't need to know what he was thinking, I certainly wanted to. I could sense nothing from him, though, neither on his face or through my gift. There was the smallest amount of intrigue, but aside from that, he was empty of emotion.

"Of course," I supposed it was her fault for not having offered her talents to the king. It was unspoken law, and abilities could be commandeered at any time if it was for the sake of the kingdom. "What do you suggest that we do with her?"

"'Do with her'?" My sister countered. "She is not an *item* to be used. Why not just ask?"

"I'm sure that was not his implication, Genevieve. We just can't guarantee that she will be willing to help if she's never offered before," my mother recovered on my behalf. I nodded my apology, and that seemed to be enough to dull the flames for a moment.

"We do not know her name, but it's the same girl. At least, as far as my soldier confirmed," the king huffed, looking at my mother. She squeezed his hand. "It seems as though I have two issues that need to be resolved: I have a king whose soldiers are far too deep into my territory for my liking, and a young lady sitting in my prison who seems to have an especially useful ability."

The queen cut in, composed as ever, and it seemed as though they had already come to this conclusion, "We need her to be escorted to King Castillo. There are some questions we'd like honest answers to, and I'm not sure she will be especially motivated to do it on her own."

"You can't make her do that," Genevieve added with the defeat evident in her tone. She didn't like it, but there wasn't much she could say.

It was the king who responded, "We can, and we must. Even more so if he wants to try to bargain for his soldier." The idea of releasing the man in any capacity was absolutely absurd, but I kept that particular thought to myself.

"Alaric can't go," I started, despite the glare that it earned me from his side of the table. "He is the heir to the throne. If he is hurt or captured, it sends an obvious message."

My father nodded, "You are correct. That's why I'm not going to send him. I'm sending you."

Somehow, I hadn't entertained that as a possibility. I wasn't entirely certain if the wave of shock I was experiencing was my own, if it came from those around me, or a mix of the two. Then, I felt anticipation rolling off Elliott like energy itself. He still looked collected. We hadn't done anything of true value in – well, ever. *Anything is better than party planning.*

"Just me?" I asked, confirming whether I'd have my friend with me.

"Just you. Bring Lieutenant Colonel Pearce if you deem it necessary. You will be emissaries on a relatively safe journey; you don't need an entourage. Your other duties will be passed onto Genevieve in your absence." She looked as though she was going to comment, but she refrained. "Haven, meet with the girl tonight. Let her know what will be required of her. I'll send a messenger to go ahead of you, but I expect you to leave in the morning. Do you understand?"

I looked to Elliott, whose eyes were lit with intrigue, then back at my king, "Yes, Your Majesty. We'll start preparing now."

Chapter Three: Selah

For a prison cell, it didn't smell nearly as bad as one would expect.

That didn't mean the floors were clean, or dry, or that the guards paid me any mind when I tried to strike up a conversation. Only twelve hours in, and I was already horrendously, hopelessly bored. I paced the suspiciously damp concrete. The movement of the chains threatened to cut deeper into my swollen wrists. My jaw was the only part of me that truly ached. His strike had been weak, but he hit bone. I tried not to let it bother me too much. The man who had inflicted such a blow had been significantly worse for wear because of it.

I could see nothing of any other prisoners from where I was kept. The room was dark: it would've been pitch black if not for a candle sitting in the far corner and a barred window that allowed in the moonlight. It could not be wise to give fire to criminals, but I supposed I appreciated the gentle glow. My first hour had been spent knocking on the creaking metal door that had been locked behind me, asking to speak with someone of reason. My request was promptly ignored, and I resorted to being left alone with my thoughts.

I allowed the anger to have a home in my chest. I helped that girl, and they locked me up. Sure, perhaps I did slightly more damage than was necessary, but some would argue that it was well earned. How could they keep me when, for all they know, he might've been luring her to her death.

It was a royal waste of my time. They were keeping me from a very important appointment with my strawberries that I had paid so much for. *They probably ate them out of spite*, I concluded. *I will reign fire and brimstone down on this entire depths-forsaken palace if they eat my strawberries.*

At long last, heavy footsteps descended the corridor toward me. Yet another guard who would ignore my request for justice. Another set of footsteps followed, and then another. I was about to move over to investigate when the latch to my cell unlocked. Just one man entered the room though, one I could have sworn I had seen before.

Sunlight personified stood before me.

He was tall, blond, and lean. The lantern he carried lit up his features, allowing me access to the honey tint of his eyes and the gentle tan of his skin. A band of gold ordained with jewels lined his forehead. Bright streaks of unkempt hair jutted each and every way like rays of light, revealing his youth. He was in the king's uniform, and green and gold outlined his coat. An usually clean sword hung at his side, ignored. It appeared it had never been used.

He also happened to be remarkably attractive.

"You're important," I muttered.

The young man grinned, and the room itself was brighter for it, "As are you, I'm told." *True.* His voice was smooth and something warm resided on the edge of his tone. "What gave it away?"

Is he teasing me?

I glanced at his forehead, "The tiara."

"It is *not* –" His brows furrowed as he interrupted himself. Concern weighed on his expression, but only for a second. "Are you still hurt?"

26

I wasn't quite sure why it mattered. "Just a bruise."

He could not be the first-born prince. I'd seen that prince once in passing, and his features were far darker. I knew the king and queen had a few children, but learning anything about them felt like tempting fate. Jewels of that sort, though, were held only for royalty. Perhaps he was the second son? Even then, I could not imagine why a prince would be sent to speak with me. They had no way of knowing about my gift, and if they did, why send a prince instead of a guard?

Likely sensing my confusion, the young man held out a hand that I did not take, "My name is Haven." I raised a brow. "Officially, Prince Haven Allicot of Elora. But just Haven is fine." *True. Depths.*

Haven. The name struck a chord somewhere in the back of my brain. I'd definitely heard it before.

"Do forgive me for not minding my manners. I should've bowed sooner." I made no effort to do so.

His smile widened, and he tucked his hands back into his pockets. Cocky, spoiled, little prince of the kingdom that had thrown me in jail for defending a child. He did not deserve my respect, I decided. "You are going to be an absolute pleasure to get acquainted with." *True. Get acquainted with?*

Jabbing you in the throat would be an absolute pleasure.

"I aim to please." Despite the fact I'd never escaped from a prison, I weighed how difficult it would be. Holding the prince hostage was certainly an option, though challenging without weapons. I also imagined that sort of thing was highly frowned upon. Alas, maybe another time. "And I am highly honored that they sent the prince to escort me home. I imagine it's stooping a little low for you, but I do appreciate the consideration."

27

He laughed. It required a notable amount of effort not to punch him in his stupid, royal face. The anger that had dissipated when he walked in returned in full force, reminding me how I ended up there to begin with. It was his father's oblivious general who had deemed me to be a threat, regardless of my testimony.

The prince relaxed a bit, settling against a wall. "That is most endearing." *True. Heavens above, he's the worst.* My only true consolation was the fact that I could vividly picture throttling him. I indulged myself for a passing moment before reigning in my attention. "But why don't we start with you giving me your account of what happened this morning."

That, I didn't mind. And it made so much sense. The man I'd apprehended hadn't been an Eloran soldier. A soldier of a sort, but certainly not one of the king's men. Personally, I hadn't recognized his uniform, but the prince might have. *Hmm.*

I held up my shackled wrists, "Would you not prefer to have this conversation elsewhere? Perhaps with fewer chains?"

To his credit, the prince considered it. He pursed his lips as he weighed my request. Amber eyes wavered on the bruising the metal bands had caused. He shook his head, "Speak with me, and then I'll decide."

Fine. I could lie, if needed, which would be alright unless the prince had the gift of detection. It was highly, wholly unlikely, but happened every few hundred years. Usually, each gift was allotted to one person at a time. There had been exceptions. Depths, I regretted paying so little attention to the royal family. Maybe his gift was merely being intolerable. I feared it would be something more bothersome.

"I went to the market this morning to visit some old friends. I bought a tub of strawberries that I will *absolutely* be expecting to be reimbursed for. I was peacefully making my way back to my home – by the river just across town, if you're wondering where to take me. I saw the man looming over a little girl and I decided to lend a hand." I plastered on a half-hearted grin and expected that to be enough. "Is that sufficient?"

"What did he say to her?" he asked, losing the humor.

"Did she not tell you herself?" It wouldn't be a total waste if all I had done was offer a healthy amount of justice, but part of me hoped she had been found.

The prince didn't bother to meet my eyes, but he nodded, "She's well, if that's what you're asking. Embarrassed that she needed saving, though, and she wasn't overly eager to give more information than necessary." *True.* I hadn't expected to feel a wash of relief. I wondered if she, like I had done when I was so vulnerable, had prayed to the god of our kingdom for help. Lukoh had listened to little of what I had poured out when I was young, though, so I was never naive enough to anticipate a response. I wondered if he favored her. Regardless, a weight that I hadn't noticed I'd been carrying left me.

Whatever the prince perceived caused the smallest wave of interest to present itself on his features, and then it was gone again. His head shook as if to rid himself of some thought, and then he was back on the subject, "What were his precise words? When we present his crimes to his king, we'll need exact statements. I'd like for you to go over it with me first."

Memories of the incident mixed with aching ones of my very own resided in the front of my mind. "He said that she would be fine, and that he wouldn't hurt her." Anger stirred about in my chest and I paused with the weight of it. "He was lying," I concluded softly.

The room was entirely silent as the prince considered what I'd said. I waited for any response, for him to recoil with disgust or to inform me how I had held a knife to a man's throat over nothing. No hint of emotion filled his features, though, and the prince of Elora had no immediate retort. I allowed him a moment, if only out of respect for the little girl.

Then, he looked at me again. Not with one of the sickly sweet grins I had been previously granted, or a smirk that told me he was aware of how he taunted me. The ghost of an expression never quite met his eyes, and something like icy anger flickered behind their golden brown tint. I needed no ability to sense the truth in his words.

"He will be dealt with accordingly."

"Good," I nodded. We found something to agree upon. I could appreciate that. Well, and that he ridded the vast boredom that had loomed in the cell for hours.

The coldness left his expression, and the cocky grin that he was much better suited for returned in its place. Tension that I hadn't noticed he was holding in his shoulders broke off as well, and he met my eyes once more, "I don't believe I know your name. It's a shame. I do make a habit of knowing all the ladies that end up in this prison."

"You know," I offered, "I recently got it inscribed on my doorstep. Take me there and find out for yourself."

He laughed, and the very sound of it filled the chamber. Years were taken off his face, and he was even more captivating than I had realized when he had first stepped into the room. I gave myself only a second to acknowledge it, and my admiration departed once I recalled who he was and where we were speaking. "We are going to have quite the journey." *True.*

I physically shook away the implication of his words, "*We* will be doing nothing. You know that I am guilty of no crime, which means it's entirely unlawful for you to hold me against my will." As far as I knew. I made no habit of getting arrested, and I spent no large amount of time studying the capital's laws.

"Really?" Amusement glinted in his features, "Is that what you think? Because the reputation that I've been made aware of is rather interesting." He stood, moving from his spot to where the candle sat. Lanky fingers danced atop the flame, never near enough for it to burn. I became suddenly and overwhelmingly nauseous. "I hear you can discern truth from deception. I have it on good authority that your talent isn't simply intuition. Lukoh has blessed you, hasn't he?"

Dread must've been apparent on my face. It must have been, or else I could have convinced him otherwise. Instead, he latched on to the flicker of a feeling, "That's a yes." He smiled at me, knowing. My fingers twitched, silently wishing for him to do something to provoke a response. "Though I cannot imagine what bloodline you are a part of. You are Eloran, aren't you?"

I readjusted, freeing my shoulders to sit straighter and tucked my arms across my chest. "Having a gift is not illegal."

His look turned even gentler, dripping with pity, "Illegal, no, of course not. You cannot control what gifts you are or are not provided with. However, as you are no doubt aware, the crown reserves the right to require your services if we are in need. I am, unfortunately, in need of you."

I decidedly *was* aware. It was half the reason I typically remained on my end of Distin and tried not to linger too long with clients. My hair was somewhat memorable, with dark black curls not being the standard in Elora, but the rest of me was entirely typical. I tried to be easy to forget. Staying hidden in the masses was meant to be simple. *How did they know about my gift?*

31

"You cannot make me stay." It was a feeble attempt at a response, but it was all I could offer.

He laughed again, "I absolutely can."

"And if I refuse?"

He waited a moment, pursing his lips. "There are two reasons that I imagine will be rather compelling."

"Enlighten me, Your Highness."

If the way I used his title bothered him, he gave no indication. I could nearly watch confidence radiate from him like the rays of light he was so suited to disperse. "First, I don't think you'd like to stay in this cell forever for refusing to aid the crown. It's rather dreary here, I think, and your candle won't last you forever."

"And?" I bristled.

"And," he crossed his arms, matching my stance. "I'm not sure you noticed, but the man you fought today was not of this kingdom. He is a soldier from Lyscott, the only neighbor of ours that we don't regularly engage with. We'd like to know exactly why the king had his men so far into Elora, and with your involvement this morning, I'd imagine you'd enjoy some answers of your own."

I considered his offer as I connected the dots, "You're wanting me to let you know when the Lyscottians are lying."

"Clever girl. I like you already." *True. Ugh.*

I bristled, "Give me back my knife, Prince. See just how much you like me then. I hear it's rather difficult to flirt with prisoners without a tongue"

He didn't so much as bat an eye at my threat, "I'm sure you'd find me just as charming."

"Perhaps even more so."

32

Yet again, and much to my dismay, another chuckle escaped from the prince. I was just a source of amusement for him, then. It was telling to see that the second born prince of Elora had nothing better to do with his time than to toy with people he had falsely imprisoned.

"You will be more than compensated for your efforts," he sobered slightly, returning his focus. He placed his hand over his heart in sincerity, "I will even personally deliver twice the number of strawberries that you have lost, if that is what it takes. But I would be more than honored to have your company, and I can guarantee it will be worth your time." *True.*

I watched him for a moment. Tufts of hair flopped onto the glinting headpiece. I wondered if he would look just as royal without it. His uniform was remarkably similar to the rest of the soldiers in Distin, but the finery that laid across his forehead was unmistakably regal. It was a bit much, honestly, especially if his plan for the evening was to visit the cell I was kept in. My clothes, still stained with blood and dirt, left me entirely underdressed.

I saw no deceit in him. He was perfectly, wholly honest. Part of me couldn't discern why that bothered me so deeply. The other half had been pulled in by his offer and found no reason to refuse. Arrogant, maybe, and irritatingly so. But I sensed nothing that labeled him as a threat. His height, towering above mine and the fit of his uniform suggested that he was strong, but he was no danger to me yet.

"What is your gift?" I asked. I would work with him if necessary, but I was not eager to do so blindly.

His warm visage remained, and he looked at me as though he knew something I didn't, "It's not too far from yours. I can sense what others feel unless I try not to, and even then it is not always optional." *True.*

I nearly changed my mind. It was a dangerous thing when someone could tell you everything you experienced. Years of effort had been concentrated into not revealing every little thing I felt. I could vividly picture the parts of me that I was unwilling to let him pick apart. So many –

"You have nothing to fear from me," he must've sensed my panic, and my thoughts were interrupted. It was true. At least he thought it was, and maybe that would be enough.

"I'll do it," I finally conceded. "Under two conditions."

Something between excitement and amusement revealed itself in his grin, "And what might those be?"

"First, you may not read what I am feeling if you are doing so for your own benefit. If it's necessary, fine. But my emotions are my own, and it is an intrusion for you to invade them without cause."

The prince nodded his response, and I continued.

"Second, I want three times the strawberries I lost, hand delivered by you. I will accept nothing less," I settled, content with my bargain.

His lips twitched with delight, "I didn't realize you so enjoyed my company." He interrupted me before I could argue. "Consider it done, then. But I have a condition of my own."

"Have you not demanded enough?"

"This should be simple," he assured, and the sincerity I felt from him seemed genuine. "Tell me your name."

He asked so gently. His volume had barely been above a whisper, and the warmth in his eyes had persisted. I wanted to tell him no, that he should shove this whole bargain and leave me be. But kindness resided in his tone, and I wasn't sure I had the nerve to refuse such a request.

"Selah Aster," I offered. It was not truly my given name. I'd taken Mariah and Eli's family name whenever it was required of me, simply because I did not have one of my own. They never minded and told anyone who asked that I was a distant relative.

His smile broadened with satisfaction. "Selah Aster, it is an honor to meet you."

True.

Chapter Four: Haven

My very soul ached while I watched the woman who stood before me.

It was no exaggeration to call her lovely, or to tell her that it was a pleasure to meet. She was a stunning mess. Black, untamed curls bounced off the top of her head and reached past her shoulders. Cutting gray-blue eyes had begun to size me up from the moment that I stepped into the cell, and they had not yet ceased. Blood had since dried on her lip, and I had sensed the pain she felt from the bruising mark on her jaw. She had to have been over half a foot shorter than me, but not once in the entire exchange had she backed away.

Even more than the fact that she was pretty enough to warrant my compliments, what I felt from her was compelling. Anger had never left her, not fully. It was as real as the heartbeat under the surface of her skin. The living, breathing rage had pulsed relentlessly, and I wondered who had earned such wrath.

Beside that anger lay a gaping, endless wound that I had sensed from few others. I could picture the hole inside her chest as well as I could see the face in front of me. Aside from the irritation, the occasional shock or persisting distaste, all I felt was a bleeding gash. She had said she wasn't hurt. She didn't appear to be injured any further than the obvious. But I felt her pain as if it were my own. After only a few minutes of it, I had to pull back. How she could handle more than that was beyond my understanding. I had opened myself up again to assess how she reacted to the suggestion that she was gifted. Once I sensed that I was correct, I let her be. It is an intrusion, of a sort, and I needed her to be willing to accompany me to Lyscott.

I wouldn't mind her liking me, either. So I did what I could.

The emotion I could not ignore was her relief. She had cared about Faye, even though she did not know who she truly was in the kingdom. If Selah hadn't recognized me, I doubted she would recognize the youngest royal. I couldn't tell if it really would've mattered. I told her that the girl she saved was safe, and it meant something to her. My sister was protected, and this stranger was glad for it. Depths, she had practically risked her life for it.

So perhaps I could look past her obvious disdain, if only to cling on to the humanity I found in what she'd felt.

"We leave in the morning," I took the forgotten lantern in my hand. My things would not pack themselves, even if I had many who would be willing to help. Our food and basic supplies would already be another's responsibility, so I had declined assistance for tucking away my own clothes. "I'll be taking you to the castle to sleep for the night. Write a list of everything you'll need. If you want items from your home, so be it, but we should have whatever you'll require."

I tapped on the door, and one of the guards slipped me the key to her chains. The skin trapped beneath the tight metal cuffs was bruised and angry, and I made a mental note to ask my father if we had a kind that was more suitable for detaining people who were cooperative. Not everyone deserved comfort, as the knowledge of the Lyscottian soldier kept only a few cells away reminded me, but she had technically done nothing wrong.

I unlocked one side, and she was silent as the other fell to the floor. "What," I asked, "no witty remark? If I'd have known all I had to do to get you quiet was let you go, I may have done it sooner."

She rubbed her wrist absentmindedly, and the defiance she had momentarily forgotten returned to her face in full force. "Did you not see the damage I caused today?"

I surely had seen it. His cell was on the path to hers, and I had peeked at his wounds. I'd heard about the gash on his leg, but that was hidden in a layer of shadows. His face, though, would have been something to pity if it had been caused for any other reason. "I'm certain I'll manage." Her features hardened into a scowl, and she glared at me as if I had three heads. "Come along then, Miss Aster. You'll need some rest before we leave."

The door creaked open behind me, and she shuffled to keep my pace. Two guards accompanied us, blending into the background of the prison. I kept towards the wall where her victim was kept. She didn't see him, fortunately, and she strutted along as if she had no other care.

We walked in silence. I held my hands tight to my sides. If I touched her, I would feel everything. She had asked me to let her be, and it was in my best interest to oblige her. Her chin remained perched in the air as I guided her through one hall, and then another. A few more silent minutes of twists and turns, and we had reached the door to the room she'd be occupying overnight.

This part of the castle was rarely touched, only tended to when we hosted the few guests we received. Regardless, it was just as pristine and ornately decorated as every other hall. The wood paneling never rattled with age, and the walls were as whole as the day they'd been built.

"This is where I leave you, Miss Aster. The guards will be here for the night, they will be more than happy to tend to your every need."

She sneered once more, looking up at me through heavy lashes, "I was under the impression that I am no longer held prisoner, and yet I am guarded?"

I shook my head. "Not like that. They serve mostly to protect you, but also to ensure that you get whatever you wish before we set off in the morning. You'll need all the rest you can get, so I can't keep you much longer."

The obvious furrow of her brow indicated her contempt, "I'm almost offended that you think I need protection."

"It's not about you. It's standard practice that we provide security to all our guests. The king has requested it," I released a heavy breath, hoping that she couldn't sense the remnants of the afternoon we'd had. All the worry and anger and fear from the table had lingered for some time after Elliott and I had left. "And he happens to have quite some power over this estate."

"I imagine so," her eyes swept around the area, absorbing the finery that she was surrounded by.

"Until tomorrow, then," I willed myself to grin despite the exhaustion that was tugging on my bones. I nodded my goodbye and left without allowing her to stop me. My head rattled with each step, anticipating the toll of the journey we'd face when the sun rose.

Familiar voices inside my bedroom reached me as I turned the handle: laughter echoed into the hall. Genevieve sat on my bed, a broad smile on her face and giggling at something Elliott had said. Elliott leaned up against my desk, holding an empty glass to his smirking lips. Alaric had joined them, still glum as ever.

Genevieve tucked long strands of straight brown hair away from her face as she acknowledged me. "Oh, Haven! How did it go? Was she angry? We've been placing bets. Elliott guessed she'd be eager to be paid, Alaric said she'd be apathetic either way, and I said she'd be angry. I'm fairly certain I won."

I met Elliott's darker gaze as I settled into the room, and amusement danced over his features. "You wouldn't happen to be encouraging my little sister to gamble, Lieutenant Colonel?"

"And your older brother," Alaric added.

Elliott shrugged. "What, she's of age! And some of us needed a bit of amusement before we set off to another kingdom." A nearly unnoticeable amount of pink revealed itself behind the dark skin of his face.

It was certainly not the first time he'd been a poor influence on the royal family, but it could have been much worse. There was the time that he talked me into traveling halfway across the nation overnight. Usually, this was impossible, but he'd stuffed me in a cart and used his ability to wheel us along. Needless to say, it was a remarkably bad idea. I've never had a worse headache. If not for the incident with the Illustri that year, my mother may have never let us forget.

I grimaced at him, "Then I hope you didn't offer your princess anything you're unwilling to part with."

"I *knew* it."

The lieutenant colonel groaned, passing her a small bag of coins. Alaric sighed heavily, handing over a similar one. The princess beamed. I guessed that she was more pleased with her own victory than with the money.

"Could it really have gone so poorly?" Elliott asked.

"No, it didn't. She was…" Heavens above. I didn't know how to describe her. She was full of anger and bitterness and pain, and yet there was something compelling about her. "Her name is Selah. She has a family name I've never heard of. She was angry that she had been detained but agreed to accompany us to Lyscott in the end."

"Rightfully so," Alaric sat back against my bed, waving his arms in the air as he spoke. "What did I tell you? Even if she had killed him, she should've gone free. I am still rather tempted, to be honest." He chuckled, "How much do you think our father would rampage if I sent the soldier's head along with you? Oh, I can only imagine the look on his face. You're not gone yet. I can still make it happen."

It was times like this when I feared for the fate of my kingdom.

"Wait," Elliott started, "a family name you've never heard of? She's Eloran, right? We know all the Eloran families with giftings."

Sure, we did. There were the Aldens from the north, a strikingly friendly bunch. The Hathaways, Eatons, Glaziers, and Pearce families all lived in Distin. The Tatton family resided near the coast, not far from the Vance family. The Danes and the Fenns settled in the east. Including our family, it made for ten gifted lineages.

I'd met the patrons of each family over my years as prince. Some were far kinder than others. I recalled the Tattons to be especially cruel, and the Aldens were a personal favorite of mine. The Eatons, Glaziers, and Vances had each never quite forgiven me for what had happened with the Illustri, regardless of who was at fault. Fortunately, I didn't interact with them much. Most families who'd been blessed were content to keep to

41

themselves. My father kept up regular correspondence, as Alaric had also started, but I saw them only during ceremonies. Well, aside from the Pearce family.

Elliott Pearce had been a constant presence for as long as I could remember. I did more with him as a child than I did with my own brother. After the attack, though, he was around far more frequently. We'd both been older than Faye's current age by that point, old enough to have started using our gifts, but not yet of the age where we'd be left to our own devices. No, especially after the attack, we were watched. For good reason, too. It took years for everything to fully return to normal. Some days, I wasn't sure it ever truly had.

I shrugged, "Her parents may not be Eloran." Though I couldn't begin to guess where she'd be from instead. Hair so curly with skin so light wasn't typical for any of our neighboring countries. "But the king said he confirmed it. Detection is a useful gift." Not good for everything, but useful. "If she'll help, I won't refuse."

Genevieve yawned. "Well, I'm happy for you. Even if it means I must triple my workload."

I cringed, "I apologize."

She waved me off. Truly, though, the event was in much better hands with her. Faye would be thrilled to hear that Gen had helped put everything together. I could manage, sure, but Gen cared exceedingly more.

Alaric, too, appeared weighed down by exhaustion, "I must retire for the evening. Not to fret. If I get a vision of you two getting stabbed, maimed, or otherwise incapacitated on your journey, I'll try to let you know in advance."

I grinned tightly, "Comforting."

As I closed the door after Gen and Alaric's exit, I drew a breath before facing Elliott. He was perched up on the desk now, shoulders slumped. His dreads now fell gently onto his shoulders as though each and every one had been thoughtfully placed. The muscles in his shoulders and back that I had witnessed him earn were only suitable for the general's son. Overbearing as that son may be.

"I do not wish to travel with someone we do not know, from a family we've never met, with an ability we've never tested," Elliott muttered.

I removed the band of gold and jewels from my forehead, appreciating the lightness I felt. *Tiara*. She was lucky I'd still been so absorbed in what she felt, or else I'd have cared far more about that humbling comment. "Then don't."

"Haven."

"Really," I looked at him again. "If you are not comfortable joining me, do not feel as though you must. There are equally qualified soldiers that can take your place. I will manage either way. But you are my friend, and I am unwilling to force you to go somewhere that you do not wish to be."

Elliott scoffed, "Of course I'm coming with you. No one else can so effectively keep your head attached to your shoulders. I simply don't like it."

"And *poor Elliott* cannot handle such distance."

He shook his head, brushing me off and throwing a vulgar gesture our parents would be ashamed of. I rolled my eyes back at him. I imagined there were many times he wished to hide what he felt from me. The years of experience together benefitted him little. Whenever I could, I allowed his feelings to be solely his own.

43

I conceded, "Test her tomorrow, if you must. But get some rest. We've a long few days ahead of us."

Chapter Five: Selah

Light shone through the pale lilac curtains far too early for my liking. For a panicked moment, I did not remember where I was or why I was there. The apprehension steadily subsided after I recalled the agreement I had made with the prince of Elora. When I reminded myself how he had led me to this room personally, and how I had spent no time at all deciding what I would need. There were few things I owned that could not be replaced, regardless of the value they held.

I relived the confusion on the guard's face when I handed him the list. Quint, his name was. He was older than me, likely by a decade or so. His eyes were the only thing that revealed his age, and the gentle wrinkles beginning to form reminded me of when I had first met Eli. Quint seemed kind, and he had not once set foot into my room. He'd caught me right after I'd gotten the chance to scrub all the dirt and grime off of me in a royal bathtub, so I was in an especially good mood.

When I handed him the parchment full of scribbles, his brows pulled together. "This is a *lot* of weapons, Miss Aster."

I had grinned at him cooly, "It will be necessary, will it not? It's quite the journey to Lyscott from here." And to stab anyone who laid a finger on me. Oh, how I had missed the chill of steel against my side while I had been holed up in the Vaults. There had been plenty of metal rubbing my wrists raw, but none that could provide comfort.

Quint was easily persuaded, and the pile of knives, swords, and all manner of sharp objects gleamed at the foot of my bed. My own dagger had rested under my pillow, and my hand had been tempted to remain on the hilt for the entirety of the night. With some convincing, I had permitted myself to relax.

The bed was far softer than my own, and the cotton sheets threatened to keep me in their grip forever. Slowly, and with an immense amount of willpower, I dragged myself up to get ready. Dawn had broken, and it was only a matter of time before the prince came trotting from wherever he resided to tell me to get moving.

I had been given a trunk to pack all my belongings into, and as the sleepiness worked itself out of my eyes, I did just that. A few outfits had come from my home, and the rest had been provided for me. I wasn't particular about what I wore, as long as it wasn't drab, nor was I especially knowledgeable about Lyscottian fashion. However, I was aware that it was no short trip. From the heart of Elora, it would take a week to travel there with a carriage. Only the heavens knew what sort of trouble we could find ourselves in. I refused to be left unprepared.

Leather leggings seemed to be the best option. They offered both protection as well as flexibility. A matching top had been provided, which happened to be remarkably effective for storing five out of the seven blades I'd requested. Three sat flush against my ribs, each sheath nestled securely into a strap. Two small daggers were readied on either wrist, with two larger ones being tucked into place by my ankles. I understood Quint's concern, as I too may be hesitant to provide someone with so many knives, but safety was far more important than his fleeting judgment. I was less eager to hear what the prince would have to say about it.

Once I was fully prepared, a rather slim and lanky servant who called himself Lars had delivered a plate to my door. The toast and eggs soothed the stomach I hadn't even realized was aching. It had been a day and a half since I'd last eaten. I was usually good enough at coping with hunger, but rarely needed to anymore.

After my stomach was full and I was momentarily content, I heard a rap at the door. I closed my eyes, willing whoever it was to leave so I could crawl back in that still warm bed. Another knock came, followed by, "Miss Aster, are you ready?"

The prince had arrived, truthfully about an hour after I had expected him. It did not make the cotton sheets look any less tempting, but I appreciated the extra rest. "If I decline to answer, will you leave?"

"Unlikely," he replied, but made no move to open my door. "May I come in?"

"Of course, Your Highness." The sarcasm leaked from my voice. "What a joy it is to begin my day with your company."

He wore the very same green and gold, holding the same untouched sword he had worn the day prior. The collar of the king's uniform was neatly tucked away, every button and stitch in perfect order. His shoes had changed, opting for hiking boots as opposed to the neat black ones he had worn the night before. His blond hair curled behind his ears and fell well over his forehead. Sunlight itself, hidden behind the colors of royalty.

"I am in complete agreement." *True.* I seethed. His gaze started at my eyes, wandered down to the weapon on my hip and then down to my boots. "You look prepared for battle."

"We are going to another nation to accuse the king of not keeping his soldiers on a tight enough leash. I'm not sure that one could take too many precautions." I tightened my worn boots, securing the laces.

Then, the prince looked at me in a way I would find that only he could. His eyes remained locked on me, but his mind was entirely elsewhere. The grin that he always seemed to wear left him. For some horrendous reason, I felt smaller than I had the moment prior. The blades that were scattered across my person didn't seem sufficient. The gold in his eyes glowed a dull amber, and his hair barely covered the jewels that laced above his brows. The hilt of my sword found its way into my hand, and I couldn't tell if it was intentional or not.

"Prince Haven," I spoke, feeling his name on my tongue for the very first time.

And he was back. His eyes had life behind them again, and the grin I couldn't seem to make him shed returned. Underneath his expression, he looked pained. Almost as though –

"Were you using your gift?" There was only an accusation in my voice.

"Yes," he admitted, much faster than I would've anticipated. His hands slipped into his pockets.

"Stop it, then," I scolded. "I am armed now, Prince. My threats from the prison are no longer so empty." I could be burned at the stake for so much as touching a perfect blond hair on the prince's perfect head, but the offer to do so was becoming more tempting by the moment.

He looked on gladly, and resentment flickered in my stomach. His mind was present and he no longer seemed as though he could see through me, but the ridiculous smile he wore irritated me to no end. I couldn't be certain I even wanted him to speak, but I was decidedly annoyed that he wouldn't. "Do you not believe me?"

His smile widened ever so slightly, "I believe that you are irked and likely have a dozen different ideas of how you'd like to solve that issue. But I am the prince, and we are running late."

"Let's be off, then." I brushed past him. I had no idea where I was meant to go.

"Left, Miss Aster. Then down the stairs and on your right," Haven guided. I silently cursed him for acknowledging how silly it was of me to get out in front of him. The scent of cinnamon and cedar wafted from behind. From him, I realized. I had been so covered in grime in the cell that I didn't notice that he smelled almost... sweet. Not feminine, but honeyed. For some odd reason, I found myself more eager to get away from him than ever.

So we walked silently down the hall, descending and turning according to his directions. The corridor led outdoors, to a fully stocked carriage accompanied by a man about my age wincing in the morning light. They had the stables so close to their guest quarters, for the sake of allowing them easy travel, I figured. Dreads fell from the grimacing man's head, falling gently onto his shoulders. He was certainly lovely to look at, but his squinting and the reek of alcohol emanating from him suggested that he'd had a bit too much fun the night prior. But his eyes, his stance, the tone of his skin, all held striking resemblance to the general who had so effortlessly rid me of my weapons.

"Is that –" I began my question, but the prince interrupted.

"Elliott Pearce, son of General Eline Pearce. I hear that you and she have... met." He glanced at me, knowing. *The Pearce Family.*

"Delightful woman, really," I muttered.

49

"First I've ever heard of it," Elliott finally spoke, his voice rumbling. "Selah, yes? I've heard only good things." *Lie, the little jerk.*

I bristled, taking in his ruffled clothes and the glimmering metal on his hip. "What a mighty soldier you have here, Your Highness." I taunted, looking him up and down. He and the prince certainly knew each other well enough.

Haven stiffened behind me, almost imperceptibly. If not from my contempt of his title, then at my antagonizing Elliott Pearce.

"Haven, can we leave her?" Elliott asked, already bored of me. *Haven.* He spoke to the prince so casually. I had hardly even said his name. The soldier crossed his arms, sizing me up at last. He glanced at the weapons I carried, the clothing fitted against my skin, and looked back at Haven for an answer.

"You'll find that Miss Selah Aster is an absolute joy once you get to know her. The mockery is simply part of her charm." My gift was silent, as though it too weighed his intention. Not fully true, but not entirely false.

The carriage itself certainly suited royalty. The Eloran colors decorated the outside, even the wheels shimmering a faint gold. Two richly black horses stood waiting patiently at the front, facing the path we would soon take. Quint, the servant from the night before, was the driver. He, of course, was making himself scarce amidst the prince's arrival.

Beyond that, the Hidran Forest loomed. Even in the light of the morning, it enveloped all the light it was offered. It was a famously eerie place, one that I had been glad to avoid on my way to Distin. The hillsides, while infinitely more treacherous, offered fewer nightmares than the forest. They had given little warmth outside of the paths thieves often stalked, but at least I had avoided being subject to that territory that absorbed so much of the sun.

Dread filled my gut, and I hoped the prince had kept his word.

"I'm afraid a nation awaits," the prince beckoned, stepping up into the carriage. It tilted from his weight, but steadied itself with no great difficulty. Pearce trudged up after him. His entrance was not quite as graceful, but it certainly did the trick. I willed my feet to take a few steps toward the carriage, consoled by the metal that was hidden away on various surfaces of my body.

I took my seat across from them, and not a moment later we were moving. The carriage had flaps on either side, letting in air and light. Packages of supplies lay strewn about in all the space we did not fill. A loaf of bread mercifully found its way into my hand, and I tore off pieces as we started toward the forest.

In lieu of conversation, I spent time in my own thoughts. When the forest finally approached, I wondered what manner of monsters it truly held. It was vast, and evergreen trees lined either edge of the dirt road. They were practically barriers; nothing could be seen but endless rows of green and brown. The leaves did suck up most of the sun, leaving us only with fragments of the midday light.

"Am I to act as a part of your court, then?" I asked the prince, whose legs were stretched far enough that they sat on the bench next to me. Elliott choked on a laugh, and the prince only wore one of his relentless grins.

"My court, Miss Aster?"

"What do we tell the Lyscottian king if he asks who I am? While 'resident expert of deceit' certainly sounds lovely, it isn't quite covert." In a perfect world, the Lsycottian king wouldn't deign to recognize my presence. But it was not a perfect world, and who could tell what he would ask.

"I will worry about that. For now, relax. Have a chat with Elliott. Tell a story. We've a long journey ahead." The aforementioned soldier did not seem at all pleased by this offer, but there wasn't much else to be done. Elliott's head fell back, leaning against the green side of the carriage.

You have nothing to fear from me, the prince had said. Yet, for hours, my hand never left the hilt of my blade. For hours, I was ready.

Chapter Six: Haven

"My least favorite animal is a duck."

"Lie."

"I had two muffins for breakfast"

"True."

"My grandmother's name is Sana."

"True."

"I care too much about others."

"A rather disheartening lie."

"*Ugh*," Elliott groaned, frustrated that he could not make her stumble. He'd been trying for half an hour. He glared at Selah, evidently not appreciating that she took up my offer to try to talk to him. Her fingers still danced along the metal at her side, but she had relaxed slightly. Only enough to be offended that Elliott was paying her no mind at all, outside of his questioning. After an entire day of their bickering on and off, we had nearly reached our destination. It was well and truly dark outside. The torches on the carriage did their best to illuminate the path ahead, but there was only so much help they could offer.

Whenever it was in my power, I stayed out of their emotions. When Selah's foot grazed mine, or when Elliott was thrown into me by a bump in the road, it was unavoidable. He had been irritated for the whole journey, and I frequently wondered why he had chosen to accompany me in the first place. She fluctuated regularly: sometimes frustrated, curious, or entertained by whatever it was going on in her head. The only consistency was the ache I had felt since I met her the day prior.

Selah chuckled in response. "Have I disappointed you? I've tried to carry a more interesting conversation for hours. You're the one who chose this."

He grunted at her, as though he couldn't muster the energy for anything more.

Steely gray eyes met my own. "If you were going to drag me to another nation, Your Highness, you could've at least brought better company," she huffed, taking her hand off her blade to cross her arms. Exhaustion weighed on her shoulders as the carriage rolled to a stop.

"Finally," Elliott sighed, the first to exit when it was finally safe to do so. After him went Selah, and I followed after them.

It was no real effort at all to get ourselves unpacked and ready to stay at the inn. Warmth radiated from the glass windows, piercing through the cool of the night. It wasn't nearly as grand as what I was used to, but there was something rather charming about its simplicity. The driver, who's name I learned was Quint, took care of the reservation and allotted us rooms. He had offered four, but Elliott and I had shared my room enough times for it to be no issue. Elliott took care of all our belongings, running them up to our individual rooms with that effortlessly inhuman speed of his.

A gasp sounded from behind me, and when I turned to look, Selah's eyes were wide with shock. "You neglected to inform me that he is..." she waved her hand in the air.

"Gifted, yes. He's not much faster than a talented horse, but it is certainly useful. I'll warn you: his impressive reflexes make him very inconvenient to spar with," I crossed my arms as I explained. Elliott loaded the last box up, huffing in my direction. So much arrogance considering the fact that I had not asked for his help. In fact, he had not even verbally volunteered for the task before beginning to haul everything away like a grumpy pack mule. With an added groan, he made his way into the inn.

The chill of the air began to penetrate through my clothes, and Selah looked no better. Teeth chattered, her curls wandered every which way in the wind, and her arms were tucked tight to herself. In all her planning with that suit of hers, she had not the foresight to consider it may not be fit for the late spring air. Unfortunate that all the steel touching her skin could not warm her.

Her glare aimed itself in my direction, and only then did I realize I was staring. I began to shrug off my coat, and her whole body cringed. "What are you doing?"

"It's only polite for me to offer," I made a truly feeble attempt at handing it to her, and she did not move an inch. "Selah," I nudged.

She scoffed, trudging into the inn instead. I paced after her, aiming to keep my steps perfectly neat and orderly despite the rocky terrain. I only nearly tumbled once but she didn't seem to care. Entirely too absorbed in her own path to notice me, fortunately.

When the door swung open, we were met with the warmth that the windows had so kindly promised us. It began to soothe the bite of the cold, and I kept my discarded jacket tucked in my arm. She, once again, did not have any idea where she was going, but I would not be the one to remind her.

As she scanned the area for any clues, I settled right next to her. "I would've been much more forthcoming, you know. I'm almost offended that you spent so much time trying to get to know him. Or is it really so difficult for me to maintain your interest?"

"And what's to say you ever held my interest?"

Her eyes still wandered throughout the room, assessing the creaking rocking chairs and the shelves of books that stood across from the fire. Her eyes landed on Quint and the proprietor of the inn. The latter was chuckling deeply at something Quint had said. Crackling of logs and soft murmurs filled the air, and the scent of bedsheets and flames followed soon after.

"Charming as ever, Miss Aster."

Elliott soon returned to lead us to our rooms. Despite his demeanor, he made no rude comment or snarky remark. Rather, once his self-appointed duties were completed, he collapsed onto his own bed. He had not even been bothered to remove his boots, and I grimaced at the dirt that fell onto his bed.

The room was cozy, really, like a grandparent had lovingly put it together. Hand stitched quilts lined the beds, and well-used dressers sat across from each of them. The posts of the bed held intricate, wooden designs that one could easily overlook if he were not paying attention. A candle was lit for us in the corner, curtains blocked the chilly evening air, and a soft wool rug rested on the floor. I never took so much care with my own space.

"A room to yourself," I motioned to Selah's door, residing just across the hall from my own and right beside Quint's. Despite her nearly overwhelming wave of relief that crashed into me, her face revealed absolutely nothing. "Preferably don't run off, if you can avoid it. It would be unbearably cold for you, and I would have to find someone else with your skill set in the kingdom. It would be a dismal task that I simply must beg you not to burden me with."

All she did was nod, and I left her on her own.

I closed our door gently behind me hoping not to wake Elliott, but he was muttering something nonetheless. I sat down on my own bed, having the decency to remove my own shoes before laying my feet across the mattress. It was deceptively comfortable, and I mourned for the version of myself that would have to leave when morning came.

Sensing I didn't hear him, he kindly repeated himself, "It wouldn't be the worst thing if she ran off. Then we could find ourselves someone who wouldn't require me to ask a million questions." He rose for a moment to glare at me. "Thank you for that, by the way."

"You didn't have to," I told him. I closed my eyes in a pause. "What is the matter with you, anyway? She answered everything thoroughly, and was much more willing to engage than you were."

"Not now, Haven," he murmured, sinking back into the pillow.

"Please?"

"No."

"Are you certain? Because I may have noticed a particular innkeeper who had an impressive ale collection. Perhaps I could go grab you a drink as a reward for your honesty." The tactic had never failed me before. For the son of such an important figure in our kingdom, he was all too easy to bribe.

As anticipated, he perked up. First, interest lit in his eyes. Then apprehension, as though he could tell it was a bribe. And finally, acceptance, due to my unparalleled bartering skills. "Fine. I'll talk once you return."

I laughed, nailing the back of his head with a stray pillow. "I refuse to fall for that. Information first, alcohol after."

He sighed with practically all his effort, and flipped around. "She's so... creepy."

My eyebrows raised in disbelief. "Creepy?" I asked, more entertained than I had been all day.

He rolled his eyes at me, the handsome and charismatic prince of Elora, second in line for the throne. His heavy hand plopped itself onto his forehead, "You won't understand."

"Enlighten me, then."

Elliott seemed all too eager to do so, propping himself up. His dark eyes bore into me, wild and open. His dreads weren't as well kept as they usually were, and a faint purple tint was beginning to appear under his lashes. "First off, we find this girl on a whim. She 'accidentally' saved the princess of our kingdom, who she claims not to know, and we are just going to blindly trust that she has no ulterior motive? It's completely foolish and painfully obvious."

I shook off that concern. "You're still paranoid. I've felt her emotions, Elliott. Obviously, that's not everything, but she seemed sincere."

"Fine," he waved, "fine. Even if that is not the case. Who needs that many weapons? She had at least five, and those were just the ones that I noticed. Didn't your father say that this is a safe journey? What is she preparing for if not readying herself to take one or both of us hostage? I understand caution, believe me, but that is excessive. It's like she doesn't want me to trust her."

"You're a foot taller than her, and twice as fast," I reminded.

Elliott Pearce, son of Eline and Igor Pearce, heir to the role of general of the most influential district in the nation of Elora, thought a girl that he practically dwarfed, was creepy. A chuckle nearly escaped, but I held it in for the sake of his dignity. I sighed after a moment and met his eyes again.

Elliott sobered.

He glanced down at his hands.

"Size and speed mean nothing once you have a knife to your neck, Haven."

I understood.

Old, forgotten grief flooded my very bones. Not just his own, though it was radiating off him like rays of light. The ghosts of shared pain filled the room, and the smell of comfort no longer lingered.

I ached with the memories.

We'd both been fourteen when the Illustri attacked, both barely old enough to have received our gifts and certainly not old enough to know how to use them. While rumors of the extremists had circulated, they were still only that. Rumors. Something to whisper about amongst friends and then forget about.

We'd snuck out to the coast. It was a three day journey from Distin, but another gifted family lived near the sea. Somehow, we'd convinced our parents to let us visit the Vance family. A handful of other gifted children also made their way towards the coast, as many as could make it. Elliott I had talked everyone into sneaking out to the sea. They all listened to us.

The party was cut short by an ambush. Brutal and quick, the Illustri had discovered where we were and that we had been blessed by Lukoh. Then, I didn't understand why it mattered to them. Now, I knew better that power was as dangerous as it was useful.

I remembered dragging Elliott away. We escaped, as well as a few others. Many of our friends didn't. A few Eloran soldiers tried to help in vain. I could recall running, and running, and running, until my lungs burned and I could carry him no further. I tried not to think of much else. Depths, I tried not to think of any of it at all.

The memories hadn't yet faded, not entirely.

"I know," I told him, rubbing a hand over my face. "I trust her enough for the time being."

He shook his head, now gentle. The combativeness had left him. "I was merely aiming to answer your question."

I leaned forward, bracing my hands on the bed. "You still do not have to come. I can send word to the castle, they would be more than happy –"

"Haven," he argued.

"I mean it."

"I know," his head tilted towards the roof, and he took a breath. "I'll be fine."

"So moody." I reached far enough to kick him. He snickered and cradled his shin. I felt the pain leave him, and he could muster the energy to be arrogant once more.

"You've more than earned that drink, I believe." I stood, brushing my hands on my pants.

His smile widened, "Such kindness. Perhaps you might even grab something for yourself."

I shook my head, but my grin matched his own. "Duty calls, I'm afraid. Only one fool can be impaired at a time." It was a silly rule, but it never felt right to have both of us unfocused. So I watched and let him have his fun.

"I'll be back," and I closed the door behind me. I heard his satisfied chuckle once it was fully sealed.

I leaned against the wood, pausing for only a second to collect myself. We hardly ever talked about such things. After the attack, we had discussed it out of necessity, but never alone. We rather spent our time remembering our friends and forgetting how they were taken from us. Gen was also always floating around, and she was just barely younger than thirteen. Old enough to hear about what happened, but still too young to hear the horrors of what we actually witnessed. It was for the best, perhaps, to not relive the memories with each other. Best, maybe, to try to imagine a world where the reminders didn't exist.

I opened my eyes, and I remembered who stayed just across from me. I took a step forward, hesitating when the floorboards creaked. Would she even want my company? She hadn't seemed too eager to chat, well, ever, but especially since we had arrived. If I had done something to offend her, I couldn't imagine what.

But her door swayed slightly open, and my feet carried me the rest of the way. I knocked, tapping twice. No response. Again, I tried, and I heard nothing. The door was already open, it was no crime to let myself in.

"Selah?" I asked, stepping in. The bed remained completely untouched, a different quilt draped across from the one I had. Her own candle was burning, but there was nothing of hers in the room aside from what I had requested from the palace staff. The trunk laid by the dresser. I would've wagered that it hadn't even been opened. No trace of the girl I had dropped off only minutes prior.

She was gone.

Chapter Seven: Selah

"Preferably don't run off, if you can avoid it. It would be unbearably cold for you, and I would have to find someone else with your skill set in the kingdom. It would be a dismal task that I simply must beg you not to burden me with."

The prince of Elora was speaking, but I hardly paid him any mind. *A room to yourself*, he had said, and it was the last thing I heard. I nearly let him see my relief. I'd never been left well and truly alone as a child, especially not with my very own space. I needed no reminder of what it felt like to have strangers too close. *Alone*. Alone to breathe, and think, and have no one watching my every step.

I nodded at him, and he sealed himself away in his own room. All I had to do was walk out of the inn, and I could go right back to the life I had left. I would not earn nearly as much money as I would in aiding the prince, and I considered if that was enough to keep me around. It would not be my only opportunity to escape, I thought, and I could always leave if I felt unsafe. I had run away a handful of times. It would be no great feat to leave someone else.

But there were shelves of books that I had not properly examined, and I didn't want to rest without exploring them.

I padded back down the stairs, silently hoping no one heard. It would be much too difficult to convince them that I was not truly trying to escape, especially when all they had seen from me were threats.

While I rarely ever had the time to sit down to read, I certainly enjoyed collecting all manner of stories. There was something about having books on a shelf that made places feel more like home. I'd bought more texts than I could ever hope to get through, and even still I found myself looking for more.

I thumped past the crackling fireplace on the other side of the room from the sweet-looking innkeeper who kept watch from her desk. Creases lined her face. Gray hair was tucked neatly into a bun, and she absentmindedly sipped from a cup of steaming tea. She waved a wrinkled hand, smiling softly at me as I walked. I nodded back and grinned politely in response.

The books were properly aging, but the spines were still intact. There were very few titles I had read, and many I had not. The ones I read were about a strange new world, art that defined the nation's history, and one about the science of the universe. I picked out one that I had only seen from afar, a mystery novel about a brilliant man and his companion solving crimes in their own city. The cover was beautiful in its simplicity. It was a deep blue with gentle copper accents, and I was nearly tempted to ask if I could take it home.

Instead, I settled into a chair before the fire, and I began to read.

I had only just found myself invested in the story when the prince of Elora peered down at me. My hopes of being unbothered were dashed. In my final attempt, I moved the book so it covered his face from my view. He chuckled, grabbing it from the spine and shutting it entirely. I audibly gasped and reached for one of my knives.

"Easy, soldier," he crooned, tucking the book under his arm.

"What do you want?" I contemplated if he would have time to recover if I tried to kick him into the fire. I then decided that perhaps being

63

known as the murderer of the prince of my nation was not the best look for my business. Who knows how many clients I would lose?

There was no harm in imagining it, though.

"I thought you'd left," he said. *True*. His posture was entirely relaxed, so clearly it didn't bother him much. Even with his body blocking the light from the fire, his perfect features were entirely visible. His perfect hair was hardly ruffled from the journey. His perfect face was twisted into curiosity. His perfect outfit concealed his stupid hands that had never touched an imperfect thing.

It made me want to vomit.

"I considered it," I admitted, plucking a different book off the shelf.

He stole that one too, placing it back just out of my reach. When I picked up another, he did the very same thing. And another, the same. "Haven –"

"Your Highness," the innkeeper appeared, interrupting. An off-white letter was tucked in her hands, and she held it out to him. "This arrived for you earlier today. And please, do try to mind your manners. Those bookshelves don't rearrange themselves," Her tone was lovely and warm. It was almost like she was teasing the prince, who was blushing with embarrassment.

"Yes, of course. Everything will be put back at once. Thank you." He took it from her, setting down my mystery book.

"Who is it from?" I asked.

"I don't know," he paused, scanning the outside of the envelope. It was just your standard, blank envelope, aside from the prince's name. There was no postage, no return address, nothing. Haven flipped it over once, then twice. His eyebrows knitted together. I lent him a knife, and he sliced the letter open with ease.

It was nothing but an emblem.

The outline of a moon was encased within a silver sun. Around the design, little specks of stars were scattered about. Geometric lines extended in every direction, the silver standing starkly out from the deep violet background. *A neighboring kingdom's seal, perhaps? Certainly not one I recognized.*

The prince shared my confusion. "Do you know who gave this to you?" he asked the innkeeper.

She shook her head. "No, Your Highness. It was just dropped off with the post earlier this evening. I had thought it to be a mistake, but then you all arrived." *True.*

Haven looked at me. After a moment I realized he was seeking confirmation. I nodded, and his answering look told me that was enough.

"Thank you, miss," he said, storing all the books back in their original homes. "Miss Aster, would you mind accompanying me upstairs? Elliott has requested a drink, and I really would appreciate some extra supervision." *Lie.* He followed the innkeeper to the desk, and she handed him a glass of something dark and amber. He offered a 'thank you,' and gently guided me upstairs by my arm.

"About time. I was beginning –" Pearce started as we walked into the room. He paused when he noticed me, looking me over again. "Doesn't she belong across the hall?"

"Have you seen this before?" Haven asked, ignoring the other comment. Elliott scanned the emblem, turning the little card over and back again. He shook his head, and Haven passed him the glass he'd grabbed from the innkeeper. Elliott drank everything down in one large gulp, and the prince scanned the envelope yet another time.

"This was sent to the inn as we arrived," Haven explained. "This trip was planned yesterday. We didn't let the innkeeper know that we were en route until we pulled in," his lips pulled together, and the jewelry on his forehead was tugged down by his expression. "But someone still organized an envelope to be delivered before we even got here."

Elliott nearly coughed up his drink. "We should leave, then. Right? Just to be cautious."

I shook my head, "It's probably nothing. More than likely, it's one of your adoring fans just trying to promote something of theirs."

Elliott cocked his head and handed the card back to Haven, "Your parents knew, as did Genevieve and Alaric. It's possible they sent it." *I've definitely heard those names before.*

"With no postage? We were just with them," Haven replied. The general's son paced across the bedroom absentmindedly, still staring at the emblem every now and then. I fought back the urge to say something comforting. His brows were still knotted in thought. Haven's mouth opened, then closed again.

Their bedroom was bigger than mine, and the rug on the floor was taking a beating from Pearce's steps. They had the very same sort of candle in the corner as I'd had in my room, and most of the trunks of stuff had been opened. His empty glass had been set aside, reflecting the dim candlelight.

"It's probably nothing," Haven repeated. *Lie.*

I bit my tongue from calling out the prince, and he gave me a pointed look. Elliott Pearce didn't seem to believe him for a moment, and resumed his pacing.

"We'll be gone in the morning," Haven reminded his overbearing friend, "and we can ask around in Lyscott to see if anyone has seen it before. There is nothing more we can do yet."

"Early in the morning," Elliott argued, "dawn at the latest."

"Dawn at the latest," the prince agreed.

They paused for a moment to look at each other. There was something weighted in their expression that I couldn't quite interpret. Pearce shook his head and stared at the ceiling for a moment. He grabbed his forgotten glass and tossed it to the prince. "If you'd be so kind."

Haven grinned, and the heaviness left him, "of course."

The prince decided it was only appropriate to escort me back to my room. After that little ordeal, I was no longer as eager to settle down by the fireplace. Exhaustion was beginning to tug at me from the thought of waking before dawn.

It was no long endeavor, walking me across the hall, but it was strange to walk in such silence. No longer heavy, but not quite a comfortable lull. His amber eyes were starting to droop. I imagined that he was as unenthusiastic about leaving so early as I had been.

"I believe this is your stop, Miss Aster," he gestured to my door with a swooping, dramatic hand. "I know you will long for me, but do try to console yourself until I am able to return."

I smacked his hand away. "Goodnight, Your Highness," I said, trying to mock him but lacking the energy.

He grinned, "Sleep well, Selah."

And then I was alone.

Only once did my body wake me up that night. I was pulled from dreams I couldn't remember to check my surroundings, and then I dozed again. My weapons were never far from me, and I found myself reaching for the dagger that I stashed under the pillow per usual.

Also per usual, nothing was amiss. The candle had burnt out, and I could only appreciate the peace that came from sitting in the dark. It was far simpler to rest where no one could see, even if it meant that I myself was blinded. Faintly, light trickled through the bottom of the door. It was only enough for me to make sense of where I was.

Morning came too quickly, and grating nausea arrived with it. A spinning world was the first thing to greet me when I finally opened my eyes, and my very bones trembled. I staggered to the bathroom, making it just in time to empty out the contents of my stomach. Then again, and a third time. My body shook and my skin gleamed with cold sweat. I was sick, thoroughly so.

I mustered up the energy to sit back against the chilled wooden walls. I didn't even attempt to stand. My head was still on an axis, and I wasn't certain if I could drag myself back to my bed. Even when there was a rap on my bedroom door, I did not bother to try to pull myself up to answer it.

"Aster?" Elliott Pearce asked for me from the other room. Of course, the very last person I'd want to chat with.

"Go away," I croaked.

"Are you –" he paused as he looked into the already open bathroom door. He bore witness to me practically collapsed on the floor. He sniffed the air, wincing. Then he glanced at me, my still quaking hands and my less than energized demeanor. "Hmm, well. Let me... let me go speak with Haven."

It was far kinder than I had expected from him, so I concluded that I must have looked as terrible as I felt. I was never sick as an adult. Like

68

most of my peers, I had built an immunity to basically every common illness under the sun when I was a child. I forgot how it felt to ache in that way, to be freezing and burning alive all at once.

As promised, the prince found his way to me a few moments later. He was in the very same uniform, but his hair was reaching in five different directions, and the band of jewelry he always wore was missing. The tunic hadn't even been tucked in, and his sword didn't sway at his side.

He pursed his lips in distaste. "The distance has truly made you ill, hasn't it?" *Lie. Ugh.* "Selah, dearest, if I had known it would have such an effect, I would've had us closer," he remarked, only amusing himself. I could've sworn the faintest amount of worry lit behind his expression.

I rolled my eyes despite the immense amount of effort it required. "I'm fine," even my gift betrayed that it was a lie. "Just … give me a moment."

The prince crouched beside me. He reached a hand for my forehead, and I shifted out of his reach the tiniest bit. He frowned, and his eyes scanned me over, "May I?"

With no small hesitation, I nodded. His hand was shockingly cool, and I nearly hissed. He grimaced and drew away after only a few seconds.

"As honored as I am that you are *actually* burning for me, I'm afraid that doesn't bode well for our morning's travel plans." He tilted his head. I looked away to avoid the pity in his gaze. I wanted none of it.

"I am *fine*," I repeated. He held out a hand that I brusquely ignored. Pulling myself up by the sink, I made it onto my feet. I was a wobbly, shaking thing, but at least I was standing.

The prince did not seem pleased.

"Selah." He stood then, arms crossed and full-fledged disbelief etched onto his face. I was glad he had not been present moments prior, when I wouldn't have had the energy to shoo him away. Even still, I was not entirely steady, but it was better than being a lump on the bathroom floor. I took a breath, and then another. My feet supported me more, even if only a little.

Let him fret, if that's what he wanted.

"I will live, Your Highness." *True*, regardless of the aching.

He didn't respond immediately. So serious, still so fully put together even when he wasn't. He retained his perfect posture. Not quite as princely as he had been, but lovely in a different way. Not as burdened, perhaps. Almost... cute. Unruly. Far more approachable.

When I found myself entertaining that train of thought, I was nearly sick again.

I picked my hands up off the counter, proving that I could stand. He shook his head in displeasure, but did not try to stop me. "You can stay here. I'll have a physician meet you –"

"Absolutely not."

His brows raised in shock, and a hint of a smile ghosted his lips, "I wasn't aware you had the authority to give me orders."

I scoffed, keeping my composure through sheer effort of will. "It is nothing but a decorated wagon. If I could rest here, I could rest there just as well. Have a physician meet us at our next stop, if you must." I looked him in the eye, willing him to believe me. I would not stay behind because the prince deemed me unfit. "It's likely caused by the unsanitary conditions I was kept in two days ago."

Nausea came back in full force. I would *not* vomit in front of the prince of my nation. I took a deep breath.

He paused to consider it, and time crawled for every second he waited, "As you wish. We'll leave whenever you're ready." Mercifully, he let himself out.

The door creaked to a close, and I rushed for the toilet. I heaved, once, twice, and then it was over. Most of the nausea subsided, and I didn't feel quite as cold either. The shaking worsened, if anything, but I felt less as though my stomach was going to escort itself out of my body.

I sat back, collecting myself for a moment. There was the cool, solid wood against my shoulders. Water dripped faintly from the ceiling, thudding in the sink. Wind howled somewhere far away, and through the window I could see the colors of morning looming over the horizon. *Dawn at the latest*, I remembered. I would not be the one to slow us down.

I dragged myself up from the floor. I rinsed out my mouth, ridding it of the taste. I dressed, albeit slowly, placing each weapon reverently into its respective hiding place. My hair was a raging mess, and I was eternally grateful to whomever had forethought to tuck away hair ties. I found many such items in the trunk the prince had someone pack for me, but that was the detail I appreciated the most by far.

I nibbled on a piece of bread that had been packed as well. My stomach growled its thanks. Still quivering, still somewhat feverish, my body at least was not as upset. I pulled back my curls, ran some water over my face, and decided that was the best I would manage for the day.

When I left my room, Pearce and Quint were each lugging trunks of their own down the stairs. The former, of course, returned within a breath. He didn't even regard me before slipping past to grab my things. At least I wasn't obligated to carry a conversation.

I trudged down the stairs, and the innkeeper greeted me from her desk. Yet again, she nursed a cup of steaming tea. No unnatural tiredness tugged at her features. Her eyes were wide and clear, and she grinned that gentle smile at me as I passed. I made a feeble attempt at returning it. Most of my efforts were spent making my way to the carriage.

71

The chill of the air grazed my cheeks, and I shuddered. Summer had not yet arrived, unfortunately, despite how late into the year it was. The mornings were still cool, and frost laced the top of the grass. The forest, at least, looked about the same. It remained soul-suckingly dark regardless of the light that was still making its way into the sky. A thin layer of fog shrouded the trees, and I wondered if someone was looking back at me.

Haven was standing beside the carriage, directing Quint and Elliott where to place the trunks they had carried. He was restored to the prince I initially met, pristine and utterly whole in appearance. I was afraid he put me to shame. My exhaustion had not even subsided, whereas he looked as though he had never experienced it. He reeked of the kind of privilege I had never known.

He regarded me with a sidelong look, "I sent for a physician. He'll meet us in Sutton." I'd never been there, but I knew of the town. From what I understood, it was a village that stood in the forest only a couple days north of Distin. Some gifted family lived in that city. "You're certain you'll make it there?"

I nodded, and it was enough for him. He held out a hand that I finally accepted, and he carefully lifted me up into the carriage. The prince sat first. The trunks had been shoved carelessly away, now taking up enough space that Elliott wouldn't fit beside him.

Not thirty seconds later, I was dreaming.

In hindsight, though, I wish I hadn't fallen asleep.

Chapter Eight: Haven

For the most part, it was a lovely day.

Quint and Elliott had been kind enough to pack all of our belongings into the carriage. The soldier, I learned, was having a birthday the next week. He'd be thirty-two, and he was about to propose to a girl he'd been with for ages. The man hummed happily as he worked, tending to the two horses and securing various trunks.

The sun had risen, and patches of yellow and purple and everything in between painted the sky. Clouds reflected the morning light, making the colors appear even more brilliant. Elora had some of the very best sunrises. Even in areas shrouded by trees, streaks of pink and orange colored the visible sky. I couldn't recall the last time I had been to Lsycott. In the back of my mind, I pictured a castle covered in sheets of ice and snow, but I couldn't tell if it was merely something my imagination had conjured.

Selah collapsed just seconds after she had sat down. I resisted the urge to move the hair out of her face, to fix all the loose strands of stray curls. I had felt her exhaustion. I withdrew enough not to feel her nausea, but the rest was difficult to avoid. Even so, her pale skin gleamed. It was an effort to keep myself still. But she was terribly stubborn, and I liked my fingers far too much to allow them to be bitten off out of spite.

The first two hours of the trip were wholly unremarkable. The world began to come alive, birds waking to chirp and sun flooding the carriage windows through the looming trees. The scent of grass and oak wafted in after it, and I wondered why we didn't travel more often. I suppose that there is little room for vacations for those needed by their country, but I pondered why it was that the king so preferred to stay in his palace.

Even Elliott had dozed off. Though, he was not nearly as graceful as Selah had been. A line of drool dripped from the corner of his mouth, and he snorted once every few minutes. He had removed his sword from his side for the sake of comfort, and the glinting metal now sat discarded on the carriage floor. He hadn't slept much either, and I had heard him stirring long before I fully woke.

We were rolling steadily, and the clomping footsteps of horses pounded along the road. The wind had begun to stir at a dull roar, but the skies were clear. Quint had assured us that there was no storm approaching to alter our traveling plans. Four hours in, we had agreed, we'd stop for lunch. But only two and a half hours had passed when the carriage slowed to a halt.

I barely made out Quint's shouting voice through the carriage walls. I hadn't even tried to sense his panic, but it was a beacon in the otherwise quiet air. I stepped over Selah and Elliott as gently as I was able. Slowly, quietly, palming my sword in my hand, I slipped out the door onto the gravel road. The lock clicked shut.

All at once, I noticed three things.

First, Quint's body was laid out face down on the ground. His chest wasn't rising, and blood was beginning to pool around him.

Second, three men in carved wooden masks and brown leathers stood on the other side of the horses. Their heads all cocked toward me at the same time. Each one grasped a thin blade of his own in one hand, and in the other, a variety of supplies. The largest man held a bundle of rope, but made no immediate move towards me. Another gripped a small cloth that he tucked into a leather pocket. The last, and smallest one, sheathed a knife into his vest. *I need Elliott*, I realized, but he was sound asleep and I'd just sealed the door shut.

Third, a woman crouched over Quint's body. She had long, straight, red hair that flowed all the way down her back. She wore a flowing, deep purple dress, and a necklace of stars was draped across her skin. She brushed back Quint's hair, a sad smile on her face. Her eyes were shades of swirling green and brown, staring up at me. The woman was older than me, but only in her late twenties or so. Her own sword was covered in my driver's blood.

"Hello, Your Highness," she nodded, and went back to looking at Quint. His lifeless body gave one final, involuntary twitch, and then became completely still.

Alarm bells rang in my head as the three men stepped closer. I ran through every training scenario Elliott and I had ever practiced, trying to recall exactly what to do. Slowly, I twisted my blade in my hand, getting accustomed to the feeling of steel in my palm. Anger of the likes I'd only felt through others started in my chest and migrated to every piece of me as I imagined splitting them apart.

It took every bit of willpower I possessed to keep my voice smooth, and even then it came out as more of a hiss, "And to what, exactly, do I owe the pleasure?"

The woman glanced up at me again. "We've come to escort you and your companions elsewhere. I was trying to explain that to this darling soul, but he wouldn't stop talking, and..." she shook her head and grinned softly. "A necessary evil, I'm sorry to say."

So flippant. So utterly unbothered.

I shrugged, hoping they didn't mistake my shaking for fear. "I've traveled alone, I'm afraid. And I've got a nation expecting me, so I regret to inform you that I will be doing nothing of the sort."

Big hazel eyes met my own, "It wasn't a request, Your Highness." She paused, still staring. "Take him."

I struck first.

I swiped at the woman, letting her dodge in time to lure in the men. The largest man came at me first, dropping the rope and gripping his sword with both hands. He was big, but he was terribly slow. It was an effort to parry his swipe, but my sword sliced clean into his shoulder. He roared and clutched his collarbone, swiping at my wrist. He missed, narrowly, and nearly knocked the sword out of my grasp. I kicked his knee and he buckled.

The smallest one engaged next, much faster but not quite as strong. I deflected, deflected, deflected, but couldn't attack in time. From the side of my vision, I saw the last man dodging around us to get into the carriage. Even a glance was too much, and the one swinging at me managed a surprisingly shallow cut on my arm. He left his chest open, and he barely blocked in time to avoid his heart being skewered. The force of the blow was enough to shove him away. I grabbed the hood of the man trying to break into the carriage and threw him back.

He hit the ground with a *thunk*, but he was up nearly as soon as he had fallen.

At the very same moment, the faster one had recovered. Unfortunately for him, I was used to supernatural speed. I was able to match him for every attack, even responding with some of my own. I had only fought once before, once when it really mattered. I was silently grateful to the god of the continent for allowing me so much preparation.

I also silently asked his forgiveness for the way I intended to tear these men into pieces.

I finally managed a solid blow to his thigh, and blood leaked as soon as I hit. He hissed, cradling the wound. The biggest man was still tearing off a stripe of his undershirt to tie around his shoulder. I made a move to reach for the man who was nearest the carriage and –

"That is enough!" The woman ordered. She was still on the far side of the carriage, a handheld torch now alit in her grasp.

The fire danced.

"Another move, Your Highness, and the carriage goes up in flames," she inched the torch closer, taunting. "Although, I'm sure that if no one is inside, it will mean little to you."

Depths.

I paused.

"Your sword, now, if you will."

Holding out my hands in surrender, I carefully laid down my sword, and pasted on my most convincing grin, "Shall we be off, then?"

Something slammed into the back of my head and my knees buckled. I only barely avoided faceplanting. The gravel stung. My wrists ached with the force. The world spun. Images of my friends bloodied and terrified flashed in my mind. A glance at Quint reminded me it had happened again.

Then a picture of my best friend, greatest ally. Then an image of the stubborn girl I had to bribe out of a prison.

It's happening again.

The woman knelt on the stone in front of me. "The carriage now, Prince Haven. Give me the key."

I laughed. Audibly, fully laughed. Part of it was in panic. Part of it was the fact that they were assuming I even had a key, that I was even able to let them in when both people inside had been fully asleep. Then, it was the idiocy of the idea that I'd simply give that up. "No," I said, still sighing.

The only man whom I hadn't injured kicked me, and I fell onto my side. I grimaced at the blow, and my ribs throbbed. The woman shook her head sadly. "I'm trying to make this easy on you. Give me the key, and we can stop with these unpleasantries."

The big one started checking Quint's body, and I prayed.

"I don't have it," I managed. Technically true.

Another kick, this time to my head. Something was bleeding.

"Such a stubborn thing," she crooned. "Come on, Prince. One little key, and we'll be done."

"Go to he –"

"Miss," the big one turned to us, and I swore under my breath. He tossed Quint's key to her, and she caught it in the air. She handed it straight to the man who stood over me. The big one started lugging me away from my sword and the carriage. Using his discarded rope, he made obnoxiously tight and quick knots around my still-sore wrists. I found myself lacking the energy to fight him off.

"See? Not hard at all," she crossed her arms as all three men entered the carriage.

I held what little breath I had.

One moment passed, then another. Elliott was pulled out first, sword at his neck. The biggest man had shoved him. He was cursing and muttering threats, but didn't fight back as they tied his hands behind him. I leaned forward slightly, trying to catch his gaze, trying to figure out a way to get them free, but he wouldn't look me in the eye.

He only paled when he glanced at Quint.

Selah was next, hair undone, looking exhausted and utterly terrified. Terrified of the sword that was held to her throat, terrified of the men who were holding her. She was wearing a different shirt that I did recognize though, only the sleeves of her outfit peaking through the sides. The smallest man had taken her, looping her hands with a different strand of rope. She shook, and beads of sweat fell down her face. My heart sank.

I reached out to try to find a way to soothe her, to try to see if somehow I could take away some of the fear she felt. But when I looked, there wasn't nearly as much as I'd expected. There was anger, wild and hot. There was true exhaustion, but probably caused by whatever ailed her. There was burning determination, but only the most vague sliver of fear.

The last man emerged, dumping the pile of weapons outside of the carriage. There was Elliott's sword, Selah's sword, and maybe a *third* of the knives Selah had carried. I remembered the small blades tucked by her wrists and by her ankles, and watching her readjust them meticulously the first day we traveled.

This trembling, pale, mess was fully armed.

I finally let out the breath I had been keeping.

"Hello, beautiful," the woman approached Selah, who truly appeared as though she was about to faint. The woman stroked Selah's hair much like she had with Quint. My face contorted with disgust. I could sense something similar in Selah, though she gave away nothing. Selah shivered, and the woman crooned, "Don't be afraid, dear. It'll be over so very soon."

The woman looked over to Elliott, glancing at him up and down, "You, I'm sure we'll enjoy. Go get the wagon, we mustn't be late."

Two of the men ran off, leaving us separated on the ground, unarmed. Selah finally met my gaze. No one was watching us, the one man too preoccupied with Elliott's whining and the woman far too busy doling out orders. Gray-blue eyes met mine, and I wondered how they hadn't seen through her act.

And, when no one was looking, Selah Aster grinned.

Chapter Nine: Selah

I woke as soon as the prince shut the carriage door.

I stirred, slowly, stretching out my tired limbs and willing life back into them. I rubbed my sore neck with absentminded fingers. The prince was no longer grinning beside me, not there to make some ridiculous comment. When I glanced over at Elliott, he was still fast asleep. His head was tilted at an awkward angle and he was certainly drooling, but at peace.

Faintly, almost imperceptibly, I heard voices murmuring outside the carriage. Strange, that we hadn't been woken up. There was a woman's voice muttering something I couldn't decipher. My gift whispered to me that she was lying, though her words didn't reach through the carriage walls.

Something's wrong.

I wiped the sleep out of my face while I debated whether to wake up Elliott. The curtain covered the carriage window, and I moved it out of the way just enough to see the prince where he stood. He was still entirely unharmed, albeit even I could sense the anger rolling off him. His blade was in his tensed hand, but he didn't move.

Only then did I see the woman crouched beside our driver's body, and the three armed men in wooden masks that stood behind her. I watched her fingers run through Quint's hair and recoiled before she saw me staring.

I peeked again, and the prince had struck.

Take him, I watched her say.

Depths.

Fear tried to build in my chest, but I clamped down on it before it became overwhelming. After a steadying breath, I looked around the carriage for something, anything to help.

Windows weren't big enough for us to crawl through and the door was the only other way out.

Elliott had a sword nearby, though difficult to use in close quarters.

Many of my weapons were visible, but not all.

A desperate plan was beginning to form. But, I'd need Elliott awake. And docile.

I tossed my sword and two of my daggers down on the floor by his. They landed with a quiet *clink*, but he did not so much as stir. I pulled up my leather sleeve and gripped a hand over his mouth.

That was enough to startle him, and his wide eyes flew open. He tried to wriggle out of my grip. My other hand slid behind his head, willing him to look at me and be quiet.

"Shhh," I hushed him, and he calmed just enough, "your prince is in danger, Pearce." He writhed again, but I held firm. "We can help him, but I need you to be quiet and to listen. Can you manage that?"

He nodded, and when I removed my hands, he shoved me off. "Where is he?" he growled, albeit quietly.

"He's right outside, but they're not gonna kill him."

"*They?* Who are *they?*"

"I don't *know* –"

Elliott reached for his sword, but I got it first. Ire lit behind his eyes, and I took one more deep breath. "Drop it, Selah, or I will gut you where you stand." *True.*

"Elliott –"

I wasn't even given the opportunity to blink before Elliott held me by my throat against the carriage walls. The sword was then in his hand, but I could still breathe and speak. I gasped, more from shock than pain.

Someone tugged at the carriage door. The lock creaked, and Elliott only glanced at it for a moment.

"You have one single *sentence*, Aster, to explain to me why I'm not wherever Haven is. A *sentence*," his sword was at my heart, but it didn't draw blood.

"Your prince trusts me."

Someone tugged at the door again.

Elliott paused. "And he is a fool."

I waited for a blow that never came.

A second passed, and then another. With a grimace, he released me. I rubbed at the marks that would undoubtedly be forming around my neck.

"What is your plan?"

I almost sighed in relief, but the exhaustion still weighed on me far too much to properly allow it. There was a trunk next to me, filled with clothes that had been packed for Haven and Elliott. The latch opened with ease, and I rummaged through for a shirt that would fit.

"The plan, Selah," Elliott reminded.

I palmed a shirt in my hand. "Whoever is after your prince knows that we're in here." The door jiggled as if in response. "I watched them say they wanted to take him. Let them capture us. I can act as the damsel in distress. You are the son of the most important district general in the nation, that training must provide some idea of how to get out of binds."

I slid one of their shirts over my own.

"I've been taught *maybe* twice, and most of my training was less than formal."

I raised a brow at him, "Twice will have to be enough, then." I picked up one of the daggers I had dropped.

"Selah, there's no point. Why not help him now?"

"You're outnumbered. These people are here for your prince, but that doesn't mean they won't kill you if you're a hassle. You have no idea how much preparation they have, what they know about us, or if they have more friends on the way." I loosed the knot in my hair, and sat back in my seat. "Besides, you wanna know why they need him? Let them tell us."

A moment passed.

"They're coming whether you like it or not, Elliott." The door rattled for a fourth time, even harder than before.

"I'm faster," he argued.

"And you also don't know what abilities they possess!" I countered, securing my hidden knives once again, gesturing for him to sit and shoving the last dagger into his hand. "I will get us out," *probably*, "I just need you to play along."

"For all I know, you are the real threat," he sat, though, reluctantly. The dagger disappeared. "Give me a reason to believe you."

"Do you have another choice?"

The lock clicked open, and three men burst in through the carriage door.

Their faces were mostly hidden behind the wooden masks they wore, but two of them were injured and bleeding. It had to have been Haven's doing. Who knew the prince of Elora could be so violent?

Elliott held his sword up, and I ducked out of his way. He swung, but the biggest of the three swiped the weapon out of Elliott's hand. It fell with a clatter. It was so unbelievably easy for them to disarm the general's son, it was almost a shock that they said nothing about it. Another man in a wooden mask patted Elliott down, slipping the dagger I had handed him out of his belt loop. He was carried out, muttering a string of curses.

I held out a small dagger, swiping every which way as the smallest of the three men approached me. I was almost offended. It was no difficult task to succumb to how terrible I felt. My pulse was pounding and adrenaline was pumping through me at full speed, but at least I kept my blades. The fear I felt was manageable. I was shaking, though, still pale and gleaming with sweat.

"Enough of this," he muttered.

When he was close enough, I made a big, flailing move to stab him. The man scoffed behind the mask. His hand clasped around my wrist and twisted, and I let myself gasp in pain. It well and truly hurt, and the sting radiated up my arm. My grip faltered and the knife fell.

In one quick move, my hand was behind my back and his sword was at my throat. I recoiled at the feeling of the sharp blade. The man chuckled, mostly under his breath, and I felt a flash of white, hot rage.

I was definitely going to stab someone. *But not yet.*

He pulled up the back of my shirt to look for any more weapons, and he found none. Content, he let it fall back down and pushed me forward out of the carriage. I stumbled, banging my knees on the trunks that were lying around. The fever I'd had that morning had begun to subside, but my body ached all over. Another shove and a hiss later, and I was out of the carriage with the rest of them.

The prince was bloodied and tied up on the gravel pavement. Red dripped down his forehead where his banded crown sat, and snaked down in a line on his bicep. An entirely new wave of anger flooded me, and my chest stung with regret. Perhaps the prince really had needed us. He was wide awake, though. His amber eyes scanned Elliott first, even as some of his own blond locks were tinted crimson.

My captor knotted a strand of rope around my wrists tight enough to hurt. *Delightful.* Even the king's soldiers had more tact, and they weren't gentle. I winced openly.

With my hands tied, my entire body trembled. I took shallow, shaking breaths. One of the men in the wooden masks roiled his eyes at me. *This is okay. This is fine. This is a good enough plan and this will work.*

Heavens above, I did not let the prince drag me from my very comfortable life just to be gutted on the side of the road. *This will work.*

The last man left the carriage, dropping our weapons out of our reach onto the ground. Only a few, as planned. I wondered if Haven would remember how many I truly carried.

The woman who had lingered over the driver's body approached me. I might have envied her stunning ginger hair or her full mouth if she hadn't been so thoroughly deranged. The sleeves of her dress blew gently in the spring breeze. A picture of elegance and grace with a bloody sword on the ground beside her.

She smiled sweetly.

Bile rose up in the back of my throat.

"Hello, beautiful," she murmured, her long nails brushing into my hair. I shivered. Her hands were freezing and brutal and far too close to my

86

face for my liking. But the prince of Elora was watching, and I had to put on a good show. "Don't be afraid, dear. This will be over so very soon." *True.*

Ugh.

She pulled her hand back, looking Elliott over instead. "You, I'm sure we'll enjoy. Go get the wagon, we mustn't be late."

The man holding me shoved me down to my knees and left with the man watching the weapons. Elliott's captor forced him to the ground as well, bickering back and forth the whole time. The woman turned to oversee her soldiers.

Amber eyes met mine. Curious, wary, and pained. Such similar features to the young girl I'd stumbled upon only days prior. How dare I permit myself to feel empathy for the most privileged children in the entirety of Elora. But he was here, and bloodied, and hurt. And I'd seen him be kind, polite, and patient.

I glanced over to see if the woman or her men were looking at me. They weren't, each too wrapped up in their own tasks to notice when I shot Haven a subtle, pointed grin. *This* will *work.*

"Careful, would you? We're traveling with the prince of your nation. Show some respect," Elliott bit, and was shoved back down again.

I pulled on years of practice to muster up a sob.

One short breath.

Then another.

Only a second later, I was in blubbering, messy tears. My chest heaved, and even Elliott stopped to see what was going on. I merely glanced at him, returning to my blatant wailing.

I had the woman's attention right away. She practically rushed to my side, her soldier pulling Elliott even further from me. *Good.* "Oh, my lovely. There's no need for any of that. Shhh, it's quite alright. We'll be home soon, and then this whole mess will be over," she soothed. I cried, fully and openly, letting her pat down strands of my wild hair as she tried to console me.

"Where –" I hiccupped, "where is home?"

She leaned in to whisper, "Home is Mallord Bay, sweet. All my friends are there waiting for us. They'll be so happy to see you before you go." *True.* I wanted to cringe at the feeling of her cool breath on my shoulder.

"Go where?" I shuddered, succumbing to a whole new bout of sobs.

Her icy hands moved to each side of my face. It was an *effort* not to recoil. "Back to Lukoh, of course. Where people like him," she gestured to the prince, "are meant to be."

True. And disgusting.

That was quite enough.

A hidden dagger on my wrist slid into my hand. The rope snapped in less than a blink, and she didn't have a chance to respond before she was pinned under me with a knife to her throat. She gasped and writhed as I inched the steel in closer.

Elliott struck at the same time, hands somehow magically freed. He kicked up at the man holding him, knocking away his mask and jerking his head back. Poor thing had been distracted by me, and Elliott was *fast.* The very next second, the man had collapsed, and Elliott had tied his hands with the same rope that had held him. Once the man was secure, Elliott moved to free the prince.

"I wore him down for you," Haven started.

"And you did so wonderfully, Highness," his friend retorted and sliced the prince's bonds loose.

My attention fell back to the woman underneath me, whose face was now aflame with rage. She was squirming still, but the blade at her neck kept her mostly steady.

"Get off of me!" she hissed.

Then Haven and Elliott reclaimed their swords, tucking the two daggers away as well.

"You are going to answer my questions." I asked, settling further, "What's your name?"

"I have nothing to say to you," she said, refusing to meet my eyes.

"Sure you do," I pushed the blade closer to her skin, close enough to hurt but not deep enough to draw blood. For some strange reason, I felt no guilt. "What is your name?"

"Let me go!" The woman tried and failed to buck me off.

A wash of something both wholly unfamiliar and yet entirely like home brushed over me. It felt... old. Ancient. Buzzing, humming around me. In my skin, in my bones, in the very air I breathed. The very feel of it was nature itself, instinct and action and everything in between.

Her eyes snapped to mine then, dazed. As if she could see whatever it was that I was feeling. Even Haven and Elliott, in the very corner of my vision, took a step back. One of them called out to me, but I wasn't really listening.

"What is your name?" I repeated, my voice uncharacteristically calm.

"Lorelai Elsborough." *True.*

"What are you doing here?"

"We were sent to bring the prince and whoever accompanied him back to Mallord Bay." *True.*

"Why?"

89

She bit down on her lip, clearly trying to fight whatever it was that she sensed. Tears fell on either side of her vacant face.

"*Why?*" I bit.

"We were sending you home." *True.* There was still no recognition in her swirling eyes, no hint that there was even life behind them.

I did not have the willpower to pry much further. Whatever happened, whatever that feeling was, it was incredibly draining.

"What home?" Haven asked, but he was met with no reply.

My head spun, and blood dripped onto Lorelai's face. My blood, I realized. I had time for one more question. Two, if I really pushed, but even that was not a guarantee. One more question.

"Is anyone else coming?" I asked.

"Yes," she nodded, "six more." *True. Depths.*

"Oh, joy," Haven muttered.

"Anything else?" Elliott asked.

She didn't meet his gaze, "We will never stop coming for him. For all of you, now." *True.*

Nausea and dizziness found me again, and blood continued to trickle down from my nose. I nodded. The ancient feeling departed, as did the last of my energy. She was limp now underneath me, unseeing eyes peering up. I sat back, catching myself on weak arms. *Weak.* Every part of me felt drained and empty. I needed to sleep for a decade and even then it might not be enough.

Lorelai didn't stir.

Elliott moved to tie her hands, and I barely shifted from where I sat. Tired, so very tired. So very drained. My nose was still bleeding, if only a little. Haven just stared at me with those curious eyes.

"We need to leave," Elliott finished the knots he made. Lorelai didn't speak a word, just sitting docile and quiet. Looking at me, no light in her face. Aside from the occasional blink, she didn't move.

"Here."

Haven offered me a steady hand, and I allowed him to pull me up. His other arm cradled his side, but he didn't wince with the force of tugging me to my feet. There was a heavy look between him and Elliott, and Haven led me by my shaking hand back into the carriage.

Unnerving, how it looked untouched. How we had been yanked out of it mere minutes prior and somehow it still seemed entirely intact.

Haven sat first, then I settled wordlessly across from him. A breath later, and the carriage was moving. Elliott, I presumed. Only then did I remember that the prince of Elora, who would not be the next king but likely another valuable position, was hurt and bleeding and yet he had still practically carried me inside. I did not want him to help me. I wanted *him* to owe *me*.

With that realization, I began digging through the trunks. Clothes, toiletries, more clothes, and then a kit to help mend wounds. Haven still watched me silently. I opened it, wiping the blood from my face and taking a quick inventory of the contents.

Then, I sat before the prince. Cedar and cinnamon. His hands remained dutifully at his sides while I rummaged to find what I needed. Water, cloths, bandages, a salve. I dabbed some water onto a cloth, set it aside and reached for the prince's forehead. He nodded, and I removed the jewelry that so regularly graced his brow. *His tiara.* It came off with a *click*, and I placed it down in his lap.

"Selah," he said quietly, as though he was trying not to frighten me. I moved towards the cloth, wiping away some of the blood from his head. It hadn't quite dried, and it came off with no difficulty. My eyes drooped and my hands were heavy, but I patted it until it was clean. I moved on to his arm, though it wasn't quite as bad as his head.

I moved for the salve, setting the now dirty cloth aside. Gently, as gently as I was able, I applied some to the prince's arm. He didn't wince, or grimace, he just stared with watching eyes. It was only when I shifted to do the same to the cut on his head that he stopped me, catching my wrist with a careful hand.

"Selah."

"Haven," I said, less than a murmur.

"What did you do to her?" His voice was breathless and reverent, and I found no judgment in his face. Concern, maybe. But no fear. No anger or disdain or apprehension. Just wonder.

I answered truthfully. "I don't know."

I tugged my hand, but he held firm.

"You are in no shape to be fixing me." *True.* Oh yes, I had forgotten. The prince's ability.

"I'm almost done."

"You're quite finished," he countered in that royal tone of his. Terribly stubborn. I lacked much more motivation to argue with him.

I wiggled the salve on my finger. "This, and a bandage, and you'll be good as new. Would you deny one of your loyal subjects the opportunity to aid her prince?" I meant for it to be light, but the sentence dragged in the air.

He shook my wrist gingerly, a reminder of his gift. "You are *exhausted*, Selah, and I have been able to tend to my own wounds since I was a child. Also, I can tell you in full honesty that you feel worse than I do." *True.* Ugh, I hated his gift. And I hated mine for giving him away. "Please."

92

"I'd be done by now if you stopped complaining."

"But oh, how my pride will never recover if a beautiful woman mistakes my injuries for weakness. I'm sure even you can see how damaging that would be to my otherwise stellar reputation," he smirked.

I smiled softly. The prince of Elora was teasing me.

When I tugged my hand back again, he allowed it. I continued applying the salve to his forehead. It smelled of mint and eucalyptus. "Your secrets are safe with me, Your Highness."

"I'm quite sure they are."

I grinned again, taping a plaster to the cut on his head and idly wrapping one around his arm. He let me, despite his previous protests. I reached to reveal the wound I knew he had cradled on his ribs, and he firmly stopped me then.

"Selah Aster," he scolded, "you will rest. This very moment, in fact." He swiped away all the supplies I had found in the kit, tossing them just out of my reach. I couldn't muster up the willpower to grab them.

"You cannot force me to."

Haven scoffed, "I most certainly can." He guided me softly by my shoulders back into my own seat. His hands were rough and calloused. I had witnessed the wounds he managed to give when it was three against one. He had watched me hold a knife to a woman's throat. But even so, he was so careful not to hurt me.

I sat back then, head falling against the carriage wall. My eyes were unbearably heavy, and I had nearly forgotten how ill I had been.

I realized I truly couldn't refuse him.

"Sleep. I'll be sure to wake you if I need someone to come to my rescue."

He had hardly finished the sentence before I was dreaming again.

93

Chapter Ten: Haven

With a king awaiting us, we carried on with our journey.

I used my gift to check on Elliott occasionally. He was always raw with worry, a healthy dose of anger and an underlying string of fear. There was never any panic, though, and that anxiety never rose above a low hum. His emotions weren't all that distant from my own.

There was no official castle protocol for what to do when a royal carriage was almost hijacked and the inhabitants nearly kidnapped. At least, if there was, I was not aware of it. Do you send word to the king? Or the guards? Was it worth being dragged back mere days into the first real task we'd ever been assigned?

Once we reached Lyscott, I decided. Then I could write a letter to the king about the threat we'd faced and discuss what to do.

Selah had stirred at one point only to grab a coat to use as a pillow. She'd curled up on the seat, knees folded and coat tucked beneath her arms. The smallest trace of blood lingered right under her nose, but she wasn't as pale as she'd been for most of the day. While I didn't imagine surprise ambushes were ideal for recovery, she was improving. Even the mark she'd received at the hand of the Lyscottian soldier was hardly noticeable.

My own side throbbed. Hints of yellow and purple revealed a developing bruise, and I applied the salve myself long after she'd fallen asleep.

Eventually, Elliott pulled the carriage off to the side of the road and slowed to a stop. My heart lurched just until I checked on him once more, and with gentle steps, I moved out of the carriage.

Elliott had pulled near a tavern, and I watched as he paced up to its entrance. No sign of men in masks, no evidence the attack had ever even occurred outside of the member of our party we'd left behind. Silently, I remembered the woman he loved and the soldiers who would have to deliver the news.

Outside the pub tucked deep within the forest, benches and tables stood under falling leaves. Some older men crowded around one, muttering amongst themselves. At another, a family scarfed down some venison. The man I could only assume was the father looked drained, but the children chewed along happily. Four young ladies rested at a third table, murmuring and pointing at a few men who trailed into the tavern after Elliott.

They knew nothing of the fight that had only just happened. Everyone else carried happily along as usual. Strange, that the world didn't stop spinning after every terrible thing. That Lukoh hadn't moved from whatever pedestal he sat upon to help. That the god I was taught who presided over my kingdom, who was endlessly kind and tirelessly merciful, chose not to spare Quint's life. Perhaps he had lent what assistance he would offer through whatever it was that Selah had done. Rather, perhaps Lorelei was right and he did have some vendetta against 'people like me.' Whatever that had meant.

A few heartbeats later, and Elliott returned with two bowls of soup in tow. I nodded toward one of the benches, making my own way over as he wandered back to join me. Heaviness exuded from him, akin to what I usually felt when I dared to open myself up to Alaric. His eyes were tired and wary. They darted from me to the carriage, from the carriage to the road we'd taken, and right to me again.

He set down the soup, handing me one as he took a spoonful of his own. "We're gonna have to talk about what happened," he mumbled.

"I know," and I did.

"And whatever Selah did to Elsborough."

"I'm aware," and I was.

"And what we are going to tell your father and the king of Lyscott."

"Nothing yet." I ate a few heaping spoonfuls, worlds hungrier than I had anticipated.

"Haven," Elliott started, "you are the prince of Elora, second in line to the throne, and there has been an attempt on your life. This could be a threat to the safety of our nation," he breathed in heavily, "and you are advising me to do *nothing*?"

"I am advising you to wait." Another spoonful. There was a very pleasant garlic flavor that really brought the dish together.

"For what, Your Highness?" It was not quite the mocking tone that Selah tended to favor, but his reference of my title was not exactly used with esteem. "Perhaps until they catch up with us and succeed in kidnapping you? When they take one of your siblings instead?"

I flinched, "Of course not. Only until we reach Lyscott. King Castillo has little need of that information, and my father can wait the five days it will take for us to make the journey. If Alaric's gift was of any use, my father may already know that something happened. Once we are settled, I

96

will write to him and give him as many details as he requires. I will offer him no excuse to pull us back home early when we are quite capable of handling ourselves."

"Look in a mirror, my prince, and then tell me how capable you are of handling yourself."

I took a deep breath and glanced at my friend, "We will manage."

Elliott shook his head, scarfing down the rest of his lunch. I understood his concern. I felt it, in him and in myself. In the weary father who kept peeking over at us every few minutes. But, save for the kidnappers, the rest of the journey was relatively safe. We had escaped them once, I thought, and they'd need time to regroup. And especially after Faye's incident, the prince and princesses would be monitored as closely as ever.

"And what of Aster? She did something to the Elsborough woman."

"I can assure you, Elliott, she was just as scared as you were. Feelings like that can be hidden, but they cannot be faked."

"With your decades of experience? Oh, I'm certain you wouldn't be easily fooled by the first pretty thing you've been near in ages. Or is it –"

"I understand."

"Do you?" He held my stare.

I nodded. The carriage still sat completely undisturbed. Utterly unmoved. A breeze brought with it the chill of the cool spring air, and my side burned with the feeling. But people could not easily defend against my gift because they tended to forget it was even there. "Keep an eye on her until and in Lyscott. There's no need to throw accusations until there is legitimate evidence of wrongdoing, but you have my full blessing to monitor her as you wish."

He nodded back in agreement. His expression was as solemn a thing as he ever mustered, and I found myself searching for the friend of mine who was unburdened.

We finished our food in relative silence, leaving as soon as we were done. Elliott argued passionately with me about who would drive, and I was only convinced when he mentioned that I was the one of us who could monitor the other. Once I finally had conceded, we were gone. Mercifully, the rest of the day's journey was wholly uneventful. I only had successfully taken over driving for an hour or so after dinner when his brooding figure returned to grab the reins again. It certainly hadn't been Selah's fault, who slept through the entirety of the day and who had barely awoken to move into the inn at night.

The physician never arrived.

The next five days were about the same. Elliott or I drove, though he much preferred to be the one in control. Selah stirred enough for us to know she lived, but the majority of her time was spent dreaming. Whatever she had done to the woman, evidently it took some vast amount of energy. Either that, or the illness she'd woken up with proved to be more severe than we expected. While I certainly missed the creativity of her threats and the regular delight of her company, I found myself enjoying the lack of tension between her and Elliott.

The sign that we had crossed over into Lyscott was the icy air that seemed to permeate my very skin. My memory really did serve me well, I realized, as I peeked up at the snow-capped mountains through the carriage windows. They leered over us, beautiful and haunting. The trees survived only a fraction of the altitude, replaced by the barren rock and falling white flakes. It was snowing in May. Even so far north should not have been so cold, but I concluded that my experience had an extent to which it could be reliable. There were no cities, no warm homes or buzzing taverns. In fact, there was no sign of civilization until we reached the capital.

When we only had about half an hour of travel left, I moved to nudge Selah. She stirred, barely.

"You've slept nearly a week of your life away" I said.

She mumbled something vulgar that I narrowly understood.

"We're approaching Lyscott, Miss Aster. I will need my trusted bodyguard to stand valiantly by my side."

With that encouragement, she shifted to a proper seated position and wiped the exhaustion from her eyes. Her gaze lingered, peering out the windows to observe the mountains and trees. Black curls stretched out at every different angle, but aside from that she looked quite alright. She bore no evident marks or bruises, which was more than I could say for myself. The purple and yellow hadn't yet faded at my side, and my face had still seen better days.

"How long do we have?" she asked, voice creaking with the roughness that only sleep could offer.

"Not too long, but time enough for you to wake properly."

She nodded, mind elsewhere. "Entire days have passed." Blue-gray orbs wandered.

I confirmed with a nod of my own, and disbelief lit up her features. "Full days? That's more than I've slept...ever. I knew I was tired, *you* knew I was tired, but that is..."

"Impressive?"

"Alarming," she yawned, squinting slightly. "Though I feel as if I could go down for another week if you offered."

"Soon, but we have a king to charm and answers to find."

99

"How could I forget?" she teased. Some unseen weight removed itself from my shoulders. It only took five days, but she was up and moving again. The weight settled right back into place once I remembered that Quint was not granted that same privilege, and I sent Lukoh a silent request to keep him.

She spent the rest of the journey preparing herself, as did I. Once more I donned the golden headpiece of my kingdom, as well as fixing the blond locks that had fallen out of place and straightening out my uniform. It was worn with use, but that was likely only noticeable to me due to the amount of time I'd spent in Elora's signature green and gold. Fortunately, I had brought the coat to match, which I was eternally glad for as I stepped outside.

The castle stood nearly as high as the surrounding mountains. Panes and panes of stone were visible as we passed through the wooden gates, glass decorating the delicately carved walls. Imagery I didn't recognize was etched into the rock. Wide oak doors were shut tightly in front of us, and the icy air bounced off them with little effort. Even still, soft light shone from inside. A retreat, somehow, in the midst of the storm.

Not a second passed before the wood creaked open. Guards dressed in Lyscottian blue and silver ushered us in, granting us access to the warmth of the palace. It was ornate in a way that my own home was only on holidays. Silver accents lined the walls, rugs that cost more than most Eloran apartments were draped across the floor, and paintings I only recognized from books were hung in all their grace. I wasn't informed that Lyscott was so wealthy. In fairness, I hadn't been told much of anything. I felt, more than witnessed, Selah and Elliott's own respective shock and admiration at the elaborate entryway.

"Your Highness," a smooth, darkened voice greeted. I was met by a man clothed in sleek navy blue, fitting in the room almost like a decoration. His skin was ashen, eerily so, as mine would've been if I was forced to hide from the elements. In contrast, his hair shone such a dark brown it was nearly ebony. His face was worn with age, but not much more than my father's. He bowed his head, "Nero Singh, advisor to His Majesty. The king has requested that I escort you to the conference room. I do hope you don't mind the company." The words were warm, but the tone was cool and empty.

Even as I reached out with my gift, there was little to note. A bit of annoyance. Anticipation. He looked up and down Elliott, then Selah. Elliott appeared as though he always did, vaguely bemused and wearing the Eloran military uniform. In the wake of realizing her outfit could easily have given her away when we were ambushed, Selah opted for more standard Eloran clothes. She was armed still, but it was only evident because I already knew where she kept her various blades. His gaze lingered a breath too many. Challenge lit in her eyes.

"It's an honor, truly. We are eager to meet His Majesty," I interjected before either of them insulted the other.

Nero turned back to me for a heartbeat, nodding before leading the way down a corridor. Neither Selah nor Elliott looked to be particularly thrilled with the gentleman's presence. At least they finally had something in common.

After a handful more steps and a few turns later, the doors opened to the king's conference room.

Five people sat at the grand oak table, three men and two women with four empty seats still available. Ten eyes stared as we entered, each watching and patiently waiting.

First, sat an older woman with warm tanned skin and dark features. Although she could easily fit into any of the countries to the south of Elora, she was there sitting quietly at the table. I felt little from her, aside from a brief wave of anxiety.

To her left sat who I could only assume was her daughter. She had the same dark hair, though one side was partially shaved, and her skin was fairer. There was no shortage of emotions there, ranging from intrigue to glee to curiosity. A feline grin lit up her face, but it didn't entirely meet her eyes.

On the other side, a man about my age reclined in his seat. His hair was a deep ebony, eyes dark and watching. He was eager, and I felt it even more when his eyes shifted to Selah. Irritation hummed in my chest almost immediately.

Then sat a young man with stark alabaster hair and a piercing gray gaze. He was wary, that was evident enough. Wary, waiting, but he only consistently felt preoccupied for the duration of the meeting. His mood shifted as he peered at us in a manner that I did not entirely understand.

And last, the king stood at the end of the table. His hair also was that same shade of white, but his nose and cheeks bore a twinge of pink. He smiled kindly, without the distance I had sensed from the others. He too was dressed in the colors of his nation, a silver crown resting atop his head.

But his grief was agonizing. It was a heavy thing, and my feet were pinned down unlike they had been when we walked into the room. I had felt pain as gnawing as his on only a few occasions and I ached to release him from it. How could he stand it? How could he grin at all with so much crushing down on him?

Almost as if he caught himself, he blinked, and the heaviness was gone. Not the pain, but the physical weight had lifted. Selah and Elliott

102

shifted on their feet as well, as though they had felt the same thing I had. But that was practically impossible, unless the king –

"You'll excuse me," he started, voice as regal as I would've expected, "my gift often has a mind of its own," he grinned. "It is a pleasure to make your acquaintance again, young prince." *Again?* I didn't recall meeting him the first time I'd visited Lyscott.

"The pleasure is mine, Your Majesty, and thank you for your hospitality on such short notice." He had a few days, maybe less, to make arrangements before we arrived.

"Nonsense, the castle could use the extra liveliness. Now, Highness, who have you brought me? Your messenger was vague, and I'd love to know who you value so highly to travel with all this way." So, the Lyscottian king was almost... polite. Both a surprise and a relief. I was relieved that the harsh climate did not seem to produce a harsh ruler.

I motioned to Elliott first, "This is Lieutenant Colonel Elliott Pearce, son of Eline Pearce, who serves as commanding general of Elora's most influential district in addition to her work in our military. His years of training do make him a valuable asset, but he is also one of my closest friends."

But there was Selah. She was going to hate me. Just when I had won an ounce of her favor, as well. Part of my mind began daydreaming explanations and apologies while the other half controlled my tongue.

"And this beautiful young woman is Lady Selah Aster of Distin. My betrothed."

Chapter Eleven: Selah

His *what?*

Oh, there would be blood. There would be fire and brimstone and whatever other misery I could possibly conjure up to torment him with. The depths of the earth would tremble if they knew the various threats that passed through my mind. *Betrothed?* To the prince of Elora? I would have sooner offered myself up to the demented human sacrifice people if I had known that this was his plan. I did not agree to that. Never would I put myself in such a monitored position.

Every bone in my body wanted to revolt, but I maintained my composure. Instead, I grinned mildly at the promise of future revenge.

To the right of the prince, the young man with the dark hair spoke first, crooning with his raspy tone. He filled out his navy shirt, and I imagined he was strong enough underneath all that arrogance. "Congratulations are in order, Your Highness. I wasn't aware you kept such a pretty pet." *True.*

"*Adiel,*" the young Lyscottian woman scolded.

Surely, stabbing him wouldn't be a war crime after that level of disrespect, would it?

My smile departed. Haven's hand was on mine before I could reach for something to skewer them both with. I writhed under his grasp just enough for him to notice, and even Elliott took a subtle step forward. Not five minutes into the meeting, and I was already filled with the burning desire to prove exactly how good of a pet I was.

But my prince answered before I was able, "I assure you, she is anything but. And she is the future of my kingdom, so I do hope that you will learn to treat her accordingly." *True.*

I recoiled at the part of me that found his interference endearing.

The king then intervened, "Please, sit. Feel free to ignore him. Young Adiel often enjoys listening to the sound of his own voice, so you have my full blessing to tune him out at will." The young man shrugged as though he was used to this sort of reaction. I wondered if Adiel would enjoy a knife buried in his neck. "The rest of my court is more pleasant. I see you've met Nero. This is Wren, his wife, and Ilse, his daughter. Their loyalty to my kingdom has been unparalleled. And my son, Prince Mekhi, the heir to the Lsycottian throne." *True.*

Wren was quiet, but her eyes were wide and searching. Her brows were knitted together in gentle concern; however, there wasn't much more to note from her. She was frail and middle aged, a bit younger than her husband.

Ilse, on the other hand, had delight written all over her features. She stared up at Haven with big, doe eyes, hanging onto his every movement like the perfect little subject of a kingdom that wasn't even hers. *Why am I here, again?* I pondered, missing the little cell the general had stuffed me into. 'Twas a simpler time, when my baseline level of annoyance was considerably lower.

Prince Mekhi gave away little. He was silent, saying nothing as he or any of the others were introduced. His eyes narrowed slightly on Haven, who was oblivious as he met the king's gaze. The Lsycottian prince looked strong and battered in a way that I hadn't seen in the others. The hands folded lazily across his abdomen held small silver scars the likes of which I'd never witnessed. He could not have been much older than me, but his face was worn. I wondered what chaos had ensued in their nation to warrant such markings, and why Elora apparently knew so little of it. He glanced my way for only a moment before moving on.

We did sit then in our respective chairs, Elliott placing himself between me and Adiel and Haven between myself and Nero. Haven kept his hand on mine, and I made no further effort to shove him away. I instead allowed the prince to feel every shred of my anger through his touch. He didn't pull back, even when it was all I focused on.

While I was pent up in my thoughts, Haven had said all the niceties. The king started, "And to what do I owe the delight of a visit from my Southern neighbors? It's been quite a long time since there's been any correspondence between our nations, although I am pleasantly surprised." *Lie.* Oh, that was something.

"My father and I agreed that it was time to open up conversation once more," Haven said. "It's been a decade and a half since we've had any real relationship, and with the coming changes," he held up our hands, "we thought it best to revisit the idea." He was lying through his teeth, but he did it with such elegance. Depths, I was nearly convinced by his performance myself.

The king sat back in his chair, features alight with consideration. "Well, I'm eager to learn more about what that looks like on your end. I'm sure you've had a long journey, though, so I don't want to keep you longer than I must." *True.*

"Ah, yes," Haven started.

Elliott pursed his lips.

"We ran into some trouble on our way, an ambush." The brunette girl gasped in a type of shock that I wasn't remotely convinced by. "We are quite alright now, but it's definitely something I'd like to pass along. If it's no burden, I'll have to send word to my father about the attack. It may be wise to have your soldiers monitoring the southern border as well." *Such diplomacy*. Who would've guessed that the prince of Elora isn't exclusively a pain in the —

The king waved him off, "It is absolutely no burden. Send me whatever details you have, and I will ensure that all is settled." King Castillo took a heavy breath. "If I recall, you don't usually train your women to defend themselves in Elora, do you?"

Oh no. Wherever that conversation was headed, I did not want to be a part of it.

Haven shook his head. "It's not generally necessary, no. Why do you ask?"

"If you'd like for your fiancée to be occupied in the time that you're here, I'd be more than happy to have my son teach her some basic techniques. He may not be remarkably talkative, but he is one of our finest fighters. He's more than capable of instructing." *True*.

I wanted to vomit, but I'd ruin my pretty outfit.

It was Elliott who piped in. "I think that's sage advice. I'd love to be involved as well, in fact. It would be a privilege to see one of Lyscott's finest warriors in action." *True*. His tone was caked with respect I wasn't accustomed to hearing from him. *Suck-up. Absolute, royal suck-up.*

The king nodded. "Consider it done then." *True*.

A brief moment was spent daydreaming about what kind of caskets I'd bury my entourage in, but I had to do something of use. Even if it was only of use to me. Or, better yet, of use for my entertainment. A breath later, and I was ready.

"If you don't mind my asking," I started, and Haven's hand twitched, "what abilities do you happen to possess? I'm sorry – I apologize. I know it can be such a personal question. It's just – well, I know it's silly, but ever since I met *my Haven*, I've been just fascinated by the kind of – what's the word you used? Giftings? Oh, everyone has a different word for it. A gift, a talent, an ability. I was wondering if that was something you were comfortable sharing. In all my days, I've never gotten used to being around people who were so extraordinary. Isn't that right, honey?"

Oh, the sweet, decadent taste of embarrassing him a fraction of the amount he had embarrassed me. It did not last very long.

His lips pulled back into a tight grin, and I realized then that I had made a mistake. "You are absolutely right, dearest. But, mind you, it isn't polite to ask in such a manner," he turned toward the king. "Even after all this time, I still get a barrage of questions whenever we meet someone with a gift. You'd think the novelty would wear off, but somehow it shocks her every time."

I was raising the price of my efforts to *four* tubs of strawberries.

"Of course, I understand how it would interest someone outside our world," the king sympathized. "My son, he can manipulate senses. He can make people deaf, blind, lose their ability to feel pain, and some more complicated maneuvers. It sounds more intense than it really is." *True.* Well, intense or not, it sounded like a pain.

"I myself can manipulate gravity, but only to an extent and only within a certain range." *True.* A very brief explanation to what I concluded was a very nuanced gift.

"Young Ilse can manifest different concoctions. Mostly we use her to fight off insomnia, but she can also make salves and poison if absolutely necessary." *True.* She grinned sweetly at Haven as the king spoke. So she was gawking over my prince, *and* she could kill any of us with no great difficulty. How comforting.

"Wren can manifest shields and wards. It's not particularly useful in everyday life, but she becomes invaluable when in need of defense. She even aided in crafting our prison system, it was a heaven-sent help." *True.* And, fortunately, not as unnerving as the others. Wren just ducked her head and nodded. Strange that she was so timid when the rest of them were bold enough.

"I'm afraid my son Adiel and I are not blessed," Nero interjected before the king could speak for them. *Lie.* He or his jerk son most certainly had a gift that he was choosing to hide. Understandable, in a way, but left me with a sinking feeling.

"Fascinating," I didn't feign most of my awe and yawned, "once we get some proper rest, I'll have a wealth of questions. I hope you'll excuse us." *And they say diplomacy is hard.*

The king grinned, "Of course. I'll have Nero walk you and Prince Haven to your room. Your friend's room is right around the corner, so he'll require no escort."

Oh no. *Oh no.* Was it far too late to return to Lorelai and give myself freely? Sure, it was a few days' journey to Mallord Bay, but certainly eternal relief would be better than the temporary agony that I was due to face. The prince squeezed my hand, and I fought to keep the color out of my face. Of course, it would be awfully suspicious if I didn't share a room with him. But being trapped in a space with any man overnight was enough to make my heart start racing. Even worse yet, I couldn't make my emotions my own again until Haven let go of my hand.

Mercifully, he did just that as we stood. "Until tomorrow, Your Majesty," I nodded my goodbye, and Haven did the same.

The king only grinned, beckoning Nero to see us off. Nero walked with fast, wide steps, then gestured for us to follow. It was an effort to keep up, however unintentional his speed may have been.

"Do you find it difficult being the one of the only ones without an ability?" I asked, hearing the lie in my own voice.

That granted me a pointed look from Haven, whose hand wandered idly to my lower back. His fingers sat not an inch above my dagger. He showed none of the difficulty with Nero's pace that I felt.

Nero cast half a glance at me before responding, "I suppose I am rather used to it by now. Indeed, and what kind of father would I be if I were jealous of my own daughter? Or what sort of advisor would I make if I couldn't make peace with the king's abilities?" *Liar.* How thankful I was for my own hidden gift. His voice grated on my skin.

"You'll have to excuse my fiancée's prodding. It's innocent interest, but I do understand that it can be overwhelming," Haven apologized. *Ugh.*

Nero gave Haven what I could only assume was a look of sympathy, "I've had my share of experience with women of the sort. It's why I went so far to find a wife. You'll find that they are much more docile south of Elora, if you ever do choose to change your mind." The hum of anger turned to a subtle roar, and once again I felt Haven pull me closer to him. Perhaps no amount of fruit would be worth the effort of keeping my mouth shut, and it had not yet been an hour.

"I'm quite content with my decision, but I do appreciate the concern."

"Noted."

A few quick, tense steps later, we reached a door with bits of snow etched into the wood. A landscape not unlike the one we'd passed through was depicted, careful to capture every detail. Had I not been so blinded by my own wrath, I would've paused longer to consider its beauty.

"This is where you'll be staying for the duration of your visit. We'll send someone to check in on you both later, but do rest if you wish. Send for whatever you need, and consider it done." He opened the door for us but did not deign to enter the room.

"Please thank the king for his hospitality," the ever-so diplomatic and professional young prince replied, and with a brief confirming nod, the door shut behind us. Nero was off.

The room itself was something out of a fairytale. The bed could fit four of me, with thin, sheer curtains draped all around it. There were shelves and shelves of books lining one wall, and enormous panes of glass on the other. Moonlight flooded in, and lanterns illuminated the places it could not reach. One corner was reserved for a vanity, another for a desk with copious amounts of writing supplies. In the other, a door led to a small kitchen and a washroom I was ready to use to rub the stain of travel off my skin. A portion of the trunks from the carriage had already been placed carefully by the foot of the bed, the rest likely under Elliott's care.

It was nearly enough to make me forget my anger. *Nearly.*

I didn't know where to begin. I was just... burning. I burned because of how blindsided I was, burned with wrath meant for the courts of two different countries, burned because I saw no way out and burned with the fear of being trapped. I had almost started to like the prince of Elora, though it certainly came as no shock that one of the most spoiled

111

children on the continent wouldn't shy away from putting me in such a position.

I was no one's *pet*.

Decidedly not his.

But I said nothing, not initially, as I debated how best to show the prince that I was having none of it. So I was quiet as I rummaged through the waiting trunks to find anything else to spend my time on.

I felt, more than saw, the prince behind me. I heard him prop himself up against the wall, and I sensed his eyes on me. He was quiet too, at first. Just watching. No quips, no comments, no remarks. Just those honey amber eyes gauging my every movement.

His patience ran out before mine did, though, as he was only content to watch for so long. "I am sorry," he said.

I would not deign to respond.

"Selah," he tried again.

"No."

Then, he was in my view. Perfectly messy tufts of hair and Eloran jewelry clouded my vision. "I, my dearest accomplice, have been blessed with the misfortune of being subject to your every emotion. You are not pleased. So, if you'd be so kind, grant me this mercy and explain to me what crime I have committed to warrant such a reaction." He wasn't quite mocking, but he wasn't entirely genuine, either.

Was he truly so blind?

"He called me your *pet*."

Haven grimaced, "I recall."

It was not callous. But regardless of his tact, the emotion bubbled up anyway. "I'm still not sure if that's better or worse than being told you

112

can *trade* me for a nice, quiet southern woman if you want someone more tolerable."

"While that offer grows increasingly tempting by the day, I think I'd bore easily. Plus, what do people do with all the time they don't spend bickering? Seems a bit much." He was playing. I was in no mood for it.

"You could've said I was a friend. An advisor. A distant cousin. A priestess. A traveling circus, for all I really care. But you decided – without me – that you were going to tell them we were engaged. Now I am –" *trapped.* I took a breath, lest I say more than I intended. "I have been put in this position. I am bound to your side. I am bound to this room. I am bound to loyalty to a country that has historically cared little about my fate. I had every right to know. But, as I should've guessed, the *esteemed* prince of Elora thought of no one but himself," I bit.

But he didn't fight back.

Ugh.

He watched me again as though I was transparent. As though, if he looked hard enough, he could glimpse my very soul. It wasn't entirely true, but I suppose he could, in a way. His brow furrowed as he stared, and eventually his expression softened, "You're afraid." *True.*

Terrified, and aching with it. I didn't want to think about any of the other scenarios I'd been trapped in. At least those men weren't princes. I wanted space. I wanted to go home. I wanted a door I could lock behind me. I wanted an armory with a bed and perhaps a nice window.

Most of those men were dead now, albeit often without my intervention. The one that remained was far from Lyscott, although the memory of his calloused, reaching hands had followed me all that distance anyway.

113

"I told you to stay out of my emotions," I retorted, but I had taken too long, and I could hear the answer in my own voice.

"Selah –"

"Nero was lying," I stared up at him, unabashedly. "He and his son more than certainly have a gift, and he's hiding it on purpose."

There was pain and longing written all over Haven's face, like he ached to say something but couldn't. It flickered away after a moment, replaced with careful consideration. "I figured as much after your prodding." *True.*

"And the king was not surprised to see us, but everything else he said was perfectly honest. Wholesome, even, on occasion," I said.

Haven nodded, and I silently wished he would return to toying with me. It was far more tolerable than the sobriety he exchanged it for, the furrowed brow and the careful gaze. "I'll keep that in mind." *True.*

I grabbed an extra blanket from the trunk. It was soft, albeit thin, but good enough. The prince didn't protest as I grabbed one of the pillows from the severely oversized bed and made myself a place to rest on the floor. The floor was largely stone, save for the large, handwoven rug that rested just below the bed. It was comfortable, as far as floors go, and with my back to the prince, I laid down without a word.

He sighed in what I could only assume was resignation. I heard some shuffling behind me, covers rustling and such. His royal majesticness was preparing himself for bed. I was *not* sharing, not even for my life, and my willingness to fight had already been depleted.

"Would you like me to keep the candles lit?" he asked.

He's trying to be nice, a quiet, airy voice whispered in the corner of my mind.

I don't care, I whispered back.

"No," just as much evil could happen in midday as it could in pitch black.

A few *puffs* later, and the moon was all that was left.

Chapter Twelve: Haven

While I was destined to end up on the floor regardless, it was significantly less tolerable when I wasn't the only one there.

It took longer than usual to fall asleep, as my unwilling roommate tossed and turned for what felt to be hours. After consistent, conscious thought, I could keep my senses to myself and stay out of her emotions. Occasionally, as I drifted closer to sleep, the concentration slipped. I would feel her hum of anxiety like it was my own, beating like a drum underneath my skin. So a group of armed, masked cult members wasn't enough to scare her, yet I was? I tried to make sense of it in the ninety or so minutes it took for me to fall asleep, but I came up with nothing.

I woke not long before she did to the sun leeching in through the towering windows and warmed a pot of tea in the small kitchenette. I remembered little of Lyscott, but I marveled at how I had forgotten its harsh beauty. The mountains cut through the morning sky, the gray of them nearly hidden by the blankets of snow. They loomed over the already foreboding castle, making their presence more than known. Now, in the daylight, I could just make out a village not far from us. It was nothing grand. There were only a few handfuls of homes and businesses scattered about. It was, if nothing else, comforting to know that there was civilization outside the castle.

As I watched the freshly fallen snow with a steaming mug in hand and contained fascination, sheets crinkled on the other side of the bed. I remained quiet and still, not moving too quickly or sipping too loudly. Not that I had anything to fear, but in an effort not to startle her. Well-rested, it was much easier to keep my gift from reaching out at will, and it often took little effort to control.

She stirred further, eventually dragging herself up and to the trunks at the foot of the bed. I didn't so much as glance in her direction, largely due to the fact that I was still enamored by the view and in part to allow her some privacy. Snow was still falling, albeit without much of the fervor it had held overnight. I had been young, but how had I not remembered such a place?

Selah paused behind me, and I braced myself for whatever criticism she was readying herself to offer.

"It's pretty," she said.

While I was taken aback by her appreciation, I tried not to let it show. A full night of rest had softened her. "It is, isn't it?" I took a careful sip from the nearly scalding mug.

She murmured her agreement. Then, after a moment, and with a heavy sigh, she sat down next to me on the floor. I said nothing. The young woman could likely stab me in ten different places, yet still I was the one treading with care.

"You could have taken the bed," Selah muttered, staring out at the falling snow. I took comfort in knowing she avoided my gaze just as I avoided hers.

"Not in good conscience," I replied, taking yet another gentle sip. It burned slightly, but it tasted sweet and warm.

"So chivalrous." There was no mocking, not in the way there was before. Her voice was quiet and hazy from sleep, but there wasn't the sarcasm that usually coated such words. Smoke from far away chimneys started to rise to signal that the day had begun.

"What can I say?" I started, "My life has been dedicated to serving my people. Even those who are too terribly stubborn to sleep in a waiting bed."

I spared her a look out of the corner of my eye to see if she caught the humor. She was a mess of curls, black hair springing in every direction. Her gaze was still fixed on the mountains, but a hint of a grin tugged on the side of her lips.

"Is this a common situation to find yourself in?" Selah Aster was finally playing along.

"You cannot possibly imagine the trouble I've faced," I hid my own smile as I sipped again.

I heard her smirk beside me, but it faded as she shifted. She faced me head on, now looking straight into my eyes. The humor was gone, but I sensed none of the anger and only a trace of the fear I had felt before.

"I'm sorry I was so angry with you," she apologized, and I nearly choked.

"It was warranted." If only in part.

"It was. You may not have earned the severity of all the things I had to say," she sighed. "So I apologize."

My mind was split between shock and admiration, and then she continued.

"But do remember that I am not here to serve you."

I paused. "What do you mean?"

"I am not here to help you, or Elliott, or your father, or your kingdom. I am not here because I am a loyal Eloran citizen who wants to serve her country. I care little for national pride, and I have no interest in aiding a government that nearly allowed me to starve as a child. Much less their royalty." She was not cruel, just blunt.

"I understand."

"I am here because I did not want to rot in a jail cell simply for the crime of stepping into a dangerous situation. I'm here because I find no fault in using my gift for money and I'm apparently rather easily bribed. And," she waved her hand flippantly, "call it curiosity, but I'd like to know what made a Lyscottian soldier think he was allowed to lay hands on a little girl. These people are also lying to you, and I am left wondering why.

"But that is the extent of my loyalty. I will use my gift when I am able, I will play my part, I will help you get whatever information you wish, and I will do what I can to make sure that you and Elliott aren't killed in the process. That is what I can offer you. If you want anything else from me, it will come at a cost. If you want me to trust you – if you want me to like you, *you need* to tell me everything. I am on your side, even if not entirely by choice, but that will change if anything like that happens again."

What should I have expected from her? For heaven's sake, I had dragged her into a different country, largely against her will, and just anticipated that she'd tolerate it. She saved my life. I felt like every bit of the entitled, rotten thing she had accused me of being. And she wasn't harsh, not nearly as callous as I deserved. A weight lifted off my shoulders and moved to my chest as I took in everything she said.

It was then that she looked off again at the mountains, speaking so quietly that I almost strained to hear, "There are few that I consider friends in this world, fewer still that I trust." She turned to me for half a second

119

before staring back out the window. "I had this... foolish inkling of hope that you would be one or the other."

My heart cracked into pieces, and it was a marvel that she didn't hear it.

"There is yet time," I said, voice coming out smooth and soft. I wished for her to hear the truth in my words. Inwardly, I clamored for what to say. There was nothing, nothing that could justify or make right all the things that I had already subjected this poor girl to. It was unfair that I shielded myself from all her fear and anger when I had been the cause of so much of it. If I had been a better man, I would have let more in. But I was not, and I had done no such thing.

"There *is* yet time," she repeated. "However, Highness, that will come later. For now, you have a king who is awfully ready to get to know you, and I have to face whatever the day holds. I'm still not sure if 'training' with the king's son will be an honor or a torture session."

I smirked at her, "Just be a remarkably less capable version of your usual, charming self. And Elliott will be there, so you'll be more than fine."

She rolled her eyes and groaned, "Torture session it is, then. Did you have to pick such a brooding creature to bring along?"

The mental image of how Elliott would've reacted to that comment had me chuckling, but I came to his defense regardless. "*Two* brooding creatures, thank you, and I am quite content with my decision."

"Good. Though, if you get sick of either of us, at least you can trade us out for some '*quiet southern women*,'" Selah mimicked Nero's deep voice and Lyscottian accent. Her eyes narrowed as she remembered the incident, and I choked on a laugh. It was almost ... endearing, how her eyebrows furrowed, and her lips formed into a slight pout.

A friend. Yes, I decided. I would like to be her friend.

After I downed the rest of the cup of tea, we each got ready for the day on our own. If I thought about it for too long, I would remember that I was a royal jerk for putting her through this ordeal, and the guilt would threaten to eat away at me. I'd make it worth her time. Regardless, we were already in Lyscott. She said she wanted to be here, for the money or because I forced her hand or otherwise. She dressed in the washroom while I put on my uniform in the calm of the morning.

Some time later, and long after I was ready, Selah came back into the room. Her curls had been tucked down into braids. She wore Eloran clothes that the palace had provided her, but the kind that wrapped tightly around her legs for full range of motion. The top was loose and it tucked in neatly to her waist. It was a deep gray set with streaks of gold, and she was stunning. Truly, thoroughly beautiful in a sense that had me turning away before my face could give away what I felt.

"Ready?" I asked her, pretending to straighten out the cuffs of my uniform to have anything else to look at.

She nodded, grabbing two small knives she had stowed away the night before and sliding them underneath her sleeves.

"Listen," I stood from where I was sitting on the edge of a bed. Pity, that it had been reduced to a fluffy, oversized chair. "I imagine much of my time will be taken up entertaining the king. If you have a chance, and if you are willing, I'd like you and Elliott to see what information the Lsycottian libraries have on Lorelai Elsborough or any cult that may be operating out of Mallord Bay. I will do what I can to keep everyone's eyes off you, just in case, but I'd like to keep the details of who attacked us as quiet as possible. Can you do that?"

While, technically, Elliott didn't need her help, it was certainly faster.

She nodded again, "And what of Nero and the king? My gift is of no use if I am not actually there."

I grimaced, "I'll see what I can sense. But I imagine they'll keep us together for dinners, so I'll revisit any subjects where I feel they aren't being entirely forthcoming." It was not a perfect arrangement, but it was temporary.

She grinned. If she was stunning before, she was far more so when she smiled. I sent a silent prayer up to Lukoh for the sake of my sanity. "Well then, I suppose we must be off. Best of luck, Highness."

"And you as well, Miss Aster."

Two Lyscottian soldiers met us at the door. They were clad with silver, leather armor that bore the Lsycottian flag's crest. Where there was not silver, there was the deep blue that decorated much of the castle. One escorted Selah to her destination, and the other held out his hand in the other direction. I nodded in silent greeting and followed him down the corridors. They were just as grand and ornate as they'd been the night before. I was still struck by it. How the king could afford such grandeur with so few villages nearby was a wonder itself.

We strode down a few more corridors before walking past the familiar meeting room of the king. In Elora, we had something similar, but it was often reserved for family meetings and very occasional diplomacy. Rarely did we entertain other nations, especially ones we weren't in active communication with, in such an intimate manner. I found myself appreciating the lack of formality. It struck me as strange, but perhaps something I'd recommend to Alaric when the time came.

I often did enjoy guessing what Alaric would be like as king. Melancholy as ever, I imagined, but likely decent. Not as friendly and decidedly not as good with people as our father had always been, but I always thought he'd do well enough. Even if he did struggle, we'd be there to help him lead. Though, it was Genevieve that I could truly picture ruling a nation. She cared much more for justice, little for all the nonsense and busywork. I considered what they would make of Lyscott, if Alaric was old enough to remember our visit.

The king was seated at a vast oak table, Nero and his daughter situated on one side of him with an open chair on the other. It was massive, bigger than the table that we had in Elora to accommodate the six members of my family and most of our friends. Food of every sort was strewn about in front of them, and a place was set for me. It smelled divine. There was fruit, pastries, all kinds of Lyscottian dishes with a few Elora breakfast items littered in between. I took my seat with no small amount of readiness as I realized that the tea only held me over for a short time.

"Good morning, Your Majesty," I nodded in greeting, and my grin was heartfelt.

"Good morning to you, Your Highness," he waved to the spread in front of him. "Please, eat. It would be a shame for you to go hungry when we have such an important day ahead of us."

I obeyed easily, dumping a few things gracefully onto my plate. Nero ate as well, dutifully quiet. Ilse merely picked at her food. Her eyes were wide and set on me, offering a sickly sweet smile when I looked at her. She was pretty by most standards. Really pretty, even, but something about her stare struck me in the wrong way.

I loosened control of my gift only to feel much of what I had sensed already. The king was at ease, but maintained that sharp undercurrent of grief. Nero was intrigued but slightly irritated and mostly bored. Ilse was eager, too much so for my own liking. Her anticipation nearly matched the king's mourning in potency. The excitement wasn't unusual, and the benefit

123

of my status was that people were often glad to see me for one reason or another. Hers was especially intense, though, and I wondered what Elliott would make of it.

Meeting the king's gaze, I prepared to take my first bite. "What did you have in mind?" I asked, carefully tearing off a piece of bread. It was still warm, and a gentle puff of steam escaped as I pulled.

"I'd like to tell you the story of my people, Prince Haven," he declared, "and ask for your hand in our war against Dobre."

Chapter Thirteen: Selah

"Morning, *Lady* Aster."

While I had not missed Elliott Pearce or his obnoxious remarks, they were far easier to tolerate after adequate amounts of rest and my conversation with the prince. I only wished we were in our own country, where I did not have to put on any sort of act. There, I could prove to Elliott just how much of a lady I could be.

But, for the time being, I was burdened with his presence.

Elliott was dressed in a variation of his usual attire. His dreads were tucked in a knot, and while he still wore a type of Eloran uniform, it was more casual than the outfit he wore when traveling. One that was meant for training, I supposed.

I smiled in a way that didn't quite reach my eyes as I entered the room the Lyscottian guard had led me to. Brown mats lined the floors, missing some of the finery that the rest of the castle held. More training equipment than I have ever seen in one place lay gracefully strewn out in the room, and weapons of all kinds were mounted on the walls. Many of them were entirely unfamiliar to me, with extra edges or strange handles. Lyscottian weaponry. Very, very beautiful, Lyscottian weaponry. I briefly pondered who I could talk into letting me take something home with me.

"Pearce," I remarked absentmindedly. I moved to the closest wall, fixed on one weapon in particular. It resembled a sword. Two blades curved over themselves at the base of the hilt, parallel to each other until the very edge. Such a lavish thing to use solely as decoration. Even the leather used for the handle I recognized as extravagant, more so than anything I had ever owned. I wanted to keep it. I was definitely going to ask if I could keep it.

Just as I reached out a hand –

"Don't touch that," a rough voice ordered. I'd been so enamored that I hadn't heard the prince of Lyscott enter the room. He paced quickly, not deigning to make eye contact with either of us while he set a waterskin down on a nearby bench. His outfit was the Lyscottian counterpart to Elliott's; most of the same fit, but different colors and made for cooler weather. My gray set made me the only one who wasn't representing my nation. Fine. I was there for myself regardless.

I glanced at Elliott. He was now wary, carefully observing and hanging a hand idly by his sword. "I'm sorry," I started, "it's just so –"

"Cut the nonsense," Prince Mekhi bit. My, my, he held none of the civility of his father. "Lose the knives too, while you're at it. You've hidden them worse today than you did last night, and that's no easy task." *True.*

I gaped briefly before regaining my composure. Then, slowly, I untucked the two daggers I had hidden beneath my sleeves and dropped them on the mat. They clattered against each other. "It's a neighboring kingdom in a foreign land. Would you not take precautions?"

"Precautions?" He finally looked at me. He was striking, handsome in a cold way and utterly callous for being so young. "First, my precautions would be much more effective than something you'd find on a dinner table.

126

Second," his gaze narrowed, "if my intentions were truly diplomatic, I'd care little for such measures."

"We were attacked on the journey, as you well know," I fought to keep my voice even. Elliott said nothing, but his lips pursed in the same displeasure I was feeling. "Clearly it was warranted."

"Hmm," Prince Mekhi murmured, indifferent. "Well, if you think those little things are enough to defend yourself, you should be grateful that my father requested for you to be taught." *True.*

They were plenty, you arrogant jerk, I thought in his direction.

"Teach me then, Your Highness," I taunted. The prince's pompous attitude was already beginning to wear me down, but at least I did not have to impress him like I had to impress his father.

The prince appeared almost animated. That was until, humming a merry tune, Nero's son strode into the room. Adiel was clad in a less-ornate version of Mekhi's attire, which immediately made me nervous. *Is he here to fight?* His black hair was tied into a small knot at the top of his head. A steady smirk was glued onto his face, and something deep inside me wanted to punch him.

"Am I interrupting something? Oh, how silly of me. I didn't consider that you all may be using this area," he remarked, seating himself comfortably on the bench. *Lie.* He was close enough for me to shove. I considered it. To my surprise, even Mekhi looked irritated.

Elliott finally spoke, "Yes, unfortunately. The king made arrangements for us to meet Prince Mekhi here."

And not the advisor's brat son, I added silently.

Adiel made a show of scoffing and shaking his head in faux innocence. "Yes, now I do recall. Well, since I'm already here, I'd be honored to teach Elora's future princess some very basic techniques. I assure you,

127

Lady Aster, I am far more polite company than my prince." *True*. Well, at least he believed it. I most certainly did not.

Mekhi sighed, sounding exhausted already, "No, Adiel. Take the soldier if you must be entertained, but I was instructed to teach the lady."

Adiel grinned regardless, shifting his attention to Elliott, "Care to join me? I'll make it quick. I know how eager the prince must be."

Elliott smiled back, but there was nothing genuine about it, "The privilege would be mine entirely."

In a manner that would rarely occur, I found myself rooting for Pearce.

The two men stepped onto the more padded section of the mats.

Reaching toward the wall, Elliott and Adiel grabbed their weapons of choice. Adiel snatched a long, heavy sword that was not nearly as graceful as the one that had initially caught my eye. It was a tool of brute force. Elliott reached for two smaller twin blades. I had seen him fight before, but I'd never been granted an opportunity to truly watch him. His dark, rough hands gripped both the swords with thorough confidence.

"Begin."

A whirlwind ensued.

Adiel struck first, a mess of rough attacks. He was quick, despite his chosen blade, fast enough that I would've strained underneath. But where I may have struggled, Elliott had been blessed with elegant speed. He ducked and struck and twirled out of reach of the shots he didn't have time to block properly. It wasn't even near the pace I'd witnessed during the ambush. He was holding back, yet it was still something to behold. Mekhi began to monitor them closely.

They exchanged blows for a minute longer before the hilt of Elliott's sword found its mark in Adiel's side. Adiel drew back. His brows

128

tugged together, and he took a breath before dropping one hand from his sword. The massive thing weighed down on his one arm. It was foolish by any means.

Mekhi relaxed as though the fight was over.

When Elliott struck again, Adiel raised his weapon. His free hand twisted in a way that I couldn't fully see. Elliott's feet were swept out from under him, and Adiel hadn't moved an inch. He was simply standing one moment and face down on the floor the next. His swords fell from his outstretched hands, and he grunted in pain as his ribs took the brunt of the fall.

The fight was over, and the general's son had lost.

A smug grin was once again plastered on Adiel's face. Somehow, he'd won, despite Elliott's gift and training. It didn't feel right.

"Better luck next time, soldier." Adiel hauled his sword back up to where it was mounted.

"Lady, Aster" the prince beckoned. It was our turn.

Elliott put away his swords with much less grace and stalked over to the bench where I had been watching. Confusion and anger were etched all over him, from clenched fists to furrowed brows. He caught my arm, lowering his voice to a level that only I could hear, "I know Haven likely advised you to hold back. However," he looked to the ceiling and sighed, "use your judgment."

I smirked and offered up a mock salute, "Yes, sir."

It was an awfully cocky thing to promise for someone with no formal fighting practice. All I had gathered in my youth came from years of feeling unsafe, often in my own skin. My teenage years were spent learning tricks to keep the more unsavory types away from me and what to do if they didn't listen. That, as well as having a thing for pretty knives, led to the making of an especially violent fake future princess. Recently, that experience saved a scared little girl as well as the prince of my nation. In times past, it served to defend me from the one abuser of mine that was still breathing.

Far from me, I reminded myself. *But still breathing.*

Regardless, I met the prince on the mat. His arms were crossed tightly, but aside from that, he appeared completely relaxed. Disinterested, even. I, for one, felt rather put out.

"Try to hit me."

"What?" I asked

"Try. To. Hit. Me." *Jerk.*

"Why?"

The prince allowed his arms to hang loosely at his sides. He looked at rest, but as someone who knows better, I could see that he was preparing himself. "Because, Lady Aster, there's no use in trying to teach you anything if you can't bring yourself to strike first."

His attitude was grating. I swung fast, as fast as I usually would, but he dodged with a step. I swung again, and again, he was just out of reach. He had moved with half of Elliott's speed, but even then, it was quick enough that he was safe from both of my attempted shots.

He didn't even seem impressed with the fact that I was better than Haven had implied. "Your form is sloppy. Who taught you this?"

I did. But it was none of his business.

I tried once more. This time, I was ready for him to slip just past where I would swing. Instead of giving it my full effort, I feigned a right hook and elbowed him in the ribs. I hit my mark. A quiet hiss of pain escaped from the prince, but he took it better than I would have. My leg shifted forward to take out his ankle. Rather than falling, he flipped me over his shoulder in a wide, practiced motion. Like it was nothing. Like I weighed nothing.

The air left my lungs as my body hit the mat. I gasped for breath. I glanced up at Elliott, whose only response was a carefully concealed grimace. Adiel had left some time before; I just hadn't noticed him. My head fell to the mat as I finally could breathe.

"Again."

That sequence went on for another hour. I would try to swing, and it would take no great amount of effort for him to toss me on the mat again. It was settled. The prince of Lyscott was a sadist. He taught me nothing. The only thing I learned was that bashing my face on the wall hurt very, very much. Remorsefully, that particular instance left a cut across my brow that would require copious amounts of makeup to conceal before dinner. It was only then that Mekhi had mercy on every one of my aching bones and excused himself from the area.

On a positive note, Lyscott was covered in snow! Thus, when I needed ice with which to nurse my throbbing wound, I merely had to step out onto the nearest balcony to find something suitable.

"Are you intact?" Elliott asked as we left the training room. As he had watched my many, many, *many* unfortunate encounters, his expressions shifted from blatant concern to fretful disappointment. It was a soldier's couth. Regardless of my state, he just wanted to know if I was in one piece.

Water dripped down my wrist as the ice began to melt against my skin. It was not the only bruise I would have, but it was certainly the most apparent. "Why, Pearce, keep asking things like that, and I'll make the mistake of assuming that it matters." My mood was no fault of his, but he hadn't stepped in, either.

He cast me a look from the corner of his eye as we walked. The prince had given us the most vague directions to the library, all of which I had immediately forgotten. It was Elliott that was marking the turns, leading us down the many hallways that were each more elaborate than the last.

"It only matters that you serve my prince." *True.* Gross. His brand of national pride was revolting.

Much to my dismay, I lacked the energy to respond. Our footsteps were the only sound. We stopped once we reached a carved birch door that was wider than both my and Elliott's shoulders combined. He tugged on it, and it slid open with all the grace I had lacked all morning.

Their library was massive. Many of the books were written in languages I could never hope to understand, but the majority of them were in the native tongue shared by much of the continent. I'd have to search for the stories I started at the inn another day, hopefully when there were less pressing matters to handle.

"What are you looking for?" Elliott watched from near a big, wooden table that was nearly as large as the one in the meeting room.

"Anything about cults from Mallord Bay. Specifically, cults that still believe in human sacrifices." I thumbed through the different sections of books, finding an entire double-shelf dedicated to Lukoh. While I hadn't had much to do with him since I was a child, it seemed as though many were still enthralled.

"Oh." *She's actually doing something useful.* The unspoken words were laced in his tone.

So he joined me. And we searched. For hours, we combed through text after text. The king was kind enough to have lunch delivered to us, because we were knee-deep in religious passages. I hadn't heard so much about Lukoh since I was forced into attending cathedral services over a decade prior.

They were all roughly the same, more or less. In all the variations, Lukoh had been around before time. He was the nurturer of mankind, helping us adapt to survive as the world evolved. The other major force, Akar, was wicked and jealous and wanted us all to rot. Every author wrote of Lukoh's kindness, compassion, and care. Where Lukoh was always depicted as sun-kissed or tawny, Akar was void of any color at all.

The only thing of any note at all were the publications that came after abilities started to surface. One author suspected that the gifts were a result of Lukoh favoring some individuals over others. I snorted as I read that particular passage, earning me yet another strange look from Elliott. It was as if all he was good for was offering judgmental glances. Another few authors guessed that, instead, gifting was another form of evolutionary adaptation: the world was perpetually changing, so humanity had to shift to keep up.

Regardless, there was no trace of Lorelai Elsborough, nor was there any mention whatsoever of Mallord Bay. Plenty of other Eloran cities were named, with Distin being an especially recurring theme, but nothing of importance from the coast.

By the end of the day, we had only managed to work our way through about a tenth of all the books on the subject between the two of us. Unfortunately, that meant we had an obscene amount of literature that we still had to investigate. At least it didn't require getting tossed around like a sweaty piece of cabbage like I had been by the prince.

So, for all my efforts that day, I merely managed to earn several dents in my ego, a rather unsightly bump on my head and a refresher on the various accounts of Lukoh's and Akar's histories.

Chapter Fourteen: Haven

"If we fight this war alone, many of our people will die."

King Castillo sat back, breathing deeply. As I sat subject to more and more of his story, his grief ebbed and flowed. It made sense, then. His agony. The pounding, trembling force that rested like a current underneath his skin. He was mourning the loss of the very kingdom he still ruled.

It took him hours to explain everything, long enough that I found myself startled when another meal was served to us at the table. Nero and Ilse didn't have much to add. What could they say, when the king was writing out the tale of how their kingdom would fall apart at the looming threat they faced? Dobre, their neighbor to the east, one that Elora shared no border with, had begun by attacking them in small ways. First, they stole resources: food, weapons, and livestock disappeared. Then, they began seizing military strongholds. There had been battles, the king claimed, that devastated the entire northeastern portion of Lyscott. Later, came threats to overtake the nation by force if the king refused to hand it over peacefully.

I knew little of Dobre. I remembered them being more callous and brutal than the more carefree nations we regularly associated with, though they usually kept to themselves. I had been told of no country that was bold enough to seize its neighboring territory solely out of boredom and cruelty. When I asked why they hadn't called for us sooner, he said that he had been in the process of reaching out when our messenger arrived. It didn't make perfect sense, especially since Selah mentioned that the king had lied about being surprised to see us. His anguish, though, was enough to convince me that he was sincere.

As the king poured out details, the weight of my limbs ebbed and flowed with the gravity of his feelings. Just like most gifts in Elora, emotions impacted his gift. King Castillo held hundreds of thousands of lives in the palm of his hand, and as the pressure dragged him down, so it also dragged the room down with him. I supposed I was glad that Alaric didn't have the ability to affect gravity, lest he succumb to it and let the rest of us fall through the floor.

"If you need more supplies, consider it done. We'd be happy to deliver whatever we can. As for soldiers –"

I was interrupted by a wave of the king's hand, stopping me from wasting any further breath. "Anything you can offer, we will appreciate. But that is not the only thing that can help."

"What are you asking?" I wished my father could have been the one to sit through the meeting. He was getting old, and the weariness had taken its toll on him, but he had been the king for decades. He would've been so much better suited for this conversation. Even Alaric, for all his faults, had much more diplomatic training. I wasn't bad at it myself, but he had mastered the strategy required.

"Our gifts have only been able to take us so far. Lukoh was generous in Elora, but he offered abilities to merely three Lyscottian families. Even then, most of us are designed for basic defense. Your family, though, could save thousands. I've done my research on the giftings of the Eloran royal house. Your father has the power to restore life with a touch, and your mother is just as capable. Prince Alaric is a seer; he could tell us what to avoid. I hear that Princess Genevieve can mend broken bones without expending a great amount of effort. You will grow to be a force to be reckoned with, and young Princess Faye," the king faltered, "will hopefully have as little involvement as necessary."

"You want *my* family to fight in your war?" I summarized. It was a simple, brief synopsis of a rather veiled request.

"I want my people to live." My gut twisted into knots. I couldn't imagine what my father would've done if he were so desperate. "Whatever that entails."

All I could do was look at the king for a moment. It was so much, so much that had gone wrong and so much suffering. He had brought out a map of where each of the major attacks had been staged, and it was devastating. They truly would need a miracle if Dobre was as strong as it appeared. But to ask the whole Eloran royal family to vacate the capital was no small request, even more so when it meant we'd have to leave the safety that it offered.

We could help, though. We could sit in the comfort of our kingdom, watching innocent people be killed, or we could step in and go down in history as the nation that cared. Perhaps it was the king's hope that gripped me, or maybe it was my own.

"I will write to my father. I cannot promise anything, but I will try."

King Castillo sighed in barely contained relief. He wiped some of the concern from his ivory complexion. Like a gust of wind, I felt it with my gift. It was swift and light, but present and powerful.

"Take all the time you need. In fact, stay until the end of the month. I'd like to have time to show you more of Lyscott before you decide whether you would be willing to defend it."

136

It was quite the journey back to Distin, considering that we had also lost our driver in the attack. At least if we remained in Lyscott for a while longer than we had originally intended, we were even further from whatever cult was operating out of Mallord Bay. I didn't even know how to begin to broach the subject of the Lyscottian soldier we kept in our prison.

Once the king was content, Ilse graciously volunteered to escort me back to my room. She gave me a shy smile that I politely returned. I couldn't quite focus. My mind was racing. In one day, I'd been presented with more responsibility than I'd had in my entire life. Additionally, this particular variety of responsibility meant that there were countless lives that could be saved or lost at the word of my father.

"It's all a bit bleak, isn't it?" Ilse spoke, her voice light and breathy.

"That it is."

"You know, it really is such an honor to have you here. Of course, I hear Elora has nicer weather, but our people are more fun to look at. Your royalty isn't half bad, though, if you are any indication," she looked me up and down.

I made the intentional decision to write off that comment as something that would only be acceptable in the north.

At last, we reached my bedroom door. She tilted her head with a small grin, "See you at dinner, Prince."

I smiled halfway and promptly locked myself into the room Selah and I shared. I had experience with women, but fake engagements made things messy.

From the washroom came a few thuds and the sound of someone rummaging around. I waited a moment to collect myself before going to investigate. There was so much weight on my chest, a nearly unbearable

137

amount of concern over Lyscott's fate and our own. If Lyscott fell, would Elora follow?

"Selah?" I finally asked, rounding the corner to the washroom. She was perched on top of the counter, looking intently into the mirror. An angry cut reached through one of her eyebrows, and Selah tended to it with a stained cloth. The only acknowledgement she gave was a sidelong glance.

"What happened?" I asked, concern lingering in my tone. I moved to gently take her chin in one of my hands, inspecting the mark. She flinched, but to my surprise, she didn't shove me off. I should've investigated what 'training' with Mekhi would've entailed before signing her up for it.

"It's nothing."

I pursed my lips, "It's not nothing. It's right here." I poked just near the wound. It really wasn't terrible, and I was more than certain that she was alright. While the wound was a jarring shade of red, I held no fear that she would bleed to death under my watch. Still, I teased, "Would you like me to have him executed? I can probably do that. I mean, I could see how that would be a diplomatic nightmare, but I'd be more than happy–"

She smirked and finally brushed me away. I had been kidding, mostly. She knew it too, if the little grin it earned me was any indication. "I'll live, Highness." Once more, Selah peeked at herself in the mirror. "But Elliott and I combed through their library for ages. We've found nothing yet."

"That's fine. The king invited us to stay until the end of the month, so you two will have plenty of chances to search." I chuckled, "Who knows? Maybe all that bonding time will turn you into the very best of friends." While I was not exactly holding my breath, it was nice to imagine.

She just rolled her eyes. "Dinner is soon, Highness. Chatter less. Prepare more."

And to think, I was her prince, yet she had the audacity to provoke me so. In actuality, I found myself quite enjoying her brand of mockery and figured that throwing her in a cell for it would severely damage both our relationship and my otherwise stellar reputation.

Dinner did arrive soon enough. While I did bring a slightly more formal version of my usual attire, I was growing weary of all the green. Instead, I picked out a white shirt with an obscene number of buttons and a pair of tan bottoms that, while not at all adequate to face the Lyscottian cold, would be suitable for a meal. I attempted to arrange my jutting locks of hair neatly to no avail.

Selah, on the other hand, had no such trouble. She had used some dark, womanly magic to make the cut on her brow nearly disappear. Her curls were tied back into a pristine, loose knot. The evening gown she wore was dark green and rendered her features even more radiant. Her lips were painted a deep shade of emerald, and I searched for anything else to busy myself with.

She was a vision. *But she's not here for you*, I reminded myself.

Selah examined herself at the vanity tucked in the corner. "I wasn't aware you owned more than one ensemble," she muttered absentmindedly, adjusting a green strap on one of her shoulders and swiping a thumb under her lip.

"Oh, I have plenty. Eloran green just makes my eyes stand out." That was not true in the slightest. It was a gesture, more than anything, to show that I was representing my people. However, while Eloran green complimented my hair well, it often made my eyes look too dark. Oh, the sacrifices one makes for his country.

139

Selah only spared me a moment's glance in response. Her eyes scanned me quickly, skimming up and down. Then, she offered her little nod of approval. "This is better. You look less entitled."

"Such flattery."

Her returning snicker was cut off by the door creaking open.

"We've been summoned," Elliott announced with a heavy sigh, strolling in. He'd opted to wear the formal version of an Eloran soldier's uniform. His otherwise calm demeanor was interrupted by the tapping of his finger against his thigh.

Apparently, I was not the only one who noticed. Selah examined him as well as she made her way to the door, "Nervous, Pearce?"

"Just ready to be done with this meal," he admitted. "I also don't find the advisor or his son to be especially pleasant company."

Despite Elliott's initial lack of enthusiasm, the king and his court were glad to see us when we finally arrived at the dining hall. The dining hall table was set much more lavishly than the meeting room table had been. A row of windows towered over one side of the room, acting as a wall that shielded us from the elements. On the other, intricate portraits of Lyscottian royalty and their ancestors were displayed. The faces of generations of rulers and their families were peering down at where we sat.

King Castillo's family portrait drew my eye. It had to have been depicted years prior. Mekhi was a young, frail thing who did not quite reach his father's shoulder. The king's features were smoother in the painting than they were in front of me, only further attesting to the years that had passed. Beside the king stood a woman. Her shoulders were set, her feet were planted, but she held the king's hand and smiled as she gazed up at him. A slightly smaller version of the crown that Castillo donned was set upon her head. *The queen.*

In her other arm, she held a sleepy little girl. The child had the same snow white hair of Mekhi and Castillo, but she was only a toddler. She rested on her mother's shoulder. *Their* mother's shoulder. *Mekhi had a sister.* But we had not met her, or the queen. I did not recall either of them ever being mentioned.

No wonder grief rushed under the surface of the king's skin. They were gone. I wondered if that was why he was so passionate about the war, if that was the thing that had taken them away.

Even as we sat, even as I greeted the men, the queen and the princess were all I could think about.

Selah sat quietly on my right, while Elliott took his place on my left side. Next to him was Adiel, then Mekhi, then the king. The spread of food was far more extravagant than it had been at lunch. There was a selection of meats and cheeses that I knew from planning a few events in Elora would have cost a small fortune. Small fruit platters were arranged for each person, and each plate was served with beautiful garnishes.

Ilse and Wren made an appearance a few moments later. Wren carried four silver goblets in her arms, and Ilse somehow managed to balance five. One by one, they handed each of the men and Selah their own goblets.

"Thank you, Wren," the king nodded to her as she took the last goblet she carried and passed it on to him.

"It's my pleasure, Your Majesty," Wren replied softly and took her own seat.

I felt a flare of curiosity beside me. Selah's face contorted into careful confusion, but she schooled her features into peaceful neutrality a moment later.

"And Ilse," the king continued, "crafts the best wine in the kingdom using that gift of hers. Drink as much as you like. A touch from her, and your glass will be full again."

Ilse bloomed under the king's praise. While I couldn't fathom the mechanics of how an ability like hers actually worked, it was excellent for parties.

And so, we ate. And we drank, though both Selah and I did so in moderation. Elliott, alternatively, enjoyed as much wine as was polite, perhaps, and then some. The king spoke, offered stories, and laughed at the absurdity of the tales he told. Mekhi had become borderline amicable, especially with Elliott, who was far chattier than he had been since Distin. Adiel even chose not to be as provocative as he had been on the night we met. Ilse and Nero often opted to chat with me instead, adding their own commentary onto the king's stories, the former refreshing empty glasses as needed.

They were so thoroughly... human. While there were often hints of sadness or pain sprinkled into conversation, it was just a king enjoying a meal with his court. With his family. I supposed I had expected some sort of northern, bull-headed brute to be ruling Lyscott, as opposed to the kind-eyed, gentle man who reclined at the head of the table. A man who was at risk of losing so much.

Both my heart and my stomach were full when we bid the king goodnight and wandered back to our rooms. Elliott's was far closer to the ornate dining room, and he was wobbling significantly more than Selah or I. Whatever Ilse put into the wine, it was strong. He said a bleary-eyed, grinning goodbye, and subsequently crashed onto his bed. The general's son was asleep in moments.

Selah and I quietly paced back to our shared lodging. She had been completely silent for most of the night, only smiling softly when it was courteous. I didn't know what to make of her disposition. Was she as moved as I was? Was the cut on her head worse than we suspected? Had she changed her mind about how angry she was with me? I had tried to give her some space after my initial request to investigate Lorelai Elsborough.

It was only when our large, wooden doors were shut tightly together that she spoke.

"I think something is wrong here, Haven," she said, removing a hidden dagger she had sheathed on her thigh and setting it on the vanity.

I balked, "Why?"

"Wren was..." she trailed off, mind clearly wandering. "Something is wrong with her, I think. Did you feel anything?"

Quite honestly, Wren had faded into the background for most of the evening. I shrugged, "She seemed normal to me. Reserved, but normal."

"And you didn't mention anything about what the king told you today. I can confirm nothing further about the war, or his kingdom, or his people," she paused thoughtfully. "Though I can confirm that Ilse's gift freaks me out."

"I have taken care of it. I felt his sincerity and his longing for his people to be safe for hours today. I have little doubt in my mind that the king is genuinely seeking our help. My help," I corrected. Not our, not with her involved, because there was no *us* with Selah. She had made her motives undeniably clear.

"We also have no idea why they sent their soldiers to Distin," she contemplated. There was no anger in her tone, present as it may be, but

143

there was something akin to concern. "Isn't that what we came to discover?"

Yes, it was, and I still had to have that painful conversation with the king. But, knowing what little I knew of the king, his hospitality, and his care, I figured that there was some reasonable explanation. "Yes, Selah. And it will be dealt with in time. But they seem like good people, and they need our help. As angry as I am about what happened, and I *am* angry, I also don't want to provoke the king with my accusations until we are on stable terms." I grinned, "Does that answer suit you, my dearest accomplice, or is there something more I can offer?" There was no harm in using what charm I had to smooth over her worry.

Some of her tension did ease due to my masterful conversation skills. "You can offer not to snore," she snickered. "It's bad enough trying to sleep on the floor. It's even worse when it sounds like a wild beast is trampling through the room."

"You can take the bed!" I gestured towards the downy pillows and the soft mattress that was soundlessly calling my name. 'Twas a shame that it was being so neglected. "Please do, in fact. It's wearing on my pride to see such a lovely lady reduced to sleeping on the carpet."

"Not gonna happen, Highness. You are more than welcome to take it for yourself." She tore off the short boots she had worn to dinner. "If you'll excuse me, I have to rest for yet another torturous morning with the prince. With any luck, hopefully a full night's recovery will make tomorrow's torment slightly more bearable."

Chapter Fifteen: Selah

It did not, in fact, make the next day any less miserable.

Actually, being torn away from sleep was far worse after finding myself so caught up in its embrace. Ilse's wine, unnerving as it may have been, had me dead asleep as soon as I was tucked under the blankets on my side of the rug. Haven had also spent the night on the floor, but at least he was chipper when he woke. I was dead on my feet as I walked to the training hall.

"Is Elliott not coming?" I asked, more to myself than to the ruthless prince who stood before me. I'd been tossed on my face about a dozen times already. Although, after studying Mehki's fighting style, I was much improved from the previous morning. He was fast and strong, but his moves were becoming predictable.

"Lieutenant Colonel Pearce has fallen ill," Mekhi confirmed, pausing to take a drink of water. *Lieutenant Colonel.* I hadn't grown accustomed to Elliott's official title. I couldn't picture him having rank over other soldiers, though I guessed that his stern gaze and steady posture could be commanding if he tried. I only really knew him as a thorn in my side who had an affinity for liquor. "It seems as though he may have drunk himself sick. Which you should not even be thinking about, because you are occupied." *True.*

He was right. A glance toward the doorway a minute before had earned me a whack to the back of the head and a biting order to focus. To my benefit, his harassment did offer adequate motivation to punch him in the face. To my detriment, none of that desire translated into successfully hitting my mark. So, on we continued, with no other instruction outside of trying to strike him.

If I was going to be stuck with him, though, I chose not to do so in complete silence.

"How does your gift work?" I asked, stretching out my aching muscles and playing the part of the fiancée who was dazzled by such things. "Manipulating senses" was a rather vague description. If nothing else, I'd get to know my second-favorite prince a little better. In the very best of circumstances, it would maybe aid in uncovering why Nero's wife was so unhappy.

Wren had lied as she told the king what a pleasure it was to serve him. That was more than enough to capture my attention.

The prince only responded with a warning look before stepping back onto the practice mat.

I continued. "Do you have to touch things, like Ilse? Or does it just work with your mind, like your father's?"

"Enough," his posture was rigid, and it blended into his tone. "When I want to chat, I will let you know. Now go again." *True.*

Oh, the prince was testy.

I threw a halfhearted jab his way, and he batted it away like it was a fly in the desert. He stared at me with a pointed, unenthusiastic glare.

"I feel like I'd try harder if I knew what I was dealing with," I complained.

"I don't care how you feel." *True.* And hurtful.

146

So, again, I struck. It was faster, fast enough to catch someone with less training. He dodged again, sidestepping me and kicking the back of my leg. It buckled, landing me firmly on one knee. He was at my back and out of my reach. I huffed. He was awful, and if I was going to be forced to tolerate his sadistic nature, he could tolerate a few questions.

I stood, turning to meet his icy stare, "Your father said you manipulated senses. Now, that description leaves a lot to the imagination. Can you create false feelings, or –"

"Keep pushing, Lady Aster, and you'll find out firsthand." *True. Tempting.*

I still hated that pretentious title.

"I just want to know –"

"Go again," he spat.

"But –"

He interrupted with a blow.

I narrowly ducked in time, and I moved to swipe his feet. He had grown accustomed to dodging punches with little variation aside from a generic strike, and I supposed I did have him to thank for my steadily improving reaction time. I shifted faster than even I had anticipated, and the joy I felt as I watched him fall was unparalleled.

However, my job was to land a hit, not just take him to the ground.

I pounced while I could, tossing myself onto his torso before he fully regained his wits. I threw a punch, which he caught in one hand. I threw another, and he caught that one, too. He bared his teeth and shifted his hips, aiming to buck me off, but my legs were clamped tight around his sides. I tried an elbow, but that merely nicked his nose. I twisted my right arm out of his and drew my hand back –

His hand reached up to touch my temple, and the world went black.

It was unlike anything I've ever experienced before. One moment, he was facing me, and the next, there was a void. It was disorienting, but not incapacitating, because I could still feel his abdomen underneath my thighs and the mat below my knees.

Until I took another breath, at least.

I felt nothing. Not Mekhi, not the mat, not my fingers, not the air leaving my lungs. There was nothing. *I* was nothing. My limbs were forgotten. I didn't know if my unseeing eyes were open or closed. I was trapped in a place where I practically didn't exist. I heard my breath quickening, and something shifting, but that was the only sensation that still remained.

"Are you not satisfied, my lady?" Mekhi's low words rumbled behind me, the Lyscottian lilt dancing in his voice. I was, but I wasn't. I heard myself gasping, but I found no relief. *I can't breathe, I can't breathe, I can't breathe.*

"You wanted to know. Aren't you glad I showed you?" he asked, frigid.

"No," I croaked from somewhere far away. *He's going to kill me. Is this going to kill me?*

"Mmmm, yeah. Most people don't react well. Something about 'hell on earth.'" *True.* He was so flippant, so unbothered by my panic. I couldn't calm down enough even to imagine the look on his face.

"Mekhi," I wheezed. Why couldn't I breathe? I heard myself heaving. Why couldn't I feel it?

"You. Shouldn't. Be. Here," he stressed, tucked close to my ear, with all the taunts leaving his voice. "It is a *very* dangerous time in a *very* dangerous place. You do not have the skills or the gifting to handle what will happen if you choose to stay. This?" he laughed dryly. "This is nothing. So run back to your prince, and tell him to run back to Elora."

True.

The prince was warning us to leave, regardless of the fact that his people's lives were on the line.

With a *whoosh*, all my senses were returned. I could see my hands again, bracing me against the floor. They were trembling, along with the rest of me, but at least I could see them shaking. The feeling returned throughout my body in an instant, and I had never been so grateful to meet the cool mat with my fingers. I tasted blood. I hadn't noticed that he had disrupted that sense, too. Mekhi was out from below me, so I felt no shame in crumpling onto the padded floor.

"Deep breath," he ordered, and I had no choice but to listen. "Better. Another."

I obeyed, and the panic dulled.

"We are finished, Lady Aster. You really need to leave. If this has not solidified how helpless you truly are, and you insist on remaining in the palace," he sighed severely, "I will teach you what I am able. Tomorrow."

I wracked my brain, searching for any reaction I could give him. A flood of questions formed on the tip of my tongue, but none of them got past my lips. It had been, what, a minute? Less? A handful of seconds, I was left quivering like a tree in a storm. But he was trying to warn me – to warn us. I stood gaping in response.

Heavy footsteps padded out the door. It probably took me the better part of ten minutes to fully come back into myself, to repeat that I was safe and that all was well. Once I could scrape my weary bones off the training mat, I trailed into the library. It was quiet, and comforting, and charming in a way that I could freshly appreciate. I had significantly less fear that the prince would find me there, tucked between shelves and huddled at a desk, than I had for the chance he would return to the training room. It didn't count as hiding if I was being productive.

I lingered in the library for hours, flipping through legend after legend concerning Lukoh and his followers. It all was the same, monotonous information that we had combed through the day prior, only with slight variations when it came to Lukoh and Akar's physical descriptions and their interactions. I had grown up reading these stories. I stared at the stack of tomes I had yet to touch with distaste.

My mind wandered as I tried to imagine Haven would make of Mekhi's admonitions. I imagined his elegant features shifting into careful confusion. He likely would've been aptly prepared to handle Mekhi in ways that I was not. He, at least, had the advantage of being able to sense Mekhi's emotions and the military training to predict his moves. The prince of Elora couldn't be a terrible fighter if he had barely been beaten by three armed men. Haven was strong, too, if the fit of his shirt around his arms at dinner last night was any indication.

Surprised by the shift in my own thought process, I slammed down on those thoughts before I could consider what those arms would feel like around me.

The library door slid open, and I choked on the air in my lungs. A couple coughs later, and my cheeks were still flushed. Small, feather-light feet roamed in, and Wren's fingertips grazed over the shelves as she stepped. Wren was beautiful in the way a song could be, though her age was revealed at the corner of her eyes and near the gentle curve of her lips. Her careful movements were borderline melodic.

Her dark eyes wandered over to me. I could only imagine I looked to be a loon, different tomes sprawled out and reaching in every direction. The volume I was reading stayed tucked in my hands, with stacks of the ones I had discarded or was yet to delve into piled around me.

Wren delicately took me in along with the poor desk that had been made subject to my mess. "That's quite the reading material, Lady Aster," she breathed.

I considered what to say. Had it been her son, her husband, or possibly even Prince Mekhi, I would have mentioned nothing. Not that the fact that we'd been attacked was any real secret, as Haven's cuts and perhaps my exhaustion had given away, but it was none of their business. Lorelai and her fun-loving companions were based in Mallord Bay, which was days away from Lyscott. Elora also had many more gifted than Lyscott, so Lyscottians would be less of a threat to them. Haven had not disclosed if he'd spoken any more about it to the king, either, and it didn't matter anyways.

Wren, though, was sweet and quiet, and altogether a mystery to me. From what little I did know of her, she was decidedly the least obnoxious of the Lyscottian court. "I'm researching the group that attacked us. They were religious, very much so, and I have unsuccessfully flipped through almost half the books in this library looking for any information about them."

She paused at a shelf near my work station, eyebrows furrowing together and her dark red lips pursing. "Loyal to Lukoh or to Akar?"

I was not even fully aware that there were any still loyal to Akar. Heavens above, I wished that I had been educated about such things as a child. Even if not for the sake of pursuing such a lifestyle, at least I may

151

have saved myself the trouble of spending days in the library. "Lukoh, but murderously loyal."

The confusion in her eyes turned to something darker, and her stare turned from me to something unseeing. "The king of light would be ashamed," she whispered, almost reverent.

True.

The king of light. One of many, many names for the god, and a very popular one among the texts I'd been pouring over. The king of light. The one who has always been. The one who always will be. The god of his people. The witness of mankind. Lukoh had titles upon titles, and I'd reverted to assuming any name that was remotely good was referring to him.

"Are you religious?" I asked her.

She nodded, and she was back with me again. "In a sense." *True.*

"Do you know anything about any groups operating out of Mallord Bay in Elora? I realize you may not be familiar with our geography, but –"

Wren's quiet response cut me off, "I know of a handful, and many from that area are terribly misled. You will find none of them in this section," she placed a hand on one pile of books. "These are religious texts, but you need more than this. Look near the history tomes instead, toward the bottom for Eloran writings. You'll have much better luck." *True.*

I sat back in my wooden chair, half amazed at her thorough knowledge and half appalled at how much time I had wasted searching in the wrong section. I laughed breathlessly, "If you're right, you may have just saved me hours. How do you know about Eloran history?"

The advisor's wife smiled softly, casting her eyes down to the carpeted floor. Her fingers wrung together. "I spend many of my days here,

Lady Aster. It's quiet, and far from the less tolerable parts of the palace. I'm sure you can imagine after the introduction you were granted." *True.*

My heart warmed with the weight of her understanding. I had been so very angry when Haven and I made it to our room the first night. I could only imagine what Wren had gone through if that was the small taste I'd been given. I pitied her much in the way one pities a bird with a broken wing. It's a dreary, hopeless thing. She wasn't happy, and perhaps would never be able to leave in the way that I could.

Her head perked up, jerking towards the door. She heard the thundering footsteps a few heartbeats before I did, then they thumped into range. Dread filled the corners of her eyes, but the expression faded as soon as it came. Eyes still not meeting mine, Wren spoke faintly, "Guard your mind, Selah. Always."

Then she left, as though that wasn't eerie as hell.

She met Nero at the door, hushed words darting back and forth between them. He looked down at his wife with something akin to disdain, and only spared me a passing glare. You'd think he'd at least be kinder to me based on my relationship with Haven, but evidently that bought me no favor with the cold advisor.

I, too, left the library some time later, after returning all the books I'd been searching through to their rightful places and setting aside Eloran history texts that I thought may have useful information. I carried as many as I was able back to the room Haven and I shared, now unnerved by Wren's warning coupled with whatever Mekhi was on about. I sat on the bed, where I had enough room to spread out like I had in the library, and I spent the rest of my day reading all about Eloran history.

Dinner was delivered to me, and I pondered whether the king had overextended himself the night prior, or if they feared that Elliott was carrying a contagious illness. I didn't mind eating in solitude, but I would've liked to check on Wren. I trusted Nero very little and, while I did not know what reason he had to be angry with her, I carried no faith in his moral compass.

Haven returned late that evening, and exhaustion weighed on every part of him. Even worn, he was unwelcomely beautiful. The blond locks that were usually unruly stood especially ruffled, and his sleeves were rolled up to his elbows. His jaw was set, and his bright amber eyes were fading. He offered me a weary grin, and all my thoughts from the library returned with such force that I felt the heat on my face.

All I could give back was a tight smile, "Long day?"

He unlatched the band of gold around his forehead and set it down on the table. "So, so much Lyscottian history. An unholy amount. More than anyone should ever have to know," He shuttered, eyes lighting up at me. I smirked, and he peered down at my work. "Any luck?"

"No, but I'm getting closer."

The prince yawned, looking entirely unroyal, "Excellent work regardless, Selah. I'd love to catch you up more about what the king had to say, but I'm afraid I'd bore us both to sleep and I'm already nearly there." *True*, and obvious.

"You are more than welcome to the bed," I glanced up at him, challenging.

He grinned again, and it was indecently attractive. "Now, what kind of fiancé would that make me? I couldn't possibly."

I focused my attention back to my work. At least, I tried to. "I'm still armed, Highness."

"I'd expect nothing less." *True.*

Haven fell asleep not long later, and I found my initial anxiety being dulled by the steadiness of his breaths. I may have been trapped, but there were worse people to be stuck with. The soft rhythm in the background was borderline soothing. Soon, I tucked myself into bed on the other side of the rug, the only sound being his deep inhaling and exhaling.

****

The library was haunting at night.

The soft sunlight that the curtains allowed by day was stolen after the sun fell. My feet were planted on the floor. Something dark and eager lingered in every shadow, watching me flip through the endless pages of countless books.

I set one tome aside in favor of another. The Glory of Akar, it was titled. It was navy blue on the outside, with silver accents and calligraphy. Had it been a different story, I might have found it stunning. But it's pages were so cold, it burnt the tips of my fingers when I tried to open it.

I dropped it with a hiss, and Wren was sitting across from me when I looked up. Her eyes were not the sweet, soft orbs that I had seen earlier in the day. They were dim and frigid, holding me down in my chair. Ice wrapped around my ankles and wrists, and the air in my lungs was stolen from me.

Guard your mind, Wren had said.

"What did I tell you?" Wren asked, sensing the thoughts that I didn't know she could hear.

"Guard my mind," I muttered past gritted teeth, straining and pulling against the ice that bound me.

Her lovely features contorted into rage, "There's no use, Selah. There is nothing you can do to keep me out."

I yanked, over and over, to no avail.

Maybe Mekhi was right. Maybe by not telling Haven about his warning, I had doomed us. I panted, but no matter how much I tugged, the ice held firm. I couldn't move, couldn't breathe, couldn't think –

Frozen, ancient nails scraped along my back.

****

I awoke with a jerk.

My breath was still caught up in my lungs, and I was upright in a second. I reached for my wrists. They were warm and unbound, and I was still in our room. Gasping, but safe. The skin around my spine stung.

Without hesitation, I jumped out from underneath the blankets and made my way into the washroom. A candle was lit, the glow just bright enough that I could see my reflection in the gilded mirror. Aching, I moved the fabric aside and twisted to see my reflection.

Clear as day, four marks traced down my back.

There's no way.

I blinked. They were real. How had they been real? Had something happened with Mekhi that I didn't realize?

From the next room, I heard Haven shuffling. "Selah?" he called, voice rough with sleep.

Depths. What would I tell the prince? That a dream monster had actually touched me? I'd sound insane.

I dropped the cloth, my mind cloudy and racing. "Go back to bed, Highness. Just a dream."

"Are you alright?"

I hesitated.

"Yes."

Whether or not he was content with that answer, the prince didn't pry. I was grateful for it. I didn't know what I'd tell him.

Eventually, after my thoughts managed to slow, I fell back asleep. No more dreams came searching for me.

Chapter Sixteen: Haven

I was no stranger to nightmares, but it had been ages since I'd been woken by someone else's terror.

When I was young, it was usually Gen's dreams that pulled me from sleep. For a few years of our lives, she'd wake up screaming nearly once a month. When I was coming into my gift, her fear was one of the first signs that I could sense emotions outside of my own. That, and our mother's exhaustion, stood as the beginning of understanding what I had been blessed with.

After the Illustri's attack, Elliott's agony-filled night terrors woke me repeatedly. For months, I would either be startled by his feelings or my own. A year of my life was spent without much rest. It was necessary, though. I didn't have the heart to leave Elliott alone and I wouldn't dare admit to myself that I needed him just as much as he needed me.

I couldn't pinpoint when it truly faded. Eventually, Elliott spent more and more nights in his own home. He remained welcome, and visited often, but no longer was his situation dire. I too calmed, nightmares becoming fewer and further between. Sleep arrived slowly, but it arrived, nonetheless.

Selah's fear was more bitter than most, and where fear usually sets its weight down on my chest, her agony also lingered on my tongue. I recognized it immediately. She was sleeping, albeit fitfully, and I wrestled with how to help. While I was deciding whether to wake her, she startled. So I waited, hoping not to scare her any further, and wondered what had induced such terror. I could not help asking, but I knew she would lie to me. Too tough and too stubborn to admit she was bothered.

When the sunlight crept in through the windows to announce it was nearly time to leave, she was still resting. As softly as I was able, I rose and started to heat some water as I prepared myself for the day. She stirred, only enough to show she was awake, but didn't move.

I poured one cup of tea for myself, and brought another to where she lay staring up at the ceiling. Selah sat up to take hold of the mug, nodding her thanks. I stood gazing at the distant village yet again. We'd see it first hand, not a few hours later. Would it be full of the wealth of the palace, or dreary with the weight of the war?

Selah's words dragged me out of my own thoughts.

"I dreamt of Wren."

Her eyes were fixed on the same far away town, where a gray pillar of smoke cut through the ivory snow. She sipped cautiously. "I'm worried about her, Haven. She's not happy here. I fear it may be for good reason. Even Mekhi thinks we're in danger, enough so to use his gift to nearly scare the life out of me to prove it."

"He did what?" I asked, turning my attention to where she sat.

I had nearly forgotten how stunning Selah Aster was. Freckles dotted along her face and splattered across her upturned nose. Her eyes were stark against the dark of her eyelashes and her pale skin stood in contrast to her ebony curls. She was half a mess, barely awake, and full of worry. Still so young, yet so clearly bothered by something painful.

I was taken by her, thoroughly, but lacked the courage to say so.

159

"He said we should leave, that we didn't belong here, and that it was a dangerous time in a dangerous place. I pushed him to use his gift, and he did. Wouldn't recommend it, but he did no lasting harm," she said, but I knew better when I felt the ghost of her panic float through the room. Consciously, I pulled myself out of her emotions. I no longer had the excuse of sleep and I'd promised her what privacy I could give.

"He should've let you be," I kept my disdain as subtle as I could. "But they're at war, Selah. I imagine it's made everything a little tense." At least, that's what I felt from the king in the days prior. I couldn't say much of how Mekhi was feeling, and I hadn't paid enough attention to Wren to know anything about her.

She shook her head, "He seemed serious."

I downed the rest of my drink in a quick gulp. Not very princely, but I knew my audience of one wouldn't be impressed with proper table etiquette. "The king has requested we accompany him to the village of Reane. Let's get through the day. If anything catches your eye, or seems off, then we'll consider our next steps. Use your gift and I'll tell you what I sense."

The compromise did not leave her entirely content, but she swallowed protests and readied herself for the day, as did I. Where I donned a warmer set of the Eloran garments I often wore, Selah appeared and I could have sworn my heart stopped. It was no fancy attire, and nothing I hadn't seen before on Gen or my mother in the colder seasons, but it was striking on her. She was wrapped in a wool coat, with leather peeking out around her sleeves and ankles. A band of fabric fit snugly around her forehead and ears for warmth, and her hair fell over it in a braid. I wondered if she had been told how alluring she was, or if she stabbed most men before they could get the words out.

"You look –"

"Armed. Heavily armed. In fact, this outfit can conceal more knives than I usually carry. Something to keep in mind," she threatened, but the steel in her voice didn't meet her eyes.

"Yes, far be it from me to make a future Princess of Elora aware of how lovely she is. My most sincere apologies."

"You should find the poor thing and tell her that yourself."

It was said almost in good faith, but landed like a punch to the stomach.

Some time later, Elliott accompanied Selah and I down to the same hall where we had met the king, Nero, Mekhi, Adiel, and Ilse. Wren was otherwise occupied, Nero explained, and Selah gave me a knowing look.

Mekhi rode in the carriage with us while the rest trotted along a few paces ahead. It was a quiet ride, though comfortable, with Mekhi not being entirely chatty and Elliott dozing off. I asked the prince nothing about what he had said to Selah the morning prior, but he did not offer much in the way of conversation. Instead, I sat back, my fake fiancée by my side and watching the snow-covered mountains pass.

When we did arrive at Reane, it was unexpectedly average. The buildings stood tall and strong, with no great amount of wealth holding them up. They were dark, heavy bricks that were built to last through powerful winds and pelting storms. Businesses were quaint but prospering, customers floating in and out in spite of the cold. Harsh, Lyscottian letters were posted on every sign, and I hadn't studied enough of this particular neighboring country's language to have any hope of knowing what the signs advertised. Men bickered in the middle of the town over something, and a handful of children snaked from one store into another.

For the majority of the morning, the king led us in and out of various shops. There were two bakeries, a tavern, an alchemist, a doctor's office, several farming supply stores, and about half a dozen lots that were selling clothes. Everyone was curt, not fearful or in awe, but amicable to the king and offered greetings to us. I forgot most of the names I was given.

It was just a village. A very cold village with sweet residents, but not a village of a nation at war. Selah was at my side through every exchange, quiet as a mouse but carefully observing every movement. The Lyscottian language rendered her gift essentially useless because, even if someone was lying, she wouldn't know what the lie was. So we passed through the village, greeting the residents. I could sense Selah's growing impatience and could not avoid Elliott's fatigue, but they were tolerant.

We paused for lunch at a bakery, and an older woman who spoke brought out plates and plates of pastries, speaking too fast for me to understand. She had practically bounded over the counter and started prattling on to the king, who took it in kind. We ate, and Elliott napped briefly on the bench while Nero and the king discussed the town's affairs: one shop had overpaid its taxes, another hadn't offered quite enough, a residence was still waiting for the pavement outside their door to be repaired, and so on.

I was content with the easy silence among the rest of our small dining party, and Mekhi, who had been subject to many marriage proposals over the course of the morning, also seemed relieved for the respite. Adiel grinned at me and winked at Selah. I took her hand in mine before she could reach for a weapon. Ilse sat in serene silence, listening to her father.

When we had all eaten our fill, the king turned his attention to me, "Highness, it's a beautiful day." Beautiful was an exaggeration. Granted, it wasn't snowing, and the sun appeared in small doses, but it was bitterly

162

cold compared to the warm Eloran weather. "There is a walking path not far from the city. It is a view that compares to few others in my kingdom. If you'd be interested, I'd love to show you more of what my country has to offer."

Selah said nothing, nor did her feelings change.

"It would be an honor, Your Majesty."

Apparently, a Lyscottian 'walking path' directly translated to being a few feet of gravel on the side of a very, very tall cliff. Smooth rock stood tall on the one side, with certain treachery on the other. In Elora, we would have ropes or fences mandated. It seemed as though the Lyscottians enjoyed living on the edge.

Due to the limited span on which we were able to walk, we were forced to split into pairs. Nero and Ilse kindly led the way, and the king and I followed closely behind. Adiel thoughtfully offered to escort Selah. If what I sensed was any indication, she narrowly avoided telling him to shove it before reluctantly agreeing. Elliott's eyes were drooping and his shoulders slumped, but he was well enough to walk and took his place in the back of the line next to Mekhi.

In spite of the peril, it was truly lovely. Snow-capped mountains and evergreen trees abounded, stretching as far as the eye could see. A few other villages roughly the size of Reane stood in the distance, similar billows of smoke emerging from their chimneys. Homes dotted the horizon, designed to keep away the cold. The silhouette of the mountains was harsh and unforgiving, but nothing less than exquisite in the light of day.

"Do you visit this area often?" I asked the king, making light conversation.

He nodded, the white of his hair blending in with the scene around us. "Reane, yes. I am far from many of my people, most of them retreating away from the mountains. Much of our territory, while the climate can still be harsh, is easier to move throughout. It's special when I can see those under my care face to face, to hear their needs from their own lips as opposed to an envoy or mere written word."

"I find it quaint," Ilse threw over her shoulder, carefully stepping over fallen rocks. While plummeting to one's death wasn't as great a risk on the near side of the path, the loose rocks and debris from the mountain rendered both sides of the path equally hazardous.

"Of course you'd find it quaint," Adiel said from behind, "you were raised in a castle."

"Quaint isn't bad!" She cast me a remorseful glance, "You'll excuse him, Prince Haven. My brother aims to make me seem arrogant. I was trying to say that it's rather endearing."

We came around the bend to a particularly precarious patch. The path continued but was blocked by a fallen boulder. It was only a foot or two in height and width, but it blocked the inside path, leaving an opening only on the face of the cliff.

Nero went first, stepping over the rock with full confidence. He evidently had a death wish or little care for the jagged edges and thorny branches that would lead to sudden doom should he misstep. He held out a hand for Ilse, who practically bounded over it herself. I imagined this was not even remotely their first time, with the ease that the first two moved. The king followed after them. He was slower than they had been, more cautious with his age, but maneuvered with little difficulty. I noted that his foot had been placed firmly in the middle of the boulder. It was flatter there, which allowed it to serve as a makeshift step.

164

Swallowing my concern, I started over the rock. It really wouldn't have been an issue, had it not been in such a treacherous spot. Regardless, I forced my feet to move and my mind to settle. My foot landed steadily. I held out a hand to brace against the mountain.

I was perfectly balanced. Wholly, entirely safe.

Until the one foot I had on the rock was swept out from underneath me, and I was falling.

"Haven!"

Two voices yelled my name, but I was dropping back, back, back, too far over the edge to reach a hold. My hands shot out toward the cliff, grabbing for something, anything, but there was nothing I could hold.

The world stopped.

At least, mine did. I was suspended, mid-air, halfway to the ascent leading to certain death. The trees waited beneath me, eager to watch me bleed. But no longer was I falling. I was stuck in the space between safety and the ground.

"What – "

I should be falling.

Where my world paused, I could see everyone else in real time. Most of the Lyscottian court stood with dropped jaws at the impossibility of it all. Elliott's arm was outstretched. His features were caught in a sharp mix of shock, fear, and steady determination. He got to me first, using every bit of that super speed of his to reach me. He pulled me back to safety, and I could move freely again.

I crouched down to my hands and knees, gasping with adrenaline. His exhaustion hit me in a wave, much like Selah's had after Lorelai. He matched me on the floor, panting.

"Was that you?" I whispered, breathless.

165

He nodded, as if that was all he could offer.

"What the hell was that?" an angry, feminine voice demanded.

Over Elliott's shoulder, I could see that Selah held a knife to Adiel's throat, teeth bared. He was pressed up against the face of the mountain, hands up at his defense. Mekhi was the only Lyscottian at this side of the rock who could help, and he merely watched with confusion lacing his pale features.

"I didn't – what do –"

"I watched you trip him!"

"I didn't! How could I –"

"You're lying." She stood firm, pushing the blade close enough that it nearly drew blood.

A spike of something between shock and realization hit me from where Mekhi shifted. *Depths.*

Did Mekhi know?

"Selah," I started.

"I'm not!" Adiel pleaded, hopeless.

"You tripped him now, and you tripped Elliott on the mat before. You are lying about not having a gift, and you just nearly killed my prince."

Adiel tried, incapable of forming a coherent word. It was Nero who then interjected on his behalf. "Lady Aster, it was just an accident. There is no need –"

"I will get to you," she bit, only sparing him a passing glance.

He puffed out his chest in anger, "I will not stand here and be disrespected by –"

"You will stand there and do whatever I please, because it is *my* prince who holds the fate of your kingdom in his hands, and it is *my* fiancé whom your son nearly killed. The very same prince, who, mind you, can do

166

nothing for your country if he is dead." She pushed Adiel against the stone wall again, "Get your brutish son under control or I will take care of him myself."

"Enough," the king took half a pace towards Selah. I helped Elliott to his feet as all the energy had seemed to leave him. He had stopped time for me. It wasn't possible. It wasn't even his gift, and yet I was living and breathing and entirely unharmed. He was steady, albeit not like he usually was. "Lady Aster, I will deal firmly with young Adiel. Any kind of behavior threatening the Eloran prince is absolutely unacceptable and will not be tolerated." He cast Adiel a pointed look. "But I do request that you let him go. Your fiancé is fine, and this is holy ground. The first of Lycott's rulers are buried underneath these stones."

Fire was lit in her gray-blue eyes as she turned back to the king.

I had been on the receiving end of her anger before, but not like this, and not with a knife to my throat. Here, now, I could vividly picture how Selah ended up in the Eloran Vaults. Perhaps I hadn't been subject to as much as I thought. She had cut their soldier to pieces for less, and for a fleeting moment, I feared for Adiel. He may have dwarfed her, but she had the knife.

She stared at the king, a war evidently raging in her mind. Her expression shifted when her eyes met mine. I was okay, I reassured her with a short nod. The movement was slight, but the flames were doused. Slowly, and with a final shove, she pulled away from Adiel and tucked the knife back to wherever it had been concealed. He cradled his throat with one hand, massaging the red mark Selah had gifted him.

"We are leaving, Your Majesty. We will meet you at the castle. When we come to a conclusion on how and if we would like to proceed, we

167

will let you know," she tugged Elliott's arm, though he wouldn't have fought her even if he had the strength to do so. I followed.

We brushed past a trembling Adiel and a notably stoic Mekhi. Selah led the way back down the trail, leaving the Lyscottian court behind. Fortunately, we weren't very far from the carriage, and we were on our way to the palace not a few minutes later.

Elliott collapsed onto the seat, eyes heavy and fighting to stay open. Gently, as gently as she'd been with me the day we were attacked, she held the back of her hand against Elliott's forehead so she could properly assess him, "You're unwell."

"Just tired," he mumbled, and didn't pull away from her.

She nodded, solemn.

Allowing him space, she moved to sit next to me instead. She met my eyes for half a second before glancing away again, and then down.

Safe, sound, and heading back to the castle, I finally had the freedom to smirk, "You were terrifying."

She huffed, "Let them be scared."

I peered down at her. "You know, if they weren't convinced you cared before, they definitely are now. You are a wonderful actress and perhaps the only security I'll ever need. Is that twice now that you've come to my aid?"

"I don't know how you're joking, Haven. You nearly died. You would've, if Elliott hadn't done – well, whatever Elliott just did. Some people would take this a bit more seriously." Her arms were firmly fixed across her chest.

"I'm alright, Selah. We're alright. End of story." Which was partially true. I would adequately process the fact that I had been suspended off the edge of a cliff when I had the energy and time to do so. But, for the time being, all I could do was try to get back to the palace.

She sighed in discontent and conceded. After another heartbeat, she rested her head against my shoulder. I sat in contained shock. I allowed it, though, grateful that we survived through most of the day and glad she trusted me a little.

We were quiet for some time, Elliott's snoring filling the silence.

"We need to figure out what's going on with our gifts, Haven." Selah's voice was soft and low.

"We will."

Chapter Seventeen: Selah

It was nearly shameful how much comfort I felt at the prince's side.

He'd almost fallen to his death. I'd almost watched it happen. Nero's jerk son was seconds from being responsible for killing the prince of Elora. I might have taken his life for it. In fact, I had been actively considering it when the king stepped in. Adiel's hand had flicked in the very same way it did on the mats with Elliott, and I just knew. His sputtering lies confirmed it. I knew it was his fault and I knew there was little I would not have done if he further threatened the prince.

Not because I cared for Haven, of course. I didn't. He was a thorn in my side, a means to an end, a horrifically needy thing who about died twice under my care. The very same entitled man who had given me the choice between being locked in a dungeon or traveling weeks with him to an entire other country. He'd intentionally blindsided me by telling them we were engaged without warning and, in doing so, trapped me in a room with him alone. I could hardly breathe the first night, much less sleep.

But then there we were, sitting in easy silence, the carriage rolling softly along the road. I leaned against him in a moment of weakness and found myself hating it far less than I would've imagined. He smelled of soil and cedar and cinnamon. He was sweet, and charming, and much more forgiving than I could ever be.

His shoulder was hard and strong against my cheek. He was here, and alive. My heart had only just settled its way back in my chest after watching his foot get swept out from under him. But it couldn't possibly have scared me, because that would mean that Haven was something more than a thing to be tolerated.

Then why was the thought of taking his hand in mine so very tempting? And why was the smell of him alone enough to set me off?

Heavens above, there must be something terribly wrong with me.

It was fine, especially because there was no conceivable way that Haven cared for me, either. Sure, he had been inconsiderate, but I'd been moody, and difficult, and had threatened his life no less than seven times. He was a flirt, and a very compelling one, but it was a *transaction*. My services in exchange for his money. I told myself that's all it was, and that this moment of comfort was merely a result of heightened emotions.

It was an effective rationalization, and one that I used for the remainder of the ride back to the palace.

I stirred again when we arrived, looking anywhere but at Haven. Fortunately, Elliott was in dire need of a hand up, and I reached out to him before the prince could. I remembered this brand of exhaustion well. Whatever I had done to Lorelai, whatever Elliott did to freeze Haven in the air, it sucked away a great amount of strength. I was out for days afterwards, and I barely recall the bits I was awake for. Mentally, I made a note to add our gifts to the list of things that needed to be researched.

The lieutenant colonel was in no shape to fight me, and he took my arm in a sloppy movement. Had I been so delirious? I helped him down, out of the carriage. Elliott was a hulking mass of a young man, built like a door from his years of military service. Keeping him upright was no easy task.

Witnessing my struggle, Haven took Elliott from me and started back towards the rooms. Pearce would sleep well, and plenty.

I remained by the carriage for a minute, watching them walk away. Haven carried Elliott with careful ease. With all our days spent away from each other, I had forgotten that they had grown up together. It caused my very soul to ache. Never, in all my years, did I have a friend that would watch out for me so thoroughly as they watched out for each other. No one would've saved my life. No one would have found it worthy of such a thing. Once we were done in Lyscott, when we returned to Distin, I would return to no one. I would have money to spend and my apartment back, but even Eli and Mariah never did more than offer me work. It was enough, of course, but it wasn't friendship. It wasn't the safety of knowing you are loved.

Haven was loved.

Perhaps he was more worthy of it. Maybe his mercy, the tenderness with which he spoke, and his underlying sweetness made him more deserving than I. His gift lent itself to such understanding, such compassion. He would return to his family, the kingdom that I had no doubt adored him, and the certainty of his home. He would be safe and happy.

And I would be wealthy and alone.

I padded my way back through the castle, up to my room. It was a wonder that I recalled which hallways to turn down. The Lyscottian palace was a labyrinth of corridors and beautiful things. Fortunately, I'd been paying extra attention the morning prior, and kept track of the art pieces lining the path to the suite Haven and I shared. I may have been jealous at the grandeur of it all, had there been space in my chest to feel such a thing. Lyscott was magnificent. Brutal, unforgiving, with the climate and the landscape, but magnificent.

Had the prince of Elora not dragged me out of a cell, albeit a cell I didn't deserve to be in, I may have never seen it. Certainly not from its own castle.

Tucked safely away, I tried to rub the longing and worry from my face. They did not budge. With a huff, I turned my attention to the assortment of blades I had hidden on my person. I slid out the ones from my ankles first, dropping them into a pile on the bed. Next, I removed the two strapped against either wrist. They were pretty, but they were small. Last, I pulled out the three I had hidden against my ribs. I had snatched the bottom one out to use against Adiel. It was the most action that particular knife had ever seen, and it was well worth the price I'd paid for it. Distin salesmen are cruel, slithering excuses of men, who charge an obnoxious amount for their goods.

I heard Haven coming long before he opened the door. His steps were solid and sure, but not heavy like Nero's or delicate like Wren's. Announcing his arrival, the hinges gently creaked.

I counted my weapons again. Still seven, just like there had been the first time I checked.

"What's wrong?" he asked. I was facing away from him, so it was impossible he knew anything from my expression.

"Get out of my head, Highness."

"I can't help hearing what is so very loud," he said, taking a seat on the bed next to all my blades, directly in my line of vision. "What is the matter?"

It was when I looked back into those ridiculous amber eyes, full of compassion and patience, that I was overcome by the urge to stab him. Who has amber eyes? It's an absurd color and I hated how they felt so inviting.

In lieu of making a mess, I grinned tightly, "All is well. If you'll excuse me, I need to continue my research."

As I moved to turn away, Haven grabbed my arm. My breath caught. His hold was gentle, but regardless I was torn between violence, shock, and anger. To his benefit, the prince didn't allow me to respond at all.

"In order to make friends, Selah – real, *true* friends – you cannot hide away everything you feel. You cannot be known if you will not allow it."

True.

Tears stung behind my eyes.

Let the record show that I allowed people to know all sorts of things. Haven knew I liked strawberries. Elliott knew about my gift. Even Adiel had recently learned about my affinity for hidden blades. How was that not enough? What more could I offer of myself?

No, maybe I had earned such a fate.

And I knew, *I knew* that my thoughts were apparent to the prince. I knew because he was touching me. I knew because he had sensed what I was feeling from the moment he stepped into the room. I knew because his face fell into a sort of hurt that I feared mirrored my own.

I could not be angry. The wrath I'd been filled with against Adiel refused to be conjured again. In my longing, I lacked the required energy. He would know that it was only to mask everything else. Instead, I offered the prince what I was able, and did so softly, to keep the grief from clawing its way into my voice, "Another time, then, I'll be worthy of your friendship."

He let go, "Selah, you know that's not –"

"I'll be back in a bit," I muttered, leaving him no time to respond as I ran off to the library. There had to be something there I could bury myself in other than the emotions that were threatening to overwhelm me. How I wished I could threaten them back. How I wished to hold them under water until they quieted into something I could tolerate. But I had a prince to avoid, and in order to keep all of us safe, we needed to know more about Lorelai and what she wanted. She ran, too. Though, I couldn't help but worry that her story was not over yet.

I snuck back into our room long after the sun had set, nearer to when it would rise again. To my great fortune, Haven was asleep. I tucked myself into the blankets on the floor and prayed that he would forget.

When I awoke, I didn't see the prince. Panic laced my chest. There was no way they had snatched him in his sleep, stolen him off to somewhere he'd never be found. I was in the room all night, and I was a light sleeper. He would've shouted; I would've heard something –

Haven turned the corner, exiting from the dressing room, entirely unharmed. It was more than an effort not to breathe out my relief. Of course he was fine. Fine, and striking in a way I could never hope to be. I remembered when I had met him in the prison, when even in the dark I had thought he looked like sunlight personified. He had his golden locks relatively tame, strands falling over the gilded head-piece he donned. The prince's tanned skin was covered by his green uniform pants and the white undershirt he wore. The matching jacket was spread over the vanity's chair, and he met my eyes before grabbing it. There they were, those eyes again. I had nothing to say to him, nothing I could muster at that hour and after the conversation we'd had.

He pulled on the jacket, glancing at me again in the mirror, "The king sent a missive last night. He wants to know how we'd like to proceed. I wish to stay, if you take no great issue with it, and I'm about to go tell him just that." *True.*

I hopped out of my covers, "Haven, that's insane. Adiel nearly killed you."

175

"But here I stand. Did Castillo mean what he said? About not tolerating any threats to my life?"

I thought back. Yes, what the king had said about Haven's protection rang true. I'd brushed over it in the heat of the moment, but I had not considered that Adiel had acted of his own will. Or, if of his own will, he hadn't intended to kill the prince at all. There were more questions than answers. "Yes, but –"

"Then that will be enough. The lives of these people are worth more than my damaged pride, are they not?"

"You're making a mistake." I argued, concern and anger equal in my voice.

"Yet it is mine to make," he said. There he was, the prince of Elora in the flesh. I'd seen Haven in a handful of ways, but never so regal as he was standing in front of me. He turned then, to look at me face on. He lacked my worry, my evident frustration. The prince tended to be even tempered, and this was no exception.

I sighed in defeat. I could not leave on my own, and he was intent on staying, "At least let me come with you."

He grinned then, twirling a strand of my hair around his finger. I was stunned still by the strange intimacy of it, then by how close we were standing. "No, my sweetest bodyguard, I think I will manage. It will be quick. After yesterday, the king is eager to give us space."

For a second, I had no worthy response. I just nodded. He dropped the piece of hair, and started towards the door.

"I like to read," I blurted, and he paused. I was a fool, a horrendous fool, but I *wanted* Haven to know me. Only a little. "I was pulled out of school too young, so I'm hopeless at higher math, but I could always read well above my grade level. The story you took from me at the inn was something I always wanted to read as a child."

If possible, he grinned wider, "I'll keep that in mind."

He finally went, then. I'd said too much. Maybe I hadn't said enough. Ugh, I didn't know what he wanted.

I needed something to do. I'd grown tired of staring at texts about gods and monsters. It was then I remembered Elliott, and how I'd felt after our encounter with Lorelai. I sent for food and tea, readied myself and set off to deliver them once they arrived.

Elliott's room was smaller than ours, less grand but filled with the expensive taste of the Lyscottians. His window was shorter, his ceilings not quite as tall, but the lieutenant colonel didn't seem the type to mind such a thing. His snores were audible from the hallway, so I didn't bother knocking to wake him. I could set the tray down by his bedside, and he would eat when he woke.

However, I was either louder than I thought or Pearce was more sensitive than I expected, because he stirred the moment I entered the room. His dreads fell like a mop around him, and his limbs were spread out in every direction. He squinted at me, "Aster. What?" he mumbled. His voice was present, but coated with sleep.

"I brought food. And tea." I held up the tray, showing him.

"Is it spiked?" groaning, he sat up.

"No, and it is not poisoned, either, as far as I'm aware. I'll admit I was tempted, but in your state it's akin to kicking a puppy," I smirked. I was kidding, of course, and hoped he wouldn't think otherwise.

"I'm thankful that your humanity prevailed," he took a hungry bite of the bread from the tray. There was a small loaf, a cup of berries, some

177

oats, and a simmering cup of peppermint tea. I looked up again, and the bread was gone. I'd woken up tired, but not nearly as ravenous.

"How are you feeling?" I asked, surprising myself because I did so in earnest. Pearce's mother had been the one to arrest me, and he did not even offer the decency of conversation on the way over. Regardless, though, we had found ourselves united in our purpose: We both wanted the prince safe and whole. We both despised Adiel and found Mekhi to be tolerable on occasion. His gift had changed. Evolved, maybe. My gift had changed, too.

If only I'd had the time to explore it.

"Tired," he said, knocking back the entire cup of berries in one fluid motion. A few more bites and a swallow later, they were gone. "Less hungry, though. I didn't understand how it was possible that you slept for five days straight. I understand now." Elliott paused thoughtfully, "But what is it that has compelled you to bring me breakfast in bed?"

I smiled slightly. "You're the man of honor, *Lieutenant Colonel* Pearce. You saved the life of the prince. This should come as no shock to you. You heroically snatched him from the brink of death."

Elliott looked at me wryly, "I wasn't aware protecting Haven would win me your favor."

I sat, though still far from him, at the foot of his bed, "You would've had my favor if you had paid me any mind. But no, *the* Elliott Pearce is too moody and brooding to lower himself to a level such as mine."

He rolled his eyes in a heavy, sweeping motion, "It's not that."

My brows pulled together. If it wasn't his status, then I could not remember what I'd done to offend him, "I don't understand how it could be anything else."

178

"Selah," he breathed, taking a greedy bite of the oats before setting them aside, "I care little for things as trivial as rank. Do you know what I do care about? The royal family. Haven. I am closer with most of them than I am with my own mother. Then, Haven decides to bring only me and you to another country at the king's behest. Me, I understand. We are rarely far apart. But you? You were in our dungeons the evening prior. You were someone who just so happened to be in the wrong place at the right time. In the course of a day, I was tied to a person I didn't know and certainly did not trust. A person who was good with a blade and who I did not know was entirely forthcoming about their gift. You will excuse my apprehension."

"Your mother arrested me. Wrongfully!" I motioned with exasperation, "And I was coerced into coming here. How am I the one to be feared?"

"There are people in this world far less scary than you who would spill your blood without mercy. It was never personal. And watching you risk your life for us – for him – helped." Elliott smirked, "Not to mention, I have rarely felt such satisfaction as I did when you held your knife to Adiel's throat. I *knew* he cheated."

I snickered then, "Eat your food, Pearce. Gather your strength so you can defeat him fairly."

There was a faint knock on Elliott's door, and Haven poked his head in not a second later. It served me right that I had left to avoid thinking of him, and yet, he had found me anyway. He looked at us sideways, taking in the scene of me and Elliot and the food I had brought him. It was rightfully out of character, and even I could not decipher what the prince made of it. "I'm glad to see my lieutenant colonel alive and well," he said. *True.*

Elliott smiled, now genuine. "I'm glad to see that the prince of Elora will live to serve another day." *True.*

"I did come to check on you. Though, if Selah is here, I'm not sure you need my protection," he grinned at me, and I mustered what I could in response. "I have news you may want to hear."

"And?" I raised a brow.

He swiped a paper out from his pocket. "I received a rather surprising letter this morning," he said, holding up the wrinkled parchment. "It seems as though Genevieve and Alaric have been sent to Lyscott. They arrive tonight."

Chapter Eighteen: Haven

Elliott's jaw nearly damaged the wooden floor as it dropped, while Selah merely watched in confusion. She hadn't met my elder brother and younger sister yet. Well, I supposed she'd met *a* younger sister, but she hadn't been introduced to Gen. I wondered if Selah would be glad to know how Genevieve fought for her against my parents. She had been the only one, actually. I'd questioned my father, but I didn't argue with the conviction of my sister. Even Elliott, though not an Allicot in name, had listened in silence.

Elliott's emotions swayed from gaping awe to outright concern, "It's not safe for them here, Haven. Alaric is the heir to the throne, and Gen –" he cut himself off with a shake of his head. "I can't believe your father allowed that."

I pursed my lips. He had to have sent them right after hearing of the attack. Maybe Alaric had a vision of something dire and convinced the king to send them off. Or, rather, the incident with Lorelai had warranted reinforcements.

"Your siblings are coming?" Selah guessed.

"You are a high-ranking soldier in my army, Elliott. You are more than capable of keeping them safe. I'm half decent with a sword. Alaric can see the future, Gen is a healer, and Selah," I gestured to her, "can stab someone, I suppose. Save for a fully-fledged siege on the castle, we can handle ourselves."

"You are perilously optimistic and today I lack the energy for it," Elliott sighed, flopping back down in his bed. Oh, the drama. In his defense, his exhaustion was entirely my fault.

It had been a strange thing, walking into a room with Elliott and Selah and watching them be civil. I hadn't seen many of their interactions, but the little I had been subject to were largely hostile on Elliott's end and antagonistic on Selah's. I thought I'd be glad when they finally got along. Why was it then rubbing me the wrong way when it was something I'd wanted?

I cast Selah a conspiratory glance and mocked a whisper, "He's only crabby because he's *very* fond of my dear sister."

She gasped in fake surprise and held a delicate hand over her heart. "Elliott! I didn't know you could be fond of people."

He threw a pillow at her that she dodged with a satisfied giggle. It stung for some odd reason. I had never earned that kind of reaction. I had no reason to be jealous. Even if Elliott were far away, she would like me just as much. She would not be the one to steal him from me, either. Neither of them were even mine.

But I consoled myself with the fact that I knew something Elliott did not: Selah Aster liked to read.

****

Genevieve and Alaric were hurried into the foyer of the Lyscottian castle where we awaited. Gen bristled, half-swallowed underneath a puffy, wool coat that was dotted with snowflakes. She gave it a tug, and all those little flakes fell to the floor. Alaric cared less for his state, only wiping a hand over his dark hair. I looked nothing like Gen, and the only matching

182

features between me and Alaric were our mother's eyes and our father's jaw. I most closely resembled Faye, who I was glad was tucked safely in the Eloran palace.

"Haven!" Genevieve hugged me tightly. How nice it was to feel at home again, even in a small way.

"Gen. Has everything been alright?"

"Of course, aside from the freezing cold," she pulled away, keeping her hands on my arms. "But what about you? We heard you were attacked on the road here! That's why we came, actually. Are you okay?"

I nodded. "We're just fine. Father sent you because of that?"

Genevieve tucked her hands back into her pockets, hesitating when she glanced at Selah. "Well, no. We sort of, in a manner, may not have overtly asked for his permission to leave. But it was Alaric's idea!"

I hugged him as well, though not quite pleased. His hold was firm but brief. "What have you done now?"

My brother waved me off, shaking Elliott's hand in greeting. "You say that as though I run off to neighboring countries often." He acknowledged Selah, "I don't, in case you're wondering. This was different. We can speak freely in private. She was the one who insisted on coming."

The culprit herself was found wrapped up in Elliott's arms, blushing like none other, "Hello again, Lieutenant Colonel. It's good to see you."

He grinned, and his pleasure was barely more contained than hers, "The pleasure is wholly mine, Princess. You've been missed."

Gen smiled straight back. "I should hope so." She turned to Selah. "And you, I don't believe I've met, though I've heard so much about. I'm Genevieve, formally known as Haven's favorite sibling, healer extraordinaire, the people's princess, or any other flattering title you may have heard."

Selah laughed and shook Gen's hand, "It is lovely to meet you. I am both shocked and appalled that I've not been told more about you. I'm in desperate need of another woman around here."

She was so friendly! The first time we had met, she was all threats and snide remarks. I should've sent Gen. Everything may have gone smoother.

"Gen, Alaric, this is Lady Selah Aster of Distin," I offered a pointed look, hoping they'd understand. The Lyscottian court was dispersed, but I was uncertain of who else could be listening. "My bride-to-be."

Gen's hand flew to cover her mouth and Alaric, too, was searching for the right words. I stopped them both with two hands in front of me. "It seems as though we have a lot to catch up on. Come, we can go to our room."

The speed at which we made it to our room was near jogging. This was due to Gen's fingers at my back, pushing me to move faster. My sister was a woman of many great qualities, but none of those were patience.

As soon as our door was shut, Gen exploded. "You're *engaged*? Why didn't we know?"

Selah sat on our desk with a content smile on her face. I would find no help from her, I concluded, "Yes. No. For appearances only. I'm afraid dear Selah would have to find my presence more tolerable for it to be real."

My sister's face lit up when she turned to Selah, "I told them arresting you was a terrible idea. I even made sure to say that it was completely unfair to drag you all the way out here. And with all the snow? It's almost inhumane. On behalf of the Eloran royal family, you have my formal apology for how you've been treated."

184

Selah beamed as she cast me a targeted glance, "Thank you! Finally, someone who understands."

They were a horrifying pair. I could not bear to try and imagine what they'd get up to in the coming days. My sister was fiery enough on her own, sweet and passionate but with a dash of cockiness. In addition to Selah's consistent desire to knife someone, I feared for Lyscott's safety.

For all of our sakes, Elliott took over the conversation. "Alaric. What happened? Is there a manhunt for you two in Elora I should know about?"

Alaric had been busy searching the cabinets, satisfied once he had found the booze. He poured himself a glass from the decanter and sipped on it. Elora's next king, everyone. "I had a vision about the cult and of Lyscott. I was here with you, staying in the palace. I was in the middle of leaving when this one," he nudged a shoulder in our sister's direction, "demanded to join me. It's okay, though. We left a note."

"Oh, well, since you left a note," an exasperated laugh left Elliott. "Alaric, you're the crown prince! You can't just leave the country."

My brother shrugged, "And, as the crown prince, I had the discernment to come when it was time. You are most welcome indeed."

Oh, the dilemma: I was torn between the dueling options of anger at their hasty departure and appreciation for their determination to come to our aid. I wasn't even aware that we needed their help; although, a healer and a seer were valuable assets. *Such* valuable assets, in fact, that they should not have been allowed to leave Elora on their own. I settled with the knowledge that, if Alaric saw himself in Lyscott, he was present for a reason.

"Wait," Selah started, "you had a vision of the cult?"

Alaric nodded, nonchalant.

185

"What did you see?"

"I saw the attack, for one," he raised his glass to me. "You fought well. It was a cheap move on her end, but you fought well."

Selah's face contorted in confusion, but Elliott spoke first. "What was a cheap move?"

I grimaced. I supposed they hadn't known how much danger they were in, or how I'd been captured. "She threatened to burn the carriage down after I'd said that there was no one inside."

They stared at me in realization.

Alaric continued. "I saw myself in Lyscott, staring out into the mountains. I also saw the cult's emblem, which I had copied down and sent to you at the inn. Did you not receive my letter?"

"That was you?" Our three voices rang out as one. I remembered how we'd paced around the room that Elliott and I had shared, fretting over the envelope and hoping it was nothing.

His brows crinkled. "Of course it was me. I told you, I'd warn you. Who else would know how to reach you?"

It made sense, unfortunately. It was also a far more comforting conclusion than that of assuming the cult had known where we'd be staying. He could have been a little less vague. But then again, what lowly creature am I to question the crown prince of Elora?

"We'll work on your communication."

Gen intervened. "It doesn't matter now. What did the king say about why his soldier was in Distin?"

If at all possible, my grimace deepened even further, "We haven't spoken of it. Yet. I've intended to, but Lyscott is at war and the king is distraught."

"Haven, that's the whole reason you're here."

186

I sighed. "I know, I know. But you've come now. We can ask the king about it together. For tonight, rest. Your rooms are near Elliott's; he can show you to them. We have a lot to figure out and nothing will be accomplished if we're all exhausted."

Elliott stole Gen and Alaric away, guiding Gen with a hand on her back. They ran away to Lyscott. Lukoh spare them, they were going to be in so much trouble when we ended up back in Distin. My mother wasn't passive, but usually not one to be riled unless the situation truly called for it. Her feelings over Faye were stronger than I'd felt from her in ages. But Alaric and Gen leaving the country without permission? How much of her wrath could I shield them from?

My father would likely be furious too, but in his more quiet manner. Where my mother was loud in her anger, he let us sit in silence with the knowledge of our actions. It was scarier, almost. To be fully aware that we disappointed him and to be left to contemplate. When he did finally vent, it was brief and precise. He was a terrifying man, but a good parent.

With the rest of them gone, it was only Selah and I left together for the night. It was an active decision to allow her space, to not allow my gift to roam as it pleased. While it did take some amount of effort, she had bargained for her privacy. I could try to give her that.

Ages passed before I fell asleep that night. Certainly, Elliott was more worried than I, just as Selah was infinitely more curious. What had Mekhi been so afraid of? Had he known that Adiel was going to try something, and that was why he warned Selah? He could have just said so. Unless there was a reason he couldn't, which was really what I wished to know.

187

I should've expected Gen to like Selah. Gen likes most people. She does not have the walls that Elliott has built or the insight of Alaric. Elliott's trepidation was absent until we were attacked those years ago. In the very depths of my memory, I recalled that Elliott had been so much like her when we were young. He'd been wild and loud, fighting for any cause he found halfway worthy.

I feared pieces of us had been buried with our friends.

****

I'll be awake 'til dawn at this rate, *I thought.*

I tossed beneath the blankets. If only Selah had taken the bed, perhaps I could've set up a wall of pillows and joined her. Of course, if she wanted the space, she could've had it. Instead, we remained in a battle of wills. My will currently felt like floorboards sticking up through the carpet, but it was unfair to blame my lack of sleep on that. I was awake because my mind hadn't yet slowed.

A lethargic, steady hand knocked at our door.

Who could possibly need something at this hour?

Dragging myself up, I stood to meet the person on the other side. I spared a glance at Selah's portion of the rug. It was empty. Surely, I would've heard her leave. I considered that I must have missed it.

What I did not miss, however, was the figure sitting on the bed.

His legs were stretched in front of him as if he'd been waiting awhile and made himself comfortable. His elbows rested on his knees, cradling his chin in one hand. The figure had long, lanky, pale fingers that tapped just below his bottom lip. His skin was devoid of color, his hair drained of pigment and eyes absent of life. Otherworldly evil tugged at the corners of my veins, trying to seep in.

I'd only seen him in photos, but I recognized him quickly.

Akar, rival of Lukoh. Divine force of destruction.

188

Run, my body urged, but my feet were frozen on the floor. The nearest weapons were Selah's knives, and even those were just out of reach.

Akar smiled, but it never reached his eyes. "Hello, princeling."

"Get out," I bit. How did he get in? The castle was well guarded, and even if he made his way past the soldiers, there were hundreds of rooms to comb through. Akar was meant to be locked away, if the legends were still true. He had been sealed into the Caves of Dobre.

The Caves of Dobre. Depths. It's not possible they found a way to free him to win the war. Is it?

If that was the case, my family's aid would not be enough.

His ivory brows crinkled in feigned offense. "Where are your manners, Highness? I've only just arrived."

"What do you want?"

Akar leaned forward with a predatory glint in his eyes. "You should know what I want. I want the princess of lies. The pretty, young thing with the gift of supernatural discernment. Bring her to me, and I'll have no further use for the Eloran royal family. You'll never have to hear from me again."

I laughed at the absurdity of his request, "Not a chance."

Akar sighed sadly, "Very well, then. Just remember that I asked nicely, Prince Haven. You've forced my hand."

A shrill scream sounded just on the other side of the door. It was agonizing and feminine. Selah's voice rang out over and over, calling my name. I could not move, I could not shift to reach her.

"Haven!"

****

I lurched up from under the blankets.

It was no longer night. Pinks and dark purples were beginning to creep out over the horizon, and the sun was well on its way into the morning sky. *It was a dream*, I reminded my aching, heaving lungs. Staring at the wicked being had felt so real, so very tangible.

But when I peeked over to the other side of the bed, Selah was there. She was whole and safe and sleeping soundly.

Heavens above, something was very, *very* wrong with Lyscott. I just didn't have the heart to leave.

Chapter Nineteen: Selah

"I'm coming with you."

The prince had woken in quite a mood.

Overnight, he'd decided that I must be monitored. Uncertain of what I'd done to be offered such a privilege, I immediately disagreed.

"Haven, it's just Mekhi. I'll be quite alright," I laced my boots as I spoke. "Doesn't the king have something for you to do today? Gen and Alaric are here, and I'd love to know what punishment he found suitable for Adiel."

He waved a flippant hand. The prince had been dressed and ready for the day long before I awoke. I stirred to the sound of him mucking about, busying himself with nothing at all. In the time we'd been in Lyscott, he'd been relatively quiet and at peace in the mornings. I wondered what had changed.

"I let him know I'll be otherwise occupied further acquainting my fiancée with my brother and sister. I'm the prince of Elora, Selah. It's not hard to sneak away," He stood there in front of me, ready and waiting. He wore a loose-fitting shirt and pants meant for training. Haven was prepared, at least. Though, his persistence struck me as odd, "What, am I really so bothersome?"

Quite the opposite. Not that it was any of his business.

What could have possibly compelled the prince to abandon his plans in favor of spending the morning with me? I did not know, but whatever it was, I didn't like it. It was especially peculiar since his siblings had just arrived. Was he avoiding them? He had no reason to. I would understand if it was the king he was shying away from, but then why run to Prince Mekhi instead?

I could use my gift to force the information out of him, or at the very least, to pry until I came up with something. It felt like cheating. If I wanted to know, maybe the best way was to reluctantly allow the prince to join me.

I shrugged, "Let's be off, then."

Mekhi took Haven's presence much better than I had. The prince of Lyscott merely eyed the prince of Elora with brief acknowledgement. I wished Mekhi wasn't so hard to read. Even Nero, for all the disgust he warranted, did not hide any of his ill intentions. The pale, stoic features of the white-haired heir, however, gave away too little.

"Your second lesson, Lady Aster. Prince Haven, if you'll join me." Mekhi beckoned not me, but my fiancé to the mat. I had no official 'first lesson', so I could only assume he was referring to using his gift to toss me on my rear and scare me to death. It was a rather effective tool, but I was glad that this lesson promised less psychological torture.

Mekhi grabbed two blades from the wall, twin silver swords that glinted in the faint light of the training room. He handed one to Haven, who toyed with the pommel in his hand. My prince took a step back, casually prepared.

From the time we'd been attacked, I'd thought Haven was captured because he didn't know how to handle a weapon. Until Alaric pressed, I had not stopped to consider that he may have put his sword down for a reason.

That also meant that the prince of Elora was capable of taking on at least three men at once.

Anticipation pulsed through my veins. It was about time the prince showed he was useful for something other than pretty nicknames.

"The first rule of a true fight is that you do not fight fair," Mekhi angled himself to the left of Haven. "If the sun is shining, then can I move to where my opponent is blinded by it. If there is a slope, I want to shift to the highest point so I have gravity on my side. And if my opponent is left-handed," he jerked his head to the sword in Haven's waiting grip. It was in his left hand. How had I not noticed? "Then I will move to his left. I will keep my hips angled towards him, and my elbows will never reach higher than my nose. Are you following?"

I nodded. Finally, even if it took Haven's company, I was learning something remotely useful.

"Technique is important, but if you don't have time to learn that, instinct will do just fine. You do not want to be gutted. Your body knows that. Reflexes will do much of the work for you." *True.* Mekhi adjusted his posture back to a fighting stance. "Prince Haven, whenever you're ready."

Haven swept out with his blade first. He was fast. Impossibly fast. In half of a blink, he was onto the next strike. Mekhi, to his credit, was keeping up. He matched every one of Haven's blows, parrying, attacking, blocking, and over again. They were a whirlwind of steel and footsteps.

Haven's brows were set, lips gently parted, entirely focused. Each of his movements were so precise, so very calculated for someone who had been nothing but gentle and easy-going. The sleeves of his shirt rolled up with all the jostling, and his forearms peeked out. Tanned muscle revealed itself, and veins traveled up his wrist to his hands. Those very same hands were wielding a sword like another limb, with all the elegance I should've expected from a prince.

You know, maybe Haven wasn't as weak as I initially thought.

He certainly didn't look bad. Heavens above, the things I would've done to get those hands on me. I wanted that attention almost as much as I wanted to get away from it.

Haven's eyes darted to mine, and Mekhi knocked him straight back down to the mat.

"And don't let a pretty young woman distract you." *True.* Mekhi smirked in what was one of the only genuine reactions I recalled seeing from him as he helped Haven back to his feet. The prince of Lyscott thought I was pretty.

The prince of Elora, however, refused to make eye contact with me, and I flushed with embarrassment. He wasn't supposed to be reading how I felt. Maybe he hadn't. Maybe something else I did had garnered his attention. Either way, I was going to forget that Haven may or may not have known what I was thinking.

"Lady Aster, if you will," Mekhi motioned for me to join him.

Haven handed back the sword he had borrowed. His lips were pursed in an effort not to chuckle. As if I wouldn't be able to tell. His fingers grazed mine as he handed off the sword.

"You *didn't –*" I stared. *He'd read my emotions.*

"No, of course not." *Lie.* The prince answered, allowing that smile to reveal itself. He really was stunning. A filthy, scheming little liar, but he grinned, and years were taken off his face. It was a boyish thing, one of which I should've known better than to appreciate.

I did not know better.

I stepped onto the mat with Mekhi. The sword was light in my hand. Heavier than the knives I favored, sturdier, but manageable. *Hips towards him. Elbows below the nose. Reflexes. Easy.*

"Watch my blade more than me. People can feign any which way, but steel doesn't lie. Are you –"

No sooner had I begun listening to Mekhi when dearest Adiel let himself in. His gait was a casual little stroll, as though he just happened to hear us and meandered over.

My blood was engulfed in flames. Had I not scared him? Had I not done enough? I was more than willing to push further, should the need arise. I eyed Haven, who was already locked onto a smirking Adiel. The Eloran prince lacked my fervor. His stance was easy, though his gaze was set.

"Focus," Mekhi urged.

I was focused. I was focused on the seven different blades against my skin, excluding the one in my hand. I was focused on my overwhelming desire to take Adiel on instead. I was focused on my prince, who stood so casually while I burned from the inside out.

"I do hope I'm not interrupting," Adiel fixed his eyes onto me. *Lie.* Rarely in my life did I regret not advertising my ability like I did then.

It was Mekhi who answered, "You are. Come back later."

Adiel scoffed with fake offense. He looked so much like his father. How did Wren, who had been so courteous with me, create such a vile thing? Even Nero was more tolerable, if only by a small margin.

"What kind of host would I be to ignore our guests?" Adiel took a few nonchalant steps towards Haven, who appeared unbothered, "Especially the prince of Elora, who found himself in *such* an unfortunate situation. And so recently! I've –"

195

There it was again.

The ancient, buzzing thing that hummed under the surface of my skin.

It was so raw, so willing to be shaped into whatever I pleased. Just once had I ever felt anything like it, in the forest with Lorelai. But I was full of the sort of anger that is not content to be ignored. Only then did Haven's attention snap to me, panic lighting briefly in his features.

"Selah," my prince warned.

I needed to stop. If Mekhi or Adiel discovered my ability, they would have to tell the king. Who knows what sort of reaction the king would have? Haven liked him, though that meant little. Would Adiel even remember if I used my gift on him? Maybe Mekhi wouldn't notice. It didn't matter. Once that power started moving, I didn't exactly know how to slow it down.

Adiel's eyes glazed over. He was staring my way, looking but entirely unseeing. It was my fault, I knew it was my fault, but I did not know what I'd done. My gift was not capable of anything like it.

"Why are you here, Adiel?" I asked. My voice was even and distant. Mekhi tensed.

He responded without a second to think, "To see you. And Prince Haven. I thought his sister might be around." *True.*

My brows furrowed, "What do you want with his sister?"

"Depends on what she looks like." *True.* And gross.

Nausea and dizziness rushed over me like a wave. My legs trembled for a heartbeat. I felt the headrush and the trickle of blood starting at the back of my nose. I knew I could look away then, release him from whatever hold he was under. We had already gone too far, though, and I had one more question.

196

"What is your gift?

Adiel paused, the only expression of his awareness being the pursing of his lips. He was fighting it. Whatever I was doing, he was trying to resist.

I took a small step forward.

"There is no name for it," he started, words tumbling out. "I can form bindings that cannot be broken. I can set simple traps that you cannot see. If my hands are free, I can manifest them at will."

I nodded. My head was pounding, and I wiped a drop of dark red from my nose. I had little energy left for him. "Leave, Adiel, and forget that we spoke."

He did so without a second thought. Perhaps without a thought at all, if the look on his face was any indication. A moment later, and the door was shut, leaving me glancing at a rigid Haven.

A hand from behind grabbed my collar and tossed me down on the mat. The sword I'd been holding clattered at Haven's feet. In a breath, I was flat on my back with Mekhi's blade hovering under my chin. In another blur of motion, Haven held my fallen weapon to the side of Mekhi's neck.

My prince's jaw was set. He hadn't been angry after Adiel nearly killed him, at least not like I had been. He hadn't really seemed to mind Adiel's presence, either. Only then, when I was finally the one with a sword at my throat, did the prince's features shift into something icy.

"That is quite enough," Haven's words were diplomatic, but his voice came out low and cold. My head was still spinning. I couldn't fight Mekhi in any state, let alone as worn and dizzy as I was. Haven could, though. He nearly had not a few minutes prior. I had little choice but to let my prince take over.

Mekhi held a hand up at Haven, "Relax, Highness. Do you really think I was not aware of her gift?" *True.*

No. I did not, in fact, think he was aware of my gift.

Mekhi went on. "You should thank whatever god you worship that I am the only one who suspected. Pray that Adiel forgets. I will say nothing. Unless," his eyes narrowed, "you ever use that ability on me."

I nodded, unable to formulate a more fitting response.

Content, Mekhi dropped his sword beside me and left without another word.

Haven set his sword down then, too, and lifted me to my feet. He steadied me with a hand on each elbow as his face searched mine, assessing the small amount of blood leaking down my face.

"You feel awful," he muttered, mostly to himself.

I coughed halfheartedly, "Words every little girl dreams of hearing."

He was not nearly as amused as I was, "Let's get you to Gen."

The princess's room was a mirror image of Elliott's. It was slightly more feminine, with pale pink drapes lingering on the edges of the windows and matching the comforter, but everything else was more or less the same. I supposed that Haven and I only received a fancier room because we were together. It was still nicer than my Distin apartment by miles, lacking none of the Lyscottian finery from the rest of the palace. Elliott had opened the door to greet us, and Alaric was sprawled out near the desk. Gen had been sitting on her bed. She perked up when we entered, head tilting slightly as she took us in. I was half a mess, and the prince at my side appeared less than thrilled.

Haven gently pushed me towards his sister, "Fix her."

"I'm fine," I assured, but Haven's frown was steady.

"What hurts?" Gen beckoned me over. Alaric said nothing, merely a careful observer. I'd never even seen the royal family before meeting Haven, but I'd expected something different. Alaric was quiet for a prince, not nearly as friendly as Haven was when we first met. In his defense, I imagine that seeing the future would leave one with much to ponder.

My prince answered for me, "Her head, but she's dizzy and trembling and fatigued."

Elliott was next to interject, "From what?"

"Nothing –"

"Her gift. It's the same thing that happened during the attack on the road and when you kept me from falling from the cliff. Both of you got sick in pretty much the same manner and your gifts manifested in ways that they should not be able to."

"Alaric?" Elliott tried.

The crown prince shrugged, "I've seen nothing of either of you."

Gingerly, I took a seat on Genevieve's bed. She took my pale, lanky fingers in her tanned, manicured hands. Her palms glowed with faint yellow light. *Her palms glowed.* It was a thing out of a storybook. A princess with the power to heal. In fairness, I'd come across many enamoring gifts in my time, but no one who *glowed.*

The spinning in my head slowly but surely subsided. The nausea was the last thing to ebb, but it too faded. I was still tired. Not like I had been, but enough to warrant a healthy nap.

"The thing where she made Lorelai tell her things?" Elliott asked, and Haven nodded. "Who did she use it on?"

I grimaced.

"Adiel."

"She did *not*," Elliott replied, letting loose a hysterical laugh. His features fell somewhere on the line between amusement and horror.

"She certainly did. In front of Mekhi, who swore not to inform anyone of the fact that we'd been less than forthcoming, so long as she doesn't use it on him. I'm not entirely sure that she can help it, but we'll be more careful."

They were speaking of me like I wasn't even in the room, "I'm right here. Present and accounted for."

My prince's expression softened.

It was a foreign thing for a man to look at me with such tenderness. I wanted it to stop just as much as I hoped it would continue, "I know, Selah. I'm sorry. We just need to figure out what is going on with you two, and how to make it stop. Your gift is of less value if they know they are being monitored."

There it was.

Of course.

My gift.

That's what the prince had brought me for, wasn't it? We were not friends, he did not care, he just needed something from me. That, I was more comfortable with. That, I could manage. It was fair enough. He did not need anyone else when he had a family, friends he'd known for his entire life. That made sense. But still, somewhere, it stung. I'd forgotten what he truly wanted me for.

Haven's attention turned away from me and back to his sister. "Can you start looking into what could be happening? Selah has spent some time researching similar things in the library, but an extra set of eyes couldn't hurt. We need to know what's going on, and we need to know before Selah accidentally reveals her gift to the entire Lyscottian court."

Chapter Twenty: Haven

Only a handful of hours later, it was time to introduce the crown prince and princess of Elora to the Lyscottian king.

Selah slept throughout much of the afternoon. Since she was unable to accompany Gen to the library, Elliott offered to join my sister instead. Far be it from me to assume that my lieutenant colonel had an ulterior motive, but I couldn't help but notice how he grinned at her. I'd heard nothing of what they'd found, or if they'd even found anything at all. I divided my time between catching up with Alaric on Eloran affairs and keeping an eye on Selah.

She woke up just before dinner, and when it was time, I escorted her down to the dining hall.

She was quiet, alarmingly so, in a mix of drowsiness and heavy thought. For fear of listening ears, I did not pry. I made a mental note to ask what she was thinking once we were back in our room.

We found Alaric and Gen in the hallway, with Elliott trailing closely behind. It was time for them to meet the king.

King Castillo grinned warmly as my siblings and I entered the dining hall. For a king, he was courteous. My father was as well, but I remembered visiting foreign nations as a child and noting how their rulers seemed so distant. Either they were haughty, prideful monarchs who cared more for themselves than their people, or they were too far removed from normal society to know how to interact with anyone who wasn't discussing politics. Castillo stood, extending a hand to my brother and sister as we joined him at the table.

"Prince Alaric, Princess Genevieve. I'm honored to have you both in Lyscott. I know it's quite the journey." He turned his admiration towards me, "your brother has spoken highly of you both. Please, sit. I'd introduce my court, but I'm sure they'll be more than happy to speak for themselves."

The rest of the Lyscottians had been quiet, though they too were gathered. My eye was drawn once again to the portrait on the wall. Mekhi was young, painfully so. I wondered how old he was when he lost his mother and sister. How could we leave them to fend for themselves when the king and the prince had already experienced so much heartache?

My brother was trained well enough in foreign affairs to know how to respond, but it was my sister who got there first. She smiled radiantly right back at the king, and spoke. "The pleasure is ours entirely. I was glad to be told we opened up communications again. I'd heard much about Lyscott's beauty. Plus, what a wonderful opportunity to get to know our future sister-in-law."

"I'm happy to hear it. Ilse, the wine, if you will." Ilse had been situated on the other side of Wren, who sat next to Selah. I wasn't sure why Selah took such interest in Wren, especially since I hadn't really noticed much from her. She was polite, but quiet, and I interacted more with her husband. The advisor's daughter hopped up from her chair at the king's behest, seeming more than thrilled.

She started with the king's cup, tracing her finger around the rim. I must have blinked, because one moment it was empty, the next it was filled to the brim with wine. She moved on to Nero's, then Mekhi's, then Elliott's, then Alaric's, then Gen's, mine, Selah's, and the rest of the Lyscottian court. Alaric and Elliott drank gleefully.

Selah cradled the chalice in her hand, but did not take more than a few sips.

"It's exquisite," Alaric noted. Fitting, that the first thing he'd spoken about was the alcohol.

Ilse blushed.

"The best in the kingdom," Castillo bragged. "Eat, chat. We have all night to get acquainted."

Per usual, Selah mostly listened. Gen and I spoke with the king, but Nero, Adiel, and Alaric interjected here and there. Ilse joined the conversation in regard to her gift, but mostly giggled at whatever Alaric said. Elliott and Mekhi shared a few words between themselves, but they were drowned out in the rest of the noise. The food was excellent, though that was no shock.

Once we had nearly finished eating, Gen shifted the conversation, "King Castillo, I am truly thrilled that this journey has reopened communications. However, may I speak freely?"

The king nodded, "You may."

"Prince Haven did not come merely for the sake of international relations, though that has been a benefit." She sighed heavily, "He was sent by my father due to some trouble caused by Lyscottian soldiers in Distin. One nearly kidnapped a young girl, and would've, if he hadn't been stopped by a brave passerby." It was a polite nod to Selah, one that I was certain I'd be hearing about later. "Not to imply that they were acting on your behalf, because I mean nothing of the sort. It was merely cause for concern. Do you know anything about it? Anything we can tell our father to give him some peace of mind would be welcome."

203

The king's brows drew together. His lips were taut, and he shook his head in steady disbelief. "I am ashamed to hear that of one of my soldiers. No, I know nothing of it. Deal with him however you wish, just have your father inform me of his name and punishment so I can pass along the news to his family."

A nearly overwhelming burst of shock and anger rippled at my right. It was enough to make me flinch. Selah's eyes narrowed slightly, and she took a small drink from her cup.

"None of your soldiers were in Elora, then?" Selah asked. *Depths.*

A flash of fear hit me from Mekhi's end of the table. His expression was stoic, but I felt his brief worry. His gaze was locked on Selah, lips slightly parted. He whispered something to Elliott. Elliott's features shifted into something of concern. He glanced at me, giving a subtle shake of his head. Whatever the king was lying about, Mekhi was afraid.

Castillo met Selah's challenge, "What reason would I have to send them? We are not enemies of Elora, nor am I in any position to antagonize yet another nation. We've enough to deal with as is, do we not?"

It was not an answer. If I was hardly content with it, I doubted my dear fiancée would be, either.

I slid my hand under the table, grabbing hers. She needed to stop. Not because she was wrong, for that was yet to be determined, but because the prince of Lyscott was afraid – afraid *for* her. No one was above fear, no soul too good for it. However, for the prince, a member of this court, to feel so strongly that I could sense it without effort, meant that it was for good reason.

"I would think that a king would keep a closer eye on those who serve him. That you would be well informed about what your own soldiers were doing," it was not quite a taunt, but it was not far from it. Heavens above, she was going to get herself imprisoned if she didn't shut up.

"We will not tolerate any disrespect to our king, Lady Aster," Nero interjected. "Do choose your next words wisely."

It was my turn, then, to come to her defense. "My fiancée is merely concerned. She means no ill intent."

Selah scoffed with mock regard, sipping from the glass she nursed. Mekhi looked at me then, silently pleading with me to get her quiet. I squeezed her hand harder. "Of course not. As the – how did you put it, Princess? The *brave passerby*? Yes, as the one who was forced to save that little girl from being taken – or worse – I find it difficult to believe that you knew absolutely nothing of it. I *personally* held the knife to your soldier's throat, Your Majesty. You can imagine my interest."

Yes. Go on, tell the king how you stabbed his soldier. What's the worst that could happen?

The king's gaze turned cold. He didn't speak at first, studying the silver chalice in his grip. "I'm well aware that you are prone to your outbursts, Lady Aster. I know of your temper. Most of us witnessed it just the other day. But you *will not* accuse me in my own home. My patience only extends so far, and I'd just hate to put you – or your prince – in such an uncomfortable situation. Do we understand each other?

He threatened her. *He threatened her?*

Icy rage flashed in Selah's expression, and I felt more fear from myself than I had from Mekhi. It was quickly replaced by something placid. She took the napkin from her lap, gently dabbing at the corners of her mouth. When she was done, she stood. "You'll excuse me, then."

She left without another word.

I rose, then, after her, and gave the king my full attention. "Your Majesty, I understand that you may feel she has spoken out of turn. So be it. But threaten her again, and Elora will offer you nothing."

My only goodbye was a brief nod. For a moment, I pitied Alaric and Gen for the position I'd left them in. Without the status of outright royalty, Elliott could easily get away with saying nothing. My siblings would not be so lucky.

I followed the remnants of Selah's fury all the way back to our bedroom. I did not even need to open the door to sense her seething on the other side. Taking a steadying breath, I set up a wall between my emotions and hers and prepared myself for whatever she would burn with.

When I entered the room, she was pacing. The poor carpet had fallen victim to her passion, wearing idly beneath her feet. Her hands wrung together in front of her, and her eyes lit with something hot when they met mine.

"Not the time," she bit out. There was nothing to be found of the detached sentiment she'd left with, just the fire leaching out of her.

"I'm not here to fight with you, Selah. I left to make sure that you are okay. Maybe teaching you a slight bit of diplomatic etiquette wouldn't hurt, but I understand." Perhaps it was poor timing for jokes.

"He was *lying*," she paused her patrolling, giving me her full attention. "He absolutely knows why those soldiers were in Distin and he's lying through his rotting teeth."

"I know. I felt it from you," my voice was soft but solid. I took a few steps closer to her, lingering within arms reach.

"That is the whole reason we're here, Haven. That's the whole reason *I'm* here. I saved that little girl, and I agreed to join you in exchange for finding out why she was in danger in the first place. Then we are finally

206

in a position to know why, he's finally saying *something,* and I am the only member of the Eloran court who seems to care. I'm not even an actual member!" She huffed in frustration. "Why do you not care? Why are you not angry?"

"I *do* care. I *am* angry. More than you understand."

"A child was nearly *taken,* Haven –"

"*I know,*" finally, some of the ire was mine, rising in my chest. My tone was stormy, not entirely because of her. "I am well aware. I was in the palace when the report came in. I felt everything from every person in the room. I was there with you the day it happened. It is not apathy. It is an effort to keep my feelings and the feelings of others from becoming something I cannot bear."

"And where did you find me that day, Haven?" She held her hands out wide. Something about her use of my name stung. "Because compassion means *nothing* if you are unwilling to act on it. I stepped in – I would do it again – but what did it earn me? Oh, yes, the choice between withering away in the Vaults of Distin – "

"I would *never* have left you there – "

" – or being dragged to a foreign nation where I would be tied to a man that I did not know. But in spite of myself, *I am angry.* I am the only one who seems to want to know – to want to press. The girl deserves better than your ridiculous pleasantries."

The only noise for a moment was our heavy breathing. She was *right,* I knew she was right, but I was not wrong. I answered her then.

"I have felt the king's pain. It is... difficult to resent people when you can see through them."

She looked at me, quiet but incredulous. She opened her mouth then paused. Again, she tried, glancing at the floor for a beat.

"The soldier would have ruined her. I've – " she exhaled, "I've been at the mercy of cruel men before. He would've ruined her."

My heart stopped.

The worst part was that *it made sense.* Her relief when we gave her a separate room at the inn. Her panic when we had spent the first night together. Her anger at me that day. Her wrath towards the king. All of it, every piece fit together. I hadn't even thought to warn her of my plan. No wonder she burned. *I lit the flame.*

Her voice lowered to just above a whisper. "And do you know what, Highness?"

I didn't dare breathe.

"I wouldn't have been so bothered if the king only threatened me. That's fine. It's an occupational hazard. But he threatened you, too." She laughed dryly, "And I swear that Lukoh must bask in my suffering, because that *mattered* to me. It matters to me now, and it mattered when Adiel nearly killed you. It should not have. I *should not* like you. I should find you haughty, and entitled, and insufferable. I do, at times. But more often than that, I find you charming, and sweet, and kind, and I *hate* it."

I could not stop myself from taking a step closer to her, from bracing my hands on her upper arms. I wanted so badly to move my palms to the sides of her face, but I kept the distance for her sake. She had already offered enough, I would not take more.

"I am sorry. On my crown, I am sorry. There is so much I would've done differently if I had known," for one of many times, I was grateful for her gift.

Unyielding, she stared right back up at me, "I do not want your pity. I want you to understand."

"I do understand."

"So why did you want me to stop? I felt your ... hand squeezes," she recreated the motion.

"I felt Mekhi's fear. He was afraid for *you*. You started prying, and he was burdened by it. I didn't know what he was scared of, or if it was worth trying to get you to back off," my chest lightened with the admission. "Elliott seemed convinced too. I trust his judgment."

Realization settled over her like a fog, "Oh."

"Even then, the king had no right to threaten you. I told him that once you left."

Her eyes widened, a hint of a grin peeking out at the corners of her mouth, "You did not."

I smiled coyly. "I let him know that if he threatens my *darling* fiancée again, he will find himself without Eloran aid in his war. I did not stick around to see how he reacted to that, but I will owe Gen and Alaric something precious after leaving them to recover that conversation."

She shook her head in disbelief. "I can't believe you. I'm *allowed* to talk back to him. I am just a lowly commoner, untrained in such political manners. You should know better."

I chuckled, gently squeezing her arms, "Evidently not, I'm afraid."

Later that night, when all was settled and we were tucked into our individual piles of floor blankets, I found myself unable to rest. Not until I'd told her one last thing.

"Selah?"

"Hmm?"

"Perhaps I should not like you, either."

Chapter Twenty-One: Selah

I should not like you, either.

The prince's words followed me long into the next day.

They accompanied me as I dressed and readied myself. They attended my lesson with Mekhi, which was notably the least eventful one we ever had. They chased me back to my room as I prepared to meet Gen and Elliott in the library. They trailed closely behind as I let myself past the shelves outfitted with books.

Gen and Elliott were seated on opposite sides of the grand desk where I often combed through the various texts. They paid little attention to each other as they read, though Gen's feet settled on the side of his chair. Both of them looked up as I entered. Gen grinned. Elliott's features were blank altogether.

"Selah!" she greeted, pulling out the wooden seat next to her. "I'm so glad you're finally here. I need someone to share in my misery."

I settled in. Stacks and stacks of tomes were set out in front of them. I too had been buried in literature, but the piles they had picked to sort through were overwhelmingly dense. Genevieve's mountain was primarily composed of texts regarding the giftings of Lukoh, whereas Elliott was knee deep in books about Eloran, Lyscottian, and Dobric history.

Gen flipped a page and huffed, "Lukoh wasn't blond! Heavens above, if I see *one* more drawing where he has straight little golden locks and pearly blue eyes, I'm burning this place down."

Elliott smirked, but didn't raise his eyes. I dragged a text to sit in front of me and swiped away the layer of dust that coated it.

I peeked over at the image she glared at. I had seen many depictions of Lukoh in recent times, mostly due to the research I'd done for Haven, but also around Distin. He was regularly shown with tawny skin, dark eyes and a mess of curly brown hair. In the book she held, he was unusually pale and, while his hair often had blond streaks or highlights, it was rarely so bleached. He looked kind. He often did.

Opening my book, I turned back to start reading. "Does it really matter what color his hair was if he's not around anymore?" I asked. The question came out more cynical than I would've liked.

Gen pursed her lips, for a moment looking much like her brother when he is unpleased. "He *is* around. He's just regaining his strength. Holding Akar takes much of his power, as you can imagine. The rest he stores for himself or shares with us." *True.*

"Oh," I muttered, averting my eyes from hers. "I didn't realize people still followed him."

The princess set her book aside, and even Elliott glanced up at us. She leaned back in her chair, supposedly tired of staring at the texts. "Most of the Eloran palace does. Do you not?"

I wondered if Haven believed in Lukoh. Heavens above, I was not ready for a conversation with him questioning my beliefs. Genevieve, though, I didn't mind so much.

I shrugged, "He was a bedtime story I was told as a child. I heard more of Akar, the monster under the bed meant to scare us into brushing our teeth and sleeping when we were told. But with Lukoh, I'm afraid that most of my prayers weren't answered and I am not entirely interested in a god who will not hear me."

She paused in thought. "It often seems that way, doesn't it?" *True*.

I nodded, resuming my work. Elliott was still quiet. I wonder what he made of all this. He didn't seem the type to blindly believe in anything.

What could the princess of Elora possibly know of unanswered prayers? She was born in a palace, for goodness' sake. What could she know of suffering? Did she know what it was to be truly cold, or hungry, or to not be able to find a safe place to sleep at night so to not sleep at all? Of course *she* believed. She clearly had never been in a situation where she needed divine intervention.

Taking a steady breath, I refocused. Genevieve was nice. She was passionate. She was the perfect, diplomatic, sweet princess. She didn't deserve my resentment. At least, maybe not as much as I was willing to offer. Lorelai deserved my anger. The king more than likely did, too.

We sat in silence for about an hour. My book was obnoxiously thick, each page more tattered than the last. It was about the regions of Elora and the different rulers. I learned that Elora was over a thousand years old, which was agreed upon by most scholars. Others wagered that it was much older, a compilation of remnants from different fallen nations. Both were likely the case, or some mixture of the two.

Most Eloran kings were decent. The Allicot line went back centuries, ruling only after they usurped the throne from another, weaker bloodline. The king in the book looked nothing like Haven. He was a homely, stocky brute who more closely resembled a bear than someone of his own lineage. I couldn't clearly picture Alaric's face, but he was slim compared to the marching figure I stared down at. In fairness, it had been a few hundred years, and time could water down any bloodline.

Evidently, what Gen said was true. The Allicot line had served Lukoh openly since their reign began. Generation after generation, each king took his turn dedicating different shrines or churches to him. When wars were won, and Elora won most conflicts, they did so in his name. Each ruler was illustrated, one after the other, all the way up until the present day.

Most recently, there was a young, dark-haired king and his blushing blonde queen. They both bore striking resemblance to their children, the king to Alaric and the queen to Haven. Especially since they appeared to be roughly Alaric's current age, if not a little older. They didn't look cruel or malicious, or anything like how I'd imagined them as I was growing up. I had imagined them to either be old and wicked or young and haughty. They just looked happy. Happy and hopeful and otherworldly in their beauty. Perhaps if either one of us deserved a peaceful childhood, it was Haven. He was good and gentle in ways that I was not and maybe that warranted such a stark difference between how we were raised.

Not to say I'd grown to be a terrible person. I hadn't, not in my opinion. I knew right from wrong. I was capable of caring for people, though I did so sparingly. I helped people. Sometimes. Usually for money. *Was* I even a good person? Do good people have to wonder if they're good? Since when did I care if I was good or not? Did it matter? I was alive, I was relatively wealthy, and goodness, I was *safe*. Maybe not from everything, and maybe not forever, but no longer was I the scared little girl I still so vividly remembered.

Depths, either the situation truly was dire or I was hopelessly bored if I was contemplating my morality.

As I was busy tearing myself back out of my own thoughts, Gen's breath caught. Elliott's gaze jerked up before mine did. She was pale, worryingly white, and her full lips were parted in shock. Her brows pulled tightly together. Gen's dark blue eyes jumped first to Elliott's, then to mine.

"What is it, Princess?" On Elliott's tongue, it sounded more like a name than a title.

"I..." she drifted, staring back down at her book with widened eyes.

"Genevieve," he nearly growled.

The words spilled out, "I found the cult from Mallord Bay." *True.*

"What?" we said in unison, but it was Elliott who jumped out of his chair. Genevieve slammed the book shut, tucking it into her lap as he approached her. Her knuckles were white as she held it from him.

"Let me see," he demanded. She was technically several ranks above him, yet still he pressed.

Her lips pursed into a thin line, "I need to speak with Alaric first."

"You can speak with *me* now."

"I am not one of your soldiers, Lieutenant Colonel. You cannot give me orders."

Elliott was unflinching before her, hovering only a few breaths away. "If it concerns your safety, Princess, I can do whatever I please. I will not ask again. Hand me the book."

Reluctantly, and with a firm stare, she stood to meet him and gave it over. Elliott opened it up on the desk, flipping through the many crisp pages. When he found the one he was looking for, his face fell. His expression then turned into something unreadable, "That's not possible."

"I'm sorry, Elliott. It lines up with everything you told me and what Alaric foresaw." She took his hands in hers, "I'm sorry."

"What isn't possible?" I asked.

I slid the book over to me, still open to the page where Elliott had left it. It spoke of a group called *The Illustri*. They were based in Mallord Bay, exactly like Lorelai said, and demanded the deaths of those with abilities as human sacrifices. Even their symbol, taking up much of the top half of the page, was the very same image that Alaric had sent Haven when we stayed in the inn. The sun and the moon, surrounded by shimmering stars and tossed onto a violet background. It was all there in writing, but I would have to wait to read it thoroughly another time.

Keeping her hand in his, Gen turned to me with a weighty look. "This is not the first time the Illustri has attacked. They came for Haven seven years ago. They... they killed a lot of people. A lot of friends." *True. Depths.*

I wracked my brain for any memory, any knowledge of reading about what happened. Seven years ago put me at thirteen. I was running most of that year, so there was little hope for me having kept up with the news.

"But Elora went after them," Elliott started. His gaze was lit with something cold, but he did not move from beside her. "My parents and their soldiers went. They eradicated them. The Illustri were little more than dust when that siege was over. There's no way that any of them would have survived, the king made sure of it. There's no way, Gen."

For a passing moment, the princess looked torn. She glanced at the page again, searching, "Well," she said, hope making a faint appearance in her tone, "when we find them – all of them – we can ask for ourselves. But who's gonna tell Haven?"

Haven. Heavens above. So maybe he hadn't had the perfect royal upbringing I'd accused him of. He wasn't much older than me, so seven years ago would've placed him only around fourteen or maybe fifteen.

Goodness, that was so young. When I pictured him that age, he was carefree, and laughing, and lanky. Not mourning the deaths of people who had been killed on his behalf. I'd been through a lot by that age, too much, but nothing like that. Perhaps we were more alike than I thought.

But he was still so... *kind.* Kind and forgiving and patient. It was possible, then. To suffer and not have the rest of your life marred by that distant pain.

My heart ached for him. I wanted to know more. I wanted to know everything, but gauging by Genevieve and Elliott's sobriety, maybe it was best left alone.

"Do we have to tell him?" I tried.

Elliott brushed me off with an open sneer, "He's the prince of Elora, Aster. Of course we have to tell him."

I wanted to taunt right back, to match his snideness with my own and take nothing in stride. But, for a fleeting breath, I could see right through him. Behind those dark eyes of his, grief and fear lingered. Fear for Haven, and perhaps even for himself. I could not know what he lived through, and I would never be the one to ask, but he carried the sort of weightiness that was not foreign to me. So I said nothing.

Our footsteps were heavy as we trudged back to the room that Haven and I shared. It was likely he wouldn't even be there. I imagined him sitting at some table with the king, grinning and utilizing every bit of his diligently practiced diplomacy. At least then, he'd be spared from the knowledge for a little while longer.

He was not with the king, however. He opened the door before we reached it. Concern breached that pretty face of his. It was a rather inconvenient thing that he could feel us coming from rooms away with his gift, but I supposed there were times that it would be useful.

216

"What happened?" he asked, searching each of our faces. I had towed the book with us, trailing behind Gen and Elliott.

Elliott placed a hand on my prince's shoulder, nudging him back into our suite. "Come. Sit."

Warily, the prince obeyed. He sat on the edge of our neglected bed, hands neatly folded in his lap while blond locks fell haphazardly over his forehead. The band of gold that marked him as royalty was hidden under his hair. He stared up at Elliott expectantly, features otherwise neutral, "Out with it, then."

Elliott's features, however, were unabashedly pained. His lips drew together in a fine line, and I had rarely seen a forehead so creased. "Genevieve found the group that Elsborough is a part of."

The prince's brows furrowed, "Then why do you three feel so terrible?" He glanced at me, then back to Elliott. "Even my dear fiancée is solemn, and she's rarely solemn."

Physically, he gave no sign he was searching my emotions, but I knew.

"Show him."

I took the tome in my hand, setting it down on the bed. As he stared over my shoulder, I felt Haven's breath on my arm. He was very, frighteningly, close. I flipped through the many pages, stopping only when I saw the violet and silver markings that I'd be searching for. I sat and passed the book to the prince, who took it into his lap.

The room was quiet as he read. The only noticeable sign of his recognition was a sharp, near silent exhale. His fingers tightened over the pages. The rest of us said nothing. What was there to say? The same people who murdered his friends had returned to try again. There were no suitable words, nothing to fix it. Though, for an unknown reason that I deeply resented, I so badly wished to make it all better.

"It's all here, isn't it? Painfully obvious," he murmured. "I'll write to my father. When we get back home, he'll have a hell of a lot of explaining to do." Amber eyes met dark brown ones, "I'm sorry, Elliott. If I had known –"

"You didn't," the lieutenant colonel replied. "It's not even sure that the king knows. My mother assured him – assured us – that they'd been dealt with. None of this is your fault, Haven." Elliott paused for a heavy, piercing moment, "Not today, nor any day before."

Haven sighed. He closed the book and set it off to the side. Every bit the prince, he spoke, "Nor has it ever been yours."

Elliott stood frozen, agony writing itself all over him. An almost imperceptible amount of dampness lit his eyes. Then, when his feet were unstuck, he gave a short nod, "If you'll excuse me."

The general's son, Lieutenant Colonel of Elora's army, ran.

Genevieve stood, eyes trailing behind him but unmoving. She tore her gaze to her brother, then back out the door. "Haven –"

"Go."

The king's daughter, Princess of Elora, ran after him.

I was left sitting on the bed that neither of us would claim with my broken prince. Still, I said nothing. I did not even meet his gaze in fear of what pain I'd find there.

He was quiet too, for a time, "Save your pity for someone who requires it."

True.

Oh, Prince.

"I would offer you no such thing," Understanding, maybe. But not pity.

His voice was raw and gravelly when he replied, "What would you offer me, then?"

I considered my words carefully under the crushing weight of his attention. "Friendship, if you so choose," I slid my hand into his. His fingers dwarfed mine, though our palms were similarly calloused. He did not pull away. In fact, if anything, his grip was firm. "And the knowledge that you are not alone."

Haven choked on a breath. I gave his hand a gentle squeeze.

"I would love nothing more than to be your friend, Selah."

True.

No *Aster, Miss Aster, Lady Aster*, no pet name or unwarranted title. Just Selah. Just me.

With delicate fingers, he tilted my face towards his. Even in his misery, he was undeniably, gut-wrenchingly beautiful. From the sharp pane of his jaw to those ethereal amber eyes, he was something to behold. I was far too close to him to pretend that he wasn't. My skin heated and nearly burned where he touched me.

He continued, "I have felt your grief, your fear, your anger. If I am not alone, then neither are you." His thumb moved absentmindedly on the side of my cheek. I wanted to pull away almost as much as I wanted to lean into him further. No one had been so near for a very long time, and even then, never so intimately. But, much to my dismay, he was enamoring. "And I will level that entire city before I ever let them touch you or Elliott, or either of my siblings again."

True.

You are safe with me, the prince had promised on the first night we spent together. It had rung true, but only in that moment had I started to believe him.

Chapter Twenty-Two: Haven

"You're not sick."

Well, then. I certainly *felt* sick.

I had fallen asleep on the bed, legs hanging off and Selah's hand still in mine. I had every intention of staying up until she was out, then returning to my floor blankets and winning the unspoken battle that had been raging since we'd arrived in Lyscott. But I'd been tired. As tired as I'd ever been, exhausted both physically and mentally. There was little hope of my victory now, having woken up hours before with a fever.

I'd peeled my clammy hand out of hers, tripping over two trunks and a rug as I made it to the washroom with mere seconds to spare. I was still dizzy, horrifically nauseous, and I had long since been relieved of the contents of my stomach. A bleary-eyed Selah found me all but passed out on the washroom tile. I was bitterly cold and burning alive all at once. She was both too small and not quite strong enough to carry me back to the bed properly, so I was half dragged there before she went to get Gen.

On the bright side, it's rather difficult to recall the traumatic deaths of those you once cared for while actively trying not to vomit.

In retrieving Gen, she had woken both Elliott and Alaric, who had made their way over as well. I was in no shape to be receiving visitors, especially since when Alaric entered, I was half certain that there were three of him. Gen had hovered her hands over me, confusion lighting in her face just as soon as she did. It was then that she made her rather bold declaration.

"You're not sick," she huffed.

"He looks sick," Alaric said, idly poking my foot.

"He's not!" She snipped at him and turned back to me. "You're not. If you were sick, I could heal you. I cannot heal you. You are not sick. It is the only logical conclusion."

"What's wrong with him then?" Selah asked, placing the tea she'd only just brewed down at my bedside and returning to put out the flame. I had little hope of being able to stomach it, but I did appreciate the gesture.

Gen's features contorted. She shared many of my father's characteristics, with his blue eyes, his fair skin, and his dark hair. However, most of her personality was borrowed from our mother. Gen was always fairly pretty and had no shortage of suitors lining up for her hand. My sister was also a remarkably good healer, blessed by the god of life himself. I hadn't been worried for my health until she was.

"I don't know," rueful, she admitted.

"*I'm fine.*"

"He's lying!" called Selah and that troublesome gift of hers from where the stove cooled.

"We can tell!" Gen called back. "Although it's nice to know that there's someone around to call your nonsense out. Have you drunk poison? I don't know much about poison. Surely my gift would still work against poison, right? Heavens above, what a bother that would be if it didn't. My gift fixes everything. Why aren't you fixed?"

221

Selah appeared over her shoulder, "Here," she offered something to my sister, but I shut my eyes tight to avoid some of the world's spinning. "We may have to do this the old fashioned way."

A cold, wet cloth was carefully placed onto my forehead. Despite their tenderness, I hissed. It felt about as icy as the heart of Akar but I lacked the energy to recoil. My head pounded in anger. After a few more moments, the pain subsided, and I was grateful for the cool compress.

"Genevieve," Alaric crooned, "you are the eldest princess of Elora, third in line for the throne, heir to the Allicot name, but you are usually much more clever than this."

Strands of her hair whipped my arm with the force she turned to him. "I'm sorry, do *you* have magical, glowing hands? Because one, you've been holding out on us, and two, now would be the time to say so."

"No. But what I lack in power, I make up for in common sense." He sighed wearily, uneager to explain himself. "Lady Aster. Your abilities have evolved as of late, have they not?"

My eyes peeled open, and I saw the very end of Selah's nod, "Yes."

"Weren't you ill only hours before?"

Her jaw dropped but she recovered quickly, "Yes, I was."

"Pearce," Alaric turned. Everyone understood, now my brother was merely enjoying himself. "Were you not also ill recently?"

"I was indeed."

"And was that not the day before you so heroically saved dear Haven from falling to his death?"

I couldn't see much of Elliott's face since he turned to Alaric. His dreads were hanging in a low knot at the nape of his neck. I'd always liked them. My hair would never be suitable, but on Elliott, they made him look strong.

222

"It was."

Alaric sat then at my feet, clearly drained from the effort of being so handsome and intelligent, "Lukoh's power is ancient. It's older than time itself. If our gifts have truly begun to evolve, and let us pray that it is Lukoh's doing, then I'd be rather disappointed if there were no growing pains."

Evolving. Gifts had been evolving since Lukoh's departure. Usually, however, they evolved only through need, and slowly, over generations. If they were changing so quickly, and so drastically, if Selah could compel people to do whatever it is she did and Elliott could hold me in the air with his mind, I was afraid of what we'd need them for.

As if my head wasn't already whirling.

"You think Haven's gift is changing?" Elliott asked.

Alaric shrugged, "Only as much as yours has. Although if you were able to fight gravity with a thought, and Selah convinced a cult member to spill all her secrets, I fear for what my brother will be able to do."

Genevieve pondered. I might've too, if I'd had the energy to do so. Selah's lips were pursed in careful distaste, while Alaric merely watched them both. I was sure that my lieutenant colonel was just as displeased.

"Maybe you'll get the ability to fly," my sister said.

"Saves me a long trip home," I muttered back.

Alaric answered then. "Oh, I'd pay good money to see the look on Adiel's face if you started hovering mid-air. I wouldn't be entirely opposed to watching the advisor squirm, either. Please, Lukoh, let it be flight."

My fiancée's indignation morphed into a subtle grin.

"Regardless," my sister held her hand to my face, unimpressed with whatever she felt. Depths, her fingers were cold. "I still know a thing or two about caring for illness. We'll keep an eye on his gift. If his case is anything like what I've heard from both of you, he'll need to rest. I'll come and check in every so often, but Selah, can you stay with him for a couple hours? I'd do it myself, but Nero and Ilse have asked Alaric and I to meet with them this morning."

"Of course."

Genevieve, Elliott, and Alaric left only once Selah convinced them that she had everything under control. It was not like I was going very far. Only so much could change in the matter of an hour or two. I was so thoroughly tired, so ready to sleep the day away, but there was a pretty girl in my room that required my attention.

I remembered how she had felt that day on the road, and when we'd found her in her room the morning before. Instead of feeling it through her, I got the pleasure of experiencing it firsthand. It sucked. I hadn't felt so miserable since I contracted the stomach flu as a child.

I'd closed my eyes for a fleeting moment when I sensed her sitting next to me on the bed. She smelled familiar, like a bush of flowers I passed often as a child but could not recall what they looked like. Maybe if having one foot in the grave was what it took to have her close to me, it was worth it.

"You need to drink, Highness," I was already halfway sitting up from when my siblings had stopped by, so when she passed me the steaming cup, I was quite capable of obeying. It smelled of honey and peppermint.

Squinting at her, I took a sip, "So bossy."

She snorted, "If being bossy is what keeps you from dying of dehydration, I doubt that the kingdom of Elora will take any issue with it. An ounce of tea is not enough. Drink more."

Idly watching her, I did as she asked. One of the first things I'd noticed about her in the Vaults was how lovely she was, even bloodied and covered in dirt. The soldier she'd fought was burly and rugged, not just some common thief. She, however slight a thing she was, may have killed him if she hadn't been stopped by General Pearce's men.

A bit of a violent streak on her, but not so difficult to look at.

I could not decide if I liked her eyes or her hair more. I didn't mind her nose either, and I could all but imagine her pretty mouth on mine. Maybe I was going mad with illness. I had rarely found her so captivating.

It was matched only by the night before, when I held her face in my hand and stared right into those blue-gray eyes. They were swirling then, wide with some mix of shock and desire. If I had not felt it so clearly from her, perhaps I could pretend that I had not noticed that she wanted me. But I *had* felt it, and I *did* notice.

And that supposedly vicious thing was sitting in bed beside me, fretting over whether or not I had drunk enough.

Apparently, I'd been staring, "What is it?"

I shook my head, regretting it immediately as the room tilted on its side, "Just thinking."

"Well," she sighed, "it seems as though I'm stuck with you this morning. Spare me from boredom and enlighten me."

I snickered, "You may be lots of things by my side, Selah Aster, even if you are only there for a time. I'd hope that none of them would be bored."

She smiled in pity. Goodness, even then I loved it. All the worry and the anger that never fully left her had melted off her face. I had to be truly exhausted if I could not fight off appreciating her in my own thoughts.

She will go home one day, I reminded myself. *She will not want you then.*

225

While we were in Lyscott, while we were far from the city we both called home and while she was here in our room, though, I could pretend she wanted me. I could pretend that she was my stunning bride-to-be who was nursing me back to health. I could pretend that she was not afraid of being too close to me. When we were home, I figured, then I could end my illusion.

I considered any number of lies before realizing she'd see straight through them. With a heavy breath, I finally answered, "I was thinking of the day we met."

Wickedly, she grinned wider, "Didn't I threaten to cut out your tongue?"

I smirked right back, then grimaced at the wave of nausea that came and went, "I was half tempted to let you try. You had quite enough bruises that day, you did not need one on your pride as well."

She scoffed, gingerly removing the cloth from my forehead. Selah brushed her fingers up against my skin. They were not as cold as my sister's, but I still buried a wince. Her emotions crept in despite how tame they were. Her persistent burning was more subtle than usual. She was less than pleased with my temperature, she was faintly sad and mildly concerned. More than any of those, she was *happy*. I had not felt her happiness before. It was warm and light, and I wanted it to stay.

"You are far hotter than you should be, Prince."

I pursed my lips together to stifle a grin. As soon as the words were out, she realized what she'd said. She tugged her hand off my head, so I only caught the very end of her embarrassment. A blush crept into her cheeks. She hopped out of the bed with the cloth in tow, moving back to the washroom. I heard distant, faint splashing sounds before she returned.

I opened my mouth to speak –

226

"Hush."

Her stormy little exterior had returned in full force.

The cloth was even colder than it had been the first time and she placed it back. I'd braced for it, so my flinch was contained. Genevieve had denied me more than a single blanket. With the added chill, I was trembling. I clamped down on my teeth to keep them from rattling.

"Stop with that."

"Stop with what?"

"With the shaking. You're being dramatic."

My chuckle was broken in pieces, but I laughed nonetheless, "Y-yes, my lady. I will s-stop at my earliest c-convenience."

She huffed, towing away my now empty cup. I shut my eyes for what I thought to be only a moment, but when I opened them again, she'd appeared with a steaming, fully brewed vessel. Selah gave it to me to hold. I did so gladly. Finally, some true warmth. It was not yet cool enough to sip, or I may have listened to her and downed the whole thing.

I could get used to lying in bed all day and being doted on by a pretty woman. When Alaric ruled, I supposed I'd have my choice of what sort of life to live. I doubted I would be so lazy, but there would be a world of options once he became king.

Depths. The king.

"I was meant to meet the k-king in the garden this afternoon," I gently blew at the rising steam.

"I'll take care of him, Highness."

"I can do it."

Unimpressed, she stared at me.

"I probably can't do it," I admitted.

She nodded. "One would think that you'd grow used to my ability after you've been in my company for weeks. It was a valiant effort. No, I'll give your most sincere apologies and I'll go in your absence. Regardless of your condition, I still have some questions for him."

With all of the passion I could muster, a frankly meager amount, I shot her a warning look, "You will have to be amicable. I can't have you angering the king of this nation when I am not there to defend you."

Truly, I wasn't sure that she needed my defense. She hadn't when we were attacked in the carriage, and she decidedly could've held her own against Adiel. However, we were meant to be mending the relationship between our nations, not igniting any new tensions.

Selah, clearly displeased with my caution, snorted in response, "I can be amicable."

"Really? With the king? I don't think you can."

Her brows furrowed together at first, then her features evened out, "You really don't, do you?"

I didn't answer.

She grinned, "I accept your challenge, Prince. Come this afternoon, I will get all the answers I seek, and the king will think so highly of me, he'll have glorious songs written in my honor. You'll see. *Amicable.*"

Before I could give a proper reply, exhaustion won over. I dreamt of a girl in a cell and all her colorful phrases.

Chapter Twenty-Three: Selah

Amicable. *I can be amicable! I am a* delight.

It was a blatant trap from the prince. If I'd sensed he was lying, I might've ignored it. But it was *true*! Haven really didn't think I would be nice to the king. If not kind, I could at the very least be civil. It was a different way of getting the answers I wanted, but I considered that it may be effective, nonetheless.

Haven slept through most of the morning. I slept for a few minutes as well in my respective area, but spent much of the day staring out at Lyscott. I sorely wished it hadn't been so beautiful. The climate was nothing to write home about, but Lyscott and everything it represented would've been far easier to resent if I had known something in my life that could do it justice. Nothing I'd seen in Elora could match the cruel loveliness of the Lyscottian mountain range.

As quietly as I could manage, I readied to meet the king. Each blade I owned was well settled into its strap, easily hidden by the extra layers of clothing I had to don to face the weather. Not a few minutes later, Gen and Elliott relieved me of my nursing duties. While the prince slept the morning away, I'd be making some real progress.

It was not just the king who met me in the garden, however, but Mekhi as well. The Lyscottian prince appeared uncharacteristically formal.

Mekhi's light features were harsh in the afternoon weather. His dress uniform was varying shades of navy and silver in true Lyscottian fashion. Oddly, he looked less like a prince than he had in our lessons alone together. I supposed that if his father had intended for him and Haven to meet, a little bit more decorum was appropriate.

The king looked like he usually did, proper and decorated but not unkind. He was decidedly a liar, but people lied for all sorts of reasons. If I was going to try to be cordial, I had – at the very least – to convince myself that there could be some valid answer for why the soldiers were in Distin. Maybe the king knew they were there, but didn't know what they were doing. Or he was a terrible person who was evil and wicked, in which case I had seven different methods of ending his life.

Yet to be determined.

"Lady Aster," the king greeted with a slight nod. "Forgive me, I had expected your fiancé. Will he be joining us?"

"Prince Haven is ill, I'm afraid. It's nothing that won't pass, but he was not yet in any shape to be around others. He asked that I attend this meeting in his place."

Prince Mekhi appeared much more apprehensive than the king, who only offered an assessing stare, "I'm sorry to hear it. Very well, then, Lady Aster. Walk with me."

I took my place alongside the king, Mekhi trailing just behind. He kept an idle hand on one of the twin swords he carried, but the rest of his stance was easy. The king walked with quiet confidence. The flecks of snow that fell upon him disappeared into the ivory tint of his hair.

Despite the cold, flowers still sprouted up around us. There was every variety of blooms, from small, yellow buds that grew on trees to purple flowers that seemed to pop straight out of the snow. My favorite, though, was a small, white flower that almost looked like a lamp. Its green stem stood straight up, and the flower pointed right back down to the snow. There had to be dozens of them in a bed we passed, each in full bloom.

Noticing where my eyes had wandered, the king stopped. "Snowdrops," he smiled sadly. "You have excellent taste. Those are – were – Annika's favorite." Gingerly, he brushed a petal with the back of his finger. "My wife planted them herself. So stubborn, my queen. I think she would've liked you. Certainly not your attitude, but your boldness, perhaps." *True.*

Queen Annika of Lyscott. The king's wife.

For a minute, I considered how to apologize in a manner that was at least somewhat genuine. Through gritted teeth, I tried, "I am sorry I was so blunt at dinner. I did not mean to offend you –"

"I think you had every intention of offending me."

True.

Well, there goes that olive branch.

"But I understand." I followed him further into the garden as the trees became more dense. "I know how desperate one can become in search of the truth. I do not blame you for your crudeness. However, I will warn you that the truth is often far more complicated than if we are doing what is right or what is wrong. If you want a simple answer from me, sincerely I can say to you that I want the best for my country, and I do not wish any unnecessary suffering on Elora." *True.*

"That being said," the king's lilting accent rang from deep in his chest. "I believe all of us have truths that we'd rather not have exposed at the dinner table. You, for example, *Miss Aster.*"

Depths. Heavens above, who told him? And my gift, there's no way – unless Adiel remembered, in which case –

231

"I'd assume you wouldn't want your future brother- and sister-in-law to know that you aren't of noble birth. While I find it remarkably endearing that the prince would think so highly of you as to deem you worthy of marrying above your station, I know how the Eloran king may disapprove of your union. Because of this, I'm sure you can understand that situations like that require discretion. That is all I ask of you. I have no intention of informing anyone of your true background, including most of my own court, so long as you are willing to respect the boundaries I have set in place." *True.*

I stifled my sigh of relief. He thought I was hiding from Gen and Alaric, not from him. The king of Elora did not yet know that Haven had pronounced us engaged and made up a fake title for me to flaunt around. Maybe Lukoh *could* be generous at times.

I paused our stroll and turned to him, "How did you know?"

King Castillo smiled back at me with evident pride. "I'm almost offended that the prince thinks that I would be so easily fooled. First, your manners are severely lacking. Any self-respecting Eloran noble would've had you trained much better." *My manners are perfectly fine, thank you.* "Second, not many proper ladies would be willing or able to hold a knife to Adiel's neck with such little hesitation. Alongside some research into Eloran noble families, it was not so difficult to uncover."

"I noticed almost immediately," Mekhi added.

Of course he did.

A subtle blush crept up my cheeks. I was so thankful that Haven and I were not truly engaged. I may not have stood much of a chance in a kingdom where I was expected to perform.

"I didn't realize I was so obvious," I muttered.

The king looked at me with something akin to pity in his eyes, "Do not fret, *Lady* Aster. Your secret is safe –

A voice rang out through the forest, loud and melodic. It called in the Lyscottian tongue. I couldn't make out a single word.

"*Depths.*"

Mekhi drew both swords, each glimmering in the snow. Briefly, he made eye contact with his father, "You need to go."

The king nodded, face grim, "Keep her alive." Only then did he turn back to me. "Stay with Prince Mekhi." He stared deeper into the woods.

That was when the shouting started.

The king fled in one direction, and Mekhi pulled me away to the other. King Castillo was a blur of snow and motion, then he was gone. The prince shoved me against one of the prettier trees, and my back cried out in protest. The screams were quickly spreading in every direction. Mekhi peeked out to where the sound first came from, bracing his hands on each of my shoulders.

His pale eyes were full of barely contained rage when they met mine again, "Can you run well?"

I nodded.

"Good. We need to get back – *move!*"

An arrow whizzed past his face, sticking into the tree right behind him. A thin stream of blood started down from his ear, but the prince did not so much as stop to bat an eye.

He yanked me from the tree, sprinting nearly as fast as I'd seen Elliott run as he weaved throughout the garden. Arrows continued to fly around us as we tore past the flowers and foliage I had only just spent time appreciating. My thigh burned where an arrow nicked me, but I did not stop chasing after the prince.

Mekhi was crashing towards the palace we'd strayed away from. As we rounded the corner to where the entrance stood, he wrenched me to the ground behind one of the more raised areas of the garden. It was just out of the way of where we'd been fleeing, but not far away enough to be safe.

"Mekh –"

The prince clamped a hand down over my mouth.

I held my breath and listened. What had to have been dozens of feet ran by us. *Dozens* of archers. Lyscott was under attack, and three of the four royal children of Elora were in the castle. *Haven.* He hadn't even been awake when I'd left him, much less suited to defend himself in battle. And Gen. Did she have any training? Surely there had to have been something, but princesses were not sent to fight in wars.

"This way!" someone shouted in an Eloran accent. *What on earth are Elorans doing here?*

The footsteps came and went too many heartbeats later. Slowly, hesitantly, Mekhi removed his fingers. I panted when I finally could get proper air, and he anchored firm hands on either side of my face.

"Listen to me," his voice was alarmingly calm and barely above a whisper. It was only then I realized I was shaking. "I need you to do everything I say, *exactly* how and when I say it, or you will die today. Repeat that back to me."

"Everything you say, how and when you say it." I heaved.

"Good. We cannot use the garden entrance. There are a lot of very unhappy people who we've just sent that way. We need to go to the main castle entrance, but that may not be safer. How many knives do you have?"

"Seven."

234

"Keep them ready." He glanced in every direction, looking or listening for something I didn't quite know. "Stay right behind me. *Right* behind me, Aster. Not a step more. Your prince will have my head if I do not return you in one piece."

My eyes widened. "The castle. They're trapped –"

Mekhi shook his head. "Wren keeps the palace warded. Only those she permits can get in and out. Your prince is fine. We need to join them."

The prince pulled me up to a low crouch. Pressing a careful finger to his lips, he didn't let go of my hand as we wandered back through the garden. There were enough trees to keep us partially hidden, but not enough to provide full cover. Blood leached out of my sliced leg. I would not die, but the sharp sting was noticeable every time we brushed against a leaf.

Our trek was slow and methodical. I could not place where the shouting came from, only that it was in more areas than I would've liked. Our steps were little more than icy crunches, so it took ages to reach from one point to another without attracting masses of unwanted attention.

Eventually, we reached a post where Mekhi stopped. Instead of just screams, there was clashing of swords and battle cries consuming each other. Mekhi's forehead strained in concern.

We'd stopped near a wall of sorts, a divider that jutted out from the rocky terrain to separate the front of the palace from the sides. Mekhi peeked over the edge of it. I moved to do so, too, but he shoved my face back and gave me a warning glare. When he finally did sit, his expression was bleak.

"Good news or bad news?" he offered, his voice slightly louder now that it would be drowned out by all the other noise.

"Good news."

"We can probably make it."

"Bad news?"

"There are very many people in our way."

When I tried for a second time to glimpse over the divider, the prince allowed it. There were dozens of Lyscottian guards met by dozens of men fighting in those depths-forsaken wooden masks.

For heaven's sake.

Mekhi must've seen me blanch, "What is it?"

"They attacked us on the road here," I explained, recalling being dragged out of the carriage to find my bloodied prince. "But there were only three or four of them. Where did all these people come from?"

"We can ask them later. Are you ready to –"

"Oh, Seeeellaaaah."

I remembered that voice. That was not a good voice. In fact, that was a very *very* bad voice.

Lorelai.

I pressed up further against the wall. The prince of Lyscott glanced at me, and I hoped the fear wasn't as apparent on my face as I thought it was. Heavens above, I needed my hands to stop trembling.

"Oh, Seeeeeelllaaaahhh," she called again. "Come on out, my friend. I know I heard that pretty voice of yours."

I squeezed my eyes shut, hoping to be invisible. She had to have been mere feet away, just on the other side of the wall. I didn't speak, I didn't breathe, I didn't so much as think.

"She's over here!" Lorelai shouted. *True.*

"Run."

I listened. I ran for my very life.

I could not tell if the prince trailed behind as the forest became a blur of snow and trees. I just ran. I did not care how much noise I made, how many people saw me fleeing. I ran to the far end of the wall, barely slowing to turn the corner. Heavens above, there were so many people between me and the castle entrance.

There, dozens of yards away, stood Lorelai. I remembered her long red hair, now tucked back into braids. I remembered her gentle cruelty. One of the hands that she'd used in a mock attempt to comfort me held a sword that had long since been bloodied. A handful of the men had answered her call, and they noticed me at the same moment she did. If I could just make it past them, I could get into the castle. If I could get into the castle, we could figure out a better plan. But it was so far, and I was armed with only knives.

Knives it would have to be, then.

Three on my ribs, one on each arm, one on each leg. Seven blades.

I took two from my ribs in each hand. Lorelai's men charged towards me, and I kept running. In the few heartbeats I had to plan before they met me, I came up with absolutely nothing.

You do not want to be gutted, Mekhi had said. *Your body knows that.*

My body did, very much so, know that.

But I didn't want to kill them if I didn't have to.

Two men reached me first. Their swords were sharp and daunting, but clunky. I sent one of my knives flying at one of their shoulders, and it hit his arm instead. It was enough, still, for him to cry out behind the wooden mask and to release his weapon.

Six.

The other was undeterred. When he made a large, sweeping motion to cut me in half, I slid to the ground and buried a blade in the back

237

of his ankle. He screamed out in agony. He turned to follow, but I'd severed the tendon. He'd live if he dealt with it soon.

Five.

I shoved myself up back to a stand. Dirt had lodged itself in my freshly bleeding wound, but I was *alive*. Alive, and running right for two more masked men. Their fury emanated through the thin pane of wood that covered their faces. I grabbed the final knife at my ribs, sending it soaring towards them.

I missed.

Four.

I slid the blades out from either wrist. When the men finally met me, I did not wait for them to try to strike. I wedged my knife as deep into one of their hips as I could manage.

Three.

When the other came in defense of his friend, I sliced through the leather of his tunic and aimed to tear through a portion of his shoulder. He jerked and I missed. The blade landed in his chest instead. His eyes widened and his sword clattered in the snow. My breath caught.

I'd never killed anyone before.

Two.

I couldn't afford to stop.

That only left Lorelai and two of her men standing in my way. I was one blade short. There was a wall on one side of them, and more of their companions on the other. I would have to go through them, or not at all. I paused only to snatch the blades from each leg. Two blades, and three people. I'd fought before, but not like this. *Nothing like this.*

I barely danced out of the way of one of the men's sweeping blows. Depths, he was fast. He struck again, and again, and it was all I could do not to be sliced in half as I stepped back, and back, and back. Only for half a second, was there an opening at his back. I lunged to reach a dagger firmly into his shoulder blade, but he elbowed me straight down onto the ground. The knife I'd almost used to stab him with flew out of my reach.

One.

His sword sailed up, up, up. The world slowed.

When the blade came crashing down, the prince of Lyscott met it just in time.

I scrambled out of Mekhi's way. He met my attacker for every strike, targeting the other man in between exchanges. His coordination looked almost choreographed in how precise the prince was. He gave up no opening, offered them no chance to land an attack.

While I was busy watching, the sharp edge of a blade pierced the back of my neck.

I froze.

"Get up, please."

Slowly, carefully, I obeyed.

"Drop your knife. I will have you cutting through no more of my men." *True.*

I hesitated, and Lorelai dug the sword deeper until I could feel the trickling stream of blood. Only then did I do as she asked, watching as my very last form of defense clattered on the icy soil. Mekhi had gotten pulled further into the fight. He would not save me.

"Good," she crooned, dragging the blade from the back of my neck to just below my chin and she circled to stand in front of me. As she pushed it towards me, I had no choice but to slowly take retreating steps. "*There you are. The frightened thing I first met. Heavens above, I worried that our entire friendship had been a lie.*" *True.*

"We are *not* friends." I bit.

She pouted, "That hurts my feelings." I tripped into the wall. I could walk back no further, and she stopped pressing. "I've heard so much about you, Selah. Some about Prince Haven and his soldier, but so very much about you." *True.* She tilted my chin up with her sword. "I know that you think yourselves to be *blessed.* I know that the Eloran royal family thinks that Lukoh has given you abilities as gifts. Oh, to be so thoroughly fooled."

I trained my mind and every bit of focus I had towards her. *Please, if there was ever a time for that new gift to come out. Please work. Please work.*

"Lukoh wants his power back. I have come to bring you to him."

True.

Well, depths.

Lorelai stared at me with manufactured pity. "Oh, don't be so glum. You are a worthy sacrifice. I wish your death would be a painless one, but everyone knows that there's only one way to kill the cursed." *True.*

"*What?*" I choked. *People believe that?* That wasn't a thing. I could die like anyone else. Someone had exhaustively lied to her, and she had bought it.

She pulled her brows together. "I think it's rather poetic. How do you disinfect an area that's been riddled with disease?" Lorelai trailed the sword down to my stomach, something lighting up in her eyes as she knowingly grinned. "With fire."

Please, please, please.

"That's a lie," I started, my traitorous voice breaking. "We are no less human than you. I can die from all sorts of things."

For a moment, she paused. I was stupid enough to allow a small bit of hope to spring up. Maybe she had come to her senses. Maybe she believed me.

"You really do think that, don't you?" she asked.

I nodded, pulling back as far into the wall as it allowed.

Lorelai Elsborough leaned in close enough to where I could feel her warm breath on my cheek. For a moment, in the midst of all of the chaos around us, it was only me, the sword, and the lethal woman who held it.

"*Watch.*"

She buried her blade into my side.

The pain was all-consuming, unlike anything I'd ever known. It was fire and ice and liquid agony all in the very same breath. My cry was drowned out in the noise of the other raging battles. Her weapon pierced all the way through me.

When she yanked the sword back out, I crumbled. The ground was more than willing to meet me as I fell. I held a hand to my leaking wound, feeling the warm blood leech past my fingers while my other palm braced against the frozen dirt.

"See? That's not so –"

Finally, all too late, that ancient feeling returned. The humming of power beneath my skin had made an appearance at last. I peered up at Lorelai. Her eyes had glazed over, unseeing in the way they'd had been in the forest. My gift had not abandoned me, it just had not come in time.

"Drop it."

The sword clanked against the ground.

"Sit," I breathed.

She listened.

With a heavy shove, I pushed myself against the stone wall. If I could stand, if I could only get inside, then Gen could heal me. The entrance door was so far away. Blood, hot and sticky, had spread across my fingers and my clothing.

And Heavens above, I was so tired.

I was so, very tired.

Chapter Twenty-Four: Haven

His fear woke me before his voice did.

It wasn't the first time I'd felt my brother's fear. It was rarely so sharp, rarely as poignant as what I was roused by. When I opened my eyes, though, only Gen and Elliott were in the room. My sister sat on the desk in the corner, muttering with Elliott in hushed voices as he sat in the chair. They looked peaceful, far more peaceful than what I was sensing.

Gen noticed my stare. "Haven! How are you feel –"

"Get the door." I croaked, the sleep having not fully left my voice.

A second later, there was pounding on the old wooden frame. My sister hopped down from her perch to answer it. As soon as Alaric entered the room, his fear became much stronger. I reigned my gift back in as I began to get up from my bed. The room spun, but not as bad as it had been that morning.

Alaric's face was pale, and he was noticeably shaken as he surveyed the area. "Where's Selah?"

"Why?" I stood.

"What's wrong?" Gen pressed, sensing what I had.

My brother began digging through the various trunks Selah and I had brought from Distin. "The Illustri are coming. A scary amount of them, too. I saw it. Where is Selah?"

243

"She went to meet the king," my sister answered.

Alaric gritted his teeth together, "And where would that put her?" He paused his search. "Why did none of us bring enough weapons?"

I opened a different crate. There was but a single blade. We really hadn't brought enough weapons if the Illustri were on their way. In our defense, it wasn't exactly diplomatic to enter a foreign nation with crates full of swords. "They were meant to be in the garden."

Alaric scoffed as he stood, "Of course they were in the garden. Why would they be anywhere other than the garden? Lukoh forbid they be *inside* when the castle is besieged."

Distantly, a voice called out. The words were Lyscottian. Gen may have caught the meaning if she were a little closer. I didn't understand, but my brother would.

If possible, he dulled further.

"Focus, Alaric." Elliott finally intervened, jaw set. "What did you see?"

Alaric sighed heavily, looking anywhere but at me. "They are coming from all sides. The advisor's wife keeps them from getting into the castle, at least as far as I saw, but at a cost. I only got a brief glimpse of Selah, but..."

My heart clenched. "But what?"

Finally, he met my eyes. "You need to go get her."

I grabbed the nearest pair of boots.

"Wait," Elliott argued. "You are the prince of Elora, Haven. You cannot just go out and fight in a battle that is not your own. I will go get Selah. Stay with Alaric and Gen."

I laced my second shoe. "I will not bother to justify that with a response."

"What weapon will you fight with? We have one sword between the four of us, and I will not let you go unarmed."

I stood to my full height. "There is a training room in this castle which has walls decorated with every type of blade. I doubt anyone will mind." I glanced back at my brother, handing him the sword I'd brought. "Where did you see her?"

"By the main entrance. But Haven –"

"We're going. Stay together, lock the door behind us, and *do not leave this room*."

And so we went.

We had to have passed half a dozen Lyscottian guards as we ran, each of them more shaken than the last. When we did make it to the training room, much of what had been on the walls was picked clean. Regardless, I managed to snatch a blade from its shelf and handed another to Elliott. They were lighter than what was standard in Elora. Were they really just made for decoration? I prayed they'd hold up.

"Go," I urged Elliott. He was blessed to be faster by miles, and I only served to slow him down.

"I will go nowhere without you."

"Well, I'm not hopping on your back, and we are running out of time. You may be able to finish the battle before I get there."

"Haven –"

"*That is an order*, Lieutenant Colonel."

He pursed his lips in unabashed distaste before darting off. Let him be irritated if it meant more of us lived through the day. I sprinted behind him, only vaguely knowing my way through the jarringly vast castle. Heavens above, at least if the Illustri *did* make it inside, they would get lost well before they made it to Gen and Alaric.

245

They will not *be making it to Gen and Alaric.*

By the time I made it to the palace entrance, the battle was raging. Of course Alaric knew that it was the Illustri. They wore those awful wooden masks. Wren too, like my brother said, was posted by the door. Weariness crept into the very edges of her features, but other than that, she appeared entirely composed. Her hands were clasped in front of her as she watched the fighting with a grim expression. She was just standing there, the door wide open, anyone able to walk right in if they made it past the Lyscottians.

An arrow flew at us, deflecting off a wall I had not seen.

I breathlessly thanked her as I crashed through the barrier.

In the distance, Elliott had taken to defending Mekhi, who was holding his own against a small barrage of attackers. The Lyscottian soldiers were fighting hard, but the amount of people the Illustri had brought with them was borderline overwhelming. Most hadn't gotten close to the castle, but they were pressing in.

I scanned the field for Selah. I didn't see her in the most brutal areas of the fighting, which was good. She wasn't next to Mekhi and if Elliott had found her, he wasn't with her anymore. *Depths.* But Alaric had said –

I saw the red hair first.

There they were, Lorelai's sword to Selah's throat, backed up against the wall. Lorelai must have been speaking, because the woman made no move as Selah glared. Where was there for her to escape to?

A man broke past the Lyscottians, running at me with a war cry in his throat. I sidestepped his wide blow and dug my sword in his side. Were these civilians? They certainly didn't fight like soldiers.

246

I felt Selah's fear, jarring and unique, from across the field. Lorelai's sword had lowered to Selah's stomach. She was still pinned to the wall, and there was nowhere for her to go without the risk of being gutted.

No.

I bolted towards her, carving through the men that stood in my way. Their swings were wide and usually predictable. Internally, I was grateful for every bit of training the General Pearce had shoved down my throat after the first attack. I remembered the exhaustion from training and thinking I'd never truly need it.

I had nearly reached her when I had to duck to avoid a barrage of arrows. Where were they coming from? They'd hit a few of their own men but plenty of Lyscottian soldiers. If we could get to the archers –

A shrill cry pierced through the garden.

Selah.

There she was, covered in blood, fighting to stand but barely moving. But it was Lorelai who knelt down before her, red-soaked sword fallen to the ground. Lorelai's eyes were foggy and distant, exactly the way they'd been in the forest. Selah was deathly pale. She clutched her side where blood leaked through her fingers. *No.*

I have never moved faster.

I slid to Selah's side. She had been stabbed, nearly gutted, the wound red and angry and unrelenting. Her face was tear-stained, her eyes were closing, and her breath was faint. Bodies had fallen around her, each wearing those pathetic, wicked wooden masks. I hated them. I hated them more than I knew I was capable of.

Selah fell easily into my arms. Her body wracked with a quiet sob when I brushed the hair out of her sweat-slickened forehead. "It's okay," she breathed harshly, "I'm okay."

My finger skimmed her skin, and it was agony. Raw, unbridled agony coursed through me for an excruciating moment. It felt like I was dying. It felt like *she* was dying. "You are. You will be." I was convincing both of us.

"You are –," she winced, "the worst liar – I've ever met."

Her eyes closed.

When I looked up, the battle still raged. Elliott was finishing off the last of the Illustri nearby, but the Lyscottian soldiers were defending the castle from the side. Mekhi rushed past us to join them, pausing only when he saw Selah bleeding in my grasp. His stoic face fell, "No."

"*Lock her up*, Mekhi. Now." My voice was little more than a hiss. I nodded to Lorelai, standing and taking Selah with me. Holding her was crippling. I could filter out some of her pain, some of her exhaustion and desperation, but not enough to keep me steady. I tucked her in closer.

He nodded, and I turned to Elliott. He was with me now, the same sort of heartbreak written all over his face. "Defend the castle, Elliott. *Do not let them in*. Do you understand?"

He looked back at me, entirely the soldier. "Go, Haven. I've got it."

I ran.

Time had never moved slower as I sprinted to the castle's entrance. Her pain was dulling by the second. It was an achingly terrible sign. If her pain was dulling, then she was fading, and if she was fading, then she was going to die.

I crossed over the threshold, and felt the after effects of Wren's ward. It was like stepping through a pane of invisible water that left you dry. I registered that she was there by the door, but took the time for nothing else. I had the time for nothing else. My companion, my ally, *my friend* was going to die if I didn't move.

When I reached our door, I pounded my fist against it over and over and over again. It was Alaric who opened it, sword in hand, who balked when he saw me. I shoved him out of the way as gently as I could manage, and set the now unconscious Selah on our bed.

Gen was there in a heartbeat, hands glowing with her gift. "Heavens above. There's so much blood. I don't –" Gen took a deep breath. "There's so much," she whispered. Her hands hovered over Selah's body, but nothing was changing.

"Is it working?"

"Quiet."

"*Is it working?*" I demanded. My hands were sticky from her blood and the blood of the soldiers I fought. She couldn't die. I would not allow it.

"Let me focus!" Gen's brows pulled together as she stared at the girl I shared the room with. The one I'd stolen from a prison and taken halfway across the continent. The girl who stared up at me with those beautiful eyes and said she wished I was her friend.

I could not fall apart, for I could not breathe well enough to even try.

The minutes crawled. I held Selah's hand while Gen worked. She wasn't dead. Air came and left her, but it was consistently too brief to be comforting. Elliott joined us eventually, cuffs stained and sword sheathed. Elliott held a hand on Gen's back, looking over her shoulder as she worked.

He stared at me with equal parts sorrow and hope in his eyes, "She'll be okay."

I would've taken some comfort in that, had I not been able to sense his fear as if it were my own. Had I not been so ill, had I just entertained the king myself, Selah would've been safely inside the castle when the Illustri struck. Sure, I may have been attacked instead, but I'd been *trained* for combat. I'd lived through it. Elliott would have come, and everything would have been fine. Selah warned me over and over again that we should leave, and my ignorance earned her injury.

I wondered how I would even begin to recover from my guilt if she died.

"Haven," Alaric started, "calm down."

Cold, icy wrath crept up my spine. I pulled my eyes up to his. "I'm sorry?"

"Can anyone else feel that?" He asked. Elliott inhaled sharply, as though he understood.

"Is that Haven?" Elliott questioned and Alaric nodded. Gen also looked up in agreement.

Confusion and worry warred within me in equal measure. "What are you talking about?"

The crown prince of Elora explained. "Everyone in this room can sense your fear, Haven. And your anger. Calm down, and you will calm us all. Including our sister, who is working on your friend."

My friend.

I took a heavy breath, lacking the will to care more than a little.

Gen stepped back, drained, "She'll live. I put her to sleep, and she needs to stay that way. She needs to rest. She'll probably be out for the next day or so, but she'll live." She drew her eyes to mine, staring intently, "She'll live. You just need to wait."

And so I waited.

The other three hovered for a long while. Gen and Alaric retired once they were confident that Selah would keep breathing. She was, in fairness, though she was still covered in blood and dirt. None of us could decide whether she would be comfortable with Gen changing her into proper clothes, so we waited for that, too.

Elliott stayed the longest by far. He did not have much to say. I certainly didn't. He just sat with me, waiting. There was little hope that she was going to wake up until the next day or later, but he stayed. He had fallen asleep in the desk chair. It could not have been remotely comfortable if the angle of his head or the stretch of his spine were any indication, but when I tried to wake him to send him to his room, he adamantly refused and fell right back asleep.

The battle had been mostly taken care of since Elliott had returned. Most of the Illustri, at least the ones that came to Lyscott, were dead. The ones who remained, including Lorelai, were locked up in the Lyscottian dungeon. Lyscott retained more soldiers than they lost, due to the inexperience of the Illustri's mob. The soldiers that were killed died more for the sheer fact that they were outnumbered than anything. Lyscott's forces were stretched thin between the Dobric borders, and if the Illustri had been aware or not, they had that advantage.

I'd been barely a few breaths too late. I was there, moments away, when the sword cut through Selah. If I had taken any longer, that may have been it. I wouldn't have been sitting next to her and waiting for those eyes to open again. There would have been no chance for such a thing.

We had only just become friends. She had only just shifted from being on edge when I stepped in the room to calming. She only just started to like me, and then she nearly died in my arms.

I had so very much I wanted to say to her and somehow there was nothing at all. So instead, I waited.

Chapter Twenty-Five: Selah

The room was terribly bright.

Light streamed idly in through the glass windows. They were usually my favorite part of our room. I might've liked the bed a little more, too, had it not been such a point of contention. The washroom wasn't bad either with its wide, ornate mirror. The windows, though, ultimately stood uncontested. Miles upon miles of Lyscott could be viewed from the safety of the carpeted floor.

But Heavens above, was it giving me a headache.

There was a rough, warm hand clutching mine. The prince appeared to have fallen asleep at my bedside, half in his chair with his face buried in the blankets next to me. The poor thing's wild blond hair was most of what I could see, little tufts sprawling out in each and every direction. A quilt had been wrapped over his shoulders. It was only us, just how it usually was. But why was I in our bed? I never slept in our bed, and last I checked, he'd been –

Blood stained our intertwined fingers.

I remembered, then.

My free hand jerked to my side. There was surely a tear in my clothes where her blade had entered and I was covered still in a thorough amount of dried blood. I only felt the ghost of what pain might've been there. My muscles were sore, but not like they'd just been sliced in half. They ached like I slept very wrong and ran about ten miles too many. Was it Gen? I hadn't been killed, then. Certainly she couldn't pull me back from the brink of death. Could she? And Lorelai –

Haven startled awake.

Frantic amber eyes met mine. They were the very same amber eyes that had so recently stared down and lied that I was going to live. But then here I was, gazing back at him.

"Hello," his voice was rough and quiet and almost reverent.

"Hello," mine was hardly more than a whisper.

The prince shifted in his chair, sitting upright. "Welcome back."

Welcome back?

"Can't have been too long."

He used his open hand to rub the sleep, and perhaps some amount of worry, out of his face. "Two days, give or take." *True.*

Two days? It felt like minutes. I guess, when facing eternity, everything feels a little bit shorter. "I'm not dead."

"You're not dead." *True.*

"You thought I was gonna die."

"I told you quite the opposite, actually."

"Did anyone –"

Haven shook his head. "No one we know." *True. Good.*

"And Lorelai?"

"In a cell. From what I understand, she's had nothing especially coherent to say. Elliott and Mekhi have been with her. I've been..." he trailed off, looking anywhere but at me. "I've been here. I'm not sure what she's said." *True.*

He'd waited with me for two days. That's a long time to sit in the same chair, especially if the bed really was big enough for us both to fit.

The prince had yet to let go of my hand. I could not very well remember a time where a man had held my hand just for the sake of holding it. But there we were, the prince of Elora clasping so tightly onto me. No one had ever cared like that, much less cared enough to stay with me for so long. People had been kind, but never that kind. At least, if I had died, I would not have been alone. I would've been with the closest friend I'd ever had.

Depths, I wanted a hug. I wanted to cry. He was so very close, and I wanted to kiss him until I could forget every tragic thing that happened. I could lose myself in him, maybe, if I tried hard enough. Then I wouldn't have to think about any of it. For a moment, I failed to remember why I ever wanted him far away. I liked him close. He smelled of cedar and cinnamon and warmth and safety.

His face shifted from worry to wanting to careful reservation. The worry made another fierce appearance when I moved to sit up. *"Selah –"*

The movement hurt, but I would not die. Apparently, I was not so easy to kill. My muscles screamed in protest as I turned to face him. I kept his hand securely in mine, slipped my legs in between his, and looked at my prince. His brows were deeply furrowed but he made no effort to move away from me.

"You normally don't feel like this," he whispered. Of course he could sense what I felt. I still kept his hand.

"I know," my voice was just as quiet as his as I moved ever so slightly closer to kissing him.

"You just almost *died*, Selah. This is not the time for –" He didn't move towards me, but still he didn't pull back.

"It certainly feels like the time." We were mere breaths away.

I could feel his eyes on me. "Your emotions are all over the place. I cannot in good conscience –"

"If you do not want me, Highness, all you have to do is say so."

Rough fingers gently tilted my chin up until my gaze was forced to his. "Wanting you has nothing to do with it and it is cruel to use my title in that tone when I have to tell you no." The prince raggedly sighed. "Heavens above, Selah. Give it a day. If this is what you want then, I will offer you whatever you ask for and more. But not today. Not when you yourself may not even know what you need."

"*Haven.*"

His pretty face was pained. His attention drifted down to my mouth and was torn back up. Idle fingers traced lines on my cheek. "Not today."

There was a knock at the door. I started towards it, but the prince pinned me with a glare. He took back both his hands and the skin that he'd been touching felt uncomfortably vacant. He stepped out to speak with whatever visitor, and I was left with my own thoughts.

Everything ached. It was so much stronger when he wasn't next to me. I had almost died. Yeah, I'd process that when I had time to bawl without threat of being seen. For the moment, I had Haven to deal with. I felt my cheeks heat with embarrassment. He wasn't right, I *didn't* normally feel like that. It couldn't have been his doing, right? Surely he didn't have the power to make me want him. No, of course he didn't. I'd nearly kissed him out of my own free will. And was he almost *okay* with it? I was so, so stupid. Getting stabbed may have been less drastic of a mistake.

It was a prince that crashed back into my room, just not the one I had expected.

Mekhi blanched at the sight of me. In his defense, I must have looked horrific. I could feel the blood that coated my skin and I had not bathed in days. I tried to kiss Haven like that. No wonder he told me no. I also was exhausted and sore and I could all but picture my demeanor.

His lips pressed in something akin to displeasure. "Your fiancé said you were not yet awake. You *look* rather awake."

Haven trailed behind him, also appearing less than thrilled. "It's a fairly recent development," I answered. "Can I help you with something?"

"*It's nothing –*"

Mekhi shot Haven a cold look before fixing back on me, "You can sense when people are lying, yes?"

It wasn't as if he wasn't already aware. I could try to talk my way around it, but I feared the prince of Lyscott knew better. His gift also happened to be really scary, and I was in no position to hold my ground, "Yes."

Both princes wore similarly unenthusiastic expressions but still Mekhi continued. "The Elsborough woman is downstairs. Most of what she's said is utter nonsense. I need you to come down and see if you can discern anything useful."

Haven shifted so that he stood between me and the Lyscottian prince. I did not know if I resented the little gesture, or if I enjoyed his coming to my defense. "She's been awake for *three minutes.* She is still exhausted and she's still in pain. Heavens above, you can at least let her rest a bit longer."

Mekhi postured slightly taller, though even then he barely reached Haven's height, "Does your fiancée always insist that you speak for her?"

My prince's head tilted ever so gently, his arms remaining firmly crossed over his chest, "Which fiancée? The one who was nearly killed under your care?"

"*Watch it –*"

"Enough," I braced a hand against my side and stood. The skin was red and angry through my torn clothes but at the very least it was intact. "I need half an hour to get cleaned up and dressed. Then I can join you."

Haven reached for my fingers, but I grabbed his forearm instead. At least there, his shirt acted as a barrier. I did not need him to know how I felt. I would be going down to speak with Lorelai regardless.

Mekhi did not wait around for me to change my mind. He left without any further remarks, though even I felt the heat of Haven's glare. My roommate, however, said nothing to me. The prince of Elora merely watched as I began to prepare myself.

I showered alone, of course, taking slightly longer than I'd told Mekhi. In fairness, scrubbing dried blood and caked-on dirt out of my hair was more difficult than I initially anticipated. When I was back in the main area, I sensed the prince's gaze on me yet again. It was heavy and poignant and required unprecedented amounts of self-control to ignore.

At first, all I spared him was a sidelong glance. My curls were especially unruly, after all, and required pointed attention. Muscles in my arms I didn't even realize existed ached with each stroke of my hairbrush, though I carefully tucked away every pained expression. The prince was overbearing enough as he was, I would offer him no more ammunition.

I would, however, offer my opinion, "You have an entire room to stare at, Highness. I fear the pillows may begin to resent me if you neglect them much longer."

My prince didn't miss a beat, "The pillows are not recovering from a near-fatal injury and insisting they question their attempted murderer, or I assure you they'd receive the same attention."

I did face him then, "I'm fine, Haven."

"Okay."

He lacked the enthusiasm I'd hoped for.

"And the sooner we get this over with, the sooner you can send people to Mallord Bay and never have to worry about creepy cult members ever again."

"I'm not stopping you, Selah." He extended a hand, "Shall we?"

And off we went. Walking down the flights of stairs was a feat of willpower. I was unaware that my legs could be so sore. The one that had been cut was exceptionally strained. I was forced to take my time, eyeing each step and gripping on to the handrail for dear life. The prince's lips were pursed in steady distaste, but he did not rush or demand to cart me away.

I was allowed plenty of space to appreciate the paintings that lined the walls. Much like most of the other Lyscottian artwork I'd seen, the paintings were framed in silver. I'd never been inside a museum as a child. Not only did I deeply lack interest, but I'd never been of the social standing where I had the time to revel in such things. Then, perhaps. My gift had made me wealthy enough and I could go on pretending to be engaged to the prince for as long as it benefitted me, I supposed. I'd read about artwork and seen distorted depictions of famous paintings in churches. I'd just never sat and stared before. Could paintings be as terrible in their beauty as Lyscott and Elora? Perhaps when I returned home, I'd purchase one to hang on my wall.

Perhaps I could talk the prince into buying one for me.

But then, I feared, I would look at it and think of him instead of appreciating the artistry. *Appreciating artistry?* I inwardly gaped at myself. It was hardly something I used to care about. I cared about feeding myself and surviving. I certainly never cared for someone enough to wish for their safety as I'm bleeding to death or waking up hoping they're alright.

He was my friend. Just a friend, but a friend, nonetheless. Maybe it was better that way. I had no interest in the disappointment a relationship would offer. He'd be a pretty distraction, sure. Visualizing his hands on me was, alarmingly, not as difficult as it should've been.

The Lyscottian dungeons were colder than the Eloran Vaults I'd been held inside. In Elora, yellow light from torches at least hinted at warmth. The Lyscottian dungeons were steel and ice, daylight filtering through cracks in the carved glacier. How did they possibly see at night? Fire would melt the ice, and unless the palace had a secret light wielder that I was not aware of, the guards would be blind if the moon was covered. Maybe they liked the mystery of it all.

Mekhi met us in the very first hallway full of frozen cells and led us down a series of corridors. Even though we had to have passed a dozen different doors, I only could make out faint outlines through walls of metal and solid ice. A steady hand on my back hurried me further along, probably hoping to get this over with as soon as possible.

Abruptly, the prince of Lyscott stopped at a cell door. A set of keys appeared in his hand, but he paused before reaching the lock. "She may be shackled, but stay out of reach. I will not let her touch you, but she has proven herself to be…" he trailed off, staring behind us towards quickly approaching footsteps.

"Unpredictable," Elliott finished, catching his breath. Strange for him to be running late with that supernatural speed he was blessed with.

259

Quickly, he scanned me, lips parting in something close to shock, "You look... alive."

I smirked. I feared that was high praise coming from the lieutenant colonel. "How could Lorelai possibly hide anything from you when you have such a way with words?"

Elliott frowned, "I liked you better unconscious."

Mekhi unlocked the cell door.

Lorelai looked oddly ethereal, even chained to a wall. The red braids that fell around her appeared to have been placed with care. Her hands, still stained with blood that was probably half mine, were folded neatly in front of her. Hazel eyes peered up through long, dark eyelashes and unblemished skin. Even her posture, sitting straight up with legs crossed beneath her, looked to be of a forgotten statue of a long-lost deity. No wonder she led. She was compelling. Totally insane, but compelling.

She stared at each of us until Mekhi sealed the door shut. It was then that her gaze settled on me. She smiled, perfect lips spreading gently, and my stomach churned, "Selah."

Never in a thousand lifetimes would I offer her the satisfaction of getting under my skin, especially after she almost killed me. I grinned steadily back, cold enough to war with the ice around us. Heavens above, my bones would freeze if we lingered. "Elsborough. Long time. What brings you to Lyscott?"

"You do, Lovely." *True.* She leaned in as if she was telling me something sacred. "I told you that you wouldn't die. I was correct, was I not?"

Haven hovered behind me, Elliott's hand resting idly on his own sword to the prince's right. Mekhi was leaning up against the door, head cocked in observation. His cold eyes were narrow and set on his prisoner.

260

I made quite the show of thinking. "Oh yes, if I recall, you mentioned something about needing us as burnt offerings."

Her chin tilted almost an imperceivable amount. Innocence rang in every feature. In another life, would I have fallen prey to her ruse? Would Haven?

"Lukoh is not pleased. Your deaths would restore balance. Your very existence is fueling Akar's return."

True. I nodded in confirmation.

Mekhi stiffened while the rest of us stood in poorly-contained shock.

Lorelai's brow furrowed, "Were you not aware?"

Haven finally stepped in, moving to my side. "Akar is nothing more than a fairytale." *Lie.* Oh.

Her stare shifted to him, jarring in its intensity. "He is as real as you and I, Prince. He is as real as the red that coated your hands while you held her bleeding body. Tell me, could you sense her agony? Did you know she would live, or did you pray to a god that would not answer you?"

Haven paled, handsome face pained.

"*Enough –*" I started.

"Were you more afraid then, or when I threatened to burn her alive?"

I stepped in front of my prince. "You are talking to me. You are not talking to him. You can answer my questions, or we'll let you rot."

"What do you want to know, Selah, that you cannot demand from me without my consent? Without my knowledge?" Her voice adopted a harsh bitterness that nearly set me back a step. But she *had* forgotten, which meant Adiel likely had as well. "You will die. It is your destiny. It is divine will. There are more than double the forces that accompanied me

261

here that are ready to take your life. They will bring you back to Mallord Bay from anywhere in the world you choose to hide. Your prince will beg for my people to show you mercy before they kill him too. A god wants you dead," Her grim expression turned to a cruel smile.

"Cain Balor wants you dead."

Cain Balor.

How could she –

There's no way.

The first man who ever hurt me.

The only one still left breathing.

A wave of emotion flooded every one of my senses. It hurt to breathe. A sob was fighting to escape my throat. I could vividly remember his hands still, as much as I had tried to bury the picture in my mind. Years of my life were spent forgetting everything he did, and suddenly every terrible moment replayed before my eyes. Arms reaching for me. The smell of sweat and salty tears. The sound of his laughter as I cried. The pool of blood he left in his wake. The tone of his voice as he announced how I should be thankful he wanted me when no one else would.

When I could see through the cloud in front of me, Lorelai's eyes were foggy. My gift had taken over. She would not see me fall apart. She would not even be aware if I did.

I mustered what strength I had left into my voice, and even then it came out quieter than I would have liked. "Prince Mekhi and Elliott are going to speak with you. You will tell them everything they want to know with as much detail as they require. Do you understand?"

I finally noticed Haven's hand in mine.

Lorelai nodded.

"Let me out, please."

262

Mekhi unlocked the door just long enough for me and Haven to pass through. I braced myself against a cool wall, battling to squeeze air into my lungs.

My prince was there in a second, palms cradling either side of my face. "Breathe. I'm right here with you."

The concern in his eyes broke me right in half.

My body wracked with messy, incoherent sobs. I could explain nothing. I didn't try. He didn't ask me to. The prince of Elora, second in line to the throne, held on to me as hot tears fell onto his shoulder. A royal hand idly rested on the back of my head while another traced circles along my spine.

I just cried. From the very depths of my being, I cried

Chapter Twenty-Six: Haven

"I can't believe that you didn't call me the *second* you realized my patient was awake. I *needed* to see her!" my sister whispered angrily.

Genevieve's foot was fiercely tapping just outside my door. Selah had fallen right into bed after seeing Lorelai. If the near-death experience hadn't been enough to knock her back out, using her ability certainly would do the trick. Shoes and all, eyes still puffy, she'd collapsed.

As we walked back, Selah had been notably quiet. We didn't wait around for Elliott and Mekhi to finish their conversation; we'd be told what happened in time. She'd grimaced at the damp spot on my shoulder to which I paid absolutely no mind. Why would it matter when I could feel her distress as if it were my own? Would I always remember what her pain felt like? Physically, it had been excruciating, but emotional agony was a different kind of torture.

"I'll come get you later, Gen. She needs to rest."

My sister's features contorted into an expression between concern and frustration. She peered around me at Selah's sleeping figure. Her feelings were never as poignant as Selah's or mellow as Elliott's, but there was a steadiness to them that I could make out in a crowd. Then, her emotions existed as a low hum of worry and irritation and an enduring sense of conflict.

She sighed, less than content, but retiring her argument. "The moment – *the breath* – anything changes, send for me. She's better now, but her body has been through more in a day than many endure in their lifetime. She's not out of the woods just yet."

When I'd nearly spent myself reassuring her that everything would be fine, she left with a less than reserved huff and a promise that she'd return. My roommate was little more than a mess of curls sprawled out in every direction. Once I was really looking, her face was slightly more red than I'd remembered and, faintly, I could see that she was shivering.

I paced the few steps to the nearest blanket and laid it over her with careful fingers. Briefly, I debated whether to take her shoes off. It couldn't be comfortable. Also, no one who can sleep well with shoes on is trustworthy. I supposed I could make an exception. Aside from that, if she woke up to it, I feared stabbing me was not entirely out of the question.

Gently, I brushed the back of my hand against her forehead. I was hot and cold and my whole body hurt all at once. That was new. She hadn't had a fever when she woke up, but she had been sick just before our first encounter with Lorelai. We had so much to figure out. Between her gift and mine and Elliott's and the Lyscottian king and the Illustri, my thoughts threatened to turn into a puddle.

Gen was right, maybe I should've let her take a look at Selah while she was awake. But she'd been better then. Well, she'd been better until meeting with Lorelai. Then everything got chaotic. I was there, in the cell, and even then, I couldn't stop her from getting under our skin.

A thumping knock at the door pushed back the guilt that loomed on the horizon.

Gen already? She'd wasted no time at all. Except, when I moved to greet her, it was not my sister at all. Instead, it was a windblown and visibly irritated Lyscottian prince.

"What happened?" I asked first.

His lips pursed in restrained frustration, "We need to talk."

The prince pushed past me into our room. It was the second time that day he'd shoved me aside. Anger bubbled for a passing moment. When he brushed my shoulder, though, I felt the anxiety that rippled off him. He spared a glance at Selah but stayed fixed on me until the door was shut.

When he spoke again, his voice was low and quiet. "You have to leave."

"Why?"

"It's not safe," he dragged an impatient hand through his hair. "It wasn't safe the second you stepped foot into the palace. I warned her already, but clearly that was not enough. On top of the inherent risk of your mere existence, half a cult followed you to my country and the other half is pissed about it. Go back to Distin. Your father's armies will be able to protect you in a way that mine is currently incapable of."

"The *inherent risk* of our existence?" It was a diplomatic journey. Our countries were at peace. There should be no 'inherent risk'.

"I have given you all the information that I am able. Pack your things. Get within your borders. Remember this kindness when you are home."

"We can't leave yet, Mekhi. Selah is in no shape to travel. Your king has hardly been introduced to my siblings. My father has yet to write back. Your nation is at war. Do you not need our help?"

"*Of course* we need your help." His voice raised, still quiet enough. "But things can – and will – get worse for you if you stay. Wait a day. Use your healer. Then you need to leave."

A new, slower hand pounded at our door, and Mekhi paled.

"It's just Gen."

"I assure you, it is not." He scanned the room, eyes fixing on the washroom entryway. "I'm really not supposed to be here."

"Go ahead."

The hand thumped again.

It took less than a breath for the prince to conceal himself and just about that same amount of time for me to crack open the door. Exactly as Mekhi had suspected, Nero stood in the hall. His spine was locked straight, his hands folded neatly in front of him, somehow peering as though I was beneath him despite the fact that I was at least three inches taller. His dark hair was meticulously slicked back in a way mine only was when I attended funerals.

Nero grinned, features full of ice, "Good evening, Prince Haven. May I come in?"

He moved to step past me, but I braced a hand in the doorway. "Evening. I'm afraid my fiancée is sound asleep, or I'd be more than happy to accommodate. Is there something I can help you with?"

With prying eyes, he squinted over my shoulder. Something about the gesture didn't sit quite right. Her guard was entirely down, and he was staring at her like a foreign puzzle. My irritation was both immediate and unprecedentedly noticeable. My gift took over when he was close enough. He was only slightly less annoyed than I felt, and something else that I didn't recognize. That wasn't normal. I recognized most emotions after

267

nearly a decade of sensing them. It carried the same gnawing beat of desperation without the panic.

I stepped in his path imperceptibly more.

"I'm looking for the prince. He's late for a meeting." Nero's gaze was still fixed on my room.

"You could check the dungeon. He was there with Lorelai just a few hours ago. A meeting at this hour, though? Is something wrong?"

Finally, I captured his attention. "Nothing of note. Who am I to question the king's timing?" Pattering, quick footsteps padded towards us. My sister, no doubt. Even blind, I could recognize her gait. Nero noticed, and his steady frustration flashed. He smiled at her when she turned the corner, "Your Highness."

She grinned, much more convincing than the Lyscottian advisor. "Evening, Nero. Is everything alright?"

"Do all of the Eloran royals fret so much?" he asked, his chuckle sounding more like a wheeze than a laugh. "All is well. In fact, I'm running late. Dream well, both of you. I'm sure the king will be eager to meet soon," with a nod and a bow, he was off.

I tugged my sister carefully into our room, sealing and locking the door behind us. Silently, I sent up a prayer that we'd receive no more visitors.

"That was odd," my sister muttered, taking a seat on the bed next to Selah. Somehow, she was still fully asleep and unbothered. "That was more than he's said to me, I suppose, ever. And he tried humor. I didn't like that."

I rounded the corner to the washroom to tell Mekhi that Nero had left. The washroom was empty. No sign of the prince even remained, not an item moved from where Selah or I had left it. There wasn't a secret entrance to our washroom, was there? Heavens above, maybe we did need to leave.

"Haven?"

Confusion must have been written on my face. "It's…" I started, but then I'd have to try to explain about Mekhi, and then why he was here, and then that Nero was looking for him, but *why was* Nero even looking for him? I had nothing to tell her. "It's nothing."

Alaric. He had to know something, right? What good is a seer if he can't – well – see? He would be able to confirm whether or not we should stay in Lyscott. "I need to speak with Alaric. Can you –

"She has a *fever*, Haven. I told you to come get me," Gen began muttering to herself. "This isn't good. Could it – no, that definitely doesn't make sense. And I already – yes, that's about the same. She should be – yes, but clearly, she's not, so –"

"Genevieve."

"Yes, go. I'm going to keep her asleep for a while longer. And *I actually will* summon you if you are needed." Forcing people to rest was one of Gen's more useful abilities as a healer.

An uneasy pit in my stomach accompanied me all the way to Alaric's room. I did not run into any more advisors or flustered princes, nor did I stumble upon any member of the Lyscottian court. I hadn't even seen Elliott for most of the day, much less my brother. Alaric was not the most social of the Allicot line, which was a shame, because monarchies required lots of mingling.

While I could have knocked, there was no need to. I welcomed myself right into his quarters. He would have done the same to me, were I not sharing a room with a young lady. That bit made his unannounced entrance unseemly. Regardless, his room was familiar in the way that all the rooms in the Lyscottian palace were familiar. They were opulent, a tad heavy-handed on the use of spruce, but tasteful enough.

On Alaric's nightstand sat an almost empty glass, amber liquid in a thin layer that coated the bottom. Next to it, my brother lay fitfully snoring. I'm told seers do not sleep well. Something about night terrors and being haunted by the future apparently makes it one of the more restless giftings. Dark circles had long since made themselves at home under his eyes, and I imagined it took the booze to get him relaxed enough to doze off. An alcoholic king was usually a miserable king. Miserable kings did not lead their countries to prosperity. Alaric would be better than that. He would have to be better than that.

Momentarily, I debated whether or not to wake him. What would I ask? *'Evening, brother. See the future recently?'* No, that didn't sound right at all. And if he already wasn't sleeping well, I didn't know if I wanted him even more irritable when I announced that we may have to leave as soon as Selah recovered.

And Selah. Gen's murmurs were not comforting. Was something even more wrong? Had she not had enough? And then there was –

"Stop leering, brother. It's unsettling."

His voice was muffled between sleepiness and pillows, so it sounded more like 'shmop leeering, broher. His unhehehing.' I had been so lost in thought that I hadn't noticed him slowly wake. He regarded me out of the corner of his eye before shutting it again.

I wasn't leering! Well, I wasn't *not* leering, but that's a poor choice of verbiage.

"I needed to speak with you."

With what appeared to be great effort, he flipped over. "I've just had the most peculiar dream. What could possibly have been so dire? Did the Illustri return? Because I may need just a little more time to collect my thoughts before –"

"No, it's not that. Mekhi says it's too dangerous for us to stay here and that we need to leave. The Lyscottian king has said nothing. I've not yet heard back from our father. Nero is acting strangely. Selah was ill when we traveled here, so it is possible that she could manage, but it would certainly not be ideal. Gen is beginning to worry about her again. I…" my voice trailed. It was overwhelming. "I need to know what to do. I need to know if you've seen anything."

Alaric lit an extra lantern as he sat up straight. Long, slender fingers scrubbed the weariness from his face. It never truly left him, though he was more attentive once he was finally upright. "What did the prince say, exactly?"

I gave him a reasonably short synopsis, but he did not respond. Pensive, he sat with legs outstretched, taking in the words as I spoke. Mekhi's warning sounded bad. He hadn't even warned of any specific danger, merely that something was wrong and that we should go. But the king's grief, his anguish, his fear for his people was so thoroughly genuine. We could leave. Elora would be fine, even if we continued not to have any real relationship with Lyscott. If they lost their war, though, Dobre's armies would then be at our doorstep. Intervention may be necessary for both of our sakes, but maybe with the Illustri behind us we'd do more harm than good.

"Your timing is convenient." He scratched the back of his head, brown hair flopping around his hand. "I just saw Lyscott's battle with Dobre. We were there, as was Gen, as were Father and Mother. Even Faye, which is the piece that's bothering me. In what universe would either of our parents allow their thirteen-year-old child to enter into a warzone? It is

271

entirely unlike them. When it was you," he sighed, "it was an accident. They would've never permitted such a thing."

"Do we stay?" I asked. "If they're gonna be here regardless, it would save us a journey."

Expression now solemn, Alaric shook his head gravely. "No. We may return eventually, but the princeling was right. Something isn't adding up. My visions are usually much more vivid, but I could see nothing of the rest of the battle outside of our involvement. Selah called out the king for lying and was nearly gutted not a full day later. If that were not enough, your gifts are morphing. That, I saw clearly. Yours, Elliott's, and, Heavens above, *certainly* Selah's gifts have already begun manifesting in new ways. Are you aware that this is unheard of? Gen is not far behind, and I pray to Lukoh that he does not bless me with yet another burden. I've had quite enough." The lanterns cast shadows on his face when he looked up at me. "We need to leave. If Gen thinks Selah is fit to travel in the morning, we'll leave then. At best, maybe we'll give her an extra day. Then we need to get to Distin."

"I'm not gonna leave her."

Alaric smirked. "Very sweet, but not what I meant. We'll just have to move her anyway and accommodate her the best we can. Even if we only made it back into Eloran borders, I'd feel better. Something is stirring here, and I am not thrilled. It's making it rather difficult to get a full night's rest. But go, speak with Gen. If she's ready, we'll gather everything to set out tomorrow."

I did go speak with Gen. In positively no way was she in favor of leaving in the morning. In fact, she was almost offended that Alaric suggested such an unfeasible expedition . Something about healers not getting enough slack and how "*Obviously* our patients don't always recover. You don't allow them an hour of proper care!"

I didn't love the implication that her patient might not recover.

I didn't realize I was in the bed next to Selah until I was already half asleep. By then, I lacked the energy or the willpower to move back to my blankets on the floor. Somehow, neglecting the bed so thoroughly made it preternaturally comfortable.

A day, then. We'd have one more day in Lyscott before starting the journey back to Distin. I'd forgotten that we were even due to return. Every day in Lyscott felt like weeks at the Eloran castle, dramatic or draining or somewhere in between.

Suddenly, I was so ready to go home.

Chapter Twenty-Seven: Selah

My bed was less comfortable than I remembered.

Perhaps the time I'd spent in the Lyscottian palace had ruined me, but the mattress no longer consumed me in the way it once had. I really needed to get up. I had an appointment, didn't I? Yes, that soldier's wife. She wanted something from me. There had been a letter...

I tore myself out of the sheets. My workspace was a room over, but even as I reentered it, I didn't notice the neatly folded piece of paper. I saw the open windows, the view of the city from my balcony. If I looked closely on a clear day, I could see the Eloran palace. It was pretty, but distant and blurry. I could see the masterfully etched hardwood that decorated my desk. I could see the dozens of weapons that brandished one wall and the hundreds of books that adorned the other. Heavens above, did I love this apartment.

Finally, I picked up a piece of parchment with my name on the outside. As I opened it, the words melded together in a mess of inky handwriting. Shame. Nonetheless, the woman would arrive soon, would she not? We had an appointment scheduled for... well, sometime in the morning.

I needed to get ready. Even if the young lady truly did not care how I looked, it often paid to appear somewhat professionally. A braid, at the very least, as well as some suitable clothing-

Knock, knock.

Well, then.

My feet padded along the stretch of rug that led me to the front door. The woman appeared frenzied, hands wringing and teeth chattering despite the warm weather. I was sure I must have said something to her, but I didn't quite remember what. She paced right in, and I sealed the door shut behind us.

"He's coming." The woman didn't dare to speak above a whisper.

"Who?"

"He –"

My front door rattled in place, the handle twisting like it was fighting against an outside force.

"Please," the woman begged. I couldn't make out any of her facial features, or her clothes. She grasped my hands, and yet I could not discern the hue of her fingertips. "You have to help me. I don't have – I need –"

The door shook again.

"It's okay. You're okay." I squeezed her hand before letting go, crossing the distance between me and the closest sword that hung on my wall. "Hide under the table."

She wasted no time at all. From underneath, she still could see my every movement, but she was partially hidden from sight behind the dining room chairs. They were remarkably comfortable chairs, from what I recalled, and also provided ample cover.

The door shuttered for a third time, and finally I looked through the peephole. The street stood empty on the other end of the thin piece of glass. There was nothing. But how – ?

"He's here," the woman whispered.

I turned to check, but my apartment was just as vacant as it was before. "I don't see him. Maybe –"

One final time, I looked through the peephole. Two harsh, beady eyes stared back at me. I jumped back, nearly dropping my sword and tripping over the rug. I moved to stand up, to barricade the door –

There he was, as real as the day I ran.

"Hello, Selah."

I jerked awake.

Hands reached for me.

A blur of motion followed.

Then, there we were. My breaths were somewhere between pants and heaving tears. The knife that I had buried underneath my pillow was resting on the edge of the prince's neck, the hilt somehow caught in my white-knuckled grip. Haven was flat on his back, with either of my knees pinned to either side of his chest. Faintly, the lines of his face were visible in the moonlight. His brows drew together as he looked up at me.

There was no panic. No fear that my hand would slip and end his life. Concern, yes. But he was not staring at my grip, or eyeing the blade, or squirming out from where I'd pinned him. There were only those same amber eyes staring right at mine, through mine, as if he understood.

"It's alright."

True.

The words were so quiet, so gentle, they were little more than a breath. Haven was always gentle.

I tossed the knife like a curse. In the darkness, I could not be entirely sure where it ended up, but the soft clatter was a sign that it landed somewhere safe. Choking on a sob, I melted right into my prince. Two warm, steady arms wrapped straight around me with no hesitation. In one fluid motion, he sat and positioned me in his lap. It had been ages since

I had been held, and never for the sole sake of comfort. Heavens above, and I had nearly stabbed him.

"I'm sorry," I squeaked, most of the tears having subsided.

His hands settled around my waist, one tracing circles on my back. "Nothing to apologize for. *I'm* sorry. I didn't mean to scare you." *True.*

We were silent for a few moments. I stared off into Lyscott, searching for lights coming from the village. At that hour, though, there were none.

Haven's next words came out unusually timid, "Are you always afraid when I am near you?"

I shifted to where I could see his face, "What?"

"When we met in the prison, I felt your fear. Then in the carriage. Then when we stayed at the inn. Then when we stayed in this room the first night. Then the next seven times that I walked in here. Then when I stood too close. I don't – I just –" he sighed, hands remaining tightly set. "I don't want you to be afraid of me."

"I…" I had no good answer. Had he really been paying that much attention? 'Fear' wasn't exactly the right word for what I felt. Maybe at first, but not then. Not with him holding onto me like I was something sacred.

"What is it, Selah?"

Haven's voice was heavy and full of something akin to pity. I was tired, so very much so. Despite Genevieve's best efforts, a ghost of pain throbbed in my chest. With sad eyes, she had promised that it would fade. But it had been days, and the ache was as present as ever.

"Haven –"

"I am your friend. Before anything, before any title, *I am your friend.* If, despite what I've felt from you earlier, that is all you ever wish I should be, then so be it. I can stay at arm's length. But your fear –" he cut himself off with a breath. "It's unbearable. I can handle your anger, I can manage your grief, but I cannot take any more of your fear. Please. Tell me what I can do. Tell me what I have done and I will fix it in." *True.* Every word of it was true.

Oh, sweet thing.

He thought it was him.

"You've done nothing wrong," I said in what was barely a whisper. His hands remained gently fixed on my waist. I loved having him so close, loved his brand of comfort, and loved how his fingers were so sure. He had saved my life, perhaps in more ways than one. If only he already knew. If only I could make him understand without having to spare a single breath.

There was nothing harsh on his face. I was silently grateful for his gift, how there was so much I didn't have to explain.

"Please."

I took a breath. Then another. Then a third, hoping it would steady me.

"I was not born in a castle," I started.

He nodded, and I continued.

"I actually am not sure where I was born, and I stopped caring a very, very long time ago."

Butterflies fluttered, but the prince did not speak. He only waited for me to go on, thumb absentmindedly moving along my side. It was so nice to be near someone, so new to be cared for in such a way, but it was as frightening as it was alluring.

"I don't know if my parents simply wanted to be rid of me, or if I was stolen from them. I was far too young to remember when I was found by some Eloran officers. They did what they were taught to do, and they

278

handed me off to a family that had volunteered to shelter me until my parents were found.

"The investigation went nowhere, and the family was not as kind as they had pretended to be. Their children were fine. Irritating, but tolerable. It was the father –" my voice broke. A sob creeped back up my throat, but I shoved it down. "He was the first. I was young, painfully young, and when he grabbed me, I didn't have the words to tell him no.

"Then he handed me over to a friend of his. Then another. There were six in total who traded me back and forth. One of them was the same Eloran officer who had found me nearly frozen to death when I was still little. But then, when I was old enough, I ran, and I ran, and I ran, until my legs were failing and lungs were ready to give out. I ran faster than I thought was even possible. I didn't know where I was going, I just knew that I didn't want to get sent back there.

"And I prayed," I could no longer stop the tears from trailing down or the cracks that wormed their way into my voice. "So many times. I begged Lukoh to make them stop. I asked him to take them away, and if not them, then me. I asked him just to let me die so that I wouldn't have to live in a world where I was used and then passed along. If I had been sent back to them, I think that would've been it.

"But I made it to Distin, in the end. I had less than nothing, but at least I was far away. And I –" I laughed humorlessly, "I got caught stealing strawberries from a cranky old lady. Mariah Aster. She was so angry – maybe more at the fact that someone so young was on the street than anything. She made me clean her booth for weeks until I'd made enough to pay her back. Then, she and her husband kept me around. I stayed on my own, and after some time I earned enough of a living to survive; eventually, I earned enough to get off the street.

"When my gift was fully developed, I eventually started exposing people's secrets for money. I don't know what family it came from. I didn't care. It's not great for making friends, but it paid well. Really well. Mostly, women wanted to know if their husbands were cheating on them, but sometimes employers or politicians would come to ask me if I'd investigate other things. It was more money than I had ever been offered in my entire life. I took it, and I bought an outrageously expensive apartment. I bought absurd locks for the doors. I bought so many weapons, half of which I've never learned how to use properly. I bought every pretty outfit I saw and tried to give myself the world.

"Then, one day, as I was returning from visiting Mariah, I saw the Lyscottian soldier looming over that little girl. I didn't think. She was the same age I had been before I ran to Distin, and my blood *boiled*. I acted on instinct. She was safe, and I was dragged away to a cell. When it was over, I wondered if she had prayed like I had. I wondered if Lukoh cared more for her than he had for me. Foolish, selfish thoughts. But I wondered what I had done so wrong for him to offer me this gift and then leave me in their hands.

"That is why I'm anxious. I have a lifetime of defense and it's especially difficult when I'm stuck in a room with someone. But it's not you, Haven. It's nothing you've done. You saved my life. You are the very best person I've ever had the pleasure of knowing. I just … forget that you are not a threat."

He wiped away the dampness that still pooled under my eyes, but his hands were shaking. He was quiet, achingly so, for one moment, then two.

"Are they still alive?" Barely contained wrath coated each word. Anger. That's why he was trembling. He was angry over me?

I nodded. "All but one met untimely ends. It seems as though someone else had a bigger vendetta against them than I did. The officer was relocated. His family moved out to Mallord Bay." *Mallord Bay. Depths.* I should've realized it sooner.

"Cain Balor," he confirmed.

I nodded again.

"I will deal with him." *True.* His hands were so gentle, so constant. It was at odds with his tone in a way that made me believe him.

I had no doubt that Haven would use every bit of his authority against Balor. If it were reversed, I would've killed someone myself over my prince. I certainly had considered it when Adiel almost knocked Haven off the side of a cliff.

"Come here," Haven beckoned, and I nearly fell back into him. A burden removed itself from my chest. He was cedar and cinnamon and warmth and the closest thing to home that I'd ever encountered. *I'm okay, I'm okay,* I repeated. Each time, I believed it more and more. The edge of fear remained if I searched for it, but I could breathe deeply. I stayed in that moment for as long as he allowed.

"Listen," he took my face in his long fingers, angling it so my eyes met his. "I cannot do much today, but here is what I can promise you, Selah Aster. You may push me away as many times as you wish, to whatever distance you prefer. Do anything you need to feel alright. However," his thumb started again, tracing little circles, "the second, the *breath* you want me back, I am yours. The moment you call, I will come. You are deserving of so much more, but that is what I can give you."

True.

True, true, true.

My heart broke in a perfect way.

"And that is more than I could ever ask for, Haven Allicot."

Chapter Twenty-Eight: Haven

Not a day too soon, a letter arrived.

The parchment had clearly seen better days. The envelope was slightly damp from the rain and snow, and the edges were crinkled from the journey. It was only a week of travel, but it was a difficult, winding road that required exceptionally nimble horses unless you wanted to add a few more days of effort. The Allicot crest was stamped boldly with green wax and faint gold accents.

If the stamp had not given it away, my father's handwriting would have. *Prince Haven Allicot* was marked with wide strokes and a pen that was seemingly running out of ink. The Eloran king wrote with a quick, broad, unmistakable hand, and excellent timing.

Selah and I had slept until early in the afternoon. She was still half tangled in my arms, half sprawled out across the bed. Such a mess, but so pretty. I was not much better off, in fairness, my own hair poking out in every direction and my clothes mussed from use.

I was greeted by messages from two kings: one, from my father, and another, King Castillo inviting us to dinner later that evening. Little did he know that it would be our final meal together, though the decision to leave was largely unanimous.

Upon receiving the letter, I sent for Elliott and my siblings. We could have gone to them, but Selah was not entirely back to her full strength, and she needed to save her energy for meeting the king. They arrived only a few minutes later. None of them were as nervous as they should have been. If we were ordered to stay, we would have to consider the risks once more. If we were ordered to leave, then we would need to break the news to the Lyscottian court that we would not be able to offer our assistance. Neither would be ideal, but it seemed as though I was the only one who truly understood the gravity of the situation.

Gen had drifted to Selah's side almost immediately, examining her in whatever way Gen needed to before they started off on their own conversation. Elliott kept a careful eye on them, but I sensed little emotion emanating from him. Alaric's expression was something between boredom and exhaustion, as though we had rudely awoken and forced him to make an appearance.

"Go on, then," Alaric muttered, peering down at the envelope I fiddled with. "We're all here."

That captured the attention of the rest of the room, whose gazes were now entirely fixed on me.

With a heavy sigh, I peeled back the wax and began to read.

"Dear Prince Haven,

First, I must offer my deepest gratitude for your faithfulness in reporting back from Lyscott. I presume that your brother and sister have already joined you at the castle, if Alaric's vision was any indication. Formally, I did not give my consent, but in all transparency, it makes little difference. While I would prefer that the crown prince of Elora remain in the country he serves, I intended for Genevieve's gift to be utilized for Lyscott's benefit. Perhaps, when she was

284

slightly older, but if war is truly as imminent as you have described, then she may be invaluable.

You have my full blessing to promise any aid you deem they are in need of. Your judgment is sound. I find it suitable that you all return first to speak with the Eloran council as a precaution before we provide any real assistance. They will be agreeable, but it is out of respect for them that you should consider their opinions. They have served Elora well, and it is vital that you seek their endorsement.

I will join you when you return to Lyscott. It is best for Alaric to remain in Distin and to write of any premonitions. I also would rather the queen remain with him to oversee Faye's education and to ensure that both the prince and princess are well taken care of. I will request Genevieve's company as well as Lieutenant Colonel Pierce. As for Lady Aster, it is up to your discretion. I cannot currently imagine what sort of help she could provide, but I know very little of what she can do.

What I do know of, however, is your engagement. Congratulations, Prince. I am not sure what you bargained for her hand in marriage, but I am certain that it must be of some great value. All of Distin is celebrating on your behalf," Selah choked on a cough, "and your people are eager to welcome you home. Do ensure that you return soon. We have much to discuss.

My sincerest wishes,

The king of Elora."

The room itself balked for a passing moment, then exploded in a fury of comments.

"The king mentioned me?"

"I can't believe he wanted me here!"

"That's not what I saw."

"All of Distin?!"

"Wait," I waved a hand, silencing the group. For the love of all that is pure, their emotions were overwhelming. Confusion was the emanating theme, but strands of shock and concern remained just as prevalent. "Alaric, one more time. What did you say?"

"That's not what I saw."

"What do you mean?" Gen asked.

"I mean," Alaric paused as though the mere act of speaking required great effort, "that I had a vision of Elora aiding Lyscott. Our father said that it would only be him, you, and Haven who came back to Lyscott. I saw all of us here, minus Elliott and Selah, though it's more than possible they are meant to join us, and I just didn't notice them. But the king said he wouldn't be bringing Faye or our mother."

"Why would he bring Faye? She's not even received her ability yet," Gen remarked. Alaric and I had only just had a similar conversation. She kept a hand near Selah, who had paled from either illness or the fact that my father had evidently announced our engagement. I was less than eager to hear what she had to say about that small piece of information. It was my fault, though. I supposed that I deserved whatever anger she may have felt.

When I reached out to her, I was surprised to find that she wasn't mad at all. Shocked, yes. Confused and worried, decidedly. But no longer did she resent me for pushing her into a betrothal.

I hadn't exactly consulted Elliott, either. He was less irritated than she had been, but he was certainly more concerned. Something about what my people would make of it and what would happen when I broke it off. I would have to end it at some point, wouldn't I? The Lyscottians knew us to be together, so if we were to pretend, how long would we have to act for? Would it ever truly be over? More importantly, did I really want our little charade to end? I was beginning to like having a roommate, and she certainly was prettier than Elliott.

Alaric held up his hands. "Don't stab the messenger. I'm just explaining what I saw, which very well may mean nothing, because the king expressly mentioned that he will not be bringing them."

"Maybe it's a vision for another time, then," Elliott commented. His posture was always unnaturally straight, and even more so as he addressed the room full of Eloran royalty. "I'm not sure which of you wants to break the news to Castillo, but we need to let him know this evening. We need to leave by dawn if we want to make it to our border at a reasonable hour."

'This evening' was quickly approaching. Perhaps if we had not slept most of the day away, we'd have been more prepared. In fairness, Selah had every reason to need rest, and I'd been thoroughly exhausted. In the first two days she'd spent recovering, I hadn't slept much at all. I had stayed up with her until she went back to sleep. It was well worth my time, but so were the extra few hours of sleep I'd managed.

I had more of a relationship with Castillo than anyone. "I'll take care of it."

We spent a few hours packing until it was time to prepare for dinner. Genevieve desperately wanted to get ready in our room with Selah, so I gave them their space. She made up some silly excuse about needing to be near her patient just in case, but really, I suspected that she was just enjoying having another young lady around to chat with.

Elliott and I prepared ourselves in silence. He wore colors vaguely reflecting Elora's royalty, white and green with gold accents and a gilded sheathe at one hip. There, he kept the only sword that we hadn't already stored for the journey. Elliott had secured drivers for each of the two carriages we'd brought, so at the very least the trip home would be easier than the way over.

"Do you like her?"

Elliott briefly paused in straightening his cuffs to look at me. His eyes narrowed, carefully weighing my intention, "Genevieve, you mean?"

I smirked and plopped down on his bed. I had long since been ready to go, though I never prepared myself as meticulously as my lieutenant colonel did. This might explain why he was on track to be General of our army and I was not. My attention to detail paled in comparison to his. "I'm quite certain I know how you feel about my sister. No, I meant Selah."

He glanced at me sideways yet again, "Why?"

"Curiosity's sake."

My best friend scoffed, "Never is it only curiosity's sake when you have that look in your eye." Regardless, he sighed heavily and turned to face me fully. "I don't mind her. She could speak less, or perhaps at better times. I can appreciate that Gen is excited to get to know her. She's clever and brave enough, and I think that I do prefer her alive. Now, should you sacrifice your kingdom for her? Absolutely not. But, for someone we picked up from a cell, we could have had much worse luck. Repeat any of that, however, and I will gladly show your sister what you'd look like as a floor rag."

I chuckled, "And whatever will you do while she's tending to me?" A clocktower chimed from somewhere far away. We were running late. "We need to get Gen and Selah. I'm sure the king will be all too eager to hear that we're leaving."

Unfortunately, I did not have time to linger on how thoroughly beautiful Selah looked. We were in too much of a rush for me to appreciate

288

how the grayish-blue of her dress somehow was a perfect match for her eyes. I decidedly didn't note how impeccably the fabric hugged her waist and trailed ever so gracefully to the floor. I surely couldn't tell that it was likely Gen who had applied her makeup from the unmitigated care that had been taken. I certainly did not get a chance to consider how difficult it would be to remove the sleeves that drifted all the way down to her decorated wrists.

She would be the end of me.

Her arm was wrapped tightly around mine as I led us to the dining hall. "You look stunning," I whispered.

In a move that was alarmingly unlike her, Selah Aster blushed.

"Doesn't she?" Gen sighed. "I had to talk her into leaving a few of the knives behind but it was well worth the debate. Really, Haven. If you are to bring your engagement back to Distin, you must let me dress her up more often."

Selah gave me an uneasy glance before we entered the dining hall at last. The Lyscottian court had taken their various places, and we exchanged greetings quickly. The king's gaze was eager but wary, and anticipation seeped from him. Though, it could also have been Nero, whose restless foot was steadily tapping under the table. Mekhi was stoic in his chair, Adiel only looked put out, and Ilse was beaming in the corner. Wren was sitting quietly, compliant as ever.

We nibbled for a short time before most of the table was engaged in quiet conversation. Only then the king started prying. "While I would love to engage in further pleasantries, I did request this meeting for a purpose. First, to see that Lady Aster has recovered," she smiled halfheartedly, "and because I was told that your father had written."

Right into it. "He has indeed."

"And what information did the king of Elora have to offer?" Nero asked.

I glanced at Elliott, who gave a quick, affirming nod. Then I spoke. "The king sends his regards. He has given me permission to offer basic aid – a handful of troops, supplies, whatever you are most in need of. He has also asked that we return to Distin at once so we can work out the details in person. If you'll have us, he'd like to come to Lyscott himself. The queen will not be able to make the journey, as she will be tending to my younger sister in Elora. Neither will Alaric."

All other dialogue stopped.

A blast of wrath rolled off the king like a tidal wave. I alone felt it, but the entire Lyscottian court suddenly fixed their wary eyes on their king. The only outward signs of his fury were the way my feet felt heavier and how his fingers wrapped tightly around his chalice. It was Mekhi who he glanced at first with a pointed look before returning his gaze to me.

"Is there an issue?" I asked. Nothing I'd said warranted such an outburst of emotion, did it?

The king smiled, now tight and forced. "Not at all, Highness. That will be perfectly suitable."

Selah grabbed my hand under the table and moved to sip from her glass.

"Are you certain?" I pressed. "If there is anything you need, this is our last night together for some time. I'm afraid you may not have another chance to ask."

Castillo took a strained breath before replying. "I'm merely shocked to hear that the queen and princess won't be arriving. We will need all the help we can get in the war with Dobre."

Selah started choking violently on her drink. The table's attention turned to her, and she was now fighting to regain her composure. A powerful pulse of shock jolted through her, which was especially poignant with her hand in mine. It was followed by confusion, then a steady beat of anger.

Selah tried to swallow her cough with another sip, but her chalice had been emptied. "Ilse, do you mind?" the king prompted, and Ilse hurried over to fill the glass again.

"Thank you," Selah croaked, swallowing slower. Once air was securely back in her lungs, she spoke. "Excuse me. I suppose I had not been told your war was with Dobre. I have some family there."

"Do you?" Adiel poked. "Are they awful? They seem awful."

"Enough, Adiel," Castillo intervened. "I'm shocked it hasn't come up yet. It's been such an ordeal for our court, I might have forgotten to mention who we were fighting. Regardless, I'm afraid I must excuse myself. There are some pressing matters that I need to attend to before you all leave in the morning. It has been a pleasure becoming acquainted. I only wish we could have had more lighthearted conversations during your time here. Perhaps your next journey will be more profitable for us both, yes?" The king said little more before retiring.

The rest of the Lyscottian court filed out after him in a contained flurry of movement. We Elorans merely looked at each other, trying to make sense out of what had just happened.

"That was quick," Alaric muttered.

Selah tugged my hand and stood. "We need to talk. All of us. Privately. Now."

Chapter Twenty-Nine: Selah

⁙

"There is no war with Dobre."

Four jaws nearly damaged the floor in front of me.

I had smuggled Elliott and the Allicot siblings back into my room as I tried to come up with a way to break the news to them. There was no war. The king had lied. Our entire trip, the king had lied, and I'd barely caught him the night before we were due to leave. I decided the best method was to be direct.

How had we been so thoroughly blind? How had it not come up already? Oh, the Lyscottians were good. Did they all know that the war was fake? Did Mekhi, as he was training me to defend myself? Or rather, was that just a diversion to keep me out of the meetings?

"But..." Haven rubbed his jaw, trying to produce an explanation. There was nothing. They'd tricked us.

"You know," Alaric started. "No wonder this place feels so wrong."

Elliott commented next. "There is no way. You cannot just make up a fake war. There's... You have to..." he sighed. "They've lied this whole time?"

"They sure have, and we let them." I scrubbed the confusion out of my face. Exhaustion loomed, but restrained itself to the corners of my mind. "They lied about the war, they lied about what their soldiers were doing in Distin with that little girl, they lied that they were surprised to see us, Adiel and Nero both lied about not having gifts and we *still* only know what Adiel's is by accident. They've been lying to our faces this whole time. But why?"

"The soldiers grabbed Faye," Gen whispered.

Faye. Was that the name of the little girl I'd saved?

Faye, with her bright blue eyes and stark blonde hair.

Genevieve's blue eyes.

Haven's blond hair.

I was going to hurt them.

"Faye," I began, "as in, Princess Faye? As in, Faye Allicot, Princess of Elora?"

Haven and Elliott locked eyes, and both winced.

"I saved the *princess of Elora?*"

Neither of the young men dared to respond.

Genevieve's head cocked, "They didn't tell you?"

"No, Gen. They didn't," I huffed in frustration. Everything made sense. Once I finally had all the information, it made so much sense! It only took a month for me to find out. "I was *arrested* for saving the *princess of Elora?*"

Haven reached for my hand, and I let him take it, "I didn't intend to hide it from you. It just... hasn't come up." *True.*

It hasn't come up?

Recognition fluttered on Elliott's face for a passing moment. He'd figured it out, too. The Allicots, though, someone needed to explain.

"*Haven,*" I breathed. "They lied about the war to buy some time until they heard from your father. The king got upset after hearing that Alaric, your mother, and Faye would not be coming. Alaric is already here,

293

he's had a chance with him, and he did not send soldiers after your mother. He wants *Faye*."

"She's a child. She doesn't even have a gift yet. What would he possibly want with her?" he asked, heartbreak in his eyes.

My tone softened, "*Yet*. What is she, twelve years old? Thirteen? Her gift will present itself soon, if she has one. And if our gifts are manifesting strangely, you can be certain that hers will likely do the same. He wants *her*."

Elliott spoke next, uncharacteristically harsh, "There are a handful of Lyscottian citizens with abilities. Castillo has shown no interest in making an enemy of us. We've been here for days. Why an Eloran princess with an unknown gift? She may not even have one, and then they've antagonized their strongest neighbor. You may as well push Haven off the side of a cliff again."

But Adiel *had* almost pushed Haven off the side of a cliff, although none of the Lyscottians had seemed overly pleased about that.

"Kill Haven, Faye would at least come to attend the funeral," Alaric muttered.

Adiel seemed convoluted enough to come up with such an absurd idea, but that wasn't what the king had wanted. Why, then? Perhaps if I'd known Faye's identity sooner, I would have known what to look for.

A slight tremor rippled through the room, which was strange, because nothing physically moved. Was it… anger? Anger isn't tangible. It was not felt in the way that a touch is felt, or in the way that wind skirts above the waves. But, oddly, I could sense it as though it were something I could hold, as though I could reach out to grab the very emotion and shape it in my hands.

"Haven," Alaric scolded.

"Sorry," all at once, the feeling was muted.

Since when could Haven do that?

The conversation was making my head spin.

I had no obligation to comfort him. Haven may not have lied to me, but he certainly had omitted a very important piece of an excessively lousy puzzle. Maybe it was the lingering betrayal on his face that swayed me. Maybe it was the fact that, for a fleeting moment, I felt his anger as if it was my own. Maybe it was the hand he still clasped in mine.

"It's not your fault," I sighed, placing a flat palm over his heart. "I mean, the whole not telling me thing *was* your fault. That was just poor judgment. But you sensed his pain. You cared. It's a good thing, Haven. The king knew you would, and he took advantage of that. That's his mistake, not yours."

The prince of Elora only nodded and rested his empty hand over mine.

Not a full moment later, a gentle *tap tap tap* of a knock sounded at our door.

Every set of eyes jerked towards it. It was too light of a rhythm to be Nero's, not urgent enough to be Mekhi's, and the king had never come to meet us on his own. Elliott's hand had twitched to one of the blades at his side and remained steadily resting there. As I just so happened to be the closest to the door, I pulled away from Haven to answer it.

It was Ilse who stood in the hallway, wide eyes searching and mildly frantic. Notably frantic, for someone who always seemed so confident in her own kingdom. Her gaze met mine first before jolting to the full room behind me. Shock passed over her face briefly until she shifted back to where I stood. "Oh, hello. I need to speak with you. Just you. Now, if at all possible." *True.*

Old nausea simmered to the surface.

I glanced at the Elorans. Haven's expression contorted into displeasure. Alaric showed only intrigue, Elliott appeared mildly cautious, and Genevieve looked outright angry. It was only Ilse. I had set her brother into place well enough, there was little doubt in my mind that I could handle her myself.

In one of the more remarkable mistakes I've made in this lifetime, I nodded in agreement.

"Let me grab my coat."

Haven snatched it up for me, his fingers grazing my shoulders as he helped me shrug it on. "Make it quick," he whispered.

I raised a brow at him.

"Please."

I squeezed one of his hands, quietly conceding. We had much to discuss.

Without much talk, I followed Ilse out of our room and sealed the door behind me. The look on her face rested somewhere between discontent and anxiety. We'd been in Lyscott for some time, and only then she wanted something.

She was aiming to lead me somewhere, but I stopped her in the hallway. I was still exhausted from my injuries. *Really* exhausted, actually. More so than I'd been when I'd first woken up.

"What is it, Ilse?" I stifled a yawn.

She smiled knowingly at me. "Are you tired, Selah?"

Something was wrong. Something was very, thoroughly wrong. My eyes were closing against my will, and suddenly the floor was not as firmly situated under me as it should have been.

"Haven will miss you," her voice, in spite of her accent, was eerily melodic. "Don't worry. I'll still be around if he needs a shoulder to cry on."

"What did you do?" I tried to ask, but the words were jumbled and I couldn't quite focus on her beautiful, wicked face.

"Only what my king required."

The world went dark.

Chapter Thirty: Haven

An hour had passed, and Selah hadn't returned.

Alaric and Elliott had trailed out first. Dinner with the king had been late enough, and with our sunrise exit in view, they decided to try to rest. Gen stayed with me a while longer. Only when her anxiety became suffocating did I recommend that she try to get some sleep as well. With bleary eyes, she excused herself.

So I waited.

And I waited.

And soon, another hour came and went. And another. And another.

With only the moonlight and the small hole I was burning in the carpet as company, I had plenty of time to think. I hadn't told Selah about Faye at first, and then somehow entirely forgot to bring it up again. But was it really so important? In hindsight, perhaps it did make the king's motive a bit clearer. But a life was a life. Did it really matter so much to her that a princess was the one she'd saved? Or was it only the fact that I *had* kept it from her?

I could hardly stand to consider my meetings with the king. I'd spent hours in his company, speaking of the threat that was Dobre. If I'd pushed a little harder, maybe I could have had Selah in the room with me.

She would've resented me for forcing her to spend any more time pretending to be engaged, but then we would have known far sooner. Heavens above, I'd been foolish. Not I, nor my siblings, nor a high-ranking soldier in Elora's army had caught on. Only Selah, and far too late.

Speaking of too late, I paced. *It's been hours. This is not making it quick. This is notably not quick.*

I debated leaving and searching around the palace. The Lyscottian castle was hauntingly vast. I could start in the library, but what business would Ilse have there? Dread made its home in my stomach as I considered what would possibly drive Ilse to want to meet with Selah in the first place. I came up with nothing good.

Dawn was soon approaching. We couldn't leave without her. I wouldn't. I'd dragged her all this way. She was my responsibility, whether she liked it or not. She was my responsibility, and she was gone, and –

My panic was interrupted by a figure bursting into my room.

Alaric's strained features were visible in the light of the lamp he'd carried with him. He was only half dressed in the same clothes he'd been in for dinner, I doubted he even bothered to change to sleep. He did not even pause in his step, setting down the light as if in dire search of something. Impossibly, my stomach dropped even further.

There was only one reasonable explanation.

"What did you see?"

He poked his head into the bathroom. "Where is Selah?"

My heart sank, "She hasn't returned."

The color drained from his face.

"What did you see?" I pressed.

Alaric did not answer right away as he scrambled through the very last of the trunks that was left in our room. The majority of our belongings were packed away into the carriages we'd been taking home, save for the most important personal items.

He stepped back, clutching five knives between his two hands. He let them fall to the floor with a stark exhale. "It's not good."

They were Selah's knives.

Alaric Allicot, Crown Prince of Elora, had been subject to foreseeing many horrors in his time. Through visions, he had witnessed every sort of wickedness under the sun. Most of those stories were passed directly to my father, who then had them documented, and records of Alaric's visions were kept in Distin for later reference. I'd read a handful of the reports. They were nauseating. He was never as shaken telling the stories as I had been merely looking at accounts of them.

Alaric's anxiety seeped through his skin. It showed in the slight tremble of his fingers as he dropped the blades. It was evident in the catch of his breath. I was not trying to sense what he felt. In fact, with my brother, I often preferred not to know, but it was painfully obvious, and it was about *her*.

Still kneeling on the floor, pinned by some invisible weight, the crown prince looked up at me with severe eyes. "The Lyscottians have taken her captive. They..." he trailed off. "She hasn't recovered yet, Haven. She didn't look well."

My chest threatened to tear in two as the barest bit of light started to peek over the horizon.

"They want *Faye*," I argued. "Selah can't help them."

My brother's voice was quiet when he spoke. "I don't know what they aimed to achieve. They just wanted her."

Heavens above, I was going to kill them.

I grabbed two of her blades and pocketed them. My sword had already been dangling on my hip. There were no other weapons I could access in time. I was going to kill them, and I was going to use Eloran blades to do it.

"Wait, stop." My brother stood and raised a hand to block me. "You can't just execute a king, Haven. There are laws –"

"I don't care." I shoved past his arm.

As I tore open the door, I nearly trampled over the prince of Lyscott. His stance was wide and set, with Gen and Elliott dimly trailing behind. Smacking into him left me subject to the full weight of Mekhi's emotions. Stifling worry, simmering anger, overwhelming regret. It was enough to make me pause before wanting to stab him.

His face, though, was void of any of what I'd sensed. The prince's harsh features remained even as he addressed me. "You need to come with me."

Now sensing my anger, Elliott glanced up at me with alarm in his eyes. "What's the matter?"

"The Lyscottians are holding Selah," I spat, never removing my stare from Mekhi.

Shock and anger rippled from where Gen and Elliott both stood.

Mekhi did not flinch, but when he spoke, the words were hollow, "That's a polite way of putting it." His hands hung readily at his sides. I had fought the prince before. I had little interest in doing so again, but my fingers were itching to move, "If you'd like to see her in this lifetime, we need to leave. My father is waiting."

"Fine."

I remained close enough to the prince that I could not stop my gift from reaching him. If Gen's fear had been suffocating, Mekhi's was outright oppressive. Rarely had I felt such strong emotion from the prince as he led us to the king. It was terrible timing. I cursed myself inwardly for letting Selah leave in the first place. I'd known, I'd *known* something was off with Ilse and I had allowed it.

As we entered the throne room of the Lyscottian palace, I braced myself.

Never in my life had I seen ceilings so high. In the early morning light, they were haunting. Pale white streams reflected from the glass and granite walls, cutting around vast marble pillars like sharp, agile blades.

For the very first time, Castillo reclined on his throne. He looked made for it. Engraved stone molded around him, carefully etched with markings I did not understand. Precious gems so light they were nearly imperceptible were embedded into the royal podium. Never before had Castillo tried so thoroughly to present himself as a king. But there he was, and Selah was missing.

Nero and Adiel flanked him on one side, while Wren and Ilse stood on the other. Nero and Adiel's expressions were hopelessly smug. I did not pay Ilse enough attention to see what she was showing because Wren's emotion pulled me so strongly in her direction. Remorse – bitter and deep and unmistakable.

My hand rested on my sword. Gen and Alaric positioned themselves beside me, her gaze as full of fire as his was full of ice.

"Where is she?"

The king stared at me, saying nothing at first. His countenance was nearly unreadable. "Do not be rash, prince. Is this any way to address your host?"

"Was I too direct?" I lazily drew my weapon. "Allow me to try again. If you do not return her, you will die. Today. This very moment."

302

The king rose, then. Slowly. Methodically, as though he was in no immense hurry. My hand twitched. His fingers tapped idly on the throne's armrest. "You risk her life with your careless words."

I took a step forward. "We've been here for *weeks*, Majesty. If your kingdom was in need of something, you've had every opportunity to ask. What could you possibly want that we have not readily offered?"

"Would you deny a god?"

The floor rattled.

Deny a god?

I shook off the confusion, "Of course not. Elora proudly serves Lukoh –

"Lukoh is a *pathetic* excuse of a deity," the king rasped, intensity flooding his voice and his features. Otherworldly intensity. He reigned himself in before he spoke again, "If you were offered everything you've ever wanted – the most precious thing you've ever lost – at a price you were more than willing to pay, would you not gladly agree?"

Alaric paled.

"*Annika*," Castillo's voice broke, his hand curling into a fist. "He offered me Annika. My queen. The light of Lyscott. Your father could have saved her. Years have been spent in this *utter* darkness. I have been blind, Prince Haven. I cannot do this without her. She –" tears welled. "You'll understand. If only you knew, you'd understand."

When Alaric spoke, his voice was almost reverent in its sobriety, "You made a bargain with Akar."

Depths.

It was so much worse than anything we'd anticipated.

"He asked so little," Castillo continued, facing us again. "'*The princess of lies*,' he said. A member of the Eloran court. That was all he wanted."

It's not possible.

That could only mean Selah. He had Selah, and he was about to –

He went on explaining. "Now, there are remarkably few Eloran princesses. There is Princess Genevieve, who has the gift of healing. That would make little sense. Young Faye, though. Her gift has not yet manifested. Detection is a powerful ability, well suited to a royal. If there will be a princess of lies, would you not assume it would be her?"

I glanced at Mekhi. He knew of Selah's gift, knew that his father had to be wrong. The prince said nothing, did not even deign to look in my direction.

"You must be mad," Gen hissed.

The king coldly grinned, "I will be borrowing Princess Faye. You will return to Distin and tell your father exactly what has happened here. You will inform him that we are on our way, and you will explain that it is in his best interest to make this a peaceful exchange. This is final. It is simply a matter of how much your brother's fiancée and the people of Elora will suffer in the process."

I raised my sword and took another step. None of the Lyscottians flinched, "We will not be leaving without her."

The king paced right up to the edge of my blade, completely unbothered by the glimmering steel. In an instant, I was pulled down to the floor of the throne room by an unseen force. My limbs were lead and the weapon clattered to the ground beside me. I could manage staying on my hands and knees, but nothing further. The king's ability. I'd only experienced it in pieces.

"Stay, then. But every minute you are still here is another minute that your bride will suffer. She's been through quite an ordeal already this week. The choice is yours."

Castillo released his hold on me.

I grabbed my sword and visualized what it would look like to chop the king into pieces. My very bones trembled. The room was too hot. Even then, even if we did manage to fight our way past the Lyscottians, then we'd have to find her in their maze of a palace. We'd seen where Lorelai was kept, so they'd be fools to hold Selah there as well. She could be dead by the time we found her. She could *already* have been dead, for all we knew.

A firm hand hauled me up. I tugged against it, but my brother held tight, "We're going."

"Are you *insane* –"

"That's one minute," the king taunted. "Take your time. I'm in no rush."

Elliott moved to assist Alaric in pulling me out. They were right. I knew they were right. In a final act of defiance, I met Castillo's stare. When I spoke, I barely recognized the sound of my own voice. "Step foot into my country, and it will be the last thing you ever do."

He only grinned, "Two minutes, Prince. See you soon."

As soon as we were clear of the throne room, out of sight of the Lyscottian court, I shoved my brother up against the nearest wall. "Are you crazy?" My heart was beating in wild bursts and I could barely catch my breath. "We are *not* leaving her here with them! *Akar* is asking for her and –"

"*Be quiet,*" Alaric spat. He gave Gen a pointed look.

She reached a hand out, but I shook it off before she made full contact.

"Don't you *dare*."

Alaric drove me back right into my sister. Delicate, cold fingers made contact with the back of my neck. The fatigue was both immediate and overwhelming.

"I'm sorry," she whispered, and quickly faded from view.

Chapter Thirty-One: Selah

Stone, cold and unforgiving, was the first thing I felt when I awoke. Then, following closely behind was the relentless pounding in my head. My bones were unusually heavy, and my limbs were reluctant to move. How had I ended up on the floor? Our room didn't even have stone tiles.

Our room doesn't have stone tiles.

I jolted to attention. While there was not an excess of light, there was enough to just barely make out my surroundings. Stained, brown cobblestone lined the floors and most of the walls. There were no windows, only dim torches on either side. There was a flimsy mattress in one corner, discolored and rotting. On the other end of the room, there was a wooden door that opened to the smallest excuse for a washroom that I'd ever seen. The only other entrance was made of solid metal with a tiny opening to see out of.

It was then I noticed that Adiel and Ilse were in the cell with me, hovering by the door but clearly not captive. Mentally, I groaned. I did *not* have the energy to fight with them.

With a great amount of effort, I shifted myself up to sit. My hands and feet had felt especially heavy because there were now chains dangling off of them. There were no locks on the chains, and therefore, no way to take them off. How had they gotten them on?

"That fatigue cocktail of yours worked wonders, Ils. I'm almost envious of how well she slept," Adiel gloated.

"I should have stabbed you when I had the chance," I rasped. My throat was dry and scratchy.

"Alas," he faked a pout, poking at the binds around my ankles with his foot. "Do you like the shackles? I designed them myself. They really bring out the hatred in your eyes."

"Oh yes," Ilse chimed in, "I was going to mention that! I do notice quite a bit more loathing than usual."

My thoughts jerked to Haven. And Gen, Elliott, and Alaric. If I was stuck in a cell, where were they?

"Where is my fiancé?"

Adiel shrugged halfheartedly, running a hand through his dark hair. "Who can say? Probably off being tortured somewhere." *Lie.*

My stomach dropped at the thought. I'd seen Haven hurt before. He'd gotten half-beaten on the road by Lorelai's men. I was the one to fix him up then since Gen was not available. More importantly, I'd been the one to get us out of there. Even when I knew Adiel was lying, it hit hard.

Ilse batted a hand at her brother, "Oh, don't be cruel. We haven't touched a hair on his royal head." *True*, thank the heavens. "More likely, he is looking for another pretty young lady to be his new bride. You're a little...*tied up*, at the moment." *Lie.*

Inwardly, a betraying pang of jealousy nagged at me. Haven was not mine, not really. In name, perhaps, but my title was a ruse and he was free to do whatever he wished. But he had held me like I was his, like he was grasping something sacred. His fingers had remained consistently, entirely reverent. He had treated me like I was something of value. I did not want him to find someone else. I wanted him to want *me*.

Outwardly, I smirked, "You think I'm pretty?"

A few heavy sets of footsteps were audible from behind the metal door. It opened with a lurch, and four figures stepped into the room. Nero, Wren, Mekhi, and Castillo. Both Ilse and Adiel moved aside to make space for the king. Wren held a tray of what appeared to be bread and water that she silently handed off to Ilse. Mekhi never met my eyes, but the king peered down at me with something akin to pity. His crown was neatly fixed atop his head, silver and glimmering in the torchlight.

"This really is the last thing I wanted," the king said. *Lie.*

"Don't condescend to me," I raised my chin. "I am here. I am listening. I am already aware that the war in Dobre was contrived to fool us. It worked, for a time. I also know that Princess Faye is important to you for some reason. Let's begin there."

Nero drew back his foot, and a sharp, shooting pain jolted through my side. "You will demand nothing from us."

"Fine," I panted through clenched teeth, considering how difficult it would be to lock my chains around his neck.

Castillo humored me, "I was offered a deal. A soul, in exchange for the Eloran princess with the gift of detection." My gut twisted. "I tried to get her peacefully to little avail. Instead, I've proposed a deal to your fiancé: your life for hers." *True.*

No.

He was trying to bargain my life for the little girl I'd saved. Haven would never, not in a million years, agree to that, no matter whether he cared for me or not. Depths, I'm not sure I even would have agreed to that. Regardless, Faye would not have the gift of detection. There was usually only one of us in a hundred years.

Was it me he was looking for?

309

"Who has the power to offer you a soul? Though it's clear that you are in need of one," I asked. Another – harder – kick landed on my ribs, and I gasped at the ache. The force of it set me onto my side. Heavens above, that would bruise.

"Akar." *True.*

You have got to be joking.

A wheezing laugh escaped me as I righted myself, broken and half-hysterical. He was crazy. Fully, deeply insane. Akar was a fairytale. "You may as well end my life now, because there is no future in which Haven agrees to that. None."

The king crouched to my level. "I can be very persuasive, Selah. The king of Elora had the chance to prevent this years ago. He chose not to do so. Really, I'd hoped that a war creeping towards their borders would be enough for them to pay a visit. It wasn't," he sighed. "I even had Nero poke around in Prince Alaric's dreams as an extra precaution." *True.*

Nero was a dreamwalker. It made so much sense. Wren's eerie warning, the dream that followed not long after, the Akar imagery. Alaric's vision of the Allicots in Dobre hadn't been real, thank goodness.

I glanced at the prince. He knew about my gift. Granted, he also knew about Nero's and Adiel's abilities and had waited for us to figure them out on our own. Had he not told his father? I was engaged to Haven. That made me an almost-Eloran princess with the gift of detection. Mekhi was clever enough to realize that they were following an empty trail. He said nothing, not even so much as glancing in my direction.

I needed to talk to him.

Castillo continued, "Don't worry, we'll be escorting you back to Elora. We'll take you, and if they won't agree to that bargain, I'll have my soldiers start picking people off the streets. The Eloran king will agree eventually, it is just a matter of how many of his citizens will be killed in the process. First, I'd like to let the Eloran royals squirm a bit before I bring you over. Make yourself comfortable. You may be here for a while."

The king did not stick around to take any more questions. Mekhi followed closely behind and Wren shot me a passing look of pity before leaving, too. Nero knocked aside the foot of mine that was closest to him with a notable amount of force as he went after his wife. Adiel lingered with Ilse, who set down the tray Wren had brought just within reach.

She smiled with faux hospitality, "Oh, and I wouldn't drink the water if I were you. Best of luck!"

In less than a breath, they were gone, too. The metal door sealed shut.

Alone, panic seized my chest. I was in a very different cell from the one Lorelai had been kept in. Even if the Allicots tried to find me, it would be of little use. *I* didn't even know where I was. Mekhi had to be well aware that I was the one they wanted to sacrifice to a god. If he decided to tell them, it would be over. Maybe I could handle that. Perhaps death was not as frightening as being at the mercy of these people.

There was no way that the Allicots would hand over Faye. *Good.* She could offer the Lyscottians nothing. If I could just let them get me into Elora, then I could find a way to get myself free. Holding me was one thing, but traveling meant that there had to be opportunities to escape. There had to be something.

I was still in the very same outfit that Gen had dressed me up in for what was meant to be our last meal in Lyscott. I'd kept two of my knives strapped to my ankles, both of which were miraculously missing. Dread pulled at me.

I could just tell them, let them hand me over to whoever they wanted, and be done. No more fighting. No more pretending. It would be final, and Elora and Distin and *Haven* would be left untouched.

Hours passed with my thoughts as my only company. I'd eaten the bread, figuring that, if they had poisoned it, they likely would have gloated about that before they left. The water, though, I was wary of. My mouth was painfully dry, and the fact that at least one of my ribs felt injured made my breaths shallow and harsh. I weighed whether or not she was bluffing.

After about an hour of careful examination and slowly increasing boredom, I tried it. It tasted fine and soothed the burning in my throat. Almost immediately, my stomach started cramping. Chills raced up and down my spine. My skin became hot and clammy. Nausea followed in full force, and suddenly I understood why they left me in a cell with a washroom.

Everything I'd had in my stomach came right back up, down to the very last bit of bile. With every heave, my ribs felt like they were ablaze. I should've believed Ilse, but I had access to no other clean water as far as I could tell. I was such a fool. I was a fool, and it was about to get me killed.

I didn't bother with the mattress. The floor was less moldy. At the very least, the cool stone soothed my burning fever. It was nearly impossible to get truly comfortable, but exhaustion tugged at me hard enough that I just barely dozed off …

Another kick jolted me awake, Nero hovering over me when I was brought back. He didn't stay long, only enough for me to know that he was there, and I was still captive.

Entire days passed like this, though I couldn't say how many. Falling asleep and being awoken by some sort of pain. Occasionally, he missed and struck my face instead. I ate whatever they slid into the cell, but

312

steered clear of the water until it became absolutely dire. Sometimes it didn't bother me. Others, I would be vomiting and feverish late into the night. Well, I suspected it was night. I had no window to be able to tell for sure, but there were some hours that I was left alone.

I didn't rest long enough to dream, but I thought of Haven often. I thought of how it felt to fall asleep in his arms. I thought of how his hands had wrapped around me. I thought of how badly I'd wanted him to kiss me when I'd woken up after getting injured, and I wondered if his gift had made me want him more. I wondered what he was thinking, or if he was thinking of me at all. I thought of what I'd say to him if I did see him again. I wondered if we'd already had our last conversation.

Once, I was lurched awake by the shutting of the metal door. It had been closed with care, but still the sound was unmistakable. In the dim torchlight, I could make out the prince of Lyscott sitting down against the steel. My breath caught, half from pain and half from relief at the sight of him. Mekhi, who had tried so hard to get us to leave before it came to this.

We were quiet for several moments as I weighed what to say.

"You knew."

He nodded wordlessly.

"Faye can't help them," I rasped. Heavens above, speaking was an effort.

"She can't," He confirmed.

"Then why –" I coughed, and agony rippled through every bone. "Why haven't you said anything?"

Mekhi's brows drew together in distaste. "You need to drink. Dehydration is a miserable way to go out."

He had to know that it was poisoned half the time. Even still, he nudged the tray towards me. What game was he playing? Staring back at him dryly, I gestured to the full, metal cup, "You first."

He reached out with long fingers, taking the smallest sip before handing me the cup back. I watched him warily for a moment. His skin retained as much color as it usually had, though he was naturally pale, and he seemed fine. I drank slowly, never looking fully away.

Heavens above, water felt good. My throat was a little less sore. My stomach was slightly fuller. It wasn't much, but it was better.

His arm remained outstretched, "Give me your hand."

I looked at him sideways. "I'm afraid I'm already spoken for."

He rolled his eyes, a painfully normal expression. Something about it stung. "I'm trying to help you, Selah. Give me your hand." *True.*

Well, it wasn't like he could make anything a whole lot worse. The second I placed my fingers in his, the pain was gone. It was pure relief. In fairness, I couldn't feel much of anything. I couldn't feel the stone beneath me, or the shackles binding me. But I wasn't hurting. I sighed, raggedly and deeply.

"I have not told them," he started quietly, "because there is a future in which everyone survives this conflict. I have little interest in your life being ended, much less the life of a child. If they knew who you were, it would not even be a question. If you can make it until we reach Elora, you may stand a chance." *True.*

"You are more than welcome to take me there now. Nero may be out of a job, but I'm sure he'll manage."

The prince shook his head. "I have to consider more than just your interest."

"Is it Wren?"

314

A blink was the only sign of shock that Mekhi showed, but she was the only person who made sense. Nero didn't strike me as a stellar husband, but Adiel and Ilse seemed happy being awful. If there was someone in the Lyscottian court who needed saving, it was her.

"Yes. Nero stole her from her home. I intend to bring her back." His gaze narrowed, "And it appears as though we've exchanged secrets."

The threat was subtle, but clear: say anything, and he'd talk as well. It was a perfectly acceptable bargain. I didn't want Wren to suffer, either. Her husband was a nuisance, and she had raised terrible children, but she'd done nothing intentionally wrong.

I nodded in agreement.

Content, Mekhi continued, "Akar has rotted my father's mind. He can offer us nothing, but the king is convinced otherwise. I cannot talk him out of it. I've tried. Once we are in Distin, with the entire Eloran army against us, he will be forced to come to his senses. Or die." *True.*

"What does Akar need me for?"

"I don't know." *True.*

Haunting silence echoed in the cell. Mekhi's optimism was as refreshing as it was pointless. If the rival of Lukoh wanted me, it was only a matter of time until I was handed over.

A flood of agony returned in full force as Mekhi released my hand. I'd forgotten just how much of me was in varying levels of pain. I gasped with the weight of it, and the prince's somber expression deepened.

"Sleep. Nero will be occupied for a few hours. We leave for Elora in the morning."

I barely managed to stay conscious until the prince left. No dreams visited me, from Nero or of my own making. Just deep, thorough sleep, the most I'd gotten since my imprisonment.

I did wake eventually with no outside intervention. Strangely, though, I was not alone. A figure had taken up the space where Mekhi had sat, but the man looked nothing like him. I recognized him immediately. Even though I'd only ever seen him in the pages of religious texts, the god was unmistakable.

Lukoh.

Chapter Thirty-Two: Haven

The days came and went in a blur.

I was never awake for more than a few minutes at a time. From what I could recall, I was only up long enough for Gen to notice and put me back to sleep. I dreamt more often than not. I dreamt of Lukoh and Akar, of kings and of nations and of battles. I dreamt of Selah.

When I was finally allowed to wake, I was sitting on a familiar, carpeted floor. A hand sewn quilt decorated the wall behind an antique dresser. The room was lit with soft candle light. I'd only stayed at the inn for a night, but you could almost make out the area where Elliott had worn through the rug with his fretting.

This time, however, one of my wrists was tied to the end of the bed. I had been sitting up against it with my legs crossed underneath me. No sword was at my side. It was then that I remembered all that had happened, and it was then that my lungs, assaulted by anger and worry, threatened to snap in half.

Alaric leaned up against the wooden door, staring keenly down at me. Elliott had perched himself onto the dresser, which was straining underneath the soldier's weight. Gen was nowhere to be found, fortunately. That meant I had a chance of staying conscious long enough to carry a conversation.

Alaric and Elliott had not spoken, but their feelings drifted towards me with surprisingly little effort. It was strange. They were more tangible than usual, almost floating in the space between us. I wondered if, even mentally, I reached out and tugged…

"Stop," Alaric ordered, wincing.

Had I done something?

I pulled on my bound wrist, "Is this really necessary?"

"We need to speak without resorting to violence," my brother dryly answered.

I looked to the soldier beside him, my very closest friend, "Are you going to allow this?"

Bitter shame leeched off Elliott like a scent. He did not move. Alaric's emotions were dampened as though he was putting a remarkable amount of work into keeping them from me. They were present, bubbling up from just underneath the surface, but not quite legible.

Finally, the implications of being back at the inn became apparent. It was, in good weather, almost a week away from where we'd been staying in Lyscott. If we were almost back to Distin…

"How long has it been?"

"Six very long days."

The words hit like a punch. Six days, Selah had been held captive by a court of people corrupted by Akar. She'd nearly stabbed Adiel when he hadn't even touched me. She was there, with them, and I'd done nothing. I'd been *forced* to do nothing.

The crown prince of Elora was seconds away from being thoroughly, brutally maimed.

His features contorted to reveal his impatience, "*Calm down.*"

My entire body shook with the force of my anger, "Come a little closer and say that again."

"You were about to get her *killed,*" His arms flew to his sides. "You were *rambling* on about how Akar needed her, and it would have taken a *second* for anyone in the Lyscottian court to turn the corner and hear you. What were you going to do, Haven? Storm the castle in search of your little lover? Tear it apart? She's not there. They are not fools. Or, rather, would you have preferred that we hand our thirteen year old sister to Akar instead?"

"Of *course* not –"

Alaric scoffed. "No, maybe you'd like to know what state they've kept your Selah in, how much worse it would be now if they only knew who she was. Should I tell you about the chains Adiel designed for her? Oh, what about the poison Ilse is shoving down her throat? Heavens above, don't get me started on Nero –"

"*Alaric,*" Elliott stopped him. It would've been less agonizing if my brother had just stabbed me. I had a lifetime of managing the pain of myself and that of others. But *this*, this knowing and being just out of reach, was so much worse. She'd already endured enough.

"The point is," Alaric huffed, "I was trying to help you. *Both* of you. If you'd been awake for the journey, if you'd heard…" he trailed. "You would have run headfirst into Lyscott and died in the process."

"Heard what?"

Finally, Elliott said something of substance, "Rumors of Akar and Castillo stirring, and the king's intent. The Lyscottians are due in Distin in a week's time. Elora's armies will be ready, but if they have Akar's power accompanying them…"

319

"They could level the city," I finished.

Alaric waved a flippant hand. "I've seen Akar. He's growing in strength, but not enough to be of real concern. Regardless, if Akar was with them, he would have already identified Selah. If the Lyscottians are still on their way, then that hasn't happened yet. And they are starting the journey soon."

Akar was meant to be evil incarnate. If he truly was returning, Elora was about to have much bigger problems than a vengeful Lyscottian king. But if Akar *was* becoming more powerful, maybe he wasn't alone.

"What about Lukoh?"

Generations of Eloran kings had pledged their lives to Lukoh the moment they took on the crown. Slowly, over the course of what must have been hundreds of years, he had become more of a superstition than a true deity. If Akar was real and powerful enough to free himself, then Lukoh had to be able to do something.

My brother shrugged, "I don't know. You can try to ask for his help, but it's been four centuries since there was any remotely credible documentation about him. It's possible, but I wouldn't bet her life on it."

"We need to consult the king and queen," Elliott hopped down from where he was perched, eyes meeting mine fully. There was a heavy weight behind the look. I had so very much to say to him, to Alaric, to *Selah*. "If people are claiming that Akar is sending them after the princess, they need to know."

I snorted. "Wouldn't be the first time we've been targeted in the name of religion."

The room was gravely silent as Elliott snatched a dagger from his waist to slice through the rope binding me. It was one of Selah's. He did not offer it to me after my hand was finally free.

I stood, rubbing my sore wrist. My clothes were warm enough. I had shoes on. Distin wasn't more than a day's walk.

I wiped the wrinkles out of my coat. "Well, I suppose I'll be seeing you all at the castle, then."

Elliott stepped in my way. I raised a brow. "It's the middle of the night and you are a prince of Elora. You cannot walk that far alone in the dark."

"Have I not rested enough?"

Pushing past Elliott, Alaric opened the door, "Suit yourself. We'll see you when we arrive."

Out the door, down the stairs, and out of the inn I went. I left Alaric with the two carriages, the one we had taken and the one my siblings brought. He'd need them more than I would. I was in no mood to sit and remember our first journey. While I was not faster than a horse, I must have been hours ahead. Surely, I'd beat them to Distin.

The air had warmed in Elora. No longer was the night chill biting at my skin how it had when we left. A soft breeze blew past, dulling the June heat. The difference in climate between the Eloran and Lyscottian border would remain forever a mystery. While their mountains were still covered in snow, ours were warm enough to hike around.

Quietly, I started the trek.

It was not long after that I heard footsteps trailing behind me. I sensed my soldier long before he spoke. I had no interest in speaking with him. I hadn't yet decided whether I was to be offended by the fact he felt it necessary to join me. So I said nothing, and he said nothing, and we walked in silence for a long while.

I tried so thoroughly not to picture Selah. What Alaric had said... Faye had narrowly been saved from that fate. That image, I quickly was able to block out of my mind. In a twisted way, I was thankful that Selah was the one at risk. She was strong. She was capable. She had a chance of recovering from whatever they'd done, even if it meant I had to walk with her through it. Children are resilient, but Faye would not have been able to heal in the same way. I barely had. Elliott claimed that he'd fully mended, but what I sensed from him usually said otherwise.

"Will you ignore me forever?"

"I'm considering it," in the moment, the option did not seem nearly as bad as his tone implied.

"Haven –"

"Is there something you'd like to discuss?" I asked, offering him nothing more than a passing glance.

Guilt leeched off of him. *Good.* He should feel bad. Never, in a million lifetimes, would I allowed him such treatment. But he did *nothing*. He did not interfere with Alaric's nonsense. It's not like he would have been punished for defying the prince. Maybe then, I'd understand. Our families were close enough though that he could have acted freely, without consequence.

He *chose* not to help.

Acknowledging that, I was angry all over again.

He only spoke once more.

"I want her back too."

I kept walking. He pushed no further.

We paced through the darkness, led by the faint glow of the moon and a barely visible path. No one passed us. Shockingly, overnight travel was not remarkably popular in Elora. The weather was fine, the road was easy, and it would get us home a few hours before Alaric and Genevieve.

In its own time, the sun rose. Distin was illuminated on the very edge of the horizon, slowly getting closer and brighter as we journeyed on. The sounds of the city began as a low hum, then a buzz, then the full force of Eloran commerce was on display. Elliott and I were granted polite nods as we passed, the occasional bow or offer of food. I had no appetite. My gut wrenched as we passed a strawberry stand tended to by a sweet older woman and her husband, wondering if they were the ones Selah had spoken of before.

The Eloran palace was just as I remembered it. Hard brick and wood adorned with the royal colors lined the walls and entrance, nearly glowing in the early morning sun. At its height, the building was among the tallest in the nation. We rarely ever used the higher floors due to the upsetting amount of stairs one needed to climb in order to reach them, but each of the lower levels were well loved. Soldiers lived in a portion of the castle, a section was designated for visitors, but our family and those we employed took up most of the space.

It took quite a while longer for us to reach the entrance, and I did not recognize the two soldiers who let us in the door. Their eyes both darted to the array of badges on Elliott's uniform, then to the metal lacing around my forehead. With an inhuman speed almost reminiscent of the lieutenant colonel, they moved out of our way. I nodded politely, not waiting for Elliott. I couldn't be bothered to.

Having somehow heard of our arrival, my parents were waiting at the entrance. My mother's features were an almost exact match of mine, with her blonde hair tied back into a knot and her amber eyes knowingly assessing. My father, though, was Genevieve's counterpart. Gray patches had started worming their way into his otherwise dark brown locks. Bright blue eyes narrowed upon our approach.

"Alaric and Genevieve?" the king asked.

"Coming," I answered, nodding to them both. "But we need to talk. Akar is returning, and the king of Lyscott is on his way here now."

Chapter Thirty-Three: Selah

He was taller than I'd expected.

I suppose that, as a god, it pays to look formidable. But sitting on the dungeon floor, he appeared nearly human. Lukoh's shoulders were broad and pulled back, even as he rested against the cool stone across from me. His hands were folded and set upon outstretched legs. His skin was the golden brown of a man who had spent his whole life working underneath the sun. Mahogany curls settled on his head just above his full, dark eyelashes and honey-amber eyes. His clothes were plain and a few decades out of style, and I could have easily mistaken him for a middle-aged Eloran citizen if there had not been something so thoroughly otherworldly simmering in his gaze.

And it was with that gaze that he stared back at me, not with judgment or disdain, but something closer to warmth.

"Hello, Selah."

I coughed, half from disbelief and half from the effort of righting myself to face him. *I haven't died, have I? Surely,* I thought, *I am not that ill.*

His head tilted ever so slightly as he cast me a sad smile. Had I said that out loud? Heavens above, he looked young. Older than me, but far younger than he'd been depicted in the books from the Lyscottian library. "No, my dear. You are most certainly alive." *True.* His eyes narrowed. "It's a strange gift that Nero has bothered you with. Not one I've ever offered him."

What?

Even now, I am not sure how I'd describe Lukoh's voice. It was low and human but still supernaturally solid and rough. It was sweet as the honey in his eyes, warm as the sunrise and as ragged as the ocean tide.

My words, on the other hand, came out as hardly more than a shaky whisper. "Tell me something he wouldn't know."

Understanding accompanied the subtle glow in the god's face.

"The prince of Elora has cared for you from the moment he stepped into the cell where you were kept."

My heart tried to shatter at the very mention of Haven, but Lukoh continued.

"I knew he would. You were witty, and brave, and unimpressed by his status. Oh, if only you could have sensed how bothered he was by your pain. But you didn't like that he was not burdened in the way that you were." *True.*

Haven. Most of what I remembered from our first meeting was that I threatened him more than I should've been allowed. I'd been so deeply angry when he waltzed into my cell with not a care in the world. If only I'd known how good he truly was, how kind and how gallant. I'd been blind enough to be caught by the enemy, and I couldn't imagine how he was handling it. If the roles were reversed …

"He'll be alright, you know." *True.* I'd forgotten for a moment that the creator of all humanity was also privy to my thoughts. Oh, the things he must have overheard. "He is afraid for you, cripplingly afraid, but I will not let it consume him. Just like I will not let you die here." *True.*

It would save everyone a lot of trouble.

"Selah," His voice hardened.

"Sorry." Tears I didn't know I was fighting began bubbling up to the surface. My very bones ached. Whatever Ilse kept giving me was taking its toll. Nero's gift kept me from resting even in my dreams. Adiel's chains felt like they grew tighter with every movement. If Akar was real, and if he wanted me dead, was there really any point in fighting him? Dozens could die if the Lyscottian king succeeded.

"He is weak," Lukoh spat, "and foolish. He is aiming for a goal that is impossible to achieve and he is making promises he cannot hope to fulfill. You do not have to let him win."

"What's the point?" I rasped. My throat started to burn. "Who cares if they serve me up as an offering? I am one person. Elora will be safe. Castillo will be happy. Gen, and Alaric, and Faye, and Haven will be left alone. The Illustri will have one less vendetta. I have no family, few friends, and a home that can be easily sold. Little would be lost."

"That is not true."

"And what if I survive?" I tried to laugh, but it was more like a wheeze. "What then? Perhaps we all make it out unscathed. I return to Distin. Maybe Haven and I will remain friends. Maybe he will forget our time together and move on. What am I left with then? Will I go back to *constantly* feeling unsafe in my own skin? Will you leave me to fend for myself like you have for the last two decades? Did I matter to you fifteen years ago, or is it only now that Akar is involved?"

"You cannot fathom how wrong you are."

"I was a *child*!" my voice broke, and finally the dam snapped in half. Hot tears fell in droves, but I could not be bothered to wipe them away. "I was weak and helpless and you are a *god*, for heaven's sake! I – I asked for your help. I was given *nothing*. Why now? Why not then?"

327

His brows were pulled tightly together. Was it pity in his expression? Could deities even feel such a thing? His beautiful features contorted in agony. For a passing moment, all I felt was shame. I had just shouted at *the* god of the continent. Granted, it seemed well earned at the time, but wasn't that an easy way to get erased from existence?

When he spoke again, his voice was quiet. Audible, but low. "There will be decades for me to explain why I did not take you away from them. We do not yet have time for me to provide my every reason. But even then, Selah, there was not a breath of yours I did not notice. I *hated* it. I hated them. Have you not questioned why so many of the men you knew met untimely ends? Balor is the only one left, and even his days are numbered. Just because I did not intervene in the way that you wanted does not mean I did not care. It does not mean I did not see. They have been repaid exactly what they are due, just as the king of Lyscott will be repaid."

True.

I lacked the energy to unpack everything Lukoh said. With food and some time, perhaps I could delve into the fact that maybe I was not abandoned. Half-broken in a cell was not the place for me to fall apart even further.

Lukoh stood, only to crouch beside me. With an ethereal hand, he gently moved a strand of hair out of my face. The touch was so soft I barely felt it. A deity was mere *inches* away. I didn't know quite what to do with myself. His expression twisted into displeasure, likely at my less than functional state. "Haven is on his way. Only for a little longer must you be brave, *nesikha*. If not for your sake, then do it for his."

I opened my mouth to answer him, but the creator of the continent was gone.

328

Chapter Thirty-Four: Haven

◆

It had hardly taken any time at all for Alaric and Genevieve to reach Distin. In fact, I realized as they pulled into the palace's side entrance, I may have been better off sleeping through the night and joining them in the carriage. My legs had started to ache, and my back had certainly seen better days. I should've been exhausted, and might have been if I hadn't been immobilized for nearly a week.

Sitting in the Eloran meeting room was surreal. The last time we'd all been gathered, it had been so different. Urgent, yes, but hopeful. I'd liked my siblings significantly more. My chest had not weighed so heavily down upon me. My thoughts were not consumed by a young lady who was being held a couple hundred miles away by a handful of manipulative, delusional psychopaths.

I sat in my assigned chair, fingers mindlessly tapping away on the vast wooden table. Only Elliott had joined me, my parents busy with Genevieve and Alaric's arrival. Depths, I couldn't stand them. Usually, I felt otherwise, but perhaps it would take time to forgive them.

The lieutenant colonel unhappily eyed my moving hand, not with disdain, but with unabashed worry. I paid him no mind. He could go on being concerned. Everyone had a good reason to be concerned. Akar was resurrecting. Well, technically, if one wished to dive into the theology of it all, he was being released. I couldn't imagine how he planned on freeing himself from the caves Lukoh had locked him inside of, or if he had already found a way out. Clearly, Akar had his limitations, as he had sent Castillo after Selah instead of searching for her himself. How long would it be until he managed to achieve free reign of the continent?

"Haven!"

A puff of blond hair nearly tackled me out of my chair. She was little, and sister-sized, and a surprisingly strong hugger for someone of her stature. Her emotions hit me with about as much force, excitement and impatience seeping through her like a rapid wind. My lungs, on the other hand, were notably compressed.

"Faye. Air. Please."

"Sorry. Hi, Elliott!"

She moved quickly over to him, although Elliott had the advantage of expecting the assault. He embraced her with a faint grin, and she bounced back again.

"Hello, Princess. Any trouble in the castle to report?"

Faye had just opened her mouth to offer him a comprehensive account before she was cut off.

"None she didn't cause, I'm afraid."

My mother entered with my father following closely behind. Perhaps it was the fact that they were no longer as young as they had once been, but the king and queen appeared to be inexplicably drained. I hadn't noticed it on my arrival, but as they took their respective places at the table, they sat down with unseen burdens tugging at them.

Has something happened?

Alaric and Genevieve finally padded in. Alaric strutted and plopped down with an irritating amount of swagger. Due to the fact that our little sister made no attempt to grapple them, I assumed the three of them had already chatted.

Upon seeing Faye, Genevieve paled slightly and grabbed our sister's hand. "This is bound to be a terribly boring conversation. Come, we can find something fun to do while I tell you about all the attractive young men who fell *madly* in love with me over the course of the journey. Oh, you would not *believe* –"

The chatter continued as they wandered down the hall. While Genevieve was still not my very favorite person, I could respect her for a moment. I agreed that informing a thirteen-year-old about how some leaders of a foreign nation wanted to kidnap and sacrifice her was not the wisest choice. She was tough, and mature enough for her age, but it was too much for anyone.

Elliott rose to seal the door shut, and my father's gaze settled on me. "I apologize, I was not quite in the space to discuss what you mentioned earlier," the king started, bracing his elbows on the wood. "What did you say about Akar?"

I told them the entire story from start to finish, which was, in fact, quite an extensive endeavor. I explained more of how we'd been attacked on the road, all about the Illustri's siege on the Lyscottian castle and how it traced back to Mallord Bay. I told them about Selah's gift, about all the little white lies she'd picked up on that I'd decided to ignore. I recalled the strange dream I had about Akar. I told of how our gifts had changed. I went into an exhaustive amount of detail concerning the king's various deceptions, their respective abilities, and how they'd ended up going after Faye. Lastly, in what felt like it was physically going to tear me apart, I told them how they had taken Selah. Alaric filled in gaps occasionally, but the story was mostly mine.

The king and queen listened in pensive silence. I'm not sure what I expected them to say. It was a month of stories, and rather complicated ones, that I was trying to retell. It would reasonably take a moment to accept.

My father rubbed a hand over his face. Strangely, his first question was not about Akar or Lorelai, not Selah or Lyscott. "Did you ever try to manipulate the king's emotions? Undo the damage that Akar has done on his mind?"

I shook my head. *Was that an option?* "No. If I did influence the king's emotions accidentally, neither of us noticed."

"He would've known," Alaric added, rubbing the back of his neck. "Your gift could be felt in Lyscott, but the first time I sensed your influence, it was evident. You tried when you woke up last night. It is...painful."

No wonder he'd complained.

"Regardless," the king continued, glancing at our mother, "I'm not sure how to proceed. We are not offering him Faye. That is non-negotiable. We could let them keep the young lady, but –"

"*Absolutely not –*"

"*But*," he waved a hand, "it is unwise. If Akar's request is truly for her, then he wants her for a reason. It would be irresponsible of us to allow that to happen."

My mother, grabbing his hand with a serious expression, spoke softly. "Faye's gift hasn't manifested yet, Malachi. While rare, it is possible that she will be granted the gift of detection."

Heavy silence fell on the room. Selah, for all she was, did not happen to be a princess. Detection was only given once in a hundred or so years, so Selah had almost made sense, but she wasn't royalty. If Faye *was* given the gift, then Akar himself would be hunting her. Without Lukoh's intervention, she would be destined to a lifetime of running away from evil.

"She won't," Alaric said with an alarming lack of confidence.

Sternly, my father looked at me. "Until Castillo breaches Eloran territory, and until we can find him, there is nothing I can do for your Selah. I have no location. I have no information concerning what he is capable of. I cannot hunt him in his own nation."

I hated that he was right, hated it more than I could handle. Reason stated that there was no way we could help. *Nothing*, while Alaric was able to describe how she was suffering.

Really, what we needed was divine intervention.

I rose from my chair.

"Understood."

No one followed me out.

I didn't know what exactly I would ask of Lukoh as I entered the cathedral. Stained glass stretched from floor to ceiling on the three main walls, with the entrance being the only portion not fully decorated. A map of Elora was hung at the very front, just above a scarcely used altar. Rows of empty pews filled the room, meticulously carved but entirely untouched.

I didn't know if the god would hear me. I didn't know if he would care. Feeling half foolish, I sat in the front row and started speaking.

Mostly, I told him about Selah. Her hair, her eyes, her attitude, the dress she wore when I saw her last, the way she'd looked at me after getting injured, how she'd fought with Adiel, how she'd tried to put me back together again after getting attacked on the road, and every tiny detail in between. If only he knew who she was, he'd help.

I couldn't get through retelling what Alaric had said. The picture was too vivid, too real. He hadn't even mentioned much, but even then. I'd seen her hurt before, so recently. How eager I would have been to trade places. How eager I would have been to suffer on her behalf.

I rested my head on folded hands, eyes closing as I tried to push it all away. How lucky was I to have a choice in whether I wanted to think of her pain. It was masochism to replay it all over and over again, but it felt equally as unjust to try to forget.

It was then that I heard a voice that, while inaudible, was so entirely outside myself. No one had entered the room; it was still only me in the vast chapel. There were no footsteps, no rustling sounds of coming or going, just me. Ethereal and otherworldly, it spoke.

Kill them quickly, Prince.

Then, in the same moment, a noise.

Thunk.

Startled, I looked up.

A knife had been buried in the Eloran map.

One of *Selah's* knives.

Chapter Thirty-Five: Selah

What, exactly, is one meant to do after speaking with a god?

I can say what *I* did. I questioned everything I've ever believed.

Lukoh was real. I'd met him. We talked. He'd called me a name in a language I didn't understand. Which meant Akar was decidedly a problem. Which meant that the stories that I'd read of them both were true, which meant Genevieve was actually right.

What am I supposed to do with that?

I was not left alone with my thoughts for long. Adiel and Ilse wandered down to me. Ilse carried a pile of clothing, while the young man's hands were empty. My strength still was nowhere near what it needed to be if I wanted to fight. I considered it. I also considered the fact that it hurt to breathe, and move, and *think*, and that I was less than eager to make it worse.

The chains disappeared, and my hands felt strangely light. The skin on my wrists was raw and bruised, but at least I could move. My ankles were not in much better shape, and the shackles were gone from them as well.

"Get dressed," Ilse tossed the pile at my feet. "It's a long journey to Distin, and I'd just hate for you to freeze on the way." *Lie.*

On second thought, maybe I could muster the energy to smack her in her stupid, beautiful face.

I snagged at the clothes, eyeing them carefully. They looked fine. Pretty, almost. Not quite the attire you'd hold a hostage in, but I was in no mood to argue any further.

Adiel noticed how I was assessing. "Are you going to need help? I'd be more than happy to supervise." *True.*

Gross. So gross.

"I'm fully capable," I muttered.

"Suit yourself," he shrugged. "You have ten minutes. Be ready. Or don't! We'll take you in as much – or as little – as you're wearing." He winked.

I contemplated whether Ilse's poison or Adiel's advances made me more nauseous. It was a remarkably close competition. They left me to change.

With about two minutes to spare, I was fully dressed. Clean, good-smelling clothes were so underrated. It had been an effort, irritating every muscle, to get them on, but it was so worthwhile. There was nowhere for me to see how I looked. I was not entirely excited to, as I could feel the puffiness of my face and I could see the bruises that speckled the rest of me.

It was Mekhi who came to escort me downstairs. His face gave away unfortunately little, and he was quiet when he entered.

His stance was set and wide, arms ready at his side, "It's time."

I tossed the dress I'd worn onto the rotting mattress. I wouldn't be wearing it again. "I spoke with Lukoh."

Concern drew his brow. He reached a hand to my forehead, and I didn't try to fight him. "You are unwell. Just a fever is perfectly manageable, but if you're hallucinating –"

I batted his arm away then. "It was real," I huffed. Heavens above, I didn't realize how much of an effort it would be to dress. I was out of breath. "I don't know how to explain it, but it was real. He called me a name – a word I've never heard before. Nes – Nesik –" I stumbled.

"*Nesikha*," Mekhi finished, paling.

I paused. *He knew?* "Is that bad?"

He sighed, "It's not good." With an outstretched arm, he opened the door behind him. "We need to leave."

I wish I could say that I remember the journey back into Elora. I don't. I know that there were eight carriages, that I was occasionally swapped back and forth between them. I don't remember if I ate or if I slept, or who kept watch of me the most. I know I was awake most of the time, little glimmers of Elora and Lyscott sitting in the very outermost edges of my mind.

Even today, I am not sure if it is a mercy that I do not know what happened. By the end of the journey, I had a few more bruises than I recalled having prior. It may have been Ilse's doing, or my own. I cannot imagine what motive she would have to make me forget – if they were kind and did not want me to know it. Or, even worse, if it had been so bad that my own conscience had worked to protect me. I imagined it was the latter.

What I do recall is only the very end of the journey. The Lyscottian carriages had vast windows on either side. I was tucked next to Mekhi, across from Ilse and Adiel. They did not say much as we trailed right in front of Nero, Wren, and the king. They were not so familiar with Elora, did not recognize the eerie forests or the winding roads.

The sun was bright and warm, and I could feel it seeping into my skin through the glass. Being in the light again felt good, felt so very human. I was nearly home. My apartment would still be waiting for me if I ever made it back to Distin. Eli and Mariah would likely have a list of questions about what the royal family, what Lyscott, was like. It was all so close, so tangible, but just out of reach.

I couldn't say how many days we'd spent traveling when our carriage lurched to a stop. Ilse and Adiel eyed each other warily, as he peeked just out of the window. Mekhi's expression was set and cold. My hands were bound once again, not with Adiel's chains, but with plain old rope. I lacked the energy or the strength to pull my way out of them, and the Lyscottians knew it. My bones ached, the fever hadn't left me, and I was still sick from Ilse's poison. It was almost over, one way or another.

I caught only a glimpse of what had stopped us before pulling back. A blockade of carriages and soldiers stood in the path.

Carriages with the Eloran royal emblem on them.

My heart jumped in my chest.

Haven, Elliott, and Gen were waiting in the middle of the road.

Chapter Thirty-Six: Haven

Lukoh had been right. The Lyscottians were exactly where he'd said they'd be.

It had been an effort to convince my father that I was serious, that my knowledge of where they were headed was guided by something other than delusion. I'd tugged him down to the chapel to show him the map, but even that had barely been enough. Regardless, it wasn't too far out of Distin, and at least if we were wrong then our forces would still be nearby.

The Lyscottian carriages were, to the shock of no one, made out of a deep navy fabric and silver metal features, so out of place in an Eloran forest. Their horses were snow white, but their flawless hooves were now covered in mud and stray blades of grass.

What struck me more than any of that was the fact that I could sense her. Barely, and I couldn't reach much of what she felt, but her presence was apparent.

One by one, the Lyscottians and their soldiers poured out of their carriages. Nero appeared first, followed by a blatantly uneasy Wren. Mekhi was the first to leave his carriage, Ilse trailing closely behind. My gut dropped as the king exited. He strutted towards us entirely composed outside of a slight tremor in his hands.

Lastly, Adiel pulled Selah out of their carriage.

As if my heart was capable of breaking any more.

She was ghost white, legs wobbling beneath her as Adiel dragged her towards the group. Layers of rope were wrapped around her wrists, marring the skin they touched. Her lip was cut, her eyes were puffy, her breaths were shaky, and she was hopelessly frail. It hadn't even been two weeks.

When they were close enough, but just out of reach, Adiel let her fall. She barely caught herself on weak hands. With all of his focus settled on us, Adiel made chains appear on the wrists of me, Gen, and Elliott. Our soldiers were untouched, meaning either it was solely a display of power, or that Adiel notably could not make that many shackles.

"Selah," I breathed.

She glanced up at me, pain and defiance evident in those pretty eyes. "Fine."

"Is she?" The king sauntered over, peering down at her. With every step of his, my feet felt more firmly glued to the floor. By the time he was close enough, the weight of it was substantially draining. "Hmm. She doesn't *look* fine. I suppose even a week in a Lyscottian dungeon will have that effect." The king's cruel gaze shifted to me. "Are you here to negotiate, Highness?"

Anger with a force I have never felt before or since flowed through me like a current. Lukoh's request to end it all did not seem so distant. Though it required a considerable amount of work, I took a steady step forward, letting the chains dangle before me. Each of their emotions were hovering just where I could reach them. Adiel, Ilse, Nero, Castillo, and Selah's were all hanging within my grasp, begging to be toyed with.

Mekhi and Wren, though, were gone. I hadn't even noticed them leave.

I clicked my tongue. "I considered telling you that your lives would be spared if you left Elora. But I am above deception, Your Majesty." I stared daggers at the king. "You and your court will die here. There is nothing to negotiate."

Castillo smirked. "You'd threaten me in chains? Very well. If violence is what you're wanting, then violence I will provide." He looked at Adiel, "Go ahead."

Adiel did not have a chance to more than reach for Selah. I singled out which emotions were his, held them with my mind, and tugged *hard*. He cried out in agony and grabbed his head. I did not let go. Immediately, the shackles vanished.

Alarm striking each of the Lyscottian soldiers' faces, they drew their swords. Adiel was too busy writhing to be bothered.

"What did you do?" Nero hissed.

I tucked my hands into my pockets and shrugged. "I haven't moved."

Selah chuckled wryly from the ground. Heavens above, I'd missed her.

The king's gift was becoming awfully burdensome, so I released Adiel. He sighed raggedly with relief, stumbling backwards. With painstaking slowness, I pulled at the king's senses. His breath caught, and my feet felt lighter, but I had not yet used much force. I only needed to sway him enough so that his gift was not as powerful.

I addressed him directly. "Call back your men, Castillo. Don't make them die with you."

"Stay *exactly* where you are!" The king ordered.

I raised a chin to the Eloran soldiers waiting behind us. "Go collect them, please. All of them."

As one wave, Elliott led the small charge of our soldiers. Right away, they pushed the Lyscottians a handful of yards back. Gen ducked back into one of the carriages, just like we'd planned.

The second she was within reach, I rushed to get to Selah. The closer I got, the more I could sense her pain. I pulled one of her knives from my waistband and reached for the binds –

"Don't," she pulled back, panting. Her eyes would barely meet mine. My gut clenched. "I'll … It'll hurt you. Let someone else –"

I took her hands and sliced the cords in half. But depths, was she right. No wonder she was having trouble breathing. My ribs were on *fire*. The weight of her exhaustion and agony were far more crippling than the king's ability. My heart stopped for a fleeting moment and I struggled to get air.

"Haven," she exhaled.

With whatever power I had, I willed her pain to lessen. It did, if only slightly. Certainly not by enough to provide her with any lasting relief, but to the point where it was bearable.

I kept her hands in one of mine and used the other to smooth stray strands of hair off her face. Her eyes squeezed tightly shut, fighting off weak tears, "It's good to see you."

Despite how my lungs tightened, I forced a smirk, "Now what sort of fiancé would I be if I hadn't gotten you back?"

"A fabricated one."

"True," I sighed, reminding myself that she was real and so close to being safe. "Here's what we're going to do," I pressed a kiss to her burning forehead, glancing at the battle raging around us. "Gen is waiting. She will take care of you while I finish with this mess."

"I can help," she argued, struggling to stand and hopelessly failing. "He's going to try to reach the city. Don't let him."

I caught her with a gentle hold, feeling the worry etch itself into my features. "You're done fighting for today, my dearest bodyguard. Grant me the honor."

Only then did Gen appear, frazzled but ready to take Selah back to the carriages, "I've got her. Go help Elliott."

Looking over, he was caught between Nero and two other Lyscottian soldiers. His supernatural speed kept him from taking any hits, but numbers forced him to stay defensive. Selah may have contended more, but she passed out as soon as I took my hands off her. Secondhand, I felt the rush of returning pain before she faded.

So soon, it would be okay.

Drawing my own weapon, I turned to join the battle.

Formally, I had only fought in two conflicts before. One, when I was a child, and a second, when the Illustri attacked the Lyscottian castle. As far as stakes, those were my only real experiences. Informally, though, General Pearce had subjected Elliott and I to every form of military training she could conjure. Alaric was the crown prince, too important to allow to fight, and the ladies were both too young at the time, so it was only us. Back then, it had been miserable. However, facing the Lyscottians, the fear I felt did not overtake me. I had only General Pearce to thank as the muscle memory took over the fight.

When the first Lyscottian started swinging, I swung right back. I was lost in the haze of battle by the third strike.

It was all blurry, practiced movements. There was not much to consider other than the clashing of the swords and anticipating each opponent's next step. It was terrifying and invigorating all at once. Around

343

me, our soldiers were gaining. Elliott had even torn down everyone he'd been fighting except Nero, who appeared to be slowly losing energy. The lieutenant colonel was more than capable. Adiel was chaining soldiers that went after him and Ilse, only to be overwhelmed by the ones he could not bind fast enough. The king, though, is who I sought out.

I reached him just as he sliced into one of my soldiers. I slashed in the same breath that he noticed me, raising his weapon to defend just fast enough to parry my blow. Blue flames seemed to dance in the king's eyes as he raged, cutting wildly through the air. I pushed him back, back, back, and he managed to nick the portion of my shoulder where two pieces of armor were tied together. I felt the slight trickle of blood, but shoved forward.

The fighting quieted around us as dozens of eyes shot to where we warred. His strikes were crazed, falling in heavy batches that took constant work to defend against. I met him, blow for blow, fighting with all my strength to knock him down. A brief reminder of the weeks he'd forced Selah through, the ones he'd planned to force Faye through, was enough for me to focus.

Castillo was strong, for all he was worth. Fighting him was draining my energy quicker than I'd anticipated. For a passing moment, I wondered if he was using his ability without even realizing.

I'd humored him quite long enough. I reached out with my gift and yanked.

The king fell back with a blood-curdling cry.

I rested my sword underneath his chin, but did not advance.

Heavy grief weighed on him so powerfully that it knocked me back a step. Castillo choked on harsh, cold, wracking sobs. The king of Lyscott had fallen, broken in half before me. My gut twisted into hundreds of tiny knots, reeling from the sheer force of all he felt.

His lament was barely audible, "I've failed her."

I bore down at him, feeling little but pity and righteous anger. "It would never have worked. Faye couldn't have helped you."

That caught his attention, and I could sense the shock of those beholding us. "What?" he exhaled.

"Would my fiancée not have been considered a princess of Elora?"

Realization fluttered in his inhumanly icy blue eyes as he put it all together. Horror wrote itself into every line of his battered face as the air visibly left from his body. "*No.*"

"*A princess of Elora with the gift of detection,*" I quoted. Hot, angry tears fell down the king's face in droves. "You've had her for *weeks.*"

He shook his head with agonizing denial. "You're lying. You're *lying.* She is no princess. She's not – it doesn't –" he wheezed in anguish.

"*She* was who you wanted," I confirmed. Watching the king crack into pieces was excruciating. I'm not sure how so many were able to bear witness to it. "Pray to your god, Castillo. He may have mercy on you. Elora will not."

He was covered in dirt and the blood of my people. I *could not* pity him. The king's chest caved in as he stared up into the sky, "My Annika has cared for our little one all by herself these past years." With those words, my own heart shattered. "It is well past time that I join her."

I had to end it. There was no better chance, no other opportunity where I'd have the king so ready, so close, so nearly dealt with. I wanted to. Heavens above, I wanted to. He was awful. He'd tried to kidnap my little sister. He'd sanctioned the torture of the woman I cared for. He'd acted on behalf of *the* very source of wickedness in the continent. He'd threatened the safety of my entire kingdom.

345

But I was staring down at him as he looked so painfully human. So broken. Snapped in half by a fate that he did not fully choose. How easily could I, could any one of us, have become him if we had suffered such a loss. If only I pushed my sword a little further, it would be done.

I couldn't.

A steady hand rested itself on my shoulder. Elliott was at my side. He had to have seen the entire encounter.

He looked at me knowingly, "I will do it."

I shook my head immediately in protest. "I can't possibly ask you to _"

"There is no need. Go direct your men, Haven. Let my conscience be stained for the sake of preserving yours."

I took in the scene around us. Most of the Lyscottians had fallen. The rest were captured or nearly so as our soldiers finished binding the last few. Ilse was screaming and clawing at the men who held her. Adiel was visibly trembling, and Nero was thoroughly bloodied but entirely stoic. In each of their eyes settled the realization that it was over.

I righted myself, staving off the emotion that threatened to overtake me. "Take them back to Distin. We will allow them a fair trial, but threatening the safety of any of the Eloran people is punishable by execution. As for the king," I glanced over to Elliott, and then to Castillo, whose face was damp and eyes squeezed tightly shut, "make it quick and painless, but final. He has suffered quite enough. There is no need for us to delay it further."

As I turned to walk away from the king, he began to recite an old, Eloran prayer.

"Heavens keep me."

I did not pause, I did not look back. I kept walking away. Even as I heard Elliott's steps in the dirt advancing towards the king, I did not look.

"Saints bless me."

Our soldiers began toting the remaining Lyscottians away. I watched as they flooded to the carriages.

"Let not my soul be discarded."

Ilse was the only one who dared to view the end of her king, and tears flooded her dark eyes.

"But perhaps death will be kinder than man."

Crack.

I stopped.

The king of Lyscott was dead.

****

As soon as the carriages were full, I'd sent all but one of them away. It took until nearly dusk for everything to settle completely. Gen had taken Selah back to the palace. Last I'd heard, they were going to set her up in my room. There was nowhere else to really put her. Injured soldiers took up the majority of the guest wing and I was more than happy to have her close.

Elliott and I had stayed behind. He'd wrapped the king's body in a cloth we'd found, and I'd borrowed two shovels from the soldiers' supplies. Maybe he did not deserve a proper burial. He certainly wouldn't have offered one to any of us. We would be *better* than that. We would be better than him and all the forces he had been influenced by. Together, in full quiet, we dug the king's grave. It was over. There was nothing to say.

When the hole was deep enough, we lowered him down into the dirt. He did not jerk back to life, did not threaten or deceive anymore. He was wholly, painfully dead. At least, from the grave, no one could corrupt his mind. Perhaps he was finally at peace.

Once there was nothing left for us to do, we paced back to the carriages. I held out a hand for him to enter, but he quietly shook his head. "I'll walk tonight, Highness. I have much to contemplate."

I nodded. I understood. With his unnatural speed, I would only slow him down. If solitude was what he needed, I could manage that.

After he had trailed off, and I was unattended in the moving carriage, I loosed the band of gold from where it rested around my forehead and cast it off to the side. It was all so much, too much.

In the emptiness of the evening, I held my face in my hands, and I wept.

Chapter Thirty-Seven: Selah

The bed smelled of cedar and cinnamon.

The room was elegant, but relatively plain. No fancy decorations lined the walls, no excessive Lyscottian artistry. The furniture was nice, regal and well made, but clearly worn down by years of use. Still functional, still pretty, but aged. I was tucked underneath a few layers of mismatched blankets, and I was alone.

It was Eloran design.

Fancy Eloran design.

I was in Elora.

That thought pulled me up in the bed. Moving didn't hurt. Not at all, actually. Not even the ache that I'd felt upon waking after being stabbed had stuck around to haunt me. My stomach rumbled fiercely, but aside from that, I was whole.

How strange it was to feel whole.

Forest green curtains concealed the windows, letting light trickle in through the very edges. Rising slowly, I approached the nearest curtain and moved it aside with timid fingers. The city of Distin, in all its glory, was bustling below me. From the very edge of my view, I could see the block of homes where my apartment was. *My* home. I hadn't been home in ages.

Judging by its distance, and the various markets I could place between us, I was in the palace. But Haven, and Gen, and Elliott, and everyone I would have known were not with me. I remembered pieces of the fight, the stuttering of my heart upon seeing that they had not forgotten me. It would take more than just a moment to realize that it was over.

I flinched when the door slowly pulled open. The prince's movements were slow and cautious as though he was earnestly trying not to wake me. He carried with him a small basket, dressed in clothes that would have seemed casual on most others, but appeared perfectly royal on him. He was stunning, and he was real, and he was truly there in front of me.

Likely sensing what I felt, his eyes jerked up.

He set the basket on the desk beside him. I took two steps in his direction, and he closed the distance in a breath. His arms slid around my waist as mine wrapped themselves around his neck. In less than a second, I was surrounded by him. His hold was firm and unyielding, and I buried my face in his hard shoulder.

When was the last time I'd been hugged? Deeply, thoroughly hugged? I could not recall a time I'd been held only for the sake of being held, except by him. It was relief, and it was warmth, and it was safety, and I would be needing a hundred more.

"Hello," my greeting was muffled in his jacket.

"Hello," his voice was low and reverent as he pulled back to look at me, keeping one hand at my side and one trailing up to the nape of my neck. "Are you alright? I mean, I know you *feel* alright – not like that – I meant –"

My fingers traced down and rested on his chest, "I'm okay."

He exhaled, "You're okay."

350

Words started bubbling up. "I'm sorry, I should've never gone with Ilse. You all knew that something was wrong and I –"

"Are you kidding?" my prince appeared to be almost offended. "I should be apologizing. If I'd actually listened when you said the king was lying, then –"

"You had mercy on him, Haven. Do not mistake your empathy for weakness. It is a strength." The steady pulse of his heartbeat thumped beneath my fingers, "Which is not to say that you were right, Highness. You *decidedly* should have listened to me. I am incredibly wise."

He chuckled quietly and planted a gentle kiss on my forehead, "And incredibly humble."

Despite his try at humor, I sensed the weight behind his tone.

"You couldn't have known."

Haven sighed, "I should've. And I didn't." Amber eyes stared out the one uncovered window. "But we are home, and I will have a lifetime to make it up to you."

A lifetime. But we weren't *actually* engaged. The Lyscottians thought we were. It had been announced to the entire city of Distin. But it wasn't real. Heavens above, I was not ready to handle that mess. I was rather fond of my anonymity. It made me *lots* of money. The last thing my poor business needed after I'd been gone for weeks was for everyone to know my face.

I was hesitant to speak, "We'll need to break it off at some point, won't we?"

His grin faded, "Oh, yes. Of course."

"Of course," I echoed.

But I really, really liked Haven. I liked being near him. I liked fighting with him. I liked that he was capable. I thoroughly enjoyed having his hands on me. I liked that he cared about me. I liked that he was sweet, and selfless, and gentle, but a significantly better swordsman than me. Marriage was far too much for either of us, but I didn't want to miss him again. I'd missed him for weeks; I had done my due diligence, and I knew that not seeing him regularly would be miserable.

"I'd like to keep you around, though," he whispered. "Not as a fiancée. Not yet. First as a friend."

"Hmmm," I nodded, deep in thought. "Do friends always stand this close?"

Haven smiled, and the entire room was a little brighter for it, "Only the very dearest of friends."

My hands slid back up, clasping behind his neck. He dropped to my waist again. Honey amber eyes were entirely focused on me. "You'll have to tell me more about this whole friendship idea. Do friends often look at each other like you're looking at me?"

Pained, Haven rested his forehead against mine. He was one sharp movement away from kissing me, and there was a battle waging in his features over it, but he did not yet try, "Selah."

"Haven."

"Can I?"

"Please."

His lips crashed into mine, and the rest of the world fell away.

Haven's hold was tight, but the kiss was almost reverent. It was as though I was something worthy of being handled with great care. His hands stayed firmly gentle, perfectly still. My skin burned wherever his fingers stayed. How I badly wanted him. How I badly wanted to soak up every detail of how it felt to be so near, so wrapped up in the prince's grasp.

For a fleeting moment, it was only him and me and every minor touch.

Then, agonizingly, he pulled back.

His lips quickly pursed together to hide his stupid, beautiful little grin. "If you'd like to reconsider the fiancée arrangement, I'm sure that we could come to an agreement –"

"*Haven.*"

"Just making sure," he planted a quick kiss on my cheek before letting me go entirely. "Alright, my loveliest companion, you are starving. It seems as though I cannot be your only form of sustenance." He snatched up the basket he'd brought and nodded towards the bed. "Come sit. There is so very much I must catch you up on."

We talked for quite some time. Haven told me of the battle on the road, filling in all the pieces that I did not remember clearly. He spoke of the journey home, and how he had yet to decide when he was going to forgive his siblings. He told me of my knife being sunken into an Eloran map. At that story, I recounted my meeting with Lukoh. The prince was keenly interested in that, and I offered him as much detail as I could. I did not tell him much of my time in the cell. There was no point for him to grieve what was already finished. But I told him of Lukoh, and of Mekhi, and of his desire to help Wren. How they'd disappeared remained a mystery. If the king was gone, Mekhi was to inherit the throne. That was another mess that neither of us quite had a solution to.

The prince had brought lots of bread, along with sliced meat and cheese. Most importantly, however, there was a wooden bowl of strawberries that was tucked into the side of the basket. He made some silly comment about being unable to forget my most unusual bargaining chip, and I took several grateful bites. They were everything I could hope

353

for and more. Heavens above, had I missed the taste of fruit. Not just any fruit, but *strawberries.*

Eventually, we slipped into comfortable silence, admiring the city below. It hummed with a sort of life that was foreign to Lyscott. When I was young, I'd run to Distin for a reason. It was an easy place to survive in, certainly. It was also so refreshing, the sort of energy that I'd been in dire need of. The sort of *hope* that I needed.

Haven tucked me underneath one arm as we stared on. How shocked the adolescent version of myself would be to see me, sitting so casually with a prince of Elora as though it was the most natural occurrence. He was thoroughly human enough that I often neglected his title.

Elora was in good hands.

The prince broke the stillness a while later, "I've spoken with my parents. I'd like to make you an offer."

I tilted my head in his direction, "Oh? Are you so pleased with how it worked out this first time?"

"You're not funny," he said roughly, but kissed my temple. "Use your gift here. In the palace. We won't take up all your time, and you'd still have plenty of hours in your day to do whatever you please, but having someone with the gift of detection is invaluable. Plus, you would be compensated fully for your efforts. As the one who'd be setting up your salary, I can personally attest that it would be more than fair."

Quietly, I pondered. The idea of being at the behest of the royal throne made me internally cringe, but a palace paycheck with the prospect of getting to see Haven, and chatting with Gen, or perhaps further training with Elliott on a regular basis was difficult to refuse.

"I accept."

He chuckled, "Good. I've already filled out all the necessary forms, so I'm glad that my many papercuts weren't wasted effort."

I smiled, but got lost in thought. What would that even entail? I did need to go back and put some more work into my business, but I wasn't sure if royal Eloran endorsement would be a blessing or a curse. I missed my work. Oftentimes, it was fulfilling. The pay didn't hurt, either.

I looked up at the prince, "So, what now?"

He loosed a breath, "Well, it depends on what you need. You are more than welcome to stay here for a few nights as you're adjusting." I contemplated it briefly. I had dreams, though, and if Haven was within a mile, I'd be waking him up constantly. As much as I appreciated his comfort, I could find no reason that he should suffer right along with me. "Ultimately, you are free to go. Compensation for this journey has already been transferred into your accounts as promised. It'll take a couple days to get everything finalized for you here, and you are welcome to do whatever you wish in the meantime."

I raised a brow, "Whatever I wish?"

Haven grinned, "Whatever you wish."

I considered it carefully. I did not want to be away from him, but I needed to go home. My apartment was likely in shambles after being away for so long. Having some time to think and to try to begin processing everything that had happened didn't sound like the very worst idea, either. Heavens above, I didn't even know how to begin to heal from all of it.

For the first time in a while, I was willing to try.

"I'd like to go home," I said.

"Then I will take you home."

Chapter Thirty-Eight: Haven

◆

Three weeks later.

We were definitely going to be late.

In our defense, Faye's gifting ceremony had been planned just after the busiest time for travel in Distin. It had taken half an hour longer than normal to cross the city, and the summer rain did not make the journey any easier. Fortunately, nothing ever started on time in the Eloran palace, and I presumed this event would be no different.

I'd been to Selah's apartment a few times in the weeks we'd been home. More often than not, I'd seen her at the castle. Most of our days had been spent getting her accustomed to working in the palace. We used her gift sparingly. Compared to our time in Lyscott, Distin was a vacation. No evil entities or corrupted kings, no bloodthirsty cults, just a steady routine.

I gently rapped on the door. Only a few moments later, gray-blue eyes peeked out from behind the small, sliding metal window in her door. By Distin's standards, it was an unusually attractive door. It was crafted out of fine oak, carved with subtle markings on each corner. If I was not mistaken, they appeared to be depictions of Lukohnian folklore.

Faintly, those eyes narrowed at me, "Cost of admission?"

I held up the wooden container I'd brought along. Eli and Mariah Aster certainly charged me more than the usual strawberry distributors, but the subtle wave of admiration that had drifted from Selah when I'd told her where I'd bought them from each time was well worth the price. "As promised."

"Hmm," The window slid shut, only for her to swing the wooden door wide open.

Selah was wrapped in an Eloran green dress. It was floor length with a slit on one side, thin straps reaching over her shoulders to accommodate for the heat, and tall, green heels. Her curls were tied up into a knot, still unruly but breathtakingly so. I could not pinpoint exactly what she had done differently with her makeup, but every piece of her was more devastating than the last.

She reached for the strawberries, and I handed them off with a kiss on her cheek. I felt her amusement, her desire, and her own appreciation. My grin only deepened, "You look stunning."

Taking a bite, she stared me up and down, "You've looked far worse."

"You're too kind." At some point, we'd have to discuss whether we truly were together. In the haze of arriving home, we'd never had that conversation. Word had spread that she would not yet be the next princess of Elora. Perhaps one day, if she stuck around and if we got on well enough, but not as she was just healing from all that Lyscott had done to her. I'd promised to allow her as much time as she needed, but how deeply I wished to present her as mine. "Shall we?"

Neither of us spoke much during the ride back to the palace. My mind was occupied with considering Faye's gift. Our parents had kept it a closely guarded secret, which generally was the custom until there could be an official gathering. Due to the nature of my gift, and the fact that I was following in Alaric's footsteps, my gifting ceremony had been underwhelming. The food was memorable, and Elliott and I had run off to climb something after all the festivities, so the night was not entirely a waste. My ability just didn't lend itself to being visible. Well, it hadn't back then. After the journey to Lyscott, our gifts had morphed into something foreign.

On the slight chance that Faye's gift truly was detection, we were in for a world of misery. Selah was an adult, and a resilient one at that. While Akar preying on her downfall certainly wasn't ideal, she could manage in a way that Faye was not yet capable of. The princess' entire young life would be spent either in hiding or heavily guarded. She would be robbed of her youth.

Because I'd spoken to Selah about this particular fear at length, she could read the worry on my face. I also tended not to hide it as well as I should have. She placed her fingers over mine, "It will be fine."

I nodded, doing my best to believe her, "If it's not?"

She gently squeezed, "Then you will manage." The few stray curls that hadn't been pulled back tickled my neck as she leaned in to whisper, "Besides, you have a very pretty and remarkably intelligent young lady at your side who is more than willing to save the day."

Slightly, I allowed a grin. She was a horrendous flirt, "That I do."

Turning the corner, we pulled into the side entrance of the Eloran palace. Dozens upon dozens of carriages were packed tightly together, with only just enough room for ours to squeeze into the very side of the lawn. For as talented as she was, Selah's shoes did not lend themselves to stability in the grass. I escorted her in with one hand that she reluctantly took. *So stubborn.*

358

Once we were tucked inside the castle, I kissed the fingers that I held. "I need to go join my family. Do you know the way?"

The roll of her eyes was enough of an answer. I could have sent Lars with her, but Selah hated being alone with most men.

With a gentle touch, she adjusted my crown, "Go be the prince."

The winding corridors that led me down to the ballroom were more familiar to me than most of the attendees that were still trickling in. The ballroom was the second tallest room in the castle, shorter only than the chapel. Large marble pillars held the glass ceiling high above our heads, and gold wiring secured the panes tightly in place. Vast hardwood flooring allowed for music to travel easily throughout the space. Hors d'oeuvres were being passed out to the bustling room full of guests, many of whose eyes drifted over me as I took my place beside our mother.

"You're late," she muttered through a grin, staring out at her people.

"Then it is most fortunate that I am one of the queen's favorite subjects, or she might've had my head for such a lapse in judgment."

She snickered, "It is most fortunate, indeed."

The royal family was positioned on a dais, where my father finally joined us. He held out a calloused hand to quiet the crowd, standing a few feet away from where my sister would soon enter. Alaric and Genevieve had long since been standing to the king's right. Faye was usually settled to my left, but not for this particular engagement.

The king's voice echoed across the open space. "Thank you all for your attendance this evening. As this is the last of our children's gifting ceremonies," he glanced at the queen, who chuckled faintly, "we are pleased to share this special moment with so many of our people. Do us the honor of warmly welcoming Princess Faye Allicot of Elora!"

The grand door behind him swung widely open, and my youngest sister took three hesitant steps forward. The growing crowd cheered loud enough to rattle the stone foundation as she emerged. Long, gilded fabric encased her, puffing out at the waist and cutting off at her elbows. It perhaps made her appear a little too old for my liking, but it was an outfit of her own choosing. Her lips had been painted bright red and green powder coated her eyelids.

Nervously, she waved. It's a lot of attention for someone so young, it had taken the older three of us quite some time to get accustomed to it. For the first time, every eye in the room was on her. I could sense the discomfort and anxiety dancing along the surface of her skin.

The queen guided Faye to the center of the stage. "Go on, darling. Whenever you're ready."

From across the room, I locked eyes with Selah. Joined by Elliott, she nursed a drink in her hand, holding the very edge to her lips as she carefully assessed. As long as it wasn't detection, everything would be alright. She had to have been thinking the same thing I was, and she held up her glass ever so subtly. *It will be fine.*

The entire room held its breath as we waited. I could hardly tell what was my sister's fear and what was my own as time itself seemed to pause. My heart threatened to beat out of my chest with the rate that it pounded. Even for my own ceremony, I hadn't been so nervous.

Seconds passed.

Faye disappeared.

A chorus of gasps reverberated as she tripped somewhere on the far side of the room. Again she vanished, only to stumble into my side. I caught her just in time. Another blink, and she was next to Gen.

She could teleport.

I choked on my relief.

Heavens above, she was going to give our parents a run for their money, but no wicked entity would pursue her. She would not be forced to live a life in hiding. I glanced at Selah and Elliott once more. They were the only ones in the crowd who understood the weight of my ease. When the crowd roared again, the two clapped and cheered along with them.

It *would* be fine.

The rest of the evening was a vision. While it took a moment for her to warm up to everyone, Faye practically glowed from all the attention she received. Alaric was content to hover wherever there was food or beverages, and even he was more chatty than usual. Gen and Elliott rarely left each other, with Gen giggling in excess at the things he said. Even my parents were visibly more relaxed. They spoke to their subjects with practiced leisure.

Luckiest of all, I got to spend the night with a strong, clever, beautiful young lady. She was a horrid dancer, nothing short of appalling, but the surprised laughs that left her every time she stepped on my feet were worth the little pain I felt. Wordlessly, I thanked the god who allowed her to be shoved in a cell for me to find. I did not wish her such a fate again, but how glad I was to have met her. Even if she was stubborn, even if she was blunt, even if she was a little too willing to draw a weapon, she was my loveliest friend.

For an evening, all was well. And, until we faced our next adventure, it would remain that way.

Acknowledgments

Oh, man. Of all the different parts of writing a book, this is one of my favorite things. All the hard work is (mostly) done by now, so I get to sit back and thank each person who helped this book transfer from an idea floating around my mind to a tangible item.

First and foremost, I owe Miss Lacy the whole world. This story would not be readable without her. As the primary editor of this book, she graciously corrected all the little mistakes I didn't realize I made. I don't know what the book would be without her. Miss Lacy, I am more than grateful for your willingness to work on this story and your gentleness when I made mistakes. The Shell family absolutely adores you!

Thanks to Mom and Dad, who listened to me ramble on about this book even when they didn't entirely understand it. Also, Mom, if you've made it this far, thank you for reading this book even though you don't like fantasy. Hopefully, this book makes you like the genre just a little more.

Special thanks to my "marketing team," Sam, Hunter, Danielle, and Noah. In reality, they are just some of my best friends who wanted to help me succeed. Also to Melinda, Nicole, and Ellena, thank you for listening every time I ran downstairs to tell you more about this story.

Last, but certainly not least, I can't possibly forget to mention Daniel Smith. I am convinced that this book would not exist without you. To say that you inspired aspects of Haven would not do you justice. His empathy was modeled after yours. Your kindness, patience, strength, and compassion have all somehow found their way into this story. Also, I just think you're really cute. I love and appreciate you with my whole heart!

About the Author

Kaitlyn Shell is currently a junior in college who resides in sunny Florida with her beloved dog, Koko. When she's not hitting the books, Kaitlyn can be found scaling rock walls, practicing jiu jitsu, or getting lost in a good book. She values time spent with friends and has a special love for rainy days, often using them as the perfect excuse for a cozy nap.

Made in the USA
Columbia, SC
10 November 2024

45901439R00221